WONDER & GLORY FOREVER

WONDER & GLORY FOREVER

AWE-INSPIRING **LOVECRAFTIAN** FICTION

EDITED AND WITH AN INTRODUCTION BY
NICK MAMATAS

DOVER PUBLICATIONS, INC.
GARDEN CITY, NEW YORK

Bibliographical Note

Wonder and Glory Forever: Awe-Inspiring Lovecraftian Fiction is a new anthology of stories,
selected and with an Introduction by Nick Mamatas, first published by Dover Publications, Inc.,
in 2020. Nick Mamatas also has written the introductions to the stories.

Library of Congress Cataloging-in-Publication Data

Names: Mamatas, Nick, editor, writer of introduction.
Title: Wonder & glory forever: awe-inspiring Lovecraftian fiction / edited and with an introduction
by Nick Mamatas.
Description: Garden City, New York: Dover Publications, Inc., 2020. | Summary: "H. P. Lovecraft's
body of work maintains a visceral influence over a host of contemporary writers. Inspired by
themes of awe and wonder, this unique collection spotlights the weird works of twelve horror
and fantasy authors, including Michael Cisco, Livia Llewellyn, Victor LaValle, Molly Tanzer,
and Masahiko Inoue. Also includes Clark Ashton Smith's 1931 'The City of the Singing Flame'
and Lovecraft's own 'The Shadow Over Innsmouth' as well as an extensive introduction by
Nick Mamatas."—Provided by publisher.
Identifiers: LCCN 2020034786 | ISBN 9780486845302 (paperback)
Subjects: LCSH: Horror tales, American. | Fantasy fiction, American.
Classification: LCC PS648.H6 W66 2020 | DDC 813/.0873808—dc23
LC record available at https://lccn.loc.gov/2020034786

Manufactured in the United States by LSC Communications
84530301
www.doverpublications.com

2 4 6 8 10 9 7 5 3 1

2020

CONTENTS

INTRODUCTION

"Hello there, little winged being in the brain of the consumer!
Thank you for coming!"

WHERE DOES one even begin with H. P. Lovecraft (1890–1937), the once obscure and now ubiquitous author of cosmic horror and science fiction? In the decades since his death, Lovecraft's work has entered the public domain. The motifs and themes he used in his work are as commonplace as the vampire or the starship. You can read about, and even read a bit of, Lovecraftian fiction in *The New Yorker*, or saddle-stitched fanzines, or the subtitles of your favorite video game's cut scenes.

Despite the truckloads of Lovecraftian fiction, comics, games, bumper stickers, memes, etc., out there, the tendency is for the stuff to express one of two things: either a sense of inescapable, inevitable doom . . . or light humor. These two extremes should come as no surprise: ultimately, Lovecraftian fiction is a type of *cult fiction*. Cult fiction inspires devotion in its readers due to its exploration of alienation, articulation of existential angst, and its offer of some level of ego gratification. You, reader, are one of the ones who *get it*, and thus you are special.

What's to get is that society, life, and perhaps the universe itself is fundamentally absurd. Cult fiction is fiction that reveals this truth, regardless of genre—thus high and low modernism, SF and noir, and visionary novels and gutter fictions can all be properly labeled "cult." Lovecraft explores the absurdity of creation in spades, overturning the divine order and revealing it to all be the willful delusions of our puny human brains. It wouldn't be an introduction to a volume of Lovecraftian fiction without this quote: "The most merciful thing in the world, I think, is the inability of the human mind to correlate all its contents. We live on a placid island of ignorance in the midst of black seas of infinity, and it was not meant that we should voyage far."

Lovecraft's vision naturally lends itself to a sense of what critic John Clute calls "vastation": "[t]o experience the malice of the made or revealed cosmos." However, Lovecraft's own personal fears and phobias—everything from non-"Aryan" races to whatever one might find washed up on the shore while strolling any New England beach at low tide—opened the door for nerdish guffaws and bad jokes. Another critic, Edmund Wilson, dismissed Lovecraft's soul-shattering horror, Cthulhu, as an "invisible whistling squid." Direct hit! But humor in the face of absurdity is also part and parcel of cult fiction. What Lovecraft made ridiculous, Lovecraftians have made whimsical, even charming. A now-famous author I helped first get published promised me a pair of Cthulhu slippers as a thank-you gift. They never arrived.

Interestingly, the once prominent Wilson is now only read thanks to cult networks: people who are interested in Lovecraft read his *New Yorker* article "Tales of the Marvellous and the Ridiculous" and grow intrigued with his style even as they disagree with his claims. Others find their way to Wilson via Frederick Exley, whose "fictional memoir" *A Fan's Notes* is a cult classic—his second, less good book, *Pages from a Cold Island*, is about his obsession with Wilson. Wilson's own remaining title that is read at all, *To the Finland Station*, is about that cult phenomenon Marxism, which has few adherents these days, but they (we!) are all voracious readers.

Though cult fictions are given to themes of existential despair, and are easy to both ridicule and reify as goofy pastiche, we just keep reading them, and there's a reason for that: Along with that experience of the malice of the made or revealed cosmos comes the experience of the sublime.

Most of us, most of the time, barring religious ecstasy, head injury, or the exact right kind of drug use, experience only a tiny sliver of the universe. We never get to see more than our senses, memory, and highly limited rationality can construct for the little homunculi riding in our skulls. Cult fiction of various sorts, and the work of H. P. Lovecraft in particular, changes that, and gives us a glimpse of what might truly be at the end of our forks. Yes, there is no invisible whistling octopus at the end of the universe, and Lovecraft knew that—he was a "mechanistic materialist" as noted by Lovecraft critic S. T. Joshi and others. The Great Old Ones are not meant to be "real" in the sense that we should believe in them, or even that they should make mimetic sense within the stories in which they appear; they represent the sublime, the marvelous, and the eternal.

Exposure and experience of the sublime is the third major thematic element of cult fiction in general, and specifically of Lovecraft's fiction. It's not as common as existential despair or absurdist humor, because it is very difficult to impress a homunculus. We are hardwired to be afraid, and hardwired to giggle inappropriately, but it takes work to get us to experience the universe in all its grandeur and *appreciate* it.

Because, the universe, that big ol' beast we're trapped in, is always trying to kill us. And it always succeeds. The audacity of the cosmos, with its endless efforts to tear us apart through earthquakes that make mountains, radiation we cannot perceive except for the thin sliver that is the rainbow, microorganisms that use us as continents even as we feel ourselves to be minute specks of flesh and time floating within the infinite, and roiling seas under which we cannot live unless we are the Robert Olmstead of "The Shadow Over Innsmouth"—oh, ho, and here we are, at the title of this anthology, *Wonder and Glory Forever*. As in, "We shall swim out to that brooding reef in the sea and dive down through black abysses to Cyclopean and many-columned Y'ha-nthlei, and in that lair of the Deep Ones we shall dwell amidst." . . . Yeah, that's the stuff.

The selections in this volume are all about finding the awe, the marvelous, and the world-shaking amidst the horror, the dark, and the degradation. So open your eyes wide and give the homunculus who surreptitiously controls your every thought and behavior a bookful of the most merciless of infinities.

—Nick Mamatas
Oakland, California
March 2020, just as the plague hit

WONDER
& GLORY
FOREVER

THE SHADOW OVER INNSMOUTH
H. P. LOVECRAFT

Lovecraft's emergence from cult author to mainstream phenomenon is a continuing process, so I don't think it odd to include here his novella The Shadow Over Innsmouth, *from which the book you hold in your hands draws its name and inspiration.*

My own introduction to Lovecraft wasn't any of his original work, but The Real Ghostbusters *episode "The Collect Call of Cathulhu," written by Michael Graves. Lovecraft is mentioned by one of the characters, and of course an ersatz Cthulhu and The Necronomicon play a role in the story. Something about it made me think,* This is real. This show is referring to something outside of itself, not just making stuff up. *When I got older, I still directly avoided Lovecraft's work, instead finding myself enamored of the British anthology* The Starry Wisdom, *which included work by Alan Moore, Grant Morrison, and Swans front man Michael Gira, all of whom I liked at the time. (I've always had a thing for cult fiction.) I didn't sit down with Lovecraft until the late 1990s, almost fifteen years after first coming across his name.*

So while you, my educated Lovecraftian pal, may have over a dozen books that feature The Shadow Over Innsmouth *in all its very damp glory, there are other readers for whom this will be their first exposure to the work after finding this title on a store shelf, or after watching* Lovecraft Country *on HBO, or or or . . . any number of twisted paths through the New England woods to find this doomed town.*

1

I

During the winter of 1927–28 officials of the Federal government made a strange and secret investigation of certain conditions in the ancient Massachusetts seaport of Innsmouth. The public first learned of it in February, when a vast series of raids and arrests occurred, followed by the deliberate burning and dynamiting—under suitable precautions— of an enormous number of crumbling, worm-eaten, and supposedly empty houses along the abandoned waterfront. Uninquiring souls let this occurrence pass as one of the major clashes in a spasmodic war on liquor.

Keener news-followers, however, wondered at the prodigious number of arrests, the abnormally large force of men used in making them, and the secrecy surrounding the disposal of the prisoners. No trials, or even definite charges, were reported; nor were any of the captives seen thereafter in the regular gaols of the nation. There were vague statements about disease and concentration camps, and later about dispersal in various naval and military prisons, but nothing positive ever developed. Innsmouth itself was left almost depopulated, and is even now only beginning to shew signs of a sluggishly revived existence.

Complaints from many liberal organisations were met with long confidential discussions, and representatives were taken on trips to certain camps and prisons. As a result, these societies became surprisingly passive and reticent. Newspaper men were harder to manage, but seemed largely to coöperate with the government in the end. Only one paper—a tabloid always discounted because of its wild policy—mentioned the deep-diving submarine that discharged torpedoes downward in the marine abyss just beyond Devil Reef. That item, gathered by chance in a haunt of sailors, seemed indeed rather far-fetched; since the low, black reef lies a full mile and a half out from Innsmouth Harbour.

People around the country and in the nearby towns muttered a great deal among themselves, but said very little to the outer world. They had talked about dying and half-deserted Innsmouth for nearly a century, and nothing new could be wilder or more hideous than what they had whispered and hinted years before. Many things had taught them secretiveness, and there was now no need to exert pressure on them. Besides, they really knew very little; for wide salt marshes, desolate and unpeopled, keep neighbours off from Innsmouth on the landward side.

But at last I am going to defy the ban on speech about this thing. Results, I am certain, are so thorough that no public harm save a shock of repulsion could ever accrue from a hinting of what was found by those horrified raiders at Innsmouth. Besides, what was found might possibly have more than one explanation. I do not know just how much of the whole tale has been told even to me, and I have many reasons for not wishing to probe deeper. For my contact with this affair has been closer than that of any other layman, and I have carried away impressions which are yet to drive me to drastic measures.

It was I who fled frantically out of Innsmouth in the early morning hours of July 16, 1927, and whose frightened appeals for government inquiry and action brought on the whole reported episode. I was willing enough to stay mute while the affair was fresh and uncertain; but now that it is an old story, with public interest and curiosity gone, I have an odd craving to whisper about those few frightful hours in that ill-rumoured and evilly shadowed seaport of death and blasphemous abnormality. The mere telling helps me to restore confidence in my own faculties; to reassure myself that I was not simply the first to succumb to a contagious nightmare hallucination. It helps me, too, in making up my mind regarding a certain terrible step which lies ahead of me.

I never heard of Innsmouth till the day before I saw it for the first and—so far—last time. I was celebrating my coming of age by a tour of New England—sightseeing, antiquarian, and genealogical—and had planned to go directly from ancient Newburyport to Arkham, whence my mother's family was derived. I had no car, but was travelling by train, trolley, and motor-coach, always seeking the cheapest possible route. In Newburyport they told me that the steam train was the thing to take to Arkham; and it was only at the station ticket-office, when I demurred at

the high fare, that I learned about Innsmouth. The stout, shrewd-faced
agent, whose speech shewed him to be no local man, seemed sympathetic
toward my efforts at economy, and made a suggestion that none of my
other informants had offered.

"You *could* take that old bus, I suppose," he said with a certain
hesitation, "but it ain't thought much of hereabouts. It goes through
Innsmouth—you may have heard about that—and so the people don't
like it. Run by an Innsmouth fellow—Joe Sargent—but never gets any
custom from here, or Arkham either, I guess. Wonder it keeps running
at all. I s'pose it's cheap enough, but I never see more'n two or three
people in it—nobody but those Innsmouth folks. Leaves the Square—
front of Hammond's Drug Store—at 10 a.m. and 7 p.m. unless they've
changed lately. Looks like a terrible rattletrap—I've never ben on it."

That was the first I ever heard of shadowed Innsmouth. Any reference
to a town not shewn on common maps or listed in recent guide-books
would have interested me, and the agent's odd manner of allusion roused
something like real curiosity. A town able to inspire such dislike in its
neighbours, I thought, must be at least rather unusual, and worthy of a
tourist's attention. If it came before Arkham I would stop off there—and
so I asked the agent to tell me something about it. He was very deliberate,
and spoke with an air of feeling slightly superior to what he said.

"Innsmouth? Well, it's a queer kind of a town down at the mouth of
the Manuxet. Used to be almost a city—quite a port before the War of
1812—but all gone to pieces in the last hundred years or so. No railroad
now—B. & M. never went through, and the branch line from Rowley
was given up years ago.

"More empty houses than there are people, I guess, and no business to
speak of except fishing and lobstering. Everybody trades mostly here or in
Arkham or Ipswich. Once they had quite a few mills, but nothing's left now
except one gold refinery running on the leanest kind of part time.

"That refinery, though, used to be a big thing, and Old Man Marsh,
who owns it, must be richer'n Croesus. Queer old duck, though, and sticks
mighty close in his home. He's supposed to have developed some skin

disease or deformity late in life that makes him keep out of sight. Grandson of Captain Obed Marsh, who founded the business. His mother seems to've ben some kind of foreigner—they say a South Sea islander—so everybody raised Cain when he married an Ipswich girl fifty years ago. They always do that about Innsmouth people, and folks here and hereabouts always try to cover up any Innsmouth blood they have in 'em. But Marsh's children and grandchildren look just like anyone else so far's I can see. I've had 'em pointed out to me here—though, come to think of it, the elder children don't seem to be around lately. Never saw the old man.

"And why is everybody so down on Innsmouth? Well, young fellow, you mustn't take too much stock in what people around here say. They're hard to get started, but once they do get started they never let up. They've ben telling things about Innsmouth—whispering 'em, mostly—for the last hundred years, I guess, and I gather they're more scared than anything else. Some of the stories would make you laugh—about old Captain Marsh driving bargains with the devil and bringing imps out of hell to live in Innsmouth, or about some kind of devil-worship and awful sacrifices in some place near the wharves that people stumbled on around 1845 or thereabouts—but I come from Panton, Vermont, and that kind of story don't go down with me.

"You ought to hear, though, what some of the old-timers tell about the black reef off the coast—Devil Reef, they call it. It's well above water a good part of the time, and never much below it, but at that you could hardly call it an island. The story is that there's a whole legion of devils seen sometimes on that reef—sprawled about, or darting in and out of some kind of caves near the top. It's a rugged, uneven thing, a good bit over a mile out, and toward the end of shipping days sailors used to make big detours just to avoid it.

"That is, sailors that didn't hail from Innsmouth. One of the things they had against old Captain Marsh was that he was supposed to land on it sometimes at night when the tide was right. Maybe he did, for I dare say the rock formation was interesting, and it's just barely possible he was looking for pirate loot and maybe finding it; but there was talk of his dealing with daemons there. Fact is, I guess on the whole it was really the Captain that gave the bad reputation to the reef.

"That was before the big epidemic of 1846, when over half the folks in Innsmouth was carried off. They never did quite figure out what the trouble was, but it was probably some foreign kind of disease brought from China or somewhere by the shipping. It surely was bad enough—there was riots over it, and all sorts of ghastly doings that I don't believe ever got outside of town—and it left the place in awful shape. Never came back—there can't be more'n 300 or 400 people living there now.

"But the real thing behind the way folks feel is simply race prejudice—and I don't say I'm blaming those that hold it. I hate those Innsmouth folks myself, and I wouldn't care to go to their town. I s'pose you know—though I can see you're a Westerner by your talk—what a lot our New England ships used to have to do with queer ports in Africa, Asia, the South Seas, and everywhere else, and what queer kinds of people they sometimes brought back with 'em. You've probably heard about the Salem man that came home with a Chinese wife, and maybe you know there's still a bunch of Fiji Islanders somewhere around Cape Cod.

"Well, there must be something like that back of the Innsmouth people. The place always was badly cut off from the rest of the country by marshes and creeks, and we can't be sure about the ins and outs of the matter; but it's pretty clear that old Captain Marsh must have brought home some odd specimens when he had all three of his ships in commission back in the twenties and thirties. There certainly is a strange kind of streak in the Innsmouth folks today—I don't know how to explain it, but it sort of makes you crawl. You'll notice a little in Sargent if you take his bus. Some of 'em have queer narrow heads with flat noses and bulgy, stary eyes that never seem to shut, and their skin ain't quite right. Rough and scabby, and the sides of their necks are all shrivelled or creased up. Get bald, too, very young. The older fellows look the worst—fact is, I don't believe I've ever seen a very old chap of that kind. Guess they must die of looking in the glass! Animals hate 'em—they used to have lots of horse trouble before autos came in.

"Nobody around here or in Arkham or Ipswich will have anything to do with 'em, and they act kind of offish themselves when they come to town or when anyone tries to fish on their grounds. Queer how fish are always thick off Innsmouth Harbour when there ain't any anywhere else around—but just try to fish there yourself and see how the folks chase you off! Those people used to come here on the railroad—walking and taking the train at Rowley after the branch was dropped—but now they use that bus.

"Yes, there's a hotel in Innsmouth—called the Gilman House—but I don't believe it can amount to much. I wouldn't advise you to try it. Better stay over here and take the ten o'clock bus tomorrow morning; then you can get an evening bus there for Arkham at eight o'clock. There was a factory inspector who stopped at the Gilman a couple of years ago, and he had a lot of unpleasant hints about the place. Seems they get a queer crowd there, for this fellow heard voices in other rooms—though most of 'em was empty—that gave him the shivers. It was foreign talk, he thought, but he said the bad thing about it was the kind of voice that sometimes spoke. It sounded so unnatural—slopping-like, he said— that he didn't dare undress and go to sleep. Just waited up and lit out the first thing in the morning. The talk went on most all night.

"This fellow—Casey, his name was—had a lot to say about how the Innsmouth folks watched him and seemed kind of on guard. He found the Marsh refinery a queer place—it's in an old mill on the lower falls of the Manuxet. What he said tallied up with what I'd heard. Books in bad shape, and no clear account of any kind of dealings. You know it's always ben a kind of mystery where the Marshes get the gold they refine. They've never seemed to do much buying in that line, but years ago they shipped out an enormous lot of ingots.

"Used to be talk of a queer foreign kind of jewellery that the sailors and refinery men sometimes sold on the sly, or that was seen once or twice on some of the Marsh womenfolks. People allowed maybe old Captain Obed traded for it in some heathen port, especially since he was always ordering stacks of glass beads and trinkets such as seafaring men used to get for native trade. Others thought and still think he'd found an old pirate cache out on Devil Reef. But here's a funny thing. The old Captain's ben dead these sixty years, and there ain't ben a good-sized ship out of the place since the Civil War; but just the same the Marshes still keep on buying a few of those native trade things—mostly glass and rubber gewgaws, they tell me. Maybe the Innsmouth folks like 'em to look at themselves—Gawd knows they've gotten to be about as bad as South Sea cannibals and Guinea savages.

"That plague of '46 must have taken off the best blood in the place. Anyway, they're a doubtful lot now, and the Marshes and the other rich folks are as bad as any. As I told you, there probably ain't more'n 400 people in the whole town in spite of all the streets they say there are. I guess they're what they call 'white trash' down South—lawless and sly, and full of secret doings. They get a lot of fish and lobsters and do exporting by truck. Queer how the fish swarm right there and nowhere else.

"Nobody can ever keep track of these people, and state school officials and census men have a devil of a time. You can bet that prying strangers ain't welcome around Innsmouth. I've heard personally of more'n one business or government man that's disappeared there, and there's loose talk of one who went crazy and is out at Danvers now. They must have fixed up some awful scare for that fellow.

"That's why I wouldn't go at night if I was you. I've never ben there and have no wish to go, but I guess a daytime trip couldn't hurt you— even though the people hereabouts will advise you not to make it. If you're just sightseeing, and looking for old-time stuff, Innsmouth ought to be quite a place for you."

And so I spent part of that evening at the Newburyport Public Library looking up data about Innsmouth. When I had tried to question the natives in the shops, the lunch room, the garages, and the fire station, I had found them even harder to get started than the ticket-agent had predicted; and realised that I could not spare the time to overcome their first instinctive reticences. They had a kind of obscure suspiciousness, as if there were something amiss with anyone too much interested in Innsmouth. At the Y.M.C.A., where I was stopping, the clerk merely discouraged my going to such a dismal, decadent place; and the people at the library shewed much the same attitude. Clearly, in the eyes of the educated, Innsmouth was merely an exaggerated case of civic degeneration.

The Essex County histories on the library shelves had very little to say, except that the town was founded in 1643, noted for shipbuilding before the Revolution, a seat of great marine prosperity in the early nineteenth century, and later a minor factory centre using the Manuxet as power. The epidemic and riots of 1846 were very sparsely treated, as if they formed a discredit to the county.

References to decline were few, though the significance of the later record was unmistakable. After the Civil War all industrial life was confined to the Marsh Refining Company, and the marketing of gold ingots formed the only remaining bit of major commerce aside from the eternal fishing. That fishing paid less and less as the price of the commodity fell and large-scale corporations offered competition, but there was never a dearth of fish around Innsmouth Harbour. Foreigners seldom settled there, and there was some discreetly veiled evidence that a number of Poles and Portuguese who had tried it had been scattered in a peculiarly drastic fashion.

Most interesting of all was a glancing reference to the strange jewellery vaguely associated with Innsmouth. It had evidently impressed the whole countryside more than a little, for mention was made of specimens in the museum of Miskatonic University at Arkham, and in the display room of the Newburyport Historical Society. The fragmentary descriptions of these things were bald and prosaic, but they hinted to me an undercurrent of persistent strangeness. Something about them seemed so odd and provocative that I could not put them out of my mind, and despite the relative lateness of the hour I resolved to see the local sample—said to be a large, queerly proportioned thing evidently meant for a tiara—if it could possibly be arranged.

The librarian gave me a note of introduction to the curator of the Society, a Miss Anna Tilton, who lived nearby, and after a brief explanation that ancient gentlewoman was kind enough to pilot me into the closed building, since the hour was not outrageously late. The collection was a notable one indeed, but in my present mood I had eyes for nothing but the bizarre object which glistened in a corner cupboard under the electric lights.

It took no excessive sensitiveness to beauty to make me literally gasp at the strange, unearthly splendour of the alien, opulent phantasy that rested there on a purple velvet cushion. Even now I can hardly describe what I saw, though it was clearly enough a sort of tiara, as the description had said. It was tall in front, and with a very large and curiously irregular periphery, as if designed for a head of almost freakishly elliptical outline. The material seemed to be predominantly gold, though a weird lighter lustrousness hinted at some strange alloy with an equally beautiful and scarcely identifiable metal. Its condition was almost perfect, and one could have spent hours in studying the striking and puzzlingly untraditional designs—some simply geometrical, and some plainly marine—chased or moulded in high relief on its surface with a craftsmanship of incredible skill and grace.

The longer I looked, the more the thing fascinated me; and in this fascination there was a curiously disturbing element hardly to be classified or accounted for. At first I decided that it was the queer other-worldly quality of the art which made me uneasy. All other art objects I had ever seen either belonged to some known racial or national stream, or else were consciously modernistic defiances of every recognised stream. This tiara was neither. It clearly belonged to some settled technique of infinite maturity and perfection, yet that technique was utterly remote from any— Eastern or Western, ancient or modern—which I had ever heard of or seen exemplified. It was as if the workmanship were that of another planet.

However, I soon saw that my uneasiness had a second and perhaps equally potent source residing in the pictorial and mathematical suggestions of the strange designs. The patterns all hinted of remote secrets and unimaginable abysses in time and space, and the monotonously aquatic nature of the reliefs became almost sinister. Among these reliefs were fabulous monsters of abhorrent grotesqueness and malignity—half ichthyic and half batrachian in suggestion—which one could not dissociate from a certain haunting and uncomfortable sense of pseudo-memory, as if they called up some image from deep cells and tissues whose retentive functions are wholly primal and awesomely ancestral. At times I fancied that every contour of these blasphemous fish-frogs was overflowing with the ultimate quintessence of unknown and inhuman evil.

In odd contrast to the tiara's aspect was its brief and prosy history as related by Miss Tilton. It had been pawned for a ridiculous sum at a shop in State Street in 1873, by a drunken Innsmouth man shortly afterward killed in a brawl. The Society had acquired it directly from the pawnbroker, at once giving it a display worthy of its quality. It was labelled as of probable East-Indian or Indo-Chinese provenance, though the attribution was frankly tentative.

Miss Tilton, comparing all possible hypotheses regarding its origin and its presence in New England, was inclined to believe that it formed part of some exotic pirate hoard discovered by old Captain Obed Marsh. This view was surely not weakened by the insistent offers of purchase at a high price which the Marshes began to make as soon as they knew of its presence, and which they repeated to this day despite the Society's unvarying determination not to sell.

As the good lady shewed me out of the building she made it clear that the pirate theory of the Marsh fortune was a popular one among the intelligent people of the region. Her own attitude toward shadowed Innsmouth—which she had never seen—was one of disgust at a community slipping far down the cultural scale, and she assured me that the rumours of devil-worship were partly justified by a peculiar secret cult which had gained force there and engulfed all the orthodox churches.

It was called, she said, "The Esoteric Order of Dagon," and was undoubtedly a debased, quasi-pagan thing imported from the East a century before, at a time when the Innsmouth fisheries seemed to be going barren. Its persistence among a simple people was quite natural in view of the sudden and permanent return of abundantly fine fishing, and it soon came to be the greatest influence on the town, replacing Freemasonry altogether and taking up headquarters in the old Masonic Hall on New Church Green.

All this, to the pious Miss Tilton, formed an excellent reason for shunning the ancient town of decay and desolation; but to me it was merely a fresh incentive. To my architectural and historical anticipations was now added an acute anthropological zeal, and I could scarcely sleep in my small room at the "Y" as the night wore away.

II

Shortly before ten the next morning I stood with one small valise in front of Hammond's Drug Store in old Market Square waiting for the Innsmouth bus. As the hour for its arrival drew near I noticed a general drift of the loungers to other places up the street, or to the Ideal Lunch across the square. Evidently the ticket-agent had not exaggerated the dislike which local people bore toward Innsmouth and its denizens. In a few moments a small motor-coach of extreme decrepitude and dirty grey colour rattled down State Street, made a turn, and drew up at the curb beside me. I felt immediately that it was the right one; a guess which the half-illegible sign on the windshield—*"Arkham-Innsmouth-Newb'port"*—soon verified.

There were only three passengers—dark, unkempt men of sullen visage and somewhat youthful cast—and when the vehicle stopped they clumsily shambled out and began walking up State Street in a silent, almost furtive fashion. The driver also alighted, and I watched him as he went into the drug store to make some purchase. This, I reflected, must be the Joe Sargent mentioned by the ticket-agent; and even before I noticed any details there spread over me a wave of spontaneous aversion which could be neither checked nor explained. It suddenly struck me as very natural that the local people should not wish to ride on a bus owned and driven by this man, or to visit any oftener than possible the habitat of such a man and his kinsfolk.

When the driver came out of the store I looked at him more carefully and tried to determine the source of my evil impression. He was a thin, stoop-shouldered man not much under six feet tall, dressed in shabby blue civilian clothes and wearing a frayed grey golf cap. His age was perhaps thirty-five, but the odd, deep creases in the sides of his neck made him seem older when one did not study his dull, expressionless face. He had a narrow head, bulging, watery blue eyes that seemed never to wink, a flat nose, a receding forehead and chin, and singularly undeveloped ears. His long, thick lip and coarse-pored, greyish cheeks seemed almost beardless except for some sparse yellow hairs that straggled and curled in irregular patches; and in places the surface seemed queerly irregular, as if peeling from some cutaneous disease. His hands were large and heavily veined, and had a very unusual greyish-blue tinge. The fingers were strikingly short in proportion to the rest of the structure, and seemed to have a tendency to curl closely into the huge palm. As he walked toward the bus I observed his peculiarly shambling gait and saw that his feet were inordinately immense. The more I studied them the more I wondered how he could buy any shoes to fit them.

A certain greasiness about the fellow increased my dislike. He was evidently given to working or lounging around the fish docks, and carried with him much of their characteristic smell. Just what foreign blood was in him I could not even guess. His oddities certainly did not look Asiatic, Polynesian, Levantine, or negroid, yet I could see why the people found him alien. I myself would have thought of biological degeneration rather than alienage.

I was sorry when I saw that there would be no other passengers on the bus. Somehow I did not like the idea of riding alone with this driver. But as leaving time obviously approached I conquered my qualms and followed the man aboard, extending him a dollar bill and murmuring the single word "Innsmouth." He looked curiously at me for a second as he returned forty cents change without speaking. I took a seat far behind

him, but on the same side of the bus, since I wished to watch the shore
during the journey.

At length the decrepit vehicle started with a jerk, and rattled noisily
past the old brick buildings of State Street amidst a cloud of vapour from
the exhaust. Glancing at the people on the sidewalks, I thought I detected
in them a curious wish to avoid looking at the bus—or at least a wish to
avoid seeming to look at it. Then we turned to the left into High Street,
where the going was smoother; flying by stately old mansions of the early
republic and still older colonial farmhouses, passing the Lower Green
and Parker River, and finally emerging into a long, monotonous stretch
of open shore country.

The day was warm and sunny, but the landscape of sand, sedge-
grass, and stunted shrubbery became more and more desolate as we
proceeded. Out the window I could see the blue water and the sandy
line of Plum Island, and we presently drew very near the beach as our
narrow road veered off from the main highway to Rowley and Ipswich.
There were no visible houses, and I could tell by the state of the road
that traffic was very light hereabouts. The small, weather-worn telephone
poles carried only two wires. Now and then we crossed crude wooden
bridges over tidal creeks that wound far inland and promoted the general
isolation of the region.

Once in a while I noticed dead stumps and crumbling foundation-
walls above the drifting sand, and recalled the old tradition quoted in
one of the histories I had read, that this was once a fertile and thickly
settled countryside. The change, it was said, came simultaneously with
the Innsmouth epidemic of 1846, and was thought by simple folk to have
a dark connexion with hidden forces of evil. Actually, it was caused by
the unwise cutting of woodlands near the shore, which robbed the soil
of its best protection and opened the way for waves of wind-blown sand.

At last we lost sight of Plum Island and saw the vast expanse of the
open Atlantic on our left. Our narrow course began to climb steeply,
and I felt a singular sense of disquiet in looking at the lonely crest ahead
where the rutted roadway met the sky. It was as if the bus were about to

keep on in its ascent, leaving the sane earth altogether and merging with the unknown arcana of upper air and cryptical sky. The smell of the sea took on ominous implications, and the silent driver's bent, rigid back and narrow head became more and more hateful. As I looked at him I saw that the back of his head was almost as hairless as his face, having only a few straggling yellow strands upon a grey scabrous surface.

Then we reached the crest and beheld the outspread valley beyond, where the Manuxet joins the sea just north of the long line of cliffs that culminate in Kingsport Head and veer off toward Cape Ann. On the far, misty horizon I could just make out the dizzy profile of the Head, topped by the queer ancient house of which so many legends are told; but for the moment all my attention was captured by the nearer panorama just below me. I had, I realised, come face to face with rumour-shadowed Innsmouth.

It was a town of wide extent and dense construction, yet one with a portentous dearth of visible life. From the tangle of chimney-pots scarcely a wisp of smoke came, and the three tall steeples loomed stark and unpainted against the seaward horizon. One of them was crumbling down at the top, and in that and another there were only black gaping holes where clock-dials should have been. The vast huddle of sagging gambrel roofs and peaked gables conveyed with offensive clearness the idea of wormy decay, and as we approached along the now descending road I could see that many roofs had wholly caved in. There were some large square Georgian houses, too, with hipped roofs, cupolas, and railed "widow's walks." These were mostly well back from the water, and one or two seemed to be in moderately sound condition. Stretching inland from among them I saw the rusted, grass-grown line of the abandoned railway, with leaning telegraph-poles now devoid of wires, and the half-obscured lines of the old carriage roads to Rowley and Ipswich.

The decay was worst close to the waterfront, though in its very midst I could spy the white belfry of a fairly well-preserved brick structure which looked like a small factory. The harbour, long clogged with sand, was enclosed by an ancient stone breakwater; on which I could begin to

discern the minute forms of a few seated fishermen, and at whose end
were what looked like the foundations of a bygone lighthouse. A sandy
tongue had formed inside this barrier, and upon it I saw a few decrepit
cabins, moored dories, and scattered lobster-pots. The only deep water
seemed to be where the river poured out past the belfried structure and
turned southward to join the ocean at the breakwater's end.

Here and there the ruins of wharves jutted out from the shore to
end in indeterminate rottenness, those farthest south seeming the most
decayed. And far out at sea, despite a high tide, I glimpsed a long, black
line scarcely rising above the water yet carrying a suggestion of odd
latent malignancy. This, I knew, must be Devil Reef. As I looked, a subtle,
curious sense of beckoning seemed superadded to the grim repulsion;
and oddly enough, I found this overtone more disturbing than the
primary impression.

We met no one on the road, but presently began to pass deserted
farms in varying stages of ruin. Then I noticed a few inhabited houses
with rags stuffed in the broken windows and shells and dead fish lying
about the littered yards. Once or twice I saw listless-looking people
working in barren gardens or digging clams on the fishy-smelling beach
below, and groups of dirty, simian-visaged children playing around
weed-grown doorsteps. Somehow these people seemed more disquieting
than the dismal buildings, for almost every one had certain peculiarities
of face and motions which I instinctively disliked without being able
to define or comprehend them. For a second I thought this typical
physique suggested some picture I had seen, perhaps in a book, under
circumstances of particular horror or melancholy; but this pseudo-
recollection passed very quickly.

As the bus reached a lower level I began to catch the steady note
of a waterfall through the unnatural stillness. The leaning, unpainted
houses grew thicker, lined both sides of the road, and displayed more
urban tendencies than did those we were leaving behind. The panorama
ahead had contracted to a street scene, and in spots I could see where
a cobblestone pavement and stretches of brick sidewalk had formerly

existed. All the houses were apparently deserted, and there were occasional gaps where tumbledown chimneys and cellar walls told of buildings that had collapsed. Pervading everything was the most nauseous fishy odour imaginable.

Soon cross streets and junctions began to appear; those on the left leading to shoreward realms of unpaved squalor and decay, while those on the right shewed vistas of departed grandeur. So far I had seen no people in the town, but there now came signs of a sparse habitation— curtained windows here and there, and an occasional battered motor-car at the curb. Pavement and sidewalks were increasingly well defined, and though most of the houses were quite old—wood and brick structures of the early nineteenth century—they were obviously kept fit for habitation. As an amateur antiquarian I almost lost my olfactory disgust and my feeling of menace and repulsion amidst this rich, unaltered survival from the past.

But I was not to reach my destination without one very strong impression of poignantly disagreeable quality. The bus had come to a sort of open concourse or radial point with churches on two sides and the bedraggled remains of a circular green in the centre, and I was looking at a large pillared hall on the right-hand junction ahead. The structure's once white paint was now grey and peeling, and the black and gold sign on the pediment was so faded that I could only with difficulty make out the words "Esoteric Order of Dagon." This, then, was the former Masonic Hall now given over to a degraded cult. As I strained to decipher this inscription my notice was distracted by the raucous tones of a cracked bell across the street, and I quickly turned to look out the window on my side of the coach.

The sound came from a squat-towered stone church of manifestly later date than most of the houses, built in a clumsy Gothic fashion and having a disproportionately high basement with shuttered windows. Though the hands of its clock were missing on the side I glimpsed, I knew that those hoarse strokes were telling the hour of eleven. Then suddenly all thoughts of time were blotted out by an onrushing image of sharp intensity and unaccountable horror which had seized me before I knew what it really was. The door of the church basement was open, revealing a rectangle of blackness inside. And as I looked, a certain object crossed or seemed to cross that dark rectangle; burning into my brain a momentary conception of nightmare which was all the more maddening because analysis could not shew a single nightmarish quality in it.

It was a living object—the first except the driver that I had seen since entering the compact part of the town—and had I been in a steadier mood I would have found nothing whatever of terror in it. Clearly, as I realised a moment later, it was the pastor; clad in some peculiar vestments doubtless introduced since the Order of Dagon had modified the ritual of the local churches. The thing which had probably caught my first subconscious glance and supplied the touch of bizarre horror was the tall tiara he wore; an almost exact duplicate of the one Miss Tilton had shewn me the previous evening. This, acting on my imagination, had supplied namelessly sinister qualities to the indeterminate face and robed, shambling form beneath it. There was not, I soon decided, any reason why I should have felt that shuddering touch of evil pseudo-memory. Was it not natural that a local mystery cult should adopt among its regimentals an unique type of head-dress made familiar to the community in some strange way—perhaps as treasure-trove?

A very thin sprinkling of repellent-looking youngish people now became visible on the sidewalks—lone individuals, and silent knots of two or three. The lower floors of the crumbling houses sometimes harboured small shops with dingy signs, and I noticed a parked truck or two as we rattled along. The sound of waterfalls became more and more distinct, and presently I saw a fairly deep river-gorge ahead, spanned by a wide, iron-railed highway bridge beyond which a large square opened out. As we clanked over the bridge I looked out on both sides and observed some factory buildings on the edge of the grassy bluff or part way down. The water far below was very abundant, and I could see two vigorous sets of falls upstream on my right and at least one downstream on my left. From this point the noise was quite deafening.

Then we rolled into the large semicircular square across the river and drew up on the right-hand side in front of a tall, cupola-crowned building with remnants of yellow paint and with a half-effaced sign proclaiming it to be the Gilman House.

I was glad to get out of that bus, and at once proceeded to check my valise in the shabby hotel lobby. There was only one person in sight—an elderly man without what I had come to call the "Innsmouth look"—and I decided not to ask him any of the questions which bothered me; remembering that odd things had been noticed in this hotel. Instead, I strolled out on the square, from which the bus had already gone, and studied the scene minutely and appraisingly.

One side of the cobblestoned open space was the straight line of the river; the other was a semicircle of slant-roofed brick buildings of about the 1800 period, from which several streets radiated away to the southeast, south, and southwest. Lamps were depressingly few and small—all low-powered incandescents—and I was glad that my plans called for departure before dark, even though I knew the moon would be bright. The buildings were all in fair condition, and included perhaps a dozen shops in current operation; of which one was a grocery of the First National chain, others a dismal restaurant, a drug store, and a wholesale fish-dealer's office, and still another, at the eastern extremity of the square near the river, an office of the town's only industry—the Marsh Refining Company. There were perhaps ten people visible, and four or five automobiles and motor trucks stood scattered about. I did not need to be told that this was the civic centre of Innsmouth. Eastward I could catch blue glimpses of the harbour, against which rose the decaying remains of three once beautiful Georgian steeples. And toward the shore on the opposite bank of the river I saw the white belfry surmounting what I took to be the Marsh refinery.

For some reason or other I chose to make my first inquiries at the chain grocery, whose personnel was not likely to be native to Innsmouth. I found a solitary boy of about seventeen in charge, and was pleased to note the brightness and affability which promised cheerful information.

He seemed exceptionally eager to talk, and I soon gathered that he did not like the place, its fishy smell, or its furtive people. A word with any outsider was a relief to him. He hailed from Arkham, boarded with a family who came from Ipswich, and went back home whenever he got a moment off. His family did not like him to work in Innsmouth, but the chain had transferred him there and he did not wish to give up his job.

There was, he said, no public library or chamber of commerce in Innsmouth, but I could probably find my way about. The street I had come down was Federal. West of that were the fine old residence streets—Broad, Washington, Lafayette, and Adams—and east of it were the shoreward slums. It was in these slums—along Main Street—that I would find the old Georgian churches, but they were all long abandoned. It would be well not to make oneself too conspicuous in such neighbourhoods—especially north of the river—since the people were sullen and hostile. Some strangers had even disappeared.

Certain spots were almost forbidden territory, as he had learned at considerable cost. One must not, for example, linger much around the Marsh refinery, or around any of the still used churches, or around the pillared Order of Dagon Hall at New Church Green. Those churches were very odd—all violently disavowed by their respective denominations elsewhere, and apparently using the queerest kind of ceremonials and clerical vestments. Their creeds were heterodox and mysterious, involving hints of certain marvellous transformations leading to bodily immortality—of a sort—on this earth. The youth's own pastor—Dr. Wallace of Asbury M. E. Church in Arkham—had gravely urged him not to join any church in Innsmouth.

As for the Innsmouth people—the youth hardly knew what to make of them. They were as furtive and seldom seen as animals that live in burrows, and one could hardly imagine how they passed the time apart from their desultory fishing. Perhaps—judging from the quantities of bootleg liquor they consumed—they lay for most of the daylight hours in an alcoholic stupor. They seemed sullenly banded together in some sort of fellowship and understanding—despising the world as if they had access to other and preferable spheres of entity. Their appearance—especially those staring, unwinking eyes which one never saw shut—was certainly shocking enough; and their voices were disgusting. It was awful to hear them chanting in their churches at night, and especially during their main festivals or revivals, which fell twice a year on April 30th and October 31st.

They were very fond of the water, and swam a great deal in both river and harbour. Swimming races out to Devil Reef were very common, and everyone in sight seemed well able to share in this arduous sport. When one came to think of it, it was generally only rather young people who were seen about in public, and of these the oldest were apt to be the most tainted-looking. When exceptions did occur, they were mostly persons with no trace of aberrancy, like the old clerk at the hotel. One wondered what became of the bulk of the older folk, and whether the "Innsmouth look" were not a strange and insidious disease-phenomenon which increased its hold as years advanced.

Only a very rare affliction, of course, could bring about such vast and radical anatomical changes in a single individual after maturity— changes involving osseous factors as basic as the shape of the skull— but then, even this aspect was no more baffling and unheard-of than the visible features of the malady as a whole. It would be hard, the youth implied, to form any real conclusions regarding such a matter; since one never came to know the natives personally no matter how long one might live in Innsmouth.

The youth was certain that many specimens even worse than the worst visible ones were kept locked indoors in some places. People sometimes heard the queerest kind of sounds. The tottering waterfront hovels north of the river were reputedly connected by hidden tunnels, being thus a veritable warren of unseen abnormalities. What kind of foreign blood—if any—these beings had, it was impossible to tell. They sometimes kept certain especially repulsive characters out of sight when government agents and others from the outside world came to town.

It would be of no use, my informant said, to ask the natives anything about the place. The only one who would talk was a very aged but normal-looking man who lived at the poorhouse on the north rim of the town and spent his time walking about or lounging around the fire station. This hoary character, Zadok Allen, was ninety-six years old and somewhat touched in the head, besides being the town drunkard. He was a strange, furtive creature who constantly looked over his shoulder as if afraid of something, and when sober could not be persuaded to talk at all with strangers. He was, however, unable to resist any offer of his favourite poison; and once drunk would furnish the most astonishing fragments of whispered reminiscence.

After all, though, little useful data could be gained from him; since his stories were all insane, incomplete hints of impossible marvels and horrors which could have no source save in his own disordered fancy. Nobody ever believed him, but the natives did not like him to drink and talk with strangers; and it was not always safe to be seen questioning him. It was probably from him that some of the wildest popular whispers and delusions were derived.

Several non-native residents had reported monstrous glimpses from time to time, but between old Zadok's tales and the malformed denizens it was no wonder such illusions were current. None of the non-natives ever stayed out late at night, there being a widespread impression that it was not wise to do so. Besides, the streets were loathsomely dark.

As for business—the abundance of fish was certainly almost uncanny, but the natives were taking less and less advantage of it. Moreover, prices were falling and competition was growing. Of course the town's real business was the refinery, whose commercial office was on the square only a few doors east of where we stood. Old Man Marsh was never seen, but sometimes went to the works in a closed, curtained car.

There were all sorts of rumours about how Marsh had come to look. He had once been a great dandy, and people said he still wore the frock-coated finery of the Edwardian age, curiously adapted to certain deformities. His sons had formerly conducted the office in the square, but latterly they had been keeping out of sight a good deal and leaving the brunt of affairs to the younger generation. The sons and their sisters had come to look very queer, especially the elder ones; and it was said that their health was failing.

One of the Marsh daughters was a repellent, reptilian-looking woman who wore an excess of weird jewellery clearly of the same exotic tradition as that to which the strange tiara belonged. My informant had noticed it many times, and had heard it spoken of as coming from some secret hoard, either of pirates or of daemons. The clergymen—or priests, or whatever they were called nowadays—also wore this kind of ornament as a head-dress; but one seldom caught glimpses of them. Other specimens the youth had not seen, though many were rumoured to exist around Innsmouth.

The Marshes, together with the other three gently bred families of the town—the Waites, the Gilmans, and the Eliots—were all very retiring. They lived in immense houses along Washington Street, and several were reputed to harbour in concealment certain living kinsfolk whose personal aspect forbade public view, and whose deaths had been reported and recorded.

Warning me that many of the street signs were down, the youth drew for my benefit a rough but ample and painstaking sketch map of the town's salient features. After a moment's study I felt sure that it would be of great help, and pocketed it with profuse thanks. Disliking the dinginess of the single restaurant I had seen, I bought a fair supply of cheese crackers and ginger wafers to serve as a lunch later on. My programme, I decided, would be to thread the principal streets, talk with any non-natives I might encounter, and catch the eight o'clock coach for Arkham. The town, I could see, formed a significant and exaggerated example of communal decay; but being no sociologist I would limit my serious observations to the field of architecture.

Thus I began my systematic though half-bewildered tour of Innsmouth's narrow, shadow-blighted ways. Crossing the bridge and turning toward the roar of the lower falls, I passed close to the Marsh refinery, which seemed oddly free from the noise of industry. This building stood on the steep river bluff near a bridge and an open confluence of streets which I took to be the earliest civic centre, displaced after the Revolution by the present Town Square.

Re-crossing the gorge on the Main Street bridge, I struck a region of utter desertion which somehow made me shudder. Collapsing huddles of gambrel roofs formed a jagged and fantastic skyline, above which rose the ghoulish, decapitated steeple of an ancient church. Some houses along Main Street were tenanted, but most were tightly boarded up. Down unpaved side streets I saw the black, gaping windows of deserted hovels, many of which leaned at perilous and incredible angles through the sinking of part of the foundations. Those windows stared so spectrally that it took courage to turn eastward toward the waterfront. Certainly, the terror of a deserted house swells in geometrical rather than arithmetical progression as houses multiply to form a city of stark desolation. The sight of such endless avenues of fishy-eyed vacancy and death, and the thought of such linked infinities of black, brooding compartments given over to cobwebs and memories and the conqueror worm, start up vestigial fears and aversions that not even the stoutest philosophy can disperse.

Fish Street was as deserted as Main, though it differed in having many brick and stone warehouses still in excellent shape. Water Street was almost its duplicate, save that there were great seaward gaps where wharves had been. Not a living thing did I see, except for the scattered fishermen on the distant breakwater, and not a sound did I hear save the lapping of the harbour tides and the roar of the falls in the Manuxet. The town was getting more and more on my nerves, and I looked behind me furtively as I picked my way back over the tottering Water Street bridge. The Fish Street bridge, according to the sketch, was in ruins.

North of the river there were traces of squalid life—active fish-packing houses in Water Street, smoking chimneys and patched roofs here and there, occasional sounds from indeterminate sources, and infrequent shambling forms in the dismal streets and unpaved lanes—but I seemed to find this even more oppressive than the southerly desertion. For one thing, the people were more hideous and abnormal than those near the centre of the town; so that I was several times evilly reminded of something utterly fantastic which I could not quite place. Undoubtedly the alien strain in the Innsmouth folk was stronger here than farther inland—unless, indeed, the "Innsmouth look" were a disease rather than a blood strain, in which case this district might be held to harbour the more advanced cases.

One detail that annoyed me was the *distribution* of the few faint sounds I heard. They ought naturally to have come wholly from the visibly inhabited houses, yet in reality were often strongest inside the most rigidly boarded-up facades. There were creakings, scurryings, and hoarse doubtful noises; and I thought uncomfortably about the hidden tunnels suggested by the grocery boy. Suddenly I found myself wondering what the voices of those denizens would be like. I had heard no speech so far in this quarter, and was unaccountably anxious not to do so.

Pausing only long enough to look at two fine but ruinous old churches at Main and Church Streets, I hastened out of that vile waterfront slum. My next logical goal was New Church Green, but somehow or other I could not bear to repass the church in whose basement I had glimpsed the inexplicably frightening form of that strangely diademed priest or pastor. Besides, the grocery youth had told me that the churches, as well as the Order of Dagon Hall, were not advisable neighbourhoods for strangers.

Accordingly I kept north along Main to Martin, then turning inland, crossing Federal Street safely north of the Green, and entering the decayed patrician neighbourhood of northern Broad, Washington, Lafayette, and Adams Streets. Though these stately old avenues were ill-surfaced and unkempt, their elm-shaded dignity had not entirely departed. Mansion after mansion claimed my gaze, most of them decrepit and boarded up amidst neglected grounds, but one or two in each street shewing signs of occupancy. In Washington Street there was a row of four or five in excellent repair and with finely tended lawns and gardens. The most sumptuous of these—with wide terraced parterres extending back the whole way to Lafayette Street—I took to be the home of Old Man Marsh, the afflicted refinery owner.

In all these streets no living thing was visible, and I wondered at the complete absense of cats and dogs from Innsmouth. Another thing which puzzled and disturbed me, even in some of the best-preserved mansions, was the tightly shuttered condition of many third-story and attic windows. Furtiveness and secretiveness seemed universal in this hushed city of alienage and death, and I could not escape the sensation of being watched from ambush on every hand by sly, staring eyes that never shut.

I shivered as the cracked stroke of three sounded from a belfry on my left. Too well did I recall the squat church from which those notes came. Following Washington Street toward the river, I now faced a new zone of former industry and commerce; noting the ruins of a factory ahead, and seeing others, with the traces of an old railway station and covered railway bridge beyond, up the gorge on my right.

The uncertain bridge now before me was posted with a warning sign, but I took the risk and crossed again to the south bank where traces of life reappeared. Furtive, shambling creatures stared cryptically in my direction, and more normal faces eyed me coldly and curiously. Innsmouth was rapidly becoming intolerable, and I turned down Paine Street toward the Square in the hope of getting some vehicle to take me to Arkham before the still-distant starting-time of that sinister bus.

It was then that I saw the tumbledown fire station on my left, and noticed the red-faced, bushy-bearded, watery-eyed old man in nondescript rags who sat on a bench in front of it talking with a pair of unkempt but not abnormal-looking firemen. This, of course, must be Zadok Allen, the half-crazed, liquorish nonagenarian whose tales of old Innsmouth and its shadow were so hideous and incredible.

III

It must have been some imp of the perverse—or some sardonic pull from dark, hidden sources—which made me change my plans as I did. I had long before resolved to limit my observations to architecture alone, and I was even then hurrying toward the Square in an effort to get quick transportation out of this festering city of death and decay; but the sight of old Zadok Allen set up new currents in my mind and made me slacken my pace uncertainly.

I had been assured that the old man could do nothing but hint at wild, disjointed, and incredible legends, and I had been warned that the natives made it unsafe to be seen talking to him; yet the thought of this aged witness to the town's decay, with memories going back to the early days of ships and factories, was a lure that no amount of reason could make me resist. After all, the strangest and maddest of myths are often merely symbols or allegories based upon truth—and old Zadok must have seen everything which went on around Innsmouth for the last ninety years. Curiosity flared up beyond sense and caution, and in my youthful egotism I fancied I might be able to sift a nucleus of real history from the confused, extravagant outpouring I would probably extract with the aid of raw whiskey.

I knew that I could not accost him then and there, for the firemen would surely notice and object. Instead, I reflected, I would prepare by getting some bootleg liquor at a place where the grocery boy had told me it was plentiful. Then I would loaf near the fire station in apparent casualness, and fall in with old Zadok after he had started on one of his frequent rambles. The youth said that he was very restless, seldom sitting around the station for more than an hour or two at a time.

A quart bottle of whiskey was easily, though not cheaply, obtained in the rear of a dingy variety-store just off the Square in Eliot Street. The dirty-looking fellow who waited on me had a touch of the staring "Innsmouth look", but was quite civil in his way; being perhaps used to the custom of such convivial strangers—truckmen, gold-buyers, and the like—as were occasionally in town.

Reëntering the Square I saw that luck was with me; for—shuffling out of Paine Street around the corner of the Gilman House—I glimpsed nothing less than the tall, lean, tattered form of old Zadok Allen himself. In accordance with my plan, I attracted his attention by brandishing my newly purchased bottle; and soon realised that he had begun to shuffle wistfully after me as I turned into Waite Street on my way to the most deserted region I could think of.

I was steering my course by the map the grocery boy had prepared, and was aiming for the wholly abandoned stretch of southern waterfront which I had previously visited. The only people in sight there had been the fishermen on the distant breakwater; and by going a few squares south I could get beyond the range of these, finding a pair of seats on some abandoned wharf and being free to question old Zadok unobserved for an indefinite time. Before I reached Main Street I could hear a faint and wheezy "Hey, Mister!" behind me, and I presently allowed the old man to catch up and take copious pulls from the quart bottle.

I began putting out feelers as we walked along to Water Street and turned southward amidst the omnipresent desolation and crazily tilted ruins, but found that the aged tongue did not loosen as quickly as I had expected. At length I saw a grass-grown opening toward the sea between crumbling brick walls, with the weedy length of an earth-and-masonry wharf projecting beyond. Piles of moss-covered stones near the water promised tolerable seats, and the scene was sheltered from all possible view by a ruined warehouse on the north. Here, I thought, was the ideal place for a long secret colloquy; so I guided my companion down the lane and picked out spots to sit in among the mossy stones. The air of death and desertion was ghoulish, and the smell of fish almost insufferable; but I was resolved to let nothing deter me.

About four hours remained for conversation if I were to catch the eight o'clock coach for Arkham, and I began to dole out more liquor to the ancient tippler; meanwhile eating my own frugal lunch. In my donations

I was careful not to overshoot the mark, for I did not wish Zadok's vinous garrulousness to pass into a stupor. After an hour his furtive taciturnity shewed signs of disappearing, but much to my disappointment he still sidetracked my questions about Innsmouth and its shadow-haunted past. He would babble of current topics, revealing a wide acquaintance with newspapers and a great tendency to philosophise in a sententious village fashion.

Toward the end of the second hour I feared my quart of whiskey would not be enough to produce results, and was wondering whether I had better leave old Zadok and go back for more. Just then, however, chance made the opening which my questions had been unable to make; and the wheezing ancient's rambling took a turn that caused me to lean forward and listen alertly. My back was toward the fishy-smelling sea, but he was facing it, and something or other had caused his wandering gaze to light on the low, distant line of Devil Reef, then shewing plainly and almost fascinatingly above the waves. The sight seemed to displease him, for he began a series of weak curses which ended in a confidential whisper and a knowing leer. He bent toward me, took hold of my coat lapel, and hissed out some hints that could not be mistaken.

"Thar's whar it all begun—that cursed place of all wickedness whar the deep water starts. Gate o' hell—sheer drop daown to a bottom no saoundin'-line kin tech. Ol' Cap'n Obed done it—him that faound aout more'n was good fer him in the Saouth Sea islands.

"Everybody was in a bad way them days. Trade fallin' off, mills losin' business—even the new ones—an' the best of our menfolks kilt a-privateerin' in the War of 1812 or lost with the *Elizy* brig an' the *Ranger* snow—both of 'em Gilman venters. Obed Marsh he had three ships afloat—brigantine *Columby*, brig *Hetty*, an' barque *Sumatry Queen*. He was the only one as kep' on with the East-Injy an' Pacific trade, though Esdras Martin's barkentine *Malay Pride* made a venter as late as 'twenty-eight.

"Never was nobody like Cap'n Obed—old limb o' Satan! Heh, heh! I kin mind him a-tellin' abaout furren parts, an' callin' all the folks stupid fer goin' to Christian meetin' an' bearin' their burdens meek an' lowly. Says they'd orter git better gods like some o' the folks in the Injies—gods as ud bring 'em good fishin' in return for their sacrifices, an' ud reely answer folks's prayers.

"Matt Eliot, his fust mate, talked a lot, too, only he was agin' folks's doin' any heathen things. Told abaout an island east of Otaheité whar they was a lot o' stone ruins older'n anybody knew anything abaout, kind o' like them on Ponape, in the Carolines, but with carvin's of faces that looked like the big statues on Easter Island. They was a little volcanic island near thar, too, whar they was other ruins with diff'rent carvin's— ruins all wore away like they'd ben under the sea onct, an' with picters of awful monsters all over 'em.

"Wal, Sir, Matt he says the natives araound thar had all the fish they cud ketch, an' sported bracelets an' armlets an' head rigs made aout of a queer kind o' gold an' covered with picters o' monsters jest like the ones carved over the ruins on the little island—sorter fish-like frogs or frog-like fishes that was drawed in all kinds o' positions like they was human bein's. Nobody cud git aout o' them whar they got all the stuff, an' all the other natives wondered haow they managed to find fish in plenty even when the very next islands had lean pickin's. Matt he got to wonderin' too, an' so did Cap'n Obed. Obed he notices, besides, that lots of the han'some young folks ud drop aout o' sight fer good from year to year, an' that they wa'n't many old folks araound. Also, he thinks some of the folks looks durned queer even fer Kanakys.

"It took Obed to git the truth aout o' them heathen. I dun't know haow he done it, but he begun by tradin' fer the gold-like things they wore. Ast 'em whar they come from, an' ef they cud git more, an' finally wormed the story aout o' the old chief—Walakea, they called him. Nobody but Obed ud ever a believed the old yeller devil, but the Cap'n cud read folks like they was books. Heh, heh! Nobody never believes me naow when I tell 'em, an' I dun't s'pose you will, young feller— though come to look at ye, ye hev kind o' got them sharp-readin' eyes like Obed had."

The old man's whisper grew fainter, and I found myself shuddering at the terrible and sincere portentousness of his intonation, even though I knew his tale could be nothing but drunken phantasy.

"Wal, Sir, Obed he larnt that they's things on this arth as most folks never heerd abaout—an' wouldn't believe ef they did hear. It seems these Kanakys was sacrificin' heaps o' their young men an' maidens to some kind o' god-things that lived under the sea, an' gittin' all kinds o' favour in return. They met the things on the little islet with the queer ruins, an' it seems them awful picters o' frog-fish monsters was supposed to be picters o' these things. Mebbe they was the kind o' critters as got all the mermaid stories an' sech started. They had all kinds o' cities on the sea-bottom, an' this island was heaved up from thar. Seems they was some of the things alive in the stone buildin's when the island come up sudden to the surface. That's haow the Kanakys got wind they was daown thar. Made sign-talk as soon as they got over bein' skeert, an' pieced up a bargain afore long.

"Them things liked human sacrifices. Had had 'em ages afore, but lost track o' the upper world arter a time. What they done to the victims it ain't fer me to say, an' I guess Obed wa'n't none too sharp abaout askin'. But it was all right with the heathens, because they'd ben havin' a hard time an' was desp'rate abaout everything. They give a sarten number o' young folks to the sea-things twict every year—May-Eve an' Hallowe'en— reg'lar as cud be. Also give some o' the carved knick-knacks they made. What the things agreed to give in return was plenty o' fish—they druv 'em in from all over the sea—an' a few gold-like things naow an' then.

"Wal, as I says, the natives met the things on the little volcanic islet— goin' thar in canoes with the sacrifices et cet'ry, and bringin' back any of the gold-like jools as was comin' to 'em. At fust the things didn't never go onto the main island, but arter a time they come to want to. Seems they hankered arter mixin' with the folks, an' havin' j'int ceremonies on the big days—May-Eve an' Hallowe'en. Ye see, they was able to live both in an' aout o' water—what they call amphibians, I guess. The Kanakys told 'em as haow folks from the other islands might wanta wipe 'em aout ef they got wind o' their bein' thar, but they says they dun't keer much, because they cud wipe aout the hull brood o' humans ef they was willin' to bother—that is, any as didn't hev sarten signs sech as was used onct by the lost Old Ones, whoever they was. But not wantin' to bother, they'd lay low when anybody visited the island.

"When it come to matin' with them toad-lookin' fishes, the Kanakys kind o' balked, but finally they larnt something as put a new face on the matter. Seems that human folks has got a kind o' relation to sech water-beasts—that everything alive come aout o' the water onct, an' only needs a little change to go back agin. Them things told the Kanakys that ef they mixed bloods there'd be children as ud look human at fust, but later turn more'n more like the things, till finally they'd take to the water an' jine the main lot o' things daown thar. An' this is the important part, young feller—them as turned into fish things an' went into the water *wouldn't never die*. Them things never died excep' they was kilt violent.

"Wal, Sir, it seems by the time Obed knowed them islanders they was all full o' fish blood from them deep-water things. When they got old an' begun to shew it, they was kep' hid until they felt like takin' to the water an' quittin' the place. Some was more teched than others, an' some never did change quite enough to take to the water; but mostly they turned aout jest the way them things said. Them as was born more like the things changed arly, but them as was nearly human sometimes stayed on the island till they was past seventy, though they'd usually go daown under fer trial trips afore that. Folks as had took to the water gen'rally come back a good deal to visit, so's a man ud often be a-talkin' to his own five-times-great-grandfather, who'd left the dry land a couple o' hundred years or so afore.

"Everybody got aout o' the idee o' dyin'—excep' in canoe wars with the other islanders, or as sacrifices to the sea-gods daown below, or from snake-bite or plague or sharp gallopin' ailments or somethin' afore they cud take to the water—but simply looked forrad to a kind o' change that wa'n't a bit horrible arter a while. They thought what they'd got was well wuth all they'd had to give up—an' I guess Obed kind o' come to think the same hisself when he'd chewed over old Walakea's story a bit. Walakea, though, was one of the few as hadn't got none of the fish blood—bein' of a royal line that intermarried with royal lines on other islands.

"Walakea he shewed Obed a lot o' rites an' incantations as had to do with the sea-things, an' let him see some o' the folks in the village as had changed a lot from human shape. Somehaow or other, though, he never would let him see one of the reg'lar things from right aout o' the water. In the end he give him a funny kind o' thingumajig made aout o' lead or something, that he said ud bring up the fish things from any place in the water whar they might be a nest of 'em. The idee was to drop it daown with the right kind o' prayers an' sech. Walakea allaowed as the things was scattered all over the world, so's anybody that looked abaout cud find a nest an' bring 'em up ef they was wanted.

"Matt he didn't like this business at all, an' wanted Obed shud keep away from the island; but the Cap'n was sharp fer gain, an' faound he cud git them gold-like things so cheap it ud pay him to make a specialty of 'em. Things went on that way fer years, an' Obed got enough o' that gold-like stuff to make him start the refinery in Waite's old run-daown fullin' mill. He didn't dass sell the pieces like they was, fer folks ud be all the time askin' questions. All the same his crews ud git a piece an' dispose of it naow and then, even though they was swore to keep quiet; an' he let his women-folks wear some o' the pieces as was more human-like than most.

"Wal, come abaout 'thutty-eight—when I was seven year' old— Obed he faound the island people all wiped aout between v'yages. Seems the other islanders had got wind o' what was goin' on, an' had took matters into their own hands. S'pose they musta had, arter all, them old magic signs as the sea-things says was the only things they was afeard of. No tellin' what any o' them Kanakys will chance to git a holt of when the sea-bottom throws up some island with ruins older'n the deluge. Pious cusses, these was—they didn't leave nothin' standin' on either the main island or the little volcanic islet excep' what parts of the ruins was too big to knock daown. In some places they was little stones strewed abaout—like charms—with somethin' on 'em like what ye call a swastika naowadays. Prob'ly them was the Old Ones' signs. Folks all wiped aout, no trace o' no gold-like things, an' none o' the nearby Kanakys ud breathe a word abaout the matter. Wouldn't even admit they'd ever ben any people on that island.

"That naturally hit Obed pretty hard, seein' as his normal trade was doin' very poor. It hit the whole of Innsmouth, too, because in seafarin' days what profited the master of a ship gen'lly profited the crew proportionate. Most o' the folks araound the taown took the hard times kind o' sheep-like an' resigned, but they was in bad shape because the fishin' was peterin' aout an' the mills wa'n't doin' none too well.

"Then's the time Obed he begun a-cursin' at the folks fer bein' dull sheep an' prayin' to a Christian heaven as didn't help 'em none. He told 'em he'd knowed of folks as prayed to gods that give somethin' ye reely need, an' says ef a good bunch o' men ud stand by him, he cud mebbe git a holt o' sarten paowers as ud bring plenty o' fish an' quite a bit o' gold. O' course them as sarved on the *Sumatry Queen* an' seed the island knowed what he meant, an' wa'n't none too anxious to git clost to sea-things like they'd heerd tell on, but them as didn't know what 'twas all abaout got kind o' swayed by what Obed had to say, an' begun to ast him what he cud do to set 'em on the way to the faith as ud bring 'em results."

Here the old man faltered, mumbled, and lapsed into a moody and apprehensive silence; glancing nervously over his shoulder and then turning back to stare fascinatedly at the distant black reef. When I spoke to him he did not answer, so I knew I would have to let him finish the bottle. The insane yarn I was hearing interested me profoundly, for I fancied there was contained within it a sort of crude allegory based upon the strangenesses of Innsmouth and elaborated by an imagination at once creative and full of scraps of exotic legend. Not for a moment did I believe that the tale had any really substantial foundation; but none the less the account held a hint of genuine terror, if only because it brought in references to strange jewels clearly akin to the malign tiara I had seen at Newburyport. Perhaps the ornaments had, after all, come from some strange island; and possibly the wild stories were lies of the bygone Obed himself rather than of this antique toper.

I handed Zadok the bottle, and he drained it to the last drop. It was curious how he could stand so much whiskey, for not even a trace of thickness had come into his high, wheezy voice. He licked the nose of the bottle and slipped it into his pocket, then beginning to nod and whisper softly to himself. I bent close to catch any articulate words he might utter, and thought I saw a sardonic smile behind the stained, bushy whiskers. Yes—he was really forming words, and I could grasp a fair proportion of them.

"Poor Matt—Matt he allus was agin' it—tried to line up the folks on his side, an' had long talks with the preachers—no use—they run the Congregational parson aout o' taown, an' the Methodist feller quit— never did see Resolved Babcock, the Baptist parson, agin—Wrath o' Jehovy—I was a mighty little critter, but I heerd what I heerd an' seen what I seen—Dagon an' Ashtoreth—Belial an' Beëlzebub—Golden Caff an' the idols o' Canaan an' the Philistines—Babylonish abominations— *Mene, mene, tekel, upharsin*—"

He stopped again, and from the look in his watery blue eyes I feared he was close to a stupor after all. But when I gently shook his shoulder he turned on me with astonishing alertness and snapped out some more obscure phrases.

"Dun't believe me, hey? Heh, heh, heh—then jest tell me, young feller, why Cap'n Obed an' twenty odd other folks used to row aout to Devil Reef in the dead o' night an' chant things so laoud ye cud hear 'em all over taown when the wind was right? Tell me that, hey? An' tell me why Obed was allus droppin' heavy things daown into the deep water t'other side o' the reef whar the bottom shoots daown like a cliff lower'n ye kin saound? Tell me what he done with that funny-shaped lead thingumajig as Walakea give him? Hey, boy? An' what did they all haowl on May-Eve, an' agin the next Hallowe'en? An' why'd the new church parsons—fellers as used to be sailors—wear them queer robes an' cover theirselves with them gold-like things Obed brung? Hey?"

The watery blue eyes were almost savage and maniacal now, and the dirty white beard bristled electrically. Old Zadok probably saw me shrink back, for he had begun to cackle evilly.

"Heh, heh, heh, heh! Beginnin' to see, hey? Mebbe ye'd like to a ben me in them days, when I seed things at night aout to sea from the cupalo top o' my haouse. Oh, I kin tell ye, little pitchers hev big ears, an' I wa'n't missin' nothin' o' what was gossiped abaout Cap'n Obed an' the folks aout to the reef! Heh, heh, heh! Haow abaout the night I took my pa's ship's glass up to the cupalo an' seed the reef a-bristlin' thick with shapes that dove off quick soon's the moon riz? Obed an' the folks was in a dory, but them shapes dove off the far side into the deep water an' never come up.... Haow'd ye like to be a little shaver alone up in a cupalo a-watchin' shapes *as wa'n't human shapes?*... Hey?... Heh, heh, heh, heh...."

The old man was getting hysterical, and I began to shiver with a nameless alarm. He laid a gnarled claw on my shoulder, and it seemed to me that its shaking was not altogether that of mirth.

"S'pose one night ye seed somethin' heavy heaved offen Obed's dory beyond the reef, an' then larned nex' day a young feller was missin' from home? Hey? Did anybody ever see hide or hair o' Hiram Gilman agin? Did they? An' Nick Pierce, an' Luelly Waite, an' Adoniram Saouthwick, an' Henry Garrison? Hey? Heh, heh, heh, heh. . . . Shapes talkin' sign language with their hands . . . them as had reel hands. . . .

"Wal, Sir, that was the time Obed begun to git on his feet agin. Folks see his three darters a-wearin' gold-like things as nobody'd never see on 'em afore, an' smoke started comin' aout o' the refin'ry chimbly. Other folks were prosp'rin', too—fish begun to swarm into the harbour fit to kill, an' heaven knows what sized cargoes we begun to ship aout to Newb'ryport, Arkham, an' Boston. 'Twas then Obed got the ol' branch railrud put through. Some Kingsport fishermen heerd abaout the ketch an' come up in sloops, but they was all lost. Nobody never see 'em agin. An' jest then our folks organised the Esoteric Order o' Dagon, an' bought Masonic Hall offen Calvary Commandery for it . . . heh, heh, heh! Matt Eliot was a Mason an' agin' the sellin', but he dropped aout o' sight jest then.

"Remember, I ain't sayin' Obed was set on hevin' things jest like they was on that Kanaky isle. I dun't think he aimed at fust to do no mixin', nor raise no younguns to take to the water an' turn into fishes with eternal life. He wanted them gold things, an' was willin' to pay heavy, an' I guess the *others* was satisfied fer a while. . . .

"Come in 'forty-six the taown done some lookin' an' thinkin' fer itself. Too many folks missin'—too much wild preachin' at meetin' of a Sunday—too much talk abaout that reef. I guess I done a bit by tellin' Selectman Mowry what I see from the cupalo. They was a party one night as follered Obed's craowd aout to the reef, an' I heerd shots betwixt the dories. Nex' day Obed an' thutty-two others was in gaol, with everbody a-wonderin' jest what was afoot an' jest what charge agin' 'em cud be got to holt. God, ef anybody'd look'd ahead . . . a couple o' weeks later, when nothin' had ben throwed into the sea fer that long. . . ."

Zadok was shewing signs of fright and exhaustion, and I let him keep silence for a while, though glancing apprehensively at my watch. The tide had turned and was coming in now, and the sound of the waves seemed to arouse him. I was glad of that tide, for at high water the fishy smell might not be so bad. Again I strained to catch his whispers.

"That awful night . . . I seed 'em . . . I was up in the cupalo . . . hordes of 'em . . . swarms of 'em . . . all over the reef an' swimmin' up the harbour into the Manuxet. . . . God, what happened in the streets of Innsmouth that night . . . they rattled our door, but pa wouldn't open . . . then he clumb aout the kitchen winder with his musket to find Selectman Mowry an' see what he cud do. . . . Maounds o' the dead an' the dyin' . . . shots an' screams . . . shaoutin' in Ol' Squar an' Taown Squar an' New Church Green . . . gaol throwed open . . . proclamation . . . treason . . . called it the plague when folks come in an' faound haff our people missin' . . . nobody left but them as ud jine in with Obed an' them things or else keep quiet . . . never heerd o' my pa no more. . . ."

The old man was panting, and perspiring profusely. His grip on my shoulder tightened.

"Everything cleaned up in the mornin'—but they was *traces.* . . . Obed he kinder takes charge an' says things is goin' to be changed . . . *others'll* worship with us at meetin'-time, an' sarten haouses hez got to entertain *guests* . . . *they* wanted to mix like they done with the Kanakys, an' he fer one didn't feel baound to stop 'em. Far gone, was Obed . . . jest like a crazy man on the subjeck. He says they brung us fish an' treasure, an' shud hev what they hankered arter. . . .

"Nothin' was to be diff'runt on the aoutside, only we was to keep shy o' strangers ef we knowed what was good fer us. We all hed to take the Oath o' Dagon, an' later on they was secon' an' third Oaths that some on us took. Them as ud help special, ud git special rewards—gold an' sech—No use balkin', fer they was millions of 'em daown thar. They'd ruther not start risin' an' wipin' aout humankind, but ef they was gave away an' forced to, they cud do a lot toward jest that. We didn't hev them old charms to cut 'em off like folks in the Saouth Sea did, an' them Kanakys wudn't never give away their secrets.

"Yield up enough sacrifices an' savage knick-knacks an' harbourage in the taown when they wanted it, an' they'd let well enough alone. Wudn't bother no strangers as might bear tales aoutside—that is, withaout they got pryin'. All in the band of the faithful—Order o' Dagon—an' the children shud never die, but go back to the Mother Hydra an' Father Dagon what we all come from onct—*Iä! Iä! Cthulhu fhtagn! Ph'nglui mglw'nafh Cthulhu R'lyeh wgah-nagl fhtagn—*"

Old Zadok was fast lapsing into stark raving, and I held my breath. Poor old soul—to what pitiful depths of hallucination had his liquor, plus his hatred of the decay, alienage, and disease around him, brought that fertile, imaginative brain! He began to moan now, and tears were coursing down his channelled cheeks into the depths of his beard.

"God, what I seen senct I was fifteen year' old—*Mene, mene, tekel, upharsin!*—the folks as was missin', an' them as kilt theirselves—them as told things in Arkham or Ipswich or sech places was all called crazy, like you're a-callin' me right naow—but God, what I seen—They'd a kilt me long ago fer what I know, only I'd took the fust an' secon' Oaths o'

Dagon offen Obed, so was pertected unlessen a jury of 'em proved I told things knowin' an' delib'rit . . . but I wudn't take the third Oath—I'd a died ruther'n take that—

"It got wuss araound Civil War time, *when children born senct 'forty-six begun to grow up*—some of 'em, that is. I was afeard—never did no pryin' arter that awful night, an' never see one of—*them*—clost to in all my life. That is, never no full-blooded one. I went to the war, an' ef I'd a had any guts or sense I'd a never come back, but settled away from here. But folks wrote me things wa'n't so bad. That, I s'pose, was because gov'munt draft men was in taown arter 'sixty-three. Arter the war it was jest as bad agin. People begun to fall off—mills an' shops shet daown—shippin' stopped an' the harbour choked up—railrud give up—but *they* . . . they never stopped swimmin' in an' aout o' the river from that cursed reef o' Satan—an' more an' more attic winders got a-boarded up, an' more an' more noises was heerd in haouses as wa'n't s'posed to hev nobody in 'em. . . .

"Folks aoutside hev their stories abaout us—s'pose you've heerd a plenty on 'em, seein' what questions ye ast—stories abaout things they've seed naow an' then, an' abaout that queer joolry as still comes in from somewhars an' ain't quite all melted up—but nothin' never gits def'nite. Nobody'll believe nothin'. They call them gold-like things pirate loot, an' allaow the Innsmouth folks hez furren blood or is distempered or somethin'. Besides, them that lives here shoo off as many strangers as they kin, an' encourage the rest not to git very cur'ous, specially raound night time. Beasts balk at the critters—hosses wuss'n mules—but when they got autos that was all right.

"In 'forty-six Cap'n Obed took a second wife *that nobody in the taown never see*—some says he didn't want to, but was made to by them as he'd called in—had three children by her—two as disappeared young, but one gal as looked like anybody else an' was eddicated in Europe. Obed finally got her married off by a trick to an Arkham feller as didn't suspect nothin'. But nobody aoutside'll hev nothin' to do with Innsmouth folks naow. Barnabas Marsh that runs the refin'ry naow is Obed's grandson by his fust wife—son of Onesiphorus, his eldest son, *but his mother was another o' them as wa'n't never seed aoutdoors.*

"Right naow Barnabas is abaout changed. Can't shet his eyes no more, an' is all aout o' shape. They say he still wears clothes, but he'll take to the water soon. Mebbe he's tried it already—they do sometimes go daown fer little spells afore they go fer good. Ain't ben seed abaout in public fer nigh on ten year'. Dun't know haow his poor wife kin feel—she come from Ipswich, an' they nigh lynched Barnabas when he courted her fifty odd year' ago. Obed he died in 'seventy-eight, an' all the next gen'ration is gone naow—the fust wife's children dead, an' the rest . . . God knows. . . ."

The sound of the incoming tide was now very insistent, and little by little it seemed to change the old man's mood from maudlin tearfulness to watchful fear. He would pause now and then to renew those nervous glances over his shoulder or out toward the reef, and despite the wild absurdity of his tale, I could not help beginning to share his vague apprehensiveness. Zadok now grew shriller, and seemed to be trying to whip up his courage with louder speech.

"Hey, yew, why dun't ye say somethin'? Haow'd ye like to be livin' in a taown like this, with everything a-rottin' an' a-dyin', an' boarded-up monsters crawlin' an' bleatin' an' barkin' an' hoppin' araoun' black cellars an' attics every way ye turn? Hey? Haow'd ye like to hear the haowlin' night arter night from the churches an' Order o' Dagon Hall, *an' know what's doin' part o' the haowlin'?* Haow'd ye like to hear what comes from that awful reef every May-Eve an' Hallowmass? Hey? Think the old man's crazy, eh? Wal, Sir, *let me tell ye that ain't the wust!*"

Zadok was really screaming now, and the mad frenzy of his voice disturbed me more than I care to own.

"Curse ye, dun't set thar a-starin' at me with them eyes—I tell Obed Marsh he's in hell, an' hez got to stay thar! Heh, heh . . . in hell, I says! Can't git me—I hain't done nothin' nor told nobody nothin'—

"Oh, you, young feller? Wal, even ef I hain't told nobody nothin' yet, I'm a-goin' to naow! You jest set still an' listen to me, boy—this is what I

ain't never told nobody. . . . I says I didn't do no pryin' arter that night—
but I faound things aout jest the same!

"Yew want to know what the reel horror is, hey? Wal, it's this—it ain't
what them fish devils *hez done, but what they're a-goin' to do!* They're
a-bringin' things up aout o' whar they come from into the taown—ben
doin' it fer years, an' slackenin' up lately. Them haouses north o' the
river betwixt Water an' Main Streets is full of 'em—them devils *an' what
they brung*—an' when they git ready. . . . I say, *when they git ready . . .* ever
hear tell of a *shoggoth?* . . .

"Hey, d'ye hear me? I tell ye *I know what them things be—I seen 'em
one night when . . .* EH—AHHHH—AH! E'YAAHHHH. . . ."

The hideous suddenness and inhuman frightfulness of the old man's
shriek almost made me faint. His eyes, looking past me toward the
malodorous sea, were positively starting from his head; while his face was
a mask of fear worthy of Greek tragedy. His bony claw dug monstrously
into my shoulder, and he made no motion as I turned my head to look at
whatever he had glimpsed.

There was nothing that I could see. Only the incoming tide,
with perhaps one set of ripples more local than the long-flung line of
breakers. But now Zadok was shaking me, and I turned back to watch
the melting of that fear-frozen face into a chaos of twitching eyelids and
mumbling gums. Presently his voice came back—albeit as a trembling
whisper.

"*Git aout o' here!* Git aout o' here! *They seen us*—git aout fer your
life! Dun't wait fer nothin'—*they know naow*—Run fer it—quick—*aout
o' this taown*—"

Another heavy wave dashed against the loosening masonry of
the bygone wharf, and changed the mad ancient's whisper to another
inhuman and blood-curdling scream.

"E—YAAHHHH! . . . YHAAAAAAA! . . ."

Before I could recover my scattered wits he had relaxed his clutch
on my shoulder and dashed wildly inland toward the street, reeling
northward around the ruined warehouse wall.

I glanced back at the sea, but there was nothing there. And when I reached Water Street and looked along it toward the north there was no remaining trace of Zadok Allen.

IV

I can hardly describe the mood in which I was left by this harrowing episode—an episode at once mad and pitiful, grotesque and terrifying. The grocery boy had prepared me for it, yet the reality left me none the less bewildered and disturbed. Puerile though the story was, old Zadok's insane earnestness and horror had communicated to me a mounting unrest which joined with my earlier sense of loathing for the town and its blight of intangible shadow.

Later I might sift the tale and extract some nucleus of historic allegory; just now I wished to put it out of my head. The hour had grown perilously late—my watch said 7:15, and the Arkham bus left Town Square at eight—so I tried to give my thoughts as neutral and practical a cast as possible, meanwhile walking rapidly through the deserted streets of gaping roofs and leaning houses toward the hotel where I had checked my valise and would find my bus.

Though the golden light of late afternoon gave the ancient roofs and decrepit chimneys an air of mystic loveliness and peace, I could not help glancing over my shoulder now and then. I would surely be very glad to get out of malodorous and fear-shadowed Innsmouth, and wished there were some other vehicle than the bus driven by that sinister-looking fellow Sargent. Yet I did not hurry too precipitately, for there were architectural details worth viewing at every silent corner; and I could easily, I calculated, cover the necessary distance in a half-hour.

Studying the grocery youth's map and seeking a route I had not traversed before, I chose Marsh Street instead of State for my approach to Town Square. Near the corner of Fall Street I began to see scattered groups of furtive whisperers, and when I finally reached the Square I saw that almost all the loiterers were congregated around the door of the

Gilman House. It seemed as if many bulging, watery, unwinking eyes looked oddly at me as I claimed my valise in the lobby, and I hoped that none of these unpleasant creatures would be my fellow-passengers on the coach.

The bus, rather early, rattled in with three passengers somewhat before eight, and an evil-looking fellow on the sidewalk muttered a few indistinguishable words to the driver. Sargent threw out a mail-bag and a roll of newspapers, and entered the hotel; while the passengers—the same men whom I had seen arriving in Newburyport that morning— shambled to the sidewalk and exchanged some faint guttural words with a loafer in a language I could have sworn was not English. I boarded the empty coach and took the same seat I had taken before, but was hardly settled before Sargent reappeared and began mumbling in a throaty voice of peculiar repulsiveness.

I was, it appeared, in very bad luck. There had been something wrong with the engine, despite the excellent time made from Newburyport, and the bus could not complete the journey to Arkham. No, it could not possibly be repaired that night, nor was there any other way of getting transportation out of Innsmouth, either to Arkham or elsewhere. Sargent was sorry, but I would have to stop over at the Gilman. Probably the clerk would make the price easy for me, but there was nothing else to do. Almost dazed by this sudden obstacle, and violently dreading the fall of night in this decaying and half-unlighted town, I left the bus and reëntered the hotel lobby; where the sullen, queer-looking night clerk told me I could have Room 428 on next the top floor—large, but without running water—for a dollar.

Despite what I had heard of this hotel in Newburyport, I signed the register, paid my dollar, let the clerk take my valise, and followed that sour, solitary attendant up three creaking flights of stairs past dusty corridors which seemed wholly devoid of life. My room, a dismal rear one with two windows and bare, cheap furnishings, overlooked a dingy courtyard otherwise hemmed in by low, deserted brick blocks, and commanded a view of decrepit westward-stretching roofs with a marshy countryside beyond. At the end of the corridor was a bathroom—a discouraging relique with ancient marble bowl, tin tub, faint electric light, and musty wooden panelling around all the plumbing fixtures.

It being still daylight, I descended to the Square and looked around for a dinner of some sort; noticing as I did so the strange glances I received from the unwholesome loafers. Since the grocery was closed, I was forced to patronise the restaurant I had shunned before; a stooped, narrow-headed man with staring, unwinking eyes, and a flat-nosed wench with unbelievably thick, clumsy hands being in attendance. The service was of the counter type, and it relieved me to find that much was evidently served from cans and packages. A bowl of vegetable soup with crackers was enough for me, and I soon headed back for my cheerless room at the Gilman; getting an evening paper and a flyspecked magazine from the evil-visaged clerk at the rickety stand beside his desk.

As twilight deepened I turned on the one feeble electric bulb over the cheap, iron-framed bed, and tried as best I could to continue the reading I had begun. I felt it advisable to keep my mind wholesomely occupied, for it would not do to brood over the abnormalities of this ancient, blight-shadowed town while I was still within its borders. The insane yarn I had heard from the aged drunkard did not promise very pleasant dreams, and I felt I must keep the image of his wild, watery eyes as far as possible from my imagination.

Also, I must not dwell on what that factory inspector had told the Newburyport ticket-agent about the Gilman House and the voices of its nocturnal tenants—not on that, nor on the face beneath the tiara in the black church doorway; the face for whose horror my conscious mind could not account. It would perhaps have been easier to keep my thoughts from disturbing topics had the room not been so gruesomely musty. As it was, the lethal mustiness blended hideously with the town's general fishy odour and persistently focussed one's fancy on death and decay.

Another thing that disturbed me was the absence of a bolt on the door of my room. One had been there, as marks clearly shewed, but there were signs of recent removal. No doubt it had become out of order, like so many other things in this decrepit edifice. In my nervousness I looked around and discovered a bolt on the clothes-press which seemed to be of the same size, judging from the marks, as the one formerly on the door. To gain a partial relief from the general tension I busied myself by transferring this hardware to the vacant place with the aid of a handy three-in-one device including a screw-driver which I kept on my key-ring. The bolt fitted perfectly, and I was somewhat relieved when I knew that I could shoot it firmly upon retiring. Not that I had any real apprehension of its need, but that any symbol of security was welcome in an environment of this kind. There were adequate bolts on the two lateral doors to connecting rooms, and these I proceeded to fasten.

I did not undress, but decided to read till I was sleepy and then lie down with only my coat, collar, and shoes off. Taking a pocket flashlight from my valise, I placed it in my trousers, so that I could read my watch if I woke up later in the dark. Drowsiness, however, did not come; and when I stopped to analyse my thoughts I found to my disquiet that I was really unconsciously listening for something—listening for something which I dreaded but could not name. That inspector's story must have worked on my imagination more deeply than I had suspected. Again I tried to read, but found that I made no progress.

After a time I seemed to hear the stairs and corridors creak at intervals as if with footsteps, and wondered if the other rooms were beginning to fill up. There were no voices, however, and it struck me that there was something subtly furtive about the creaking. I did not like it, and debated whether I had better try to sleep at all. This town had some queer people, and there had undoubtedly been several disappearances. Was this one of those inns where travellers were slain for their money? Surely I had no look of excessive prosperity. Or were the townsfolk really so resentful about curious visitors? Had my obvious sightseeing, with its frequent map-consultations, aroused unfavourable notice? It occurred to me that I must be in a highly nervous state to let a few random creakings set me off speculating in this fashion—but I regretted none the less that I was unarmed.

At length, feeling a fatigue which had nothing of drowsiness in it, I bolted the newly outfitted hall door, turned off the light, and threw myself down on the hard, uneven bed—coat, collar, shoes, and all. In the darkness every faint noise of the night seemed magnified, and a flood of doubly unpleasant thoughts swept over me. I was sorry I had put out the light, yet was too tired to rise and turn it on again. Then, after a long, dreary interval, and prefaced by a fresh creaking of stairs and corridor, there came that soft, damnably unmistakable sound which seemed like a malign fulfilment of all my apprehensions. Without the least shadow of a doubt, the lock on my hall door was being tried—cautiously, furtively, tentatively—with a key.

My sensations upon recognising this sign of actual peril were perhaps less rather than more tumultuous because of my previous vague fears. I had been, albeit without definite reason, instinctively on my guard—and that was to my advantage in the new and real crisis, whatever it might turn out to be. Nevertheless the change in the menace from vague premonition to immediate reality was a profound shock, and fell upon me with the force of a genuine blow. It never once occurred to me that the fumbling might be a mere mistake. Malign purpose was all I could think of, and I kept deathly quiet, awaiting the would-be intruder's next move.

After a time the cautious rattling ceased, and I heard the room to the north entered with a pass-key. Then the lock of the connecting door to my room was softly tried. The bolt held, of course, and I heard the floor creak as the prowler left the room. After a moment there came another soft rattling, and I knew that the room to the south of me was being entered. Again a furtive trying of a bolted connecting door, and again a receding creaking. This time the creaking went along the hall and down the stairs, so I knew that the prowler had realised the bolted condition of my doors and was giving up his attempt for a greater or lesser time, as the future would shew.

The readiness with which I fell into a plan of action proves that I must have been subconsciously fearing some menace and considering possible avenues of escape for hours. From the first I felt that the unseen fumbler meant a danger not to be met or dealt with, but only to be fled from as precipitately as possible. The one thing to do was to get out of that hotel alive as quickly as I could, and through some channel other than the front stairs and lobby.

Rising softly and throwing my flashlight on the switch, I sought to light the bulb over my bed in order to choose and pocket some belongings for a swift, valiseless flight. Nothing, however, happened; and I saw that the power had been cut off. Clearly, some cryptic, evil movement was afoot on a large scale—just what, I could not say. As I stood pondering with my hand on the now useless switch I heard a muffled creaking on the floor below, and thought I could barely distinguish voices in conversation. A moment later I felt less sure that the deeper sounds were voices, since the apparent hoarse barkings and loose-syllabled croakings bore so little resemblance to recognised human speech. Then I thought with renewed force of what the factory inspector had heard in the night in this mouldering and pestilential building.

Having filled my pockets with the flashlight's aid, I put on my hat and tiptoed to the windows to consider chances of descent. Despite the state's safety regulations there was no fire escape on this side of the hotel, and I saw that my windows commanded only a sheer three-story drop to the cobbled courtyard. On the right and left, however, some ancient brick business blocks abutted on the hotel; their slant roofs coming up to a reasonable jumping distance from my fourth-story level. To reach either of these lines of buildings I would have to be in a room two doors from my own—in one case on the north and in the other case on the south—and my mind instantly set to work calculating what chances I had of making the transfer.

I could not, I decided, risk an emergence into the corridor; where my footsteps would surely be heard, and where the difficulties of entering the desired room would be insuperable. My progress, if it was to be made at all, would have to be through the less solidly built connecting doors of the rooms; the locks and bolts of which I would have to force violently, using my shoulder as a battering-ram whenever they were set against me. This, I thought, would be possible owing to the rickety nature of the house and its fixtures; but I realised I could not do it noiselessly. I would have to count on sheer speed, and the chance of getting to a window before any hostile forces became coördinated enough to open the right door toward me with a pass-key. My own outer door I reinforced by pushing the bureau against it—little by little, in order to make a minimum of sound.

I perceived that my chances were very slender, and was fully prepared for any calamity. Even getting to another roof would not solve the problem, for there would then remain the task of reaching the ground and escaping from the town. One thing in my favour was the deserted and ruinous state of the abutting buildings, and the number of skylights gaping blackly open in each row.

Gathering from the grocery boy's map that the best route out of town was southward, I glanced first at the connecting door on the south side of the room. It was designed to open in my direction, hence I saw—after drawing the bolt and finding other fastenings in place—it was not a favourable one for forcing. Accordingly abandoning it as a route, I cautiously moved the bedstead against it to hamper any attack which might be made on it later from the next room. The door on the north was hung to open away from me, and this—though a test proved it to be locked or bolted from the other side—I knew must be my route. If I could gain the roofs of the buildings in Paine Street and descend successfully to the ground level, I might perhaps dart through the courtyard and the adjacent or opposite buildings to Washington or Bates—or else emerge in Paine and edge around southward into Washington. In any case, I would aim to strike Washington somehow and get quickly out of the Town Square region. My preference would be to avoid Paine, since the fire station there might be open all night.

As I thought of these things I looked out over the squalid sea of decaying roofs below me, now brightened by the beams of a moon not much past full. On the right the black gash of the river-gorge clove the panorama; abandoned factories and railway station clinging barnacle-like to its sides. Beyond it the rusted railway and the Rowley road led off through a flat, marshy terrain dotted with islets of higher and dryer scrub-grown land. On the left the creek-threaded countryside was nearer, the narrow road to Ipswich gleaming white in the moonlight. I could not see from my side of the hotel the southward route toward Arkham which I had determined to take.

I was irresolutely speculating on when I had better attack the northward door, and on how I could least audibly manage it, when I noticed that the vague noises underfoot had given place to a fresh and heavier creaking of the stairs. A wavering flicker of light shewed through my transom, and the boards of the corridor began to groan with a ponderous load. Muffled sounds of possible vocal origin approached, and at length a firm knock came at my outer door.

For a moment I simply held my breath and waited. Eternities seemed to elapse, and the nauseous fishy odour of my environment seemed to mount suddenly and spectacularly. Then the knocking was repeated—continuously, and with growing insistence. I knew that the time for action had come, and forthwith drew the bolt of the northward connecting door, bracing myself for the task of battering it open. The knocking waxed louder, and I hoped that its volume would cover the sound of my efforts. At last beginning my attempt, I lunged again and again at the thin panelling with my left shoulder, heedless of shock or pain. The door resisted even more than I had expected, but I did not give in. And all the while the clamour at the outer door increased.

Finally the connecting door gave, but with such a crash that I knew those outside must have heard. Instantly the outside knocking became a violent battering, while keys sounded ominously in the hall doors of the rooms on both sides of me. Rushing through the newly opened connexion, I succeeded in bolting the northerly hall door before the lock could be turned; but even as I did so I heard the hall door of the third room—the one from whose window I had hoped to reach the roof below—being tried with a pass-key.

For an instant I felt absolute despair, since my trapping in a chamber with no window egress seemed complete. A wave of almost abnormal horror swept over me, and invested with a terrible but unexplainable singularity the flashlight-glimpsed dust prints made by the intruder who had lately tried my door from this room. Then, with a dazed automatism which persisted despite hopelessness, I made for the next connecting door and performed the blind motion of pushing at it in an effort to get through and—granting that fastenings might be as providentially intact as in this second room—bolt the hall door beyond before the lock could be turned from outside.

Sheer fortunate chance gave me my reprieve—for the connecting door before me was not only unlocked but actually ajar. In a second I was through, and had my right knee and shoulder against a hall door which was visibly opening inward. My pressure took the opener off guard, for the thing shut as I pushed, so that I could slip the well-conditioned bolt as I had done with the other door. As I gained this respite I heard the battering at the two other doors abate, while a confused clatter came from the connecting door I had shielded with the bedstead. Evidently the bulk of my assailants had entered the southerly room and were massing in a lateral attack. But at the same moment a pass-key sounded in the next door to the north, and I knew that a nearer peril was at hand.

The northward connecting door was wide open, but there was no time to think about checking the already turning lock in the hall. All I could do was to shut and bolt the open connecting door, as well as its mate on the opposite side—pushing a bedstead against the one and a bureau against the other, and moving a washstand in front of the hall door. I must, I saw, trust to such makeshift barriers to shield me till I could get out the window and on the roof of the Paine Street block. But even in this acute moment my chief horror was something apart from the immediate weakness of my defences. I was shuddering because not one of my pursuers, despite some hideous pantings, gruntings, and subdued barkings at odd intervals, was uttering an unmuffled or intelligible vocal sound.

As I moved the furniture and rushed toward the windows I heard a frightful scurrying along the corridor toward the room north of me, and perceived that the southward battering had ceased. Plainly, most of my opponents were about to concentrate against the feeble connecting door which they knew must open directly on me. Outside, the moon played on the ridgepole of the block below, and I saw that the jump would be desperately hazardous because of the steep surface on which I must land.

Surveying the conditions, I chose the more southerly of the two windows as my avenue of escape; planning to land on the inner slope of the roof and make for the nearest skylight. Once inside one of the decrepit brick structures I would have to reckon with pursuit; but I hoped to descend and dodge in and out of yawning doorways along the shadowed courtyard, eventually getting to Washington Street and slipping out of town toward the south.

The clatter at the northerly connecting door was now terrific, and I saw that the weak panelling was beginning to splinter. Obviously, the besiegers had brought some ponderous object into play as a battering-ram. The bedstead, however, still held firm; so that I had at least a faint chance of making good my escape. As I opened the window I noticed that it was flanked by heavy velour draperies suspended from a pole by brass rings, and also that there was a large projecting catch for the shutters on the exterior. Seeing a possible means of avoiding the dangerous jump, I yanked at the hangings and brought them down, pole and all; then quickly hooking two of the rings in the shutter catch and flinging the drapery outside. The heavy folds reached fully to the abutting roof, and I saw that the rings and catch would be likely to bear my weight. So, climbing out of the window and down the improvised rope ladder, I left behind me forever the morbid and horror-infested fabric of the Gilman House.

I landed safely on the loose slates of the steep roof, and succeeded in gaining the gaping black skylight without a slip. Glancing up at the window I had left, I observed it was still dark, though far across the crumbling chimneys to the north I could see lights ominously blazing

in the Order of Dagon Hall, the Baptist church, and the Congregational
church which I recalled so shiveringly. There had seemed to be no one
in the courtyard below, and I hoped there would be a chance to get away
before the spreading of a general alarm. Flashing my pocket lamp into
the skylight, I saw that there were no steps down. The distance was slight,
however, so I clambered over the brink and dropped; striking a dusty
floor littered with crumbling boxes and barrels.

The place was ghoulish-looking, but I was past minding such
impressions and made at once for the staircase revealed by my flashlight—
after a hasty glance at my watch, which shewed the hour to be 2 a.m.
The steps creaked, but seemed tolerably sound; and I raced down past a
barn-like second story to the ground floor. The desolation was complete,
and only echoes answered my footfalls. At length I reached the lower
hall, at one end of which I saw a faint luminous rectangle marking the
ruined Paine Street doorway. Heading the other way, I found the back
door also open; and darted out and down five stone steps to the grass-
grown cobblestones of the courtyard.

The moonbeams did not reach down here, but I could just see my
way about without using the flashlight. Some of the windows on the
Gilman House side were faintly glowing, and I thought I heard confused
sounds within. Walking softly over to the Washington Street side I
perceived several open doorways, and chose the nearest as my route out.
The hallway inside was black, and when I reached the opposite end I saw
that the street door was wedged immovably shut. Resolved to try another
building, I groped my way back toward the courtyard, but stopped short
when close to the doorway.

For out of an opened door in the Gilman House a large crowd of
doubtful shapes was pouring—lanterns bobbing in the darkness, and
horrible croaking voices exchanging low cries in what was certainly not
English. The figures moved uncertainly, and I realised to my relief that
they did not know where I had gone; but for all that they sent a shiver
of horror through my frame. Their features were indistinguishable, but
their crouching, shambling gait was abominably repellent. And worst of

all, I perceived that one figure was strangely robed, and unmistakably surmounted by a tall tiara of a design altogether too familiar. As the figures spread throughout the courtyard, I felt my fears increase. Suppose I could find no egress from this building on the street side? The fishy odour was detestable, and I wondered I could stand it without fainting. Again groping toward the street, I opened a door off the hall and came upon an empty room with closely shuttered but sashless windows. Fumbling in the rays of my flashlight, I found I could open the shutters; and in another moment had climbed outside and was carefully closing the aperture in its original manner.

I was now in Washington Street, and for the moment saw no living thing nor any light save that of the moon. From several directions in the distance, however, I could hear the sound of hoarse voices, of footsteps, and of a curious kind of pattering which did not sound quite like footsteps. Plainly I had no time to lose. The points of the compass were clear to me, and I was glad that all the street-lights were turned off, as is often the custom on strongly moonlit nights in unprosperous rural regions. Some of the sounds came from the south, yet I retained my design of escaping in that direction. There would, I knew, be plenty of deserted doorways to shelter me in case I met any person or group who looked like pursuers.

I walked rapidly, softly, and close to the ruined houses. While hatless and dishevelled after my arduous climb, I did not look especially noticeable; and stood a good chance of passing unheeded if forced to encounter any casual wayfarer. At Bates Street I drew into a yawning vestibule while two shambling figures crossed in front of me, but was soon on my way again and approaching the open space where Eliot Street obliquely crosses Washington at the intersection of South. Though I had never seen this space, it had looked dangerous to me on the grocery youth's map; since the moonlight would have free play there. There was no use trying to evade it, for any alternative course would involve detours of possibly disastrous visibility and delaying effect. The only thing to do was to cross it boldly and openly; imitating the typical shamble of the

Innsmouth folk as best I could, and trusting that no one—or at least no pursuer of mine—would be there.

Just how fully the pursuit was organised—and indeed, just what its purpose might be—I could form no idea. There seemed to be unusual activity in the town, but I judged that the news of my escape from the Gilman had not yet spread. I would, of course, soon have to shift from Washington to some other southward street; for that party from the hotel would doubtless be after me. I must have left dust prints in that last old building, revealing how I had gained the street.

The open space was, as I had expected, strongly moonlit; and I saw the remains of a park-like, iron-railed green in its centre. Fortunately no one was about, though a curious sort of buzz or roar seemed to be increasing in the direction of Town Square. South Street was very wide, leading directly down a slight declivity to the waterfront and commanding a long view out at sea; and I hoped that no one would be glancing up it from afar as I crossed in the bright moonlight.

My progress was unimpeded, and no fresh sound arose to hint that I had been spied. Glancing about me, I involuntarily let my pace slacken for a second to take in the sight of the sea, gorgeous in the burning moonlight at the street's end. Far out beyond the breakwater was the dim, dark line of Devil Reef, and as I glimpsed it I could not help thinking of all the hideous legends I had heard in the last thirty-four hours—legends which portrayed this ragged rock as a veritable gateway to realms of unfathomed horror and inconceivable abnormality.

Then, without warning, I saw the intermittent flashes of light on the distant reef. They were definite and unmistakable, and awaked in my mind a blind horror beyond all rational proportion. My muscles tightened for panic flight, held in only by a certain unconscious caution and half-hypnotic fascination. And to make matters worse, there now flashed forth from the lofty cupola of the Gilman House, which loomed up to the northeast behind me, a series of analogous though differently spaced gleams which could be nothing less than an answering signal.

Controlling my muscles, and realising afresh how plainly visible I was, I resumed my brisker and feignedly shambling pace; though keeping my eyes on that hellish and ominous reef as long as the opening of South Street gave me a seaward view. What the whole proceeding meant, I could not imagine; unless it involved some strange rite connected with Devil Reef, or unless some party had landed from a ship on that sinister rock. I now bent to the left around the ruinous green; still gazing toward the ocean as it blazed in the spectral summer moonlight, and watching the cryptical flashing of those nameless, unexplainable beacons.

It was then that the most horrible impression of all was borne in upon me—the impression which destroyed my last vestige of self-control and set me running frantically southward past the yawning black doorways and fishily staring windows of that deserted nightmare street. For at a closer glance I saw that the moonlit waters between the reef and the shore were far from empty. They were alive with a teeming horde of shapes swimming inward toward the town; and even at my vast distance and in my single moment of perception I could tell that the bobbing heads and flailing arms were alien and aberrant in a way scarcely to be expressed or consciously formulated.

My frantic running ceased before I had covered a block, for at my left I began to hear something like the hue and cry of organised pursuit. There were footsteps and guttural sounds, and a rattling motor wheezed south along Federal Street. In a second all my plans were utterly changed— for if the southward highway were blocked ahead of me, I must clearly find another egress from Innsmouth. I paused and drew into a gaping doorway, reflecting how lucky I was to have left the moonlit open space before these pursuers came down the parallel street.

A second reflection was less comforting. Since the pursuit was down another street, it was plain that the party was not following me directly. It had not seen me, but was simply obeying a general plan of cutting off my escape. This, however, implied that all roads leading out of Innsmouth were similarly patrolled; for the denizens could not have known what route I intended to take. If this were so, I would have to make my retreat across country away from any road; but how could I do that in view of the marshy and creek-riddled nature of all the surrounding region? For a moment my brain reeled—both from sheer hopelessness and from a rapid increase in the omnipresent fishy odour.

Then I thought of the abandoned railway to Rowley, whose solid line of ballasted, weed-grown earth still stretched off to the northwest from the crumbling station on the edge of the river-gorge. There was just a chance that the townsfolk would not think of that; since its brier-choked desertion made it half-impassable, and the unlikeliest of all avenues for a fugitive to choose. I had seen it clearly from my hotel window, and knew about how it lay. Most of its earlier length was uncomfortably visible from the Rowley road, and from high places in the town itself; but one could perhaps crawl inconspicuously through the undergrowth. At any rate, it would form my only chance of deliverance, and there was nothing to do but try it.

Drawing inside the hall of my deserted shelter, I once more consulted the grocery boy's map with the aid of the flashlight. The immediate problem was how to reach the ancient railway; and I now saw that the safest course was ahead to Babson Street, then west to Lafayette—there edging around but not crossing an open space homologous to the one I had traversed—and subsequently back northward and westward in a zigzagging line through Lafayette, Bates, Adams, and Bank Streets—the latter skirting the river-gorge—to the abandoned and dilapidated station I had seen from my window. My reason for going ahead to Babson was that I wished neither to re-cross the earlier open space nor to begin my westward course along a cross street as broad as South.

Starting once more, I crossed the street to the right-hand side in order to edge around into Babson as inconspicuously as possible. Noises still continued in Federal Street, and as I glanced behind me I thought I saw a gleam of light near the building through which I had escaped. Anxious to leave Washington Street, I broke into a quiet dog-trot, trusting to luck not to encounter any observing eye. Next the corner of Babson Street I saw to my alarm that one of the houses was still inhabited, as attested by curtains at the window; but there were no lights within, and I passed it without disaster.

In Babson Street, which crossed Federal and might thus reveal me to the searchers, I clung as closely as possible to the sagging, uneven buildings; twice pausing in a doorway as the noises behind me momentarily increased. The open space ahead shone wide and desolate under the moon, but my route would not force me to cross it. During my second pause I began to detect a fresh distribution of the vague sounds; and upon looking cautiously out from cover beheld a motor-car darting across the open space, bound outward along Eliot Street, which there intersects both Babson and Lafayette.

As I watched—choked by a sudden rise in the fishy odour after a short abatement—I saw a band of uncouth, crouching shapes loping and shambling in the same direction; and knew that this must be the party guarding the Ipswich road, since that highway forms an extension of Eliot Street. Two of the figures I glimpsed were in voluminous robes, and one wore a peaked diadem which glistened whitely in the moonlight. The gait of this figure was so odd that it sent a chill through me—for it seemed to me the creature was almost *hopping*.

When the last of the band was out of sight I resumed my progress; darting around the corner into Lafayette Street, and crossing Eliot very hurriedly lest stragglers of the party be still advancing along that thoroughfare. I did hear some croaking and clattering sounds far off toward Town Square, but accomplished the passage without disaster. My greatest dread was in re-crossing broad and moonlit South Street—with its seaward view—and I had to nerve myself for the ordeal. Someone might easily be looking, and possible Eliot Street stragglers could not fail to glimpse me from either of two points. At the last moment I decided I had better slacken my trot and make the crossing as before in the shambling gait of an average Innsmouth native.

When the view of the water again opened out—this time on my right—I was half-determined not to look at it at all. I could not, however, resist; but cast a sidelong glance as I carefully and imitatively shambled toward the protecting shadows ahead. There was no ship visible, as I had half expected there would be. Instead, the first thing which caught my eye was a small rowboat pulling in toward the abandoned wharves and laden with some bulky, tarpaulin-covered object. Its rowers, though distantly and indistinctly seen, were of an especially repellent aspect. Several swimmers were still discernible; while on the far black reef I could see a faint, steady glow unlike the winking beacon visible before, and of a curious colour which I could not precisely identify. Above the slant roofs ahead and to the right there loomed the tall cupola of the Gilman House, but it was completely dark. The fishy odour, dispelled for a moment by some merciful breeze, now closed in again with maddening intensity.

I had not quite crossed the street when I heard a muttering band advancing along Washington from the north. As they reached the broad open space where I had had my first disquieting glimpse of the moonlit water I could see them plainly only a block away—and was horrified by the bestial abnormality of their faces and the dog-like sub-humanness of their crouching gait. One man moved in a positively simian way, with long arms frequently touching the ground; while another figure—robed and tiaraed—seemed to progress in an almost hopping fashion. I judged this party to be the one I had seen in the Gilman's courtyard—the one, therefore, most closely on my trail. As some of the figures turned to look in my direction I was transfixed with fright, yet managed to preserve the casual, shambling gait I had assumed. To this day I do not know whether they saw me or not. If they did, my stratagem must have deceived them, for they passed on across the moonlit space without varying their course—meanwhile croaking and jabbering in some hateful guttural patois I could not identify.

Once more in shadow, I resumed my former dog-trot past the leaning and decrepit houses that stared blankly into the night. Having crossed to the western sidewalk I rounded the nearest corner into Bates Street, where I kept close to the buildings on the southern side. I passed two houses shewing signs of habitation, one of which had faint lights in upper rooms, yet met with no obstacle. As I turned into Adams

Street I felt measurably safer, but received a shock when a man reeled out of a black doorway directly in front of me. He proved, however, too hopelessly drunk to be a menace; so that I reached the dismal ruins of the Bank Street warehouses in safety.

No one was stirring in that dead street beside the river-gorge, and the roar of the waterfalls quite drowned my footsteps. It was a long dog-trot to the ruined station, and the great brick warehouse walls around me seemed somehow more terrifying than the fronts of private houses. At last I saw the ancient arcaded station—or what was left of it—and made directly for the tracks that started from its farther end.

The rails were rusty but mainly intact, and not more than half the ties had rotted away. Walking or running on such a surface was very difficult; but I did my best, and on the whole made very fair time. For some distance the line kept on along the gorge's brink, but at length I reached the long covered bridge where it crossed the chasm at a dizzy height. The condition of this bridge would determine my next step. If humanly possible, I would use it; if not, I would have to risk more street wandering and take the nearest intact highway bridge.

The vast, barn-like length of the old bridge gleamed spectrally in the moonlight, and I saw that the ties were safe for at least a few feet within. Entering, I began to use my flashlight, and was almost knocked down by the cloud of bats that flapped past me. About half way across there was a perilous gap in the ties which I feared for a moment would halt me; but in the end I risked a desperate jump which fortunately succeeded.

I was glad to see the moonlight again when I emerged from that macabre tunnel. The old tracks crossed River Street at grade, and at once veered off into a region increasingly rural and with less and less of Innsmouth's abhorrent fishy odour. Here the dense growth of weeds and briers hindered me and cruelly tore my clothes, but I was none the less glad that they were there to give me concealment in case of peril. I knew that much of my route must be visible from the Rowley road.

The marshy region began very shortly, with the single track on a low, grassy embankment where the weedy growth was somewhat thinner.

Then came a sort of island of higher ground, where the line passed through a shallow open cut choked with bushes and brambles. I was very glad of this partial shelter, since at this point the Rowley road was uncomfortably near according to my window view. At the end of the cut it would cross the track and swerve off to a safer distance; but meanwhile I must be exceedingly careful. I was by this time thankfully certain that the railway itself was not patrolled.

Just before entering the cut I glanced behind me, but saw no pursuer. The ancient spires and roofs of decaying Innsmouth gleamed lovely and ethereal in the magic yellow moonlight, and I thought of how they must have looked in the old days before the shadow fell. Then, as my gaze circled inland from the town, something less tranquil arrested my notice and held me immobile for a second.

What I saw—or fancied I saw—was a disturbing suggestion of undulant motion far to the south; a suggestion which made me conclude that a very large horde must be pouring out of the city along the level Ipswich road. The distance was great, and I could distinguish nothing in detail; but I did not at all like the look of that moving column. It undulated too much, and glistened too brightly in the rays of the now westering moon. There was a suggestion of sound, too, though the wind was blowing the other way—a suggestion of bestial scraping and bellowing even worse than the muttering of the parties I had lately overheard.

All sorts of unpleasant conjectures crossed my mind. I thought of those very extreme Innsmouth types said to be hidden in crumbling, centuried warrens near the waterfront. I thought, too, of those nameless swimmers I had seen. Counting the parties so far glimpsed, as well as those presumably covering other roads, the number of my pursuers must be strangely large for a town as depopulated as Innsmouth.

Whence could come the dense personnel of such a column as I now beheld? Did those ancient, unplumbed warrens teem with a twisted, uncatalogued, and unsuspected life? Or had some unseen ship indeed landed a legion of unknown outsiders on that hellish reef? Who were they? Why were they there? And if such a column of them was scouring the Ipswich road, would the patrols on the other roads be likewise augmented?

I had entered the brush-grown cut and was struggling along at a very slow pace when that damnable fishy odour again waxed dominant. Had the wind suddenly changed eastward, so that it blew in from the sea and over the town? It must have, I concluded, since I now began to hear shocking guttural murmurs from that hitherto silent direction. There was another sound, too—a kind of wholesale, colossal flopping or pattering which somehow called up images of the most detestable sort. It made me think illogically of that unpleasantly undulating column on the far-off Ipswich road.

And then both stench and sounds grew stronger, so that I paused shivering and grateful for the cut's protection. It was here, I recalled, that the Rowley road drew so close to the old railway before crossing westward and diverging. Something was coming along that road, and I must lie low till its passage and vanishment in the distance. Thank heaven these creatures employed no dogs for tracking—though perhaps that would have been impossible amidst the omnipresent regional odour. Crouched in the bushes of that sandy cleft I felt reasonably safe, even though I knew the searchers would have to cross the track in front of me not much more than a hundred yards away. I would be able to see them, but they could not, except by a malign miracle, see me.

All at once I began dreading to look at them as they passed. I saw the close moonlit space where they would surge by, and had curious thoughts about the irredeemable pollution of that space. They would perhaps be the worst of all Innsmouth types—something one would not care to remember.

The stench waxed overpowering, and the noises swelled to a bestial babel of croaking, baying, and barking without the least suggestion of human speech. Were these indeed the voices of my pursuers? Did they have dogs after all? So far I had seen none of the lower animals in Innsmouth. That flopping or pattering was monstrous—I could not look upon the degenerate creatures responsible for it. I would keep my eyes shut till the sounds receded toward the west. The horde was very close now—the air foul with their hoarse snarlings, and the ground almost shaking with their alien-rhythmed footfalls. My breath nearly ceased to come, and I put every ounce of will power into the task of holding my eyelids down.

I am not even yet willing to say whether what followed was a hideous actuality or only a nightmare hallucination. The later action of the government, after my frantic appeals, would tend to confirm it as a monstrous truth; but could not an hallucination have been repeated under the quasi-hypnotic spell of that ancient, haunted, and shadowed town? Such places have strange properties, and the legacy of insane legend might well have acted on more than one human imagination amidst those dead, stench-cursed streets and huddles of rotting roofs and crumbling steeples. Is it not possible that the germ of an actual contagious madness lurks in the depths of that shadow over Innsmouth? Who can be sure of reality after hearing things like the tale of old Zadok Allen? The government men never found poor Zadok, and have no conjectures to make as to what became of him. Where does madness leave off and reality begin? Is it possible that even my latest fear is sheer delusion?

But I must try to tell what I thought I saw that night under the mocking yellow moon—saw surging and hopping down the Rowley road in plain sight in front of me as I crouched among the wild brambles of that desolate railway cut. Of course my resolution to keep my eyes shut had failed. It was foredoomed to failure—for who could crouch blindly while a legion of croaking, baying entities of unknown source flopped noisomely past, scarcely more than a hundred yards away?

I thought I was prepared for the worst, and I really ought to have been prepared considering what I had seen before. My other pursuers had been accursedly abnormal—so should I not have been ready to face a *strengthening* of the abnormal element; to look upon forms in which there was no mixture of the normal at all? I did not open my eyes until the raucous clamour came loudly from a point obviously straight ahead.

Then I knew that a long section of them must be plainly in sight where the sides of the cut flattened out and the road crossed the track—and I could no longer keep myself from sampling whatever horror that leering yellow moon might have to shew.

It was the end, for whatever remains to me of life on the surface of this earth, of every vestige of mental peace and confidence in the integrity of Nature and of the human mind. Nothing that I could have imagined—nothing, even, that I could have gathered had I credited old Zadok's crazy tale in the most literal way—would be in any way comparable to the daemoniac, blasphemous reality that I saw—or believe I saw. I have tried to hint what it was in order to postpone the horror of writing it down baldly. Can it be possible that this planet has actually spawned such things; that human eyes have truly seen, as objective flesh, what man has hitherto known only in febrile phantasy and tenuous legend?

And yet I saw them in a limitless stream—flopping, hopping, croaking, bleating—surging inhumanly through the spectral moonlight in a grotesque, malignant saraband of fantastic nightmare. And some of them had tall tiaras of that nameless whitish-gold metal . . . and some were strangely robed . . . and one, who led the way, was clad in a ghoulishly humped black coat and striped trousers, and had a man's felt hat perched on the shapeless thing that answered for a head. . . .

I think their predominant colour was a greyish-green, though they had white bellies. They were mostly shiny and slippery, but the ridges of their backs were scaly. Their forms vaguely suggested the anthropoid, while their heads were the heads of fish, with prodigious bulging eyes that never closed. At the sides of their necks were palpitating gills, and their long paws were webbed. They hopped irregularly, sometimes on two legs and sometimes on four. I was somehow glad that they had no more than four limbs. Their croaking, baying voices, clearly used for articulate speech, held all the dark shades of expression which their staring faces lacked.

But for all of their monstrousness they were not unfamiliar to me. I knew too well what they must be—for was not the memory of that evil tiara at Newburyport still fresh? They were the blasphemous fish-frogs of the nameless design—living and horrible—and as I saw them I knew also of what that humped, tiaraed priest in the black church basement had so fearsomely reminded me. Their number was past guessing. It seemed to me that there were limitless swarms of them—and certainly my momentary glimpse could have shewn only the least fraction. In another instant everything was blotted out by a merciful fit of fainting; the first I had ever had.

V

It was a gentle daylight rain that awaked me from my stupor in the brush-grown railway cut, and when I staggered out to the roadway ahead I saw no trace of any prints in the fresh mud. The fishy odour, too, was gone. Innsmouth's ruined roofs and toppling steeples loomed up greyly toward the southeast, but not a living creature did I spy in all the desolate salt marshes around. My watch was still going, and told me that the hour was past noon.

The reality of what I had been through was highly uncertain in my mind, but I felt that something hideous lay in the background. I must get away from evil-shadowed Innsmouth—and accordingly I began to test my cramped, wearied powers of locomotion. Despite weakness, hunger, horror, and bewilderment I found myself after a long time able to walk; so started slowly along the muddy road to Rowley. Before evening I was in the village, getting a meal and providing myself with presentable clothes. I caught the night train to Arkham, and the next day talked long and earnestly with government officials there; a process I later repeated in Boston. With the main result of these colloquies the public is now familiar—and I wish, for normality's sake, there were nothing more to tell. Perhaps it is madness that is overtaking me—yet perhaps a greater horror—or a greater marvel—is reaching out.

As may well be imagined, I gave up most of the foreplanned features of the rest of my tour—the scenic, architectural, and antiquarian diversions on which I had counted so heavily. Nor did I dare look for that piece of strange jewellery said to be in the Miskatonic University Museum. I did, however, improve my stay in Arkham by collecting some genealogical notes I had long wished to possess; very rough and hasty data, it is true, but capable of good use later on when I might have time to collate and codify them. The curator of the historical society there—Mr. E. Lapham Peabody—was very courteous about assisting me, and expressed unusual interest when I told him I was a grandson of Eliza Orne of Arkham, who was born in 1867 and had married James Williamson of Ohio at the age of seventeen.

It seemed that a maternal uncle of mine had been there many years before on a quest much like my own; and that my grandmother's family was a topic of some local curiosity. There had, Mr. Peabody said, been considerable discussion about the marriage of her father, Benjamin Orne, just after the Civil War; since the ancestry of the bride was peculiarly puzzling. That bride was understood to have been an orphaned Marsh of New Hampshire—a cousin of the Essex County Marshes—but her education had been in France and she knew very little of her family. A guardian had deposited funds in a Boston bank to maintain her and her French governess; but that guardian's name was unfamiliar to Arkham people, and in time he dropped out of sight, so that the governess assumed his role by court appointment. The Frenchwoman—now long dead—was very taciturn, and there were those who said she could have told more than she did.

But the most baffling thing was the inability of anyone to place the recorded parents of the young woman—Enoch and Lydia (Meserve) Marsh—among the known families of New Hampshire. Possibly, many suggested, she was the natural daughter of some Marsh of prominence—she certainly had the true Marsh eyes. Most of the puzzling was done after her early death, which took place at the birth of my grandmother—her only child. Having formed some disagreeable impressions connected with the name of Marsh, I did not welcome the news that it belonged on my own ancestral tree; nor was I pleased by Mr. Peabody's suggestion that I had the true Marsh eyes myself. However, I was grateful for data which I knew would prove valuable; and took copious notes and lists of book references regarding the well-documented Orne family.

I went directly home to Toledo from Boston, and later spent a month at Maumee recuperating from my ordeal. In September I entered Oberlin for my final year, and from then till the next June was busy with studies and other wholesome activities—reminded of the bygone terror only by occasional official visits from government men in connexion with the campaign which my pleas and evidence had started. Around the middle of July—just a year after the Innsmouth experience—I spent a week with my late mother's family in Cleveland; checking some of my new genealogical data with the various notes, traditions, and bits of heirloom material in existence there, and seeing what kind of connected chart I could construct.

I did not exactly relish the task, for the atmosphere of the Williamson home had always depressed me. There was a strain of morbidity there, and my mother had never encouraged my visiting her parents as a child, although she always welcomed her father when he came to Toledo. My Arkham-born grandmother had seemed strange and almost terrifying to me, and I do not think I grieved when she disappeared. I was eight years old then, and it was said that she had wandered off in grief after the suicide of my uncle Douglas, her eldest son. He had shot himself after a trip to New England—the same trip, no doubt, which had caused him to be recalled at the Arkham Historical Society.

This uncle had resembled her, and I had never liked him either. Something about the staring, unwinking expression of both of them had given me a vague, unaccountable uneasiness. My mother and uncle Walter had not looked like that. They were like their father, though poor little cousin Lawrence—Walter's son—had been an almost perfect duplicate of his grandmother before his condition took him to the permanent seclusion of a sanitarium at Canton. I had not seen him in four years, but my uncle once implied that his state, both mental and physical, was very bad. This worry had probably been a major cause of his mother's death two years before.

My grandfather and his widowed son Walter now comprised the Cleveland household, but the memory of older times hung thickly over it. I still disliked the place, and tried to get my researches done as quickly as possible. Williamson records and traditions were supplied in abundance by my grandfather; though for Orne material I had to depend on my uncle Walter, who put at my disposal the contents of all his files, including notes, letters, cuttings, heirlooms, photographs, and miniatures.

It was in going over the letters and pictures on the Orne side that I began to acquire a kind of terror of my own ancestry. As I have said, my grandmother and uncle Douglas had always disturbed me. Now, years after their passing, I gazed at their pictured faces with a measurably heightened feeling of repulsion and alienation. I could not at first understand the change, but gradually a horrible sort of *comparison* began to obtrude itself on my unconscious mind despite the steady refusal of my consciousness to admit even the least suspicion of it. It was clear that the typical expression of these faces now suggested something it had not suggested before—something which would bring stark panic if too openly thought of.

But the worst shock came when my uncle shewed me the Orne jewellery in a downtown safe-deposit vault. Some of the items were delicate and inspiring enough, but there was one box of strange old pieces descended from my mysterious great-grandmother which my uncle was almost reluctant to produce. They were, he said, of very grotesque and almost repulsive design, and had never to his knowledge been publicly worn; though my grandmother used to enjoy looking at them. Vague legends of bad luck clustered around them, and my great-grandmother's French governess had said they ought not to be worn in New England, though it would be quite safe to wear them in Europe.

As my uncle began slowly and grudgingly to unwrap the things he urged me not to be shocked by the strangeness and frequent hideousness of the designs. Artists and archaeologists who had seen them pronounced the workmanship superlatively and exotically exquisite, though no one seemed able to define their exact material or assign them to any specific art tradition. There were two armlets, a tiara, and a kind of pectoral; the latter having in high relief certain figures of almost unbearable extravagance.

During this description I had kept a tight rein on my emotions, but my face must have betrayed my mounting fears. My uncle looked concerned, and paused in his unwrapping to study my countenance. I motioned to him to continue, which he did with renewed signs of reluctance. He seemed to expect some demonstration when the first piece—the tiara—became visible, but I doubt if he expected quite what actually happened. I did not expect it, either, for I thought I was thoroughly forewarned regarding what the jewellery would turn out to be. What I did was to faint silently away, just as I had done in that brier-choked railway cut a year before.

From that day on my life has been a nightmare of brooding and apprehension, nor do I know how much is hideous truth and how much madness. My great-grandmother had been a Marsh of unknown source whose husband lived in Arkham—and did not old Zadok say that the daughter of Obed Marsh by a monstrous mother was married to an Arkham man through a trick? What was it the ancient toper had muttered about the likeness of my eyes to Captain Obed's? In Arkham, too, the curator had told me I had the true Marsh eyes. Was Obed Marsh my own great-great-grandfather? Who—or what—then, was my great-great-grandmother? But perhaps this was all madness. Those whitish-gold ornaments might easily have been bought from some Innsmouth sailor by the father of my great-grandmother, whoever he was. And that look in the staring-eyed faces of my grandmother and self-slain uncle might be sheer fancy on my part—sheer fancy, bolstered up by the Innsmouth shadow which had so darkly coloured my imagination. But why had my uncle killed himself after an ancestral quest in New England

For more than two years I fought off these reflections with partial success. My father secured me a place in an insurance office, and I buried myself in routine as deeply as possible. In the winter of 1930–31, however, the dreams began. They were very sparse and insidious at first, but increased in frequency and vividness as the weeks went by. Great watery spaces opened out before me, and I seemed to wander through titanic sunken porticos and labyrinths of weedy Cyclopean walls with grotesque fishes as my companions. Then the *other shapes* began to appear, filling me with nameless horror the moment I awoke. But during the dreams they did not horrify me at all—I was one with them; wearing their unhuman trappings, treading their aqueous ways, and praying monstrously at their evil sea-bottom temples.

There was much more than I could remember, but even what I did remember each morning would be enough to stamp me as a madman or a genius if ever I dared write it down. Some frightful influence, I felt, was seeking gradually to drag me out of the sane world of wholesome life into unnamable abysses of blackness and alienage; and the process told heavily on me. My health and appearance grew steadily worse, till finally I was forced to give up my position and adopt the static, secluded life of an invalid. Some odd nervous affliction had me in its grip, and I found myself at times almost unable to shut my eyes.

It was then that I began to study the mirror with mounting alarm. The slow ravages of disease are not pleasant to watch, but in my case there was something subtler and more puzzling in the background. My father seemed to notice it, too, for he began looking at me curiously and almost affrightedly. What was taking place in me? Could it be that I was coming to resemble my grandmother and uncle Douglas?

One night I had a frightful dream in which I met my grandmother under the sea. She lived in a phosphorescent palace of many terraces, with gardens of strange leprous corals and grotesque brachiate efflorescences, and welcomed me with a warmth that may have been sardonic. She had changed—as those who take to the water change—and told me she had never died. Instead, she had gone to a spot her dead son had learned about, and had leaped to a realm whose wonders—destined for him as well—he had spurned with a smoking pistol. This was to be my realm,

too—I could not escape it. I would never die, but would live with those
who had lived since before man ever walked the earth.

I met also that which had been her grandmother. For eighty thousand
years Pth'thya-l'yi had lived in Y'ha-nthlei, and thither she had gone back
after Obed Marsh was dead. Y'ha-nthlei was not destroyed when the
upper-earth men shot death into the sea. It was hurt, but not destroyed.
The Deep Ones could never be destroyed, even though the palaeogean
magic of the forgotten Old Ones might sometimes check them. For the
present they would rest; but some day, if they remembered, they would
rise again for the tribute Great Cthulhu craved. It would be a city greater
than Innsmouth next time. They had planned to spread, and had brought
up that which would help them, but now they must wait once more. For
bringing the upper-earth men's death I must do a penance, but that would
not be heavy. This was the dream in which I saw a *shoggoth* for the first
time, and the sight set me awake in a frenzy of screaming. That morning
the mirror definitely told me I had acquired *the Innsmouth look*.

So far I have not shot myself as my uncle Douglas did. I bought an
automatic and almost took the step, but certain dreams deterred me. The
tense extremes of horror are lessening, and I feel queerly drawn toward
the unknown sea-deeps instead of fearing them. I hear and do strange
things in sleep, and awake with a kind of exaltation instead of terror. I
do not believe I need to wait for the full change as most have waited. If
I did, my father would probably shut me up in a sanitarium as my poor
little cousin is shut up. Stupendous and unheard-of splendours await me
below, and I shall seek them soon. *Iä-R'lyeh! Cthulhu fhtagn! Iä! Iä!* No, I
shall not shoot myself—I cannot be made to shoot myself!

I shall plan my cousin's escape from that Canton madhouse, and
together we shall go to marvel-shadowed Innsmouth. We shall swim out
to that brooding reef in the sea and dive down through black abysses to
Cyclopean and many-columned Y'ha-nthlei, and in that lair of the Deep
Ones we shall dwell amidst wonder and glory for ever.

SEVEN MINUTES IN HEAVEN
NADIA BULKIN

It will probably take you all of seven minutes to read this story, to live the life of a living dead girl. There's no kissing here, nothing but a cosmic mystery that will forever remain unsolved—why did the town next-door to mine die, while my town got to live?

Because we spend very little time actually perceiving the universe as it is, we instead hallucinate that on some level the universe is just. God or karma or virtue will mean that the good people of Earth will get their just deserts, as will the vile. All the evidence points to the contrary, so we invent reasons why we are God's favored or why others have been cursed by the activities of our past lives or our recent poor decisions. But in those moments of clarity that come few and far between, we get a glimpse of the truth: Just universes are hells like any other.

A GHOST town lived down the road from us. Its bones peeked out from over the tree line when we rattled down Highway 51 in our cherry red pick-up. I could see a steeple, a water tower, a dome for a town hall. It was our shadow. It was a ghost town because there was an accident, a long time ago, that turned it into a graveyard.

I used to wonder: what kind of accident kills a whole town? Was it washed away in a storm? Did God decide, "away with you sinners," with a wave of His hand—did He shake our sleeping Mt. Halberk into life? My parents said I was "morbid" when I asked these questions, and told me to play outside. So I would go outside, and play Seven Minutes in Heaven—freeze tag with a hold time of seven minutes, the length of time it takes for a soul to fly to God—with Allie Moore and Jennifer Trudeau. When the sky turned dark orange we would run back to our houses and slam our screen doors, and after my parents tucked me in I would sketch a map of the ghost town by the glow of my Little Buzz flashlight: church on the bottom of Church Street instead of the top, school on the east of the railroad tracks instead of the west. Then I would draw Mt. Halberk, and take a black Sharpie, and rain down black curlicues on those little Monopoly houses until every single one was blanketed by the dark. When I got older, and madder, I would draw stick-people too—little stick-families walking little stick-dogs, little stick-farmers herding little stick-cows. And last, the darkness.

When I was in junior high school they told us the truth: the accident was industrial. The principal stood up in the auditorium and said there used to be a factory over there, in *that town,* and one day there was a leak of toxic gas, and people died over there, in *that town.* A long time ago, he said, nothing to worry about now. Some parents were angry; they said kids were getting upset. But gas leak sounds a lot less scary than a volcano, ask any kid.

Nobody would talk about it, except when we needed to dwell on something bad. Some families said a little prayer for the ghost town during Thanksgiving, so they could be grateful for something. My uncle Ben, the asshole, told my cousins that he would leave them there if they misbehaved. Politicians in mustard suits pointed across the stage of the town hall and said, "My opponent supports the kind of policies that lead to the kind of accidents that empty out towns like Manfield." That was the ghost's name: Manfield. I lived in Hartbury.

✳ ✳ ✳

ALLIE MOORE was afraid of bats; she didn't like the way they crawl. Jennifer Trudeau was afraid of ice cream trucks, and nobody knew why. We only knew that when she heard the ring-a-ling song coming around the corner she'd rub her scarab amulet, to remember the power of God.

Me, I was afraid of skeletons. It was mostly the skull, the empty hugeness of the eye sockets and the missing nose and the grin of a mouth that could bite but couldn't kiss. But I also hated the rib cage and the pelvic butterfly and the knife-like fingers splayed apart in perpetual pain. It made me sick to think about what waited for me on the other side: the ugliness, the suffering. My parents took me to church and Pastor Joel promised that there would be none of that in Heaven, when I finally exhausted the cherished life that Almighty God had given me, when I finally decided my seven minutes were up and I was ready to go. "But that won't be for a long, long time from now," he said, patting my head. "So run along."

That was all well and good, but Pastor Joel didn't stop the nightmares. He didn't stop that Hell-sent skeleton from crawling out from under my box spring, clacking its teeth, tearing my sheets and then my skin. I would try to run but could never move, and those rotten bones would clamp like pliers around my neck, squeezing and squeezing until I woke up. I stopped telling my parents; their solution to everything was sleeping pills. The only thing that calmed me down was drawing and destroying Manfield, to remember that I wasn't dead like them.

It was Miss Lucy who stopped the nightmares. Miss Lucy loved Halloween, and come October she decked the classroom in pumpkins and sheet-ghosts and purple-caped vampires. She also hung a three-foot skeleton decal from the American flag above the white board. I could not stop staring at it, because it would not stop staring at me. "I know ol' Mr. Bones is kind of creepy," Miss Lucy whispered after I refused to go to the board to answer a math problem. "But you shouldn't be scared of skeletons, Amanda. You've already got one inside you." Then she reached out her finger and poked me in the chest, in what I suddenly realized was bone. I'm proud to say that I only wanted to dig myself apart for a few gory seconds before I realized that Miss Lucy was right, that a skeleton couldn't hurt me if it was already part of me.

"Memento mori," Miss Lucy said. My parents thought she was witchy, and corrected things she told us about the Pacific Wars—*we never promised that we would help Japan, we never threatened Korea.* She was gone by next September, and a woman with puppy-patterned vests had taken over her class. Mrs. Joan didn't like Halloween. Parents liked her, though.

∗ ∗ ∗

I WAS seventeen the first time I went to Manfield. Allie Moore's boyfriend, Jake Felici, decided it would be a hardcore thing to do for Halloween. Jake was a moody, gangly boy who played bass guitar, and Allie's hair had turned a permanent slime-green from years on the swim team. They were the captains of hardcore. Allie invited me and Jennifer Trudeau. Jake invited Brandon Beck, who I loved so frantically that I thought it might kill me. So while other kids in Hartbury were drinking screwdrivers in somebody's basement or summoning demons with somebody's Ouija board, we piled into Jake's beat-up Honda Accord and drove down Highway 51, Brandon and his perfect chestnut hair smashed between me and Jennifer Trudeau.

We were expecting something like those old Western gold-miner towns—wood shacks, rusted roadsters, a landscape still dominated by barrels and wheelbarrows. We were expecting something that had been cut down a hundred years ago, when companies were still playing around with chemicals like babies with guns, before regulations would have kept them in line. But that was not Manfield. Manfield had ticky-tacky houses and plastic lawn gnomes and busted minivans. There was a Java Hut coffee house, a Quick Loan, a Little Thai restaurant. That is, Manfield looked just like Hartbury—only dead. Only dark.

We were standing in what had once been the town's beating heart. Jake's flashlight found a now-blinded set of traffic lights. Allie's flashlight found something called Ram's Head Tavern. Taped to the inside of the tavern's windows were newspaper clippings from twelve years back: the local high school had won a track meet; an old man had celebrated sixty years at the chemical plant that would kill them all; and they had held a harvest fair not so different from the one we celebrated in early October. Kids in flannel struggled to hoist blue-ribbon pumpkins, white-haired grandparents held out homemade pies, a blonde girl with a sash that read *Queen of Mount Halberk* waved, smirking, to the camera. Hartbury was the only town on Mt. Halberk now.

"Are you sure this is safe?" asked Jennifer. "What if there's still poison in the air?"

"It's not like it was radiation," said Jake, trying to muster up the certainty to be our Captain Courage. "Gas dissipates, so it's all gone now."

Allie echoed him enthusiastically, but she also pulled her plaid scarf higher up her neck. I looked at Brandon, but he wasn't looking at me. No, Brandon was hanging back with meek, slight, big-eyed Jennifer—telling her that it would be all right, kicking pebbles in her direction. None of it seemed real. I saw the five of us standing like five scarecrows, five finger-puppets, five propped-up people-like things that were, nevertheless, not people. My heart was pounding like a wild animal inside my chest. I wanted to get out—out of Manfield, out of my body. I don't know what I thought was coming after me. I could only feel its rumbling, unstoppable and insurmountable, like the black volcanic clouds I had once drawn descending upon this town.

No one else seemed worried about the fact that everyone had lied about how recently the accident destroyed Manfield, and in the years to come we would never ask our parents why. I suppose we assumed that they had been so traumatized, so saddened by the loss of their sister-town, that they decided to push Manfield backward into the soft underbelly of history. "They never said when it was exactly," Jake said, in their defense, "just that it was a while ago."

A while. All our understanding of time is made up of slipshod words that you can rearrange to cover up the fact that somewhere, somebody was wrong. In a while, Brandon Beck started dating Jennifer Trudeau. In a while, I decided to leave the state for college. For a while, I dreamt of my parents driving five-year-old me to a harvest festival, buying me a pumpkin, crowning me Queen of Manfield, and then leaving me to vanish into a gently-swirling fog.

* * *

I GAVE myself an education at Rosewood College. I learned that Seven Minutes in Heaven was not, in fact, a kind of freeze tag, because it was not, in fact, the length of time it took for a dead soul to reach God. I learned that boys would lie to you about hitchhiking across the Pampas to get you to sleep with them, and I learned they probably wouldn't call. I learned that I had no memory of several headliner incidents that took place the year I turned six—not the three-hundred-person Chinese passenger aircraft that was mistakenly shot down over Lake Dover a hundred miles from where I grew up, not the earthquake that killed sixty in Canada, not the Great Northeastern Chemical Disaster that saw a pesticide gas cloud submerge Manfield and then float westward toward Hartbury—and that I actually had no memory of kindergarten at all.

My parents couldn't help me. I would call and they would grunt and hum and rummage through the kitchen drawers; when they got anxious, they needed to fix things. My mother remembered so many of my little childhood calamities—how I once tied our puppy Violet to my Radio Flyer and made her pull me "like a hearse"—but she didn't remember much from the year that Manfield gave up the ghost. So I tried to forget that I'd ever forgotten anything by drinking, making sure I met enough new people at each party that I'd be invited to another. I'd eventually cycle through everything and everyone, throw up in every floor's bathroom, memorize every vintage poster for every French and Italian liqueur on every dorm room wall.

I had hoped to get along with my freshman year roommate, a poker-faced redhead named Georgina Hanssen who was also from a small town, but Georgina was not the bonding type. She lived and breathed only anthropology. She had pictures of herself holding spears in Africa and monkeys in Asia, and eventually the truth came out that her parents had been missionaries, and she had been raised Mennonite. Sometimes she ate dinner with me in the white-walled cafeteria, and we would take turns insulting the slop that passed for food, but she didn't give me any ways in, and at night she would turn down hall parties to hunch over her weird yellow books and munch her mother's homemade granola bars. One morning I woke up drunk, half-in half-off my bed, and found her staring at me like a feral animal, like she was seeing me for the first time. "What are you reading," I asked, the only question that could start a conversation with her.

"A History of Forgotten Christianity," she said. Her finger scratched an itch on the open page. "For Professor Kettle's class. I'm on the chapter about cults of universal resurrection." She paused, then started reading. "Cults of universal resurrection have experienced cyclical fortunes throughout American history, typically reaching peak popularity during periods of economic depression. An estimated three hundred and fifty such communities have been documented across the Northeastern region. They are commonly found in small towns with high mortality rates due to exposure to natural disasters, poor medicine, and unsafe industrial conditions."

Something slithered around my shoulders. "So?"

Georgina took a deep breath. "Cult-followers believed that God had bestowed upon them the power to return the dead to life. When an untimely death occurred in the community, church pastors and town elders would quickly perform a ritual to prevent the soul from leaving the dead person's body, holding it in a state of 'limbo' until the more elaborate resurrection ritual—often involving a simulated burial and rebirth— could be performed. Although resurrection rituals varied, all cults of universal resurrection held the dung beetle—famously worshipped by ancient Egyptians for similar reasons—in high symbolic standing, as the insect's eggs emerge from a ball of its waste. Rather than Christ the divine worm, cultists worshipped Christ . . ."

"Christ the divine scarab," I finished. Yes, I had learned that line in Sunday school, along with *God bestows the gift of life unto those who have faith*, and yes, we hung scarabs on our Christmas tree, but only as a reminder that God was all-giving and we were His life-possessing children, and I had no idea what *that* had to do with bringing people back from the fucking dead.

"So? What happened to them?"

"During the Great Evangelical Revival, they were mostly pressured to convert to mainstream Christianity." A fingernail scraped a page. Something tore inside me. *"Mostly."*

I LEFT school after my freshman year. There didn't seem to be much point in staying. I went into the city, because I couldn't go home—not to that town full of the walking dead. Not to Pastor Joel and whatever he had done to us on the night of the gas leak. Not to my parents. Before I burned their pictures I would search their frozen smiles for some sign, some hollowness, some fakery, some *deadness* in their eyes. Depending on how much time I'd spent with Brother Whiskey and Sister Vodka, I sometimes found it, sometimes didn't. Regardless, I took their money— I had to, what with the economy and the price of liquor. They sent me Christmas cards with green-and-gold scarabs on them, and on the off-chance that they had the right address I burned those cards along with a lock of my poisoned bleached hair, because Lily Twining said she was a witch and that was how you severed family ties. "Doesn't purify your blood, though," Lily warned me, cigarette jammed between her teeth. "Believe me, I've tried."

When I was twenty-three my Aunt Rose, wife to Uncle Ben the asshole, died of a stroke. My parents picked me up at the bus station with glassy eyes and the old red pick-up, and oh how I longed to slide back into a gentler, dumber time when I could simply be their daughter, Amanda Stone, twenty-three years old. It did not work. *Memento mori.* I remembered.

Things had changed in Hartbury. My favorite Italian restaurant on Church Street had gone out of business, replaced by a plasma donation center. Everyone looked like ghouls, the skeletons that we all should have turned to grinning through their sagging skin. And a new dog—a black and white spaniel—came bounding off the porch. "Where's Violet?" I asked.

"Violet died last year," said my mother, without a hint of sadness in her voice.

"Life is cheap," I replied, rubbing New Dog behind its ears.

My parents didn't know what was happening to me. They were frightened by my tattoos: a black outline of my sternum where Miss Lucy poked me, followed by three black ribs on each side. They were worried about Brother Whiskey and Sister Vodka, not realizing that those two had seen me through a lot of darkness. They were embarrassed by how I behaved at Aunt Rose's funeral. They didn't understand why Pastor Joel's numb routine of *o death where is thy sting* and *o grave where is thy victory* made me hysterical with terror and laughter. I went to Manfield on my final night in town, and took New Dog with me—like Violet, this mutt had immediately adopted me, apparently willing to overlook the question of whether or not I was undead. I said I was going to see a friend, as in *hello darkness my old friend,* and my mother asked if I was going to see Allie Felici and her new baby. "Sure," I said, and slammed the screen door.

Manfield looked beaten-up. Windows had been broken into, storefronts had been tagged with unimaginative graffiti—a reversed pentagram here, a forever love there. Another car with an unfamiliar set of self-indulgent high school stickers was already parked at the mouth of the main street, and it didn't take me and New Dog long to find the occupants trudging along in the half-light, posing for pictures while making stretched-out corpse-faces. We crept behind at a safe distance,

New Dog and I, just close enough to hear the sharp edges of words.

"You hear about that other town that got hit with the same stuff, except nobody died?"

"Why? They closed their windows?"

"No, joker. Look, my mom was a 911 operator. They got so many calls from Hartbury that she thought the whole town was toast, just like Manfield. But when the rescue workers got there, freaking Hartbury just closed up and told them to go home, said everything was fine."

At Aunt Ruth's funeral, my father told me that I had no respect for the life this town gave me. I said that he had no respect for death. I said that if he respected life so much then why didn't he just dig up Aunt Ruth and bring her back? His face collapsed like a withered orange. "Aunt Ruth was ready to go," he said. I flailed out of his grasp like a wildcat. I ran to the parking lot over the graves of strangers who had decided to stay dead, under the watchful eye of the great green stained-glass scarab in the window of the church. *But I am a scarab, and no man.*

* * *

IT SOUNDS romantic when you first hear it: seven minutes in heaven, seven minutes for your soul to board its tiny interstellar ship and set the coordinates for God. Seven minutes for you to change your mind. But that time is spent in nothing but the dark. The empty. Just like underneath Manfield's carefully preserved skin, behind the Ram's Head Tavern sign forever creaking in the wind, there's nothing but gas masks and body bags.

The world was changing, very fast. I had stolen food out of children's mouths, helped a man I loved pilfer from plague corpses, thanked God I wasn't pregnant because I didn't want a calcified stone baby at the bottom of my stomach. I'd seen a lot of skeletons, but only on a cross-country bus in the dead of summer did my own return to me—howling, ushered in by smoke. Its bones were just as coarse as I remembered, but its agony was so much deeper, that much richer. My skeleton had grown up. That time, I let it win. I unclenched my fists and let go. I let God.

I woke up when we stopped to let new passengers barter their way on in exchange for gas. Outside my window, one man was beating another to death for whatever the dead man had in his bag—soldiers who couldn't have been older than fifteen ran off the survivor, the killer. I might have tried to see what I could salvage from the dead one, as ghouls go after corpses, but was interrupted by an old man on the other side of the aisle with rotting teeth and a black fedora. He called me young lady, though I felt like I'd lived forever, and asked where I was from.

It was a question I hated answering. Sometimes I named the state. Sometimes I lied. Sometimes I said something crazy—"outer space" or "hell" or "beyond." That time I told the truth. *Memento mori*—the skeleton made me. I told him about Hartbury, about the harvest festival. I told him about Seven Minutes in Heaven. I told him about playing dead—laying frozen in time in a bed of fallen leaves, waiting for someone to pluck you back to life.

"Can I tell you a secret? I died there." The shadows of nearly all my bones were tattooed across my body—I wanted to command the world to pay witness to my death. "I've died."

The old man grinned and wiggled deeper into his suit, as if he and I and every other loser on that bus were buckled into a fantastic Stairway to Heaven. "Join the club, living dead girl."

✳ ✳ ✳

THE THIRD time I went to Manfield, I was thirty-four. I walked, because my sponsor was big on cold night walks with a backpack filled with stones, to symbolize the burdens we all carry in our Pilgrim's Progress. I was alone, save for the county dogs that smiled at me with bloody gums as they trotted up and down the cracked remains of the interstate. New Dog, whose name turned out to be Buttons, had been hit by a car on Highway 51. I invited my parents, but they frowned sadly and wondered why on Earth I'd want to go. "That's a dead town," they said.

How strange I must have always seemed to them. They must have spent my life blaming themselves for my choices, wondering why I wasn't more like sweet little Jennifer Trudeau, who had her head wrenched off in a freak accident with an ice cream truck. Seven minutes in heaven can't undo that kind of fatality. "It's peaceful there," I said.

So it was. There was a stillness in Manfield that you couldn't find in Hartbury, because when the blanket of death came for us we kicked it off and were left naked and shivering in the world. But in Manfield there was grass carpeting what had once been the sidewalk, vines crawling up Ram's Head Tavern, rabbits nesting in the seats of long-gone drivers. Rehab always stressed peace in our time—there are some dragons you must appease, my sponsor said, because there's no fighting them. And truth's one such dragon.

A new flock of teenagers had landed in Manfield. Two girls, three boys, all on crippled bicycles whose parts had been cannibalized for the war effort. I hid behind a termite-eaten column as they wobbled past.

"You know this place is haunted. My older brother knew a guy who went up here on a dare and saw a ghost . . . a girl with a dog. One of them red-eyed demon hellhounds." In hiding, I smiled. Buttons was going to live forever. "I think that guy got deployed." As had Brandon Beck, his perfect hair shorn down to the scalp before he left for the front. The town used to hold candlelight vigils for his never-recovered body, before his parents passed and so many others followed in his footsteps. "I think he's dead."

Everyone was dead; everyone was alive. A fighter jet roared overhead, right on time for its appointment with the grim reaper. The teenagers stopped their pedaling to watch the angel pass and I took the occasion to run silent and deep, head down, fire in the belly.

VASTATION
Laird Barron

Ah, a story with something for everyone. Laird Barron's monologue of a very peculiar superhuman's life and times (and times and times . . .). Perhaps if we were better, stronger, more intelligent, and gifted with the ability to better perceive and even manipulate space and time, we would be immune from infinity, inured to eternity. And perhaps we would be so bored that even the awe-inspiring scale of the universe wouldn't mean anything. Vastation, as in Clute's usage of the term, would be just another item on a shopping list of emotions and experiences we could arrange for ourselves.

Barron is a writer known for careful scene-setting and slow burns. "Vastation" is the exact opposite of his usual weird fiction style, and it needs to be, to cram one-third of the multiverse into a short story.

WHEN I was six, I discovered a terrible truth: I was the only human being on the planet. I was the seed and the sower and I made myself several seconds from the event horizon at the end of time—at the x before time began. Indeed, there were six billion other carbon-based sapient life forms moiling in the earth, but none of them were the real McCoy. *I'm* the real McCoy. The rest? Cardboard props, marionettes, grist for the mill. After I made me, I crushed the mold under my heel.

When I was six million, after the undying dreamers shuddered and woke and the mother continent rose from the warm, shallow sea and the celestial lights flickered into an alignment that cooked far flung planets and turned our own skies red as the bloody seas themselves, I was, exiled-potentate status notwithstanding, as a flea.

Before the revelation of flea-ishness, I came to think of myself as a god with a little G. Pontiff Sacrus was known as Ted in those days. I called him Liberace—he was so soft and effete, and his costumes.... I think he was going for the Fat Elvis look, but no way was I going to dignify my favorite buffoon by comparing him to incomparable E.

Ted was a homicidal maniac. He'd heard the whispers from the vaults of the Undying City that eventually made mush of his sensibilities. He was the sucker they, my pals and acolytes, convinced to carry out the coup. Ted shot me with a Holland & Holland .50; blasted two slugs, each the size and heft of a lead-filled cigar, through my chest. Such bullets drop charging elephants in their tracks, open them up like a sack of rice beneath a machete. Those bullets exploded me and sawed the bed in half. Sheets burst into flame and started a fire that eventually burned a good deal of Chicago to the ground.

Bessy got a bum rap.

In sleep, I am reborn. Flesh peels from the bones and is carried at tachyon velocity toward the center of the universe. I travel backward or forward along my personal axis, never straying from the simple line—either because that's the only way time travel works, or because I lack the balls to slingshot into a future lest it turn out to be a day prior to my departure.

As much as I appreciate Zen philosophy, my concentrated mind resembles nothing of perfect, still water, nor the blankness of the moon. When I dream, my brain is suspended in a case of illimitable darkness. The gears do not require light to mesh teeth in teeth, nor the circuits to chain algorithms into sine waves of pure calculation.

In that darkness, I am the hammer, the Emperor of Ice Cream's herald, the polyglot who masticates hidden dialects—the old tongues that die when the last extant son of antiquity is assimilated by a more powerful tribe. I am the eater of words and my humor is to be feared. I am the worm that has turned and I go in and out of the irradiated skulls of dead planets; a writhing, slithering worm that hooks the planets of our system together like beads on a string. When all is synchronized and the time comes to resurface, a pinhole penetrates the endless blackness, it dilates and I am purged into a howling white waste. I scream, wet and angry as a newborn until the crooked framework of material reality absorbs the whiteness and shapes itself around me.

My artificial wife is unnerved at how I sleep. I sleep, smiling, eyes bright as glass. The left eye swims with yellow milk. The pupil is a distorted black star that matches its immense, cosmic twin, the portal to the blackest of hells. That cosmic hole is easily a trillion magnitudes larger than Sol. Astronomers named it Ur-Nyctos. They recorded the black hole via X-ray cameras and the process of elimination—it displaces light of nearly inconceivable dimensions; a spiral arm of dark matter that inches ever nearer. It will get around to us, sooner or later. We'll be long gone by then, scooped up into the slavering maw of functionally insensate apex predators, or absorbed into the folds of the great old inheritors of the Earth who revel and destroy, and scarcely notice puny us at all. Or, most likely, we'll be extinct from war, plague, or ennui. We mortal fleas.

The milkman used to come by in a yellow box van, although I seldom saw him. He left the milk bottles on the step. The bottles shone and I imagined them as the poet Charles Simic said, glowing in the lowest circle of Hell. I imagined them in Roman catapults fired over the ramparts of some burning city of old Carthage, imagined one smashing in the skull of my manager, and me sucking the last drops through the jagged red remnants while flies gathered.

I think the milkman fucked my wife, the fake one, but that might've been my imagination. It works in mysterious ways; sometimes it works at cross purposes to my design. I gave up fucking my wife, I'm not sure when. Somebody had to do it. Better him than me.

The flagellants march past the stoop of my crumbling home every day at teatime. We don't observe teatime here in the next to last extant Stateside bubble-domed metropolis. Nonetheless, my artificial wifey makes a pot of green tea and I take it on the steps and watch the flagellants lurch past, single file, slapping themselves about the shoulders with belts studded with nails and screws and the spiny hooks of octopi. They croak a dirge copped from ancient tablets some anthropologists found and promptly went mad and that madness eagerly spread and insinuated itself in the brainboxes of billions. They fancy themselves Openers of the Way, and a red snail track follows them like the train of a skirt made of meat. Dogs skulk along at the rear, snuffling and licking at the blood. Fleas rise in black clouds from their slicked and matted fur.

I smoke with my tea. I exhale fire upon the descending flea host and most scatter, although a few persist, a few survive and attach. I scratch at the biting little bastards crawling beneath the collar of my shirt. They establish beachheads in the cuffs of my trousers, my socks. And damn me if I can find them; they're too small to see and that's a good metaphor for how the Old Ones react to humanity. More on that anon, as the bards say.

At night I hunch before the bedroom mirror and stroke bumps and welts. It hurts, but I've grown to like it.

I killed a potter in Crete in the summer of 45 BC. I murdered his family as well. I'd been sent by Rome to do just that. No one gave a reason. No one ever gave reasons, just names, locations, and sometimes a preferred method. They paid me in silver that I squandered most recklessly on games of chance and whores. Between tasks, I remained a reliable drunk. I contracted a painful wasting disease from the whores of Athens. My sunset years were painful.

The potter lived in the foothills in a modest villa. He grew grapes and olives, which his children tended. His goats were fat and his table settings much finer than one might expect. His wife and daughter were too lovely for a man of such humble station and so I understood him to be an exiled prince whose reckoning had come. I approached him to commission a set of vases for my master. We had dinner and wine. Afterward, we lounged in the shade of his porch and mused about the state of the Empire, which in those days was prosperous.

The sun lowered and flattened into a bloody line, a scored vein delineating the vast black shell of the land. When the potter squatted to demonstrate an intricacy of a mechanism of his spinning wheel I raised a short, stout plank and swung it edgewise across the base of his skull. His arms fell to his sides and he pitched facedown. Then I killed the wife and the daughter who cowered inside the villa between rows of the potter's fine oversized vases I'd pretended to inspect. Then the baby in the wicker crib, because to leave it to starvation would've been monstrous.

Two of the potter's three sons were very young and the only trouble they presented was tracking them down in a field on the hillside. Only the eldest, a stripling youth of thirteen or fourteen, fought back. He sprang from the shadows near the well and we struggled for a few moments. Eventually, I choked him until he became limp in my arms. I threw him down the well. Full darkness was upon the land, so I slept in the potter's bed. The youth at the bottom of the well moaned weakly throughout the evening and my dreams were strange. I dreamt of a hole in the stars and an angry hum that echoed from its depths. I dreamt someone scuttled on all fours across the clay tiles of the roof, back and forth, whining like a fly that wanted in. Back. And Forth. Occasionally, the dark figure spied upon my restless self through a crack in the ceiling.

The next morning, I looted what valuables I could from the house. During my explorations, I discovered a barred door behind a rack of jars and pots. On the other side was a tiny cell full of scrolls. These scrolls were scriven with astronomical diagrams and writing I couldn't decipher. The walls were thick stone and a plug of wood was inset at eye level. I worked the cork free, amazed at the soft, red light that spilled forth. I finally summoned the courage to press my eye against the peephole.

I suspect if a doctor were to give me a CAT scan, to follow the optic nerve deep into its fleshy backstop, he'd see the blood red peephole imprinted in my cerebral cortex, and through the hole, Darkness, the quaking mass at the center of everything where a sonorous wheedling choir of strings and lutes, flutes and cymbals crashes and shrieks and echoes from the abyss, the foot of the throne of an idiot god. The potter had certainly been a man of many facets.

I set out for the port and passage back to my beloved Rome. Many birds gathered in the yard. Later, in the city, my old associates seemed surprised to see me.

Semaphore. Soliloquy. Solipsism. That's a trinity a man can get behind. The wife never understood me, and the first A.I. model wasn't any great shakes either. Oh, Wife 2.0 said all the right things. She was soft and her hair smelled nice, and her programming allowed for realistic reactions to my eccentricities. Wife 2.0 listened *too* much, had been programmed to receive. She got weird; started hiding from me when I returned home, and eventually hanged herself in the linen closet. That's when they revealed her as a replica of the girl I'd first met in Lincoln Park long ago. Unbeknownst to me, that girl passed away from a brain embolism one summer night while we vacationed in the Bahamas and They, my past and future pals and acolytes and current dilettante sycophants of those who rule the Undying City, slipped her replacement under the covers while I snored. Who the hell knows what series of android spouse I'm up to now.

I killed most of my friends and those that remain don't listen, and never have. The only one left is my cat Softy-Cuddles. Cat version one million and one, I suspect. The recent iterations are black. Softy-Cuddles wasn't always a Halloween cat (or a self-replicating cloud of nano-bots), though, he used to be milk white. Could be, I sliced the milkman's throat and stole his cat. In any event, I found scores of pictures of both varieties, and me petting them, in a rusty King Kong lunchbox some version of me buried near the—what else?—birdbath in the back yard. When I riffle that stack of photos it creates a disturbing optical effect.

The cat is the only thing I've ever truly loved because he's the only being I'm convinced doesn't possess ulterior motives. I'll miss the little sucker when I'm gone, nano-cloud or not.

During the Dark Ages, I spent twenty-nine years in a prison cell beneath a castle in the Byzantine Empire. Poetic justice, perhaps. It was a witchcraft rap—not true, by any means. The truth was infinitely more complicated as I've amply demonstrated thus far. The government kept me alive because that's what governments do when they encounter such anomalous persons as myself. In latter epochs, my type are termed "materials." It wouldn't do to slaughter me out of hand; nonetheless, I couldn't be allowed to roam free. So, down the rabbit hole I went.

No human voice spoke my name. I shit in a hole in the corner of the cell. Food and drink was lowered in a basket, and occasionally a candle, ink, quill and parchment. The world above was changing. They solicited answers to questions an Information Age mind would find anachronistic. There were questions about astronomy and quantum physics and things that go bump in the night. In reply, I scrawled crude pictures and dirty limericks. Incidentally, it was likely some highly advanced iteration of lonely old me that devised the questions and came tripping back through the cosmic cathode to plague myself. One day (or night) they bricked over the distant mouth of my pit. How my bells jangled then, how my laughter echoed from the rugged walls. For the love of God!

Time well spent. I got right with the universe, which meant I got right with its chief tenant: me. One achieves a certain equilibrium when one lives in a lightless pit, accompanied by the squeak and rustle of vermin and the slow drip of water from rock. The rats carried fleas and the fleas feasted upon me before they expired, before I rubbed out their puny existences. But these tiny devils had their banquet—while I drowsed, they sucked my blood, drowned and curdled in tears of my glazed eyes. And the flies.

Depending upon who I'm talking to, and when, the notion of re-growing lost limbs and organs, of reorganizing basic genetic matrices to build a better mousetrap, a better *mouse*, will sound fantastical, or fantastically tedious. Due to the circumstances of my misspent youth, I evolved outside the mainstream, avoided the great and relentless campaigns to homogenize and balance every unique snowflake into a singular aesthetic. No clone mills for me, no thought rehabilitation. I come by my punctuated equilibrium honestly. I'm the amphibian that finally crawled ashore and grew roots, irradiated by the light of a dark star.

I pushed my best high school bud off the Hoover Dam. Don't even recall why. Maybe we were competing for the girl who became my wife. My pal was a smooth operator. I could dial him up and ask his quantum self for the details, but I won't. I've only so many hands, so many processes to run at once, and really, it's more fun not knowing. There are so few secrets left in the universe.

This I do recall: when I pushed him over the brink, he flailed momentarily, then spread his arms and caught an updraft. He twirled in the clouds of steam and spray, twisting like a leaf until he disappeared. Maybe he actually made it. We hadn't perfected molecular modification, however. We hadn't even gotten very far with grafts. So I think he went into the drink, went straight to the bottom. Sometimes I wonder if he'd ever thought of sending me hurtling to a similar fate. I have this nagging suspicion I only beat him to the punch.

The heralds of the Old Ones came calling before the time of the terrible lizards, or in the far-flung impossible future while Man languished in the throes of his first and last true Utopian Era. Perspective; Relativity. Don't let the Law of Physics fool you into believing she's an open book. She's got a *whole* other side.

Maybe the Old Ones sent them, maybe the pod people acted on their own. Either way, baby, it was Night of the Living Dead, except exponentially worse since it was, well, real. Congruent to Linear Space Time (what a laugh that theory was) Chinese scientists tripped backward to play games with a supercollider they'd built on Io while Earth was still a hot plate for protoplasmic glop. Wrap your mind around that. The idiots were fucking with making a pocket universe, some bizarre method to cheat relativity and cook up FTL travel. Yeah, well, just like any disaster movie ever filmed, something went haywire and there was an implosion. What was left of the moon zipped into Jupiter's gravity well, snuffed like spit on a griddle. A half million researchers, soldiers, and support personnel went along for the ride.

Meanwhile, one of the space stations arrayed in the sector managed to escape orbit and send a distress call. Much later, we learned the poor saps had briefly generated their pocket universe, and before it went kablooey, they were exposed to peculiar extra dimensional forces, which activated certain genetic codes buried in particular sectors of sentient life, so the original invaders were actually regular Joe Six-packs who got transmogrified into yeasty, fungoid entities .

The rescue team brought the survivors to the Colonies. Pretty soon the Colonies went to the Dark. We called the hostiles Pod People, Mushrooms, Hollow Men, The Fungus Among Us, etc., etc. The enemy resembled us. This is because they *were* us in every fundamental aspect except for the minor details of being hollow as chocolate bunnies, breeding via slime attack and sporination, and that they were hand puppets for an alien intellect that in turn venerated The Old Ones who sloth and seep (and dream) between galaxies when the stars are right. Oh, and hollow and empty are more metaphorical than useful: burn a hole in a Pod Person with a laser and a thick, oily blackness spewed forth and made goo of any hapless organics in its path.

The Mushroom Man agenda? To liquefy our insides and suck them up like a kid slobbering on a milkshake, and pack our brains in cylinders and ship them to Pluto for R&D. The ones they didn't liquefy or dissect joined their happy, and rapidly multiplying family. Good times, good times.

I was the muckety-muck of the Territorial Intelligence Ministry. I was higher than God, watching over the human race from my enclave in the Pyrenees. But don't blame me; a whole slew of security redundancies didn't do squat in the face of this invasion that had been in the planning stages before men came down from the trees. Game, Set, and Match. Okay, that's an exaggeration. Nonetheless, I think a millennia to repopulate and rebuild civilization qualifies as a Reset at least. I came into contact with them shortly after they infiltrated the Pyrenees compound. My second in command, Jeff and I were going over the daily feed, which was always a horror show. The things happening in the metropolises were beyond awful. Funny the intuitive leap the brain makes. My senses were heightened, but even that failed to pierce the veil of the Dark. On a hunch, mid-sentence, I crushed his forehead with a moon rock I used as a paper weight. Damned if there wasn't a gusher of tar from that eggshell crack. Not a wise move on my part—that shit splattered over half the staff sitting at the table and ate them alive. I regenerated faster than it dissolved my flesh and that kept me functional for a few minutes. Oh, Skippy day.

A half dozen security guards sauntered in and siphoned the innards from the remainder of my colleagues in an orgy of spasms and gurgles. I zapped several of the baddies before the others got hold and sucked my body dry.

I'd jumped into a custodian named Hank who worked on the other side of the complex, however, and all those bastards got was a lifeless sack of meat. I went underground, pissed and scared. Organizing the resistance was personal. It was on.

We (us humans, so-called) won in the end. Rope-a-dope!

Once most of us were wiped from existence, the invaders did what any plague does after killing the host—it went dormant. Me and a few of the boys emerged from our bunkers and set fire to the house. We brought the old orbital batteries online and nuked every major city on the planet. We also nuked our secret bunkers, exterminating the human survivors. Killing off the military team that had accompanied me to the surface was regrettable—I'd raised every one of them from infancy. I could've eliminated the whole battalion from the control room with an empathic pulse, but that seemed cowardly. I stalked them through the dusty labyrinths, and killed them squad by squad. Not pretty, although I'm certain most of my comrades were proud to go down fighting. They never knew it was me who did them dirt: I configured myself into hideous archetypes from every legend I could dream up.

None of them had a noggin full of tar, either. I checked carefully.

I went into stasis until the nuclear bloom faded and the ozone layer regenerated. Like Noah, I'd saved two of everything in the DNA Repository Vault inside the honeycombed walls of Mare Imbrium. The machines mass produced in vitro bugs, babies and baby animals with such efficiency, Terra went from zero to overpopulation within three centuries.

The scientists and poets and sci-fi writers alike were all proved correct: I didn't need to reproduce rats or cockroaches. They'd done just fine.

The layers of Space & Time are infinite; I've mastered roughly a third of them. What's done can't be undone, nor would I dream of trying; nonetheless, it's impossible to resist all temptation. Occasionally, I materialize next to Chief Science Officer Hu Wang while he's showering, or squatting on the commode, or masturbating in his bunk, and say howdy in Cantonese, which he doesn't comprehend very well. I ask him compromising questions such as, how does it feel to know you're going to destroy the human race in just a few hours? Did your wife really leave you for a more popular scientist?

Other times, I find him in his village when he's five or six and playing in the mud. I'm the white devil who appears and whispers that he'll grow into a moderately respected bureaucrat, be awarded a plum black ops research project and be eaten alive by intergalactic slime mold. And everyone will hate him—including his ex-wife and her lesbian lover. Until they're absorbed by the semi-infinite, that is.

I have similar talks with Genghis Khan, Billie Jean King, Elvis (usually during his final sit-down), and George Bush Jr. Don't tell anyone, but I even visit myself, that previous iteration who spent three decades rotting in a deep, dark hole. I sit on the rim of his pit and smoke a fat one and whisper the highlights of *The Cask of Amontillado* while he screams and laughs. I've never actually descended to speak with him. Perhaps someday.

Dystopian Days, again. That fiasco with the creatures from Dimension X was just the warm up match. Whilst depopulating Terra, our enemies were busy laying the groundwork for the return to primacy of their dread gods. Less than a millennium passed and the stars changed. The mother continent rose from primordial muck and its rulers and their servitors took over the regions they desired and we humans got the scraps.

It didn't even amount to a shooting war—Occasionally one or another cephalopodan monstrosity lumbered forth from the slimy sea and Hoovered up a hundred thousand from the crowded tenements beneath an atmospheric dome or conculcated another half billion of them to jelly. The Old Ones hooted and cavorted and colors not meant to be seen by human eyes drove whole continental populations to suicide or catatonia. Numerous regions of the planet became even more polluted and inhospitable to carbon-based life. But this behavior signified nothing of malice; it was an afterthought. Notable landmarks survived in defiance of conventional Hollywood Armageddon logic—New York, Paris, Tokyo. What kind of monsters eat Yokohama and leave Tokyo standing? There wasn't a damned thing mankind could do to affect these shambling beings who exist partially in extra dimensional vaults of space-time. The Old Ones didn't give a rat's ass about our nukes, our neutron bombs, our anthrax, our existence in general.

Eventually, we did what men do best and aimed our fear and rage at one another. The Pogroms were a riot, literally. I slept through most of them. My approval rating was in the toilet; a lot of my constituent children plotted to draw and quarter their Dear Leader, their All Father, despite the fact the masses had everything. *Everything* except what they most desired—the end of the Occupation. I was a god emperor who didn't measure up to the real thing lurching along the horizon two hundred stories high.

Still, you'd think superpowers and the quenching of material hunger might suffice. Wrongo. Sure, sure, everybody went bonkers for molecular modifications when the technology arrived on the scene. It was my booboo to even drop a hint regarding that avenue of scientific inquiry—and no, I'm not an egghead. Stick around long enough to watch civilization go through the rinse cycle and you start to look smarter than you really are.

On one of my frequent jaunts to ye olden times I attended a yacht party thrown by Caligula. Cal didn't make an appearance; he'd gone with a party of visiting senators to have an orgy at the altar of Artemis. I missed the little punk. I was drunk as a lord and chatting up some prime Macedonian honeys, when one of Cal's pet mathematicians started holding forth primitive astrophysical theories I'd seen debunked in more lifetimes than I care to count. One argument led to another and the next thing I know, me and Prof Toga are hanging our sandals over the stern and I'm trying to explain; via my own admittedly crude understanding, the basics of molecular biology and how nanobots are the wave of the future.

Ha! We know how that turned out, don't we? The average schmuck acquired the ability to modify his biological settings with the flip of a mental switch. Everybody fooled around with sprouting extra arms and legs, bat wings and gigantic penises, and in general ran amok. A few even joined forces and blew themselves up large enough to take on our overlords of non-Euclidian properties. Imagine a Macy Day float filled to the stem with blood. Then imagine that float in the grip of a flabby, squamous set of claws, or an enveloping tentacle—and a big, convulsive squeeze. Not pretty.

Like fries with a burger, this new craze also conferred a limited form of immortality. I say limited because hacking each other to bits, drinking each other's blood, or committing thrill kills in a million different ways remained a game ender. The other drawback was that fucking around with one's DNA also seemed to make Swiss cheese of one's brain. So, a good percentage of humanity went to work on their brothers and sisters hammer and tong, tooth and claw, in the Mother of All Wars, while an equal number swapped around their primal matter so much they gradually converted themselves to blithering masses of effluvium and drifted away, or were rendered unto ooze that returned to the brine.

It was a big old mess, and as I said, arguably my fault. A few of my closest, and only, friends (collaborators with the extra dimensional monster set) got together and decided to put me out of my misery—for the sake of all concerned, which was everyone in the known universe, except me. The sneaky bastards crept into the past and blasted me while I lay comatose from a semi-lethal cocktail of booze, drugs, and guilt. That's where you, or me, came in. I mean, no matter who you are, you're really me, in drag or out.

Afterward, the gang held a private wake that lasted nearly a month. There were lovely eulogies and good booze and a surprising measure of crocodile (better than nothing!) grief. I was impressed and even a little touched.

For a couple thousand years I played dead. And once bored with my private version of Paradise Lost, I reorganized myself into material form and began a comeback that involved a centuries-long campaign of terror through proxy. I had a hell of a time tracking down my erstwhile comrades. Those who'd irritated me most, I kept trapped in perpetual stasis. Mine is the First Power, and to this day I, or one of my ever exponentially replicating selves, revive a traitor on occasions that I'm in a pissy mood and torment him or her in diabolical ways I've perfected past, present, and future.

Now, it amuses me to walk among mortals in disguise of a fellow commoner. I also feel a hell of a lot safer—the Old Ones sometimes rouse from their obliviousness to humanity and send questing tendrils to identify and extract those who excite their obscene, yet unknowable interest.

I'm going to wait them out.

Seven or eight of us still celebrate Fourth of July despite the fact the United States is of no more modern relevance than cave paintings by hominids. Specialist historians and sentimental fools such as myself are the only ones who care.

This year, Pontiff Sacrus, Lord High Necromancer bought me a hotdog, heavy on the mustard, from an actual human vendor, and we sat on a park bench. Fireworks cracked over the lake. Small red and green paper lanterns bobbed on the water. The lanterns were dogs and cats and, Paul Revere and his Horse. The city had strung wires along the thoroughfares. American flags chattered in a stiffening breeze. I breathed in the smoke and petted Softy-Cuddles who'd appeared from nowhere to settle in my lap.

The Pogroms were finished. Pontiff Sacrus had overseen the Stonehenge Massacre that spring and there weren't any further executions scheduled. According to my calculations exactly six hundred and sixty-seven unmodified Homo sapiens remained extant, although none were aware the majority of the billions who populated the planet were replicants, androids, and remote-operated clones. Pontiff Sacrus's purge squads had eradicated the changelings and shifters and the gene-splicers and any related medical doctors who might conspire to reintroduce that most diabolical technology. He'd reversed the Singularity and lobotomized the once nigh universal A.I. Super job, Pontiff, old bean. He purported himself to be the High Priest of the Undying Ones, but they ignored him pretty much the same as every priest of every denomination has ever been ignored by his deity.

Now, the Pontiff has been around for ages and ages. He's kept himself ticking by the liberal application of nano-enhanced elixirs, molecular tomfoolery, and outdated cloning tech. Probably the only remaining shred of his humanity lies within that mystical force that animates us monkeys. His is the face of a gargoyle bust or the most Goddamned beautiful, dick stiffening angel ever to walk the Earth. He's moody, like me. That's to be expected, since on the molecular level he is me. Right?

Man, oh man, was he shocked when I appeared in a puff of sulfurous smoke after all these eons. I'm a legend; a boogeyman that got assimilated by pop culture and shat out, forgotten by the masses. *Every* devil is forgotten once a society falls far enough. But Pontiff Sacrus remembered. His fear rushed through him like fire; he smelled as if he were burning right there beside me on the bench. He finally grasped that it was I who'd tormented and slain, one by one, our inner circle.

We watched the fireworks, and when the show wound down, I told him I'd decided to reach back and erase his entire ancestry from the Space Time Continuum. The honorable High Necromancer would cease to exist. The spectacle of the god's anguish thrilled me in ways I hadn't anticipated. Naturally, I never planned to actually nullify his existence. Instead, I made him gaze into the Hell of my left eye. He shrieked as I manually severed his personal timeline at the culmination of the fireworks display and set it for continual loop with a delay at the final juncture so he might fraternize with his accumulating selves before the big rewind.

Last I checked, the crowd of Sacruses has overflowed the park. He'll be/is a city of living nerves, each thread shrieking for eternity. My kind of music.

Crete, 45 B.C., again. The Universe is a cell. I travel by osmosis. Randomly, to and fro betwixt the poles that fuse everything. It's dark but for a candle within the potter's house. The blood odor is thick. My prior self snores within, sleeping the sleep of the damned. I alight upon the slanted roof; I peep through chinks and spy our restless form in the shadows. He whimpers.

Because I'm bored to tears with my existence, and just to see what will happen, I slip down through the cracks and smother him. His eyes snap open near the end. They shine with blind energy and his bowels release, and he is finished. Then I toss his corpse into the well, and return to the bed and fall asleep in his place.

I've gone back a hundred times to perpetrate the same self-murder. I've sat upon the hillside and watched with detached horror as a dozen of my selves scrabble across the roof like ungainly crows, and one by one enter the house to do the dirty deed, then file in and out to and from the well like a stream of ants. This changes nothing. The problem is, the Universe is constantly in motion. The Universe stretches to a smear and cycles like a Slinky reversing through its own spine. No matter what I do, stuff keeps happening in an uninterruptable stream.

How I wish the Pod People could give me a hand, help me explore self annihilation or ultimate enlightenment, which I'm certain are one and the same. Alas, their alien intellect, a fungal strain that resists the vagaries of vacuum, light and dark, heat and cold, remains supremely inscrutable. That goes double for their gargantuan masters. Like me, the fungal tribe and their monster gods (and ours?) exist at all points south of the present. It's enough to drive a man insane.

After epochs that rival the reign of the dinosaurs, the stars are no longer right. Yesterday the black continent and its black house sank beneath the sallow, poison waves and the Old Ones dream again in the dread majesty of undeath. I wonder how long it will be before the dregs of humanity venture from the bubble-domed metropolises they've known for ages beyond reckoning. The machines are breaking down, and they need them since after the Pogroms all bio modifications were purged. Just soft, weak Homo sapiens as God intended. The population is critically low and what with all those generations of inbreeding and resultant infertility I don't predict a bounce back this time. Another generation or two and it'll be over. Enter (again) the rats, the cockroaches and the super beetles.

I sigh. I'm shaving. Wife is in the kitchen chopping onions while the tiny black and white television broadcasts a cooking show. The morning sky is the color of burnt iron. If I concentrate, I can hear, yet hundreds of millions of light years off, the throb and growl of Ur-Nyctos as it devours strings of matter like a kid sucking up grandma's pasta.

I stare at my freakish eyeball, gaze into the distorted pupil until it expands and fills the mirror, fills my brain and I'm rushing through vacuum. Wide awake and so far at such speed I flatten into a subatomic contrail. That grand cosmic maw, that eater of galaxies, possesses sufficient gravitational force to rend the fabric of space and time, to obliterate reality, and in I go, bursting into trillions of minute particles, quadrillions of whining fleas, consumed. Nanoseconds later, I understand everything there is to understand. Reduced to my "essential saltes" as it were, I'm the prime mover seed that gets sown after the heat death of the universe when the Ouroboros swallows itself and the cycle begins anew with a big bang.

Meanwhile, back on Earth in the bathroom of the shabby efficiency flat, my body teeters before the mirror. Lacking my primal ichor and animating force that fueled the quasi immortal regeneration of cells that in turn thwarted the perfect pathogen, the latent mutant gene of the Pod People activates and transmogrifies the good old human me into one of Them. Probably the last self-willed fungus standing—but not for long; this shit does indeed spread like wildfire. My former guts, ganglion, reproductive organs, and whatnot, dissolve into a thick, black stew while my former brain contracts and fossilizes to the approximate size of a walnut and adopts an entirely new set of operating principles.

Doubtless, it has a plan for the world. May it and my android wife be very happy together. I hope they remember to feed the cat.

YOU WILL NEVER BE THE SAME
Erica L. Satifka

If there is a writer as cultish as Lovecraft once was before he burst wide open like a spore from the outer reaches of the solar system, it is Cordwainer Smith. The characters in Smith's stories struggle against galactic perfection, they revolt against utopia, perhaps just for fun, or individual fulfillment. The stories themselves are clipped and elliptical; they demand you fill in the blanks. Smith is in many ways the opposite of Lovecraft. "You Will Never Be the Same" is the iterary synthesis of Smith's thesis and Lovecraft's antithesis—ably smashed together, combined, and transformed by Erica L. Satifka's dialect. This is a very short story, but it contains volumes.

1

It is a dreadful thing, the up-and-out, the Stop-captain thought, as he paced the planoforming room. He never had gotten used to it, not in twenty years of space travel and almost as many crews.

The Stop-captain knew that to the dashing crew of the *Wong-Danforth*, he was a milquetoast, but his job was important in its own way. The ship couldn't run without his maintenance checks. And of course, he was also there for the sake of the passengers, to reassure them. Neither the heroic Go-captains nor the pinlighters in their crowns of telepathic amplifiers could keep the passengers from truly understanding that they were literally between dimensions: only a few millimeters away from death or insanity.

Only the Stop-captain could do that.

Except I'm not any better at dealing with this than they are, he mused, wiping his forehead with a handkerchief. Space still scared him. The formless, mindless up-and-out.

He straightened the epaulets on his captain's jacket and stepped through the door into the main part of the ship, done up in a simulacrum of a lovely beach at low-tide. Passengers strolled about, laughing. Further up the shore, four adolescents played volleyball. The Stop-captain much preferred this view to the sights of the planoforming room, even if he knew it wasn't real.

Then a strange thing happened.

Thunder cracked the sky.

2

The Stop-captain opened the door to the planoforming room. Inside, pinlighters with the crust of colored lights on their heads jerked about spasmodically. The Go-captain sat in his usual trance, his eyes crossed at the locksheets, mouth slightly open.

"Sir and Master, what is the meaning of this?"

The Go-captain's head swiveled, giving the Stop-captain as much mind as one would give a bug. *"Pardon me?"*

"The ship, Sir. The programming seems to be off."

"All is well."

"All is *not* . . . I've just never seen this before. Not in twenty years."

"Just a little interference. Go back to your part of the ship. Calm the people down."

The Stop-captain sighed. He could do this. He had no choice but to do this. On his way out of the planoforming room, he felt a jolt as one of the pinlighters spun into him. Both toppled to the floor.

"Ph'nglui mglw'nafh . . ." The pinlighter's words were drowned in a chorus of babbles.

Crazy telepath. The Stop-captain pushed through the door. He had to get back to his own duties.

3

THE DISCOVERY of planoforming had finally unlocked the galaxy for mankind. No longer would humans have to slumber for decades in adiabatic pods in order to colonize the worlds. You simply got into a large structure not unlike a warehouse, lived for a few subjective hours in a simulated world, and walked out onto another planet.

The passengers knew—objectively—that traversing the galaxy meant skipping between dimensions. They knew that it was the job of the Go-captain and his crew of pinlighters to keep them from the madness that surely awaited any human when exposed to whatever it was that dwelled between the stars.

But they didn't *really* know anything.

The Stop-captain knew. A little. He had seen pinlighters rip out their eyes after a poor calculation sent extra-dimensional forces slamming into their telepathic senses. He had signed off on the medical forms after his last Go-captain had requested that his brain be shut off.

That Go-captain's last words before the leucotome's healing slash had been cryptic. "Mad men with horse heads, and golden their eyes were— oh! Oh! Oh!" He shivered, now, thinking of it.

The Stop-captain patrolled the beach, feeling ridiculous in his maroon-and-gold captain's uniform. Overhead, the sky whirled like a pinwheel. All the colors in the simulacrum looked flat and washed out. The Stop-captain listened to the fervently whispered conversations with concern.

"—*something's gone wrong*—"

"—*getting colder*—"

"—*thought I saw something on the breakers, right out there*—"

A woman wearing nothing but a bathing suit jogged up to the Stop-captain. "Captain, is something wrong?"

He thought of the crew, toiling away in a room fifty yards and one layer of reality away. "Just a bit of interference, my dear. Don't be alarmed."

"But the sky! Haven't you listened?"

The Stop-captain cocked his head. He listened.

The sky was groaning.

4

THE STOP-CAPTAIN begged off and went back into the planoforming room. Instead of an orderly, clinical environment, he'd come into a disaster.

He'd seen men go insane in the up-and-out before.

But not like this.

The pinlighters danced in a devilish quartet, the array of augments flashing like an insane carnival ride. One of the women had taken off her clothes, and the Stop-captain clapped a hand over his eyes. This was most indecent.

He turned to the Go-captain in his trance. But the Go-captain wasn't even looking at the locksheets anymore, the printed guides that helped him navigate the *Wong-Danforth* from one safe region of the galaxy to another, that got them through the endless abyss of uncharted space.

He was looking at the Stop-captain.

"*This is the space which is not space.*"

"Sir and Master?"

"*Man rules now where They ruled once. They will rule again.*"

"Who, sir?"

The Go-captain swiveled his head toward the fallen locksheets, which had gathered in a clutter on the floor.

"*The Great Old Ones. They have lived in the up-and-out eons before man's ancestors were even born. And we . . . we have gone to them.*" The Go-captain threw back his head and laughed.

The Stop-captain slowly backed away.

5

WITHOUT THE locksheets, and a sane man to follow them, there would be no way to return to the charted regions of space. He reached for the fallen sheets, only to be kicked aside by one of the Go-captain's legs.

"*This is not for you.*"

"With all due respect, Sir and Master, I disagree." The Stop-captain had watched all his life as greater men and women than him had taken the spotlight. He had seen these remarkable talents guide passengers from one end of the galaxy to the other, through the heartless void of the up-and-out. He had trusted people like this with his life hundreds of times.

But he would not let them lead him into madness.

The Stop-captain had no telepathy, no talents of any kind. Maybe that was the key. Maybe a mundane person could guide the *Wong-Danforth* through this patch of "interference."

I have to try, he thought.

The Stop-captain wound back his fist, and sent it slamming into the side of the Go-captain's head. His knuckles split at the impact, but the once-heroic navigator was out cold.

The gibbering pinlighters sat on the floor, talking to one another in a strange, ugly language. He could only hope that they were continuing to monitor the ship with some portion of their lunatic brains.

The Stop-captain gathered up the locksheets and put them back into what he thought was the right order. He could be wrong. But right now there was no order at all.

He bit his lip. "Have to *try*," he said.

The Stop-captain dragged the Go-captain's prone body into a corner of the planoforming room, tying his hands together with a scrap of cord. Then he settled back into the Go-captain's chair and crossed his eyes at the locksheets pinned to the wall.

"Go," he said, then screamed as the room melted—

6

LATER, THE Stop-captain could only recall fragments of what he had seen.

He remembered the lamentations of horned madmen as they danced about a fire whose smoke seemed to spell out something of the greatest importance, if only he could make it out . . .

He remembered the grinding of an inhuman voice below a sheet of ice, beckoning him to come closer, whispering in his ear, with a voice that seemed to encircle his brain like a thick webbing . . .

He remembered pleading for mercy at a tribunal with thousands of other men and women, facing the backs of iron gods who never turned, never reacted, until one of them shifted slightly to the side and oh God, the face, *the face* . . .

All of these scenes he remembered as he sat in the planoforming room of the *Wong-Danforth*, the pins sticking from his head like cactus needles, hot tears streaming into his mouth, but alive. Alive.

He had made it through the up-and-out.

When he came to the second time, it was in a hospital. The Go-captain was in the bed across from him, a bandage over his left eye. The Stop-captain reflexively looked down at his fist.

The smiling nurse entered, a cup of bright pink pills in his hand. "That was a close one," he said. "We found the Go-captain knocked out on the floor, and you in the chair. Isn't that funny? The pinlighters are in the next room." He jerked his thumb.

"And the passengers?" *My people.*

"Oh, they're fine, of course. A little more rattled than usual. They said something about a storm."

The Stop-captain stared into the pill cup. "Just a bit of dimensional interference."

"They were asking about you. I told them you made it off the ship just fine." The nurse looked back at the Go-captain. "You're doing a lot better than him, I can tell you that much. We had to shock him. He may never captain again."

"A pity." The Stop-captain couldn't imagine *wanting* to climb back in the chair after this. He didn't even know how he would be able to perform his mundane Stop-captain's duties, after seeing what truly dwelt between the dimensions through which ships like the *Wong-Danforth* sailed.

"Get your rest," the nurse said. "You should be out of here in a few days."

The Stop-captain asked the nurse to close the curtain around him. In the privacy of his hospital bed, the Stop-captain turned over all the things in his mind. Is this what the Go-captain and the pinlighters saw every time the ship dropped into extra-dimensional space? Did he have enough saved to retire? Could he even stand to be a *passenger* on a planoforming ship?

The Stop-captain's eyes roamed over the curtain. Such an unusual pattern. He couldn't stop looking at it. As he watched, the curtain seemed to twist and bend, the shapes within to press out from the surrounding fabric like a holovid. He felt his mouth move without conscious control, his lips bending around unfamiliar sounds.

"Cthulhu R'lyeh wgah'nagl fhtagn," the Stop-captain muttered. "He has risen, he has risen."

The dimensions were coming undone. No more would man travel into the up-and-out. The up-and-out had come to Mankind.

Night Voices, Night Journeys
Masahiko Inoue
Translated by Edward Lipsett

Awe most often comes in a flash—as in the imperialist gambit of "shock and awe," or the epiphanies at the end of modernist short stories where nothing happens until the very end, when that shattered teacup or finally opened letter from the war utterly transforms a middle-class neurotic's life. But sometimes awe comes upon us slowly. Sometimes it crawls, like something out of the sea, or like a black stretch limousine taking its time in the fog as it traces the lip of a city canal.

This story plays tricks on you, and not just the obvious ones of spreading references to this or that Lovecraftian motif like sesame seeds sprinkled over rice. Read slowly, read carefully, giggle when directed, and keep your eyes—all three of them—open.

AUTHOR'S NOTE

The city where this story takes place is quite unlike the real one, and exists only in the land of the imagination. I made reference to numerous books in touring and writing about these dream excursions, which are becoming a daily infatuation of mine.

LOVINGLY, THOSE fingers toyed with her ear.

Those fingertips, moving so skillfully, soothed along the perfectly-sculpted rim of her ear, cupping; the trace of a fingernail. Sound faded, and then inundated her again. The extravagant seats of the limousine. From the sound system came the crystal clarity of old jazz, the elegant music vanishing, surging back to a head, fading again. Sound—silence—sound—silence . . . just like the singing crickets in the casino. Or perhaps a different nighttime insect? Fragments of jazz sketched poems through her elegant lines.

Perhaps voices from that night so long ago, or a requiem for a nighthawk of the forest? Or, maybe, cheek-to-cheek in the dance hall. Dancing together, so intimately, are life and death . . . Sound—silence—sound—silence. The rhythm of his fingers. She lay on the bench seat, facing upward, body stretched out to him. To his fingers. His incessant, gentle, ravenous fingers.

Of course, the fingers would love not only her ear. He would surely walk them elsewhere. From her ear, on down, to other parts. Those unique fingertips, slick with saliva pungent with the scent of myrrh, would glide from that other place to yet another spot, rich in so many secrets, never ceasing their mysterious dance. The hot, brilliant garnet of her self would dull under his distorted fingerprints. The mark of his possession. She was his possession, just like this museum-class limousine, and the audio system that was in itself a work of art; she knew. How well she understood the ways of this man, her master. As an *objet d'art*, he would savor her entirety, her all, until he was fulfilled.

This obsession, almost sad, was not his alone. All of the men who had possessed her had been awed by her very existence, and possessed in turn by the secrets of her flesh. Those that opened her body lost themselves in obscene pursuits. As if falling into cosmic chaos. And yet, it was nothing she desired; nothing she could comprehend. Not even her own existence, nor the terrible fate that awaited them. She could merely drift, on a night voyage, on so many endless night voyages.

She could hear the voices of the night, there on the bench seat. The singing crickets gathering on her skin; the poetry of the night-hawk. The garnet grew feverish, and the song swelled, hot enough for the dead to embrace the living. And then, his fingers froze. He stopped moving his fingertips. Feeling an unmistakable presence, she looked at him. He was holding the fingers of both hands up, staring at his fingers as if they were some strange organs he had seen for the very first time.

The deformation of his hands had progressed considerably.

In the streaming lights of the night his fingers looked like some translucent organism of the ocean depths. Aware of her openness, perhaps, he returned to himself, lowering his twitching hands again, and softly covered her face as if murmuring "Nothing to fear."

His fingers, newly elongated, bizarrely entangled one in the other, made his hands like a soft-bodied organism in shape as well as translucency. She felt the touch of countless tiny suckers on her face, but what she felt was not fear. She had suffered uglier and more fearsome things than this, crawling across her flesh.

The jazz was approaching its end. You could tell that he loved this song so very, very much from the name he gave to this million-dollar tank of a limousine. He flashed a sign to the chauffeur's compartment, separated from the rear seats by an etched glass panel, and "The A–Train" quietly began to slow. She knew that the night's drive was drawing to its conclusion . . . as had so many other drives of the long night . . .

"It's been a long time, hasn't it? The smell of the tide . . ." he said, his hand in its black deerskin glove wrapped around her spine. "Strange that the fog should be so thick here in Wai Tan. Because I brought you, perhaps?"

She shivered, silently.

"It may have drifted here from some distant land . . ."

The sound of his cane echoed on the paving stones of the Bund wharf road. Her field of vision was obscured dangerously, even at her foot. Even the immobile limousine had sunk its huge body into the milky white sea of cloud, only the gleams from the horns of the René Lalique hood ornament shining through the mist.

"Those who come here from the sea," he said, back to the broad canal. "They always see this scene, first."

Sensing the shadow that drew across his face, she gazed up.

"It's not bad . . . this view."

In the grayish-white darkness they waited, indigo.

". . . As beautiful as the spirits of the dead . . ."

Spirits, tall and blue. Towering castles, worthy of the name skyscraper. The ghosts of art deco, stretching linear into the sky. Other specters soared in Victorian gothic, pointed towers to the heavens. And yet others, neo-baroque shades in dazzling curves. And Queen Anne revivals, with their glossy brick reliefs; spirits in colonial architecture, with maze-like stone roofs. The stone giants of countless ages of Europe, entombed here, looked as if they had awakened, reborn, to the call of a gong. The indigo spirits of the cityscape, elegant, reaching into the clouds . . .

"The ghosts of the modern world," he murmured. "The very essence of modern civilization, from every era, has possessed this city, driven by the passion of those on the leading edges of culture. Imprisoned here, they count the passing of eternal hours."

It was true. The original bold modernity of the blue, shadowed city—the Chinese called it Yi Cheng, the "Foreigner's Castle": it was a collection of mansions and buildings erected by cosmopolitans pursuing their colonial dreams of the very latest style—was now covered by ancient growths, revealing the grand visages of the dead, trapped in frozen time.

It was as if a long-dead European metropolis had been wrapped in the ocean fog, and transformed, over time, into a beautiful waxen corpse. Their blue faces were as handsome as death itself.

Still. She knew.

She knew what hid behind the peaceful city streets. Behind the façade.

She knew that behind the handsome chalk death mask raged the rawness of the banquet. The chaos of Asia, ever ready to well up from the alleys running like cracks through the Western-style castles. The formless desire, eating through those graceful, deathly faces. Giant mandibles, antennae, pseudopods and beaks squirming, wriggling, sucking up the blood and meat and mucus, secreting, mating, snaring prey, spawning, reproducing in the gorgeous and sacred banquet of darkness.

And so it was called "City of Demons." This second name of the "Paris of the Orient" derived from its dark, hidden side. He, none other, had explained it to her. The man who was her master. An inhabitant of the *société noire*, the society of darkness; bastard of chaos. When she first met him—when he tore her away from her previous owner—he had already been the master of the port. A Napoleon, ruling over the Paris of the Orient. Though already in his prime, he was richer in welling vitality than any youth she had ever met.

"You are the image of Shanghai," he said, running his fingers over her surface, his face so like the king of spades. "Underneath this chill skin, as cool as a corpse, you hold the unfathomable treasure of the cosmos. You are like my woman, but yet refuse to give me your all. You excite the hearts of all who see you, invite them, and lure them to leap into Hell to possess you.

"Just like this city . . . a beautiful curse," he murmured.

Like a wolf feasting on raw flesh, he continued his loving. And as he did with her form, so he pressed his hot fingerprints into every crevice of the city.

Still, she knew. She knew that this night journey was drawing to an end.

"It's not at all bad, is it? This view."

Looking up at the deep blue of the skyscrapers, with his hand still in its deerskin glove encircling her, he spoke into the smothering fog, but his words were no longer those of a conquering Napoleon. They recalled, rather, the defeated general, exiled to a lonely isle. This man himself understood that the journey was drawing to a close. His pale face under the Borsalino still showed the character of the king of spades, even the clear-cut lines of a waxen carving, but his cheeks and lips quivered like ripples on the sea.

"This view—I took it all, all of it, with these hands."

Those hands, black deerskin gloves, twisted into an unnatural shape.

"And yet . . ."

He shielded his face, like a vampire in the sun, and through his fingers his bitter eyes stared away from the skyscrapers, off into the distant reaches of the Huang Pu River.

On the other side of the canal stood a bizarrely shaped tower, like a space rocket in a science drama: the business district of Pu Dong surrounding the Oriental Pearl Broadcasting Tower filled the nighttime scenery of the twenty-first century.

"There are things I cannot win," he rasped, his voice thin and pinched, as if the words burned his throat. "I can understand it, now; I can understand the feelings of Shi Huang Di, the First Emperor, searching for immortality. Even though this Shanghai is still rich in new culture, new innovations I have not yet devoured . . ."

He chuckled, rasping, "For me, there is . . . no more time."

Like a doll with a broken neck, he crumpled, but even collapsing called to her: "Azia . . . Azia . . ."

She could not even respond to that, the name that he had given her.

"At the least . . . you."

She shuddered yet again at her fate.

The same conclusion, the same end for every journey. The fate of the men who had loved her flesh, had been intoxicated by the poison of her cursed skin, and had passed away, calling her name.

"Your all . . . My Azia."

His silver cane slid down, a dry clatter against the paving stones.

The limousine door opened, the shape of the burly driver bursting out, realizing something had happened.

The man's Borsalino skittered away; one of his black gloves slipped off and fell.

She saw them clearly, then—that pair of eyes.

She clearly saw those eyelids of fog blink, rending the white film.

The silent eyes, watching them, piercing them from the depths of the darkness.

Someone had been watching.

No, they were still watching . . .

She sat in the limousine as it sped home, shaken to the core.

Her master lay on the rear seat, on the other side of the rosewood table. He wasn't on the verge of death, but he lay like a shadow, limp and deep. He looked as if he might begin to rot before her eyes. Half-covered by the Borsalino, his face could almost be glowing with phosphorescence.

This journey was drawing to a close. Soon, someone else would take her.

She thought back on her oft-repeated fate.

So . . . perhaps that was her next master, watching?

"They'll want you, Azia," her possessor had said, his white teeth tearing at a bloody fillet steak. "They all know that your skin, your body, is worth more than the blessings of the axis of the heavens."

He had swept his eyes across the western-style room watchfully. The guests at the French restaurant, popular since the first days of the settlement, had looked elsewhere, as if frozen.

"And that only he who commands you can rule this city—no, the world!"

Every time, washing the territory in blood. At the time, this man had been watching a newly emerging organization that was rising in the south.

"It is always the south that interferes with the unity of the Empire."

He entreated his underlings, too: "The children of Cao Cao and Kublai Khan both fought the flames of uprisings from the south. The Red Cliffs of the Three Kingdoms and the Red Turbans of the Mongols are not a thing of the past. Be vigilant! And especially when their territory, their port, is returned from the British."

Perhaps, then, those eyes belonged to one from the south port.

Those that her master had called "denizens of the other castle that knows no night."

In any case, her fate would play itself out, again.

She looked at the chauffeur, on the other side of the glass partition. The broad-backed driver had shared, to a lesser extent, her strange fate. Hired as a driver–bodyguard by her master for his tough, almost ape-like body, he was yet another spoil of conquest. Like her, he had been taken by force from a former master. His taciturn face was reflected in the rearview mirror, and under his chauffeur's cap was the face that had earned him his new name from his new master. He was "Qing Wa," "the green frog." The other "Qing Wa" was a three-legged incense stand, one of her master's many curiosities. His melancholy visage, somehow a mixture of toad and prehistoric fish, had not been at all uncommon in one harbor town where she had lived, years ago. Boys in their teens, beginning to masturbate, would already begin showing those features. Some Westerners believed it was just an Asian face, and her former master had been one. He first noticed his mistake when he met the Napoleon of the Orient, come to buy heroin and opium, but by the time his skull had been shattered with a candelabra by his guest, he himself had had a fearsome expression indeed.

Still. She had to admit that her present master's face was undergoing an even more grotesque transformation. Inside those black deerskin gloves, and elsewhere.

The toxins of her skin? The cost of power? The abominable fate that overtook all who partook of her mystery was cursed, indescribable. But she—she suffered an even harsher curse, unable to escape the prison of her eternal form.

The limousine quietly arrived at The Castle.

It was one of the hotels the master owned; another skyscraper, looking out over the Huang Pu River where it merged with the sea. The front entrance was grand, imposing; the private entranceway opened instead, looking somehow like the door to a seamen's clubhouse. The hotel manager, with white hair and moustache, opened the limousine door, smiling like honey. And his smiling face instantly stiffened with tension. From inside the hotel seeped the sounds of old jazz. The master sat up, the king of spades looking out from under his Borsalino.

The air filled with the balm of jazz.

The music echoed as they walked along the hotel hallway, decorated in art deco style. Like water seeping up through the hull of a ship, the resplendent sounds of saxophone and trombone boiled up around them. She felt a slight sense of relief as they waded through his Castle, flooded with music. The chandeliers with their parallel cubes and pentagons, and the *objets d'art* like roses painted by a cubist, brilliantly illuminated them. The unique geometry of the art deco designs created the lines and planes that the master loved, as he leaned on his silver cane, protected by the decidedly non-geometrical frog-faced chauffeur, and led by the manager. The enormous Castle, like a bell tower right up to its gargoyles, looked like a crystalline mineral.

"Tonight is a very special night," said the master, looking up at the red, inverted pentagram of the lampshade suspended from the high-vaulted ceiling. "I must change to formal attire, to match you."

His black-gloved hand fingered the silver chain adorning her. The garnet, set into the ebony and silver arabesque, pulsed crimson. His voice came again, as if tormented by a demon: "I'll return shortly, Azia."

She felt a flash of ineffable apprehension, but behind her there were no watching eyes to terrify. This was the heart of her master's domain. Standing near the polyhedral statuary was a black-garbed servant, like a Tang funerary statue, a terracotta warrior guarding its master. There was no gap in the defenses for the southern barbarians to penetrate.

Qing Wa nodded, and the snow-haired manager smiled again, dripping honey.

"I'll return shortly . . ."

The doors, decorated with a double-happiness symbol drawn in cubist style, closed in front of her, and the elevator with its golden cage carried him upward along the wall, flashing in mother-of-pearl and tortoise shell marquetry.

"I'll return shortly . . ."

The image frozen in the brandy snifter, endless eons passing.

. . . Eternity. She smiled her twisted smile. Compared to the night journeys she had come through thus far, a short wait. Only three short requests by the live jazz band in the basement café.

Not even long enough for the ice to melt, in glasses she and Qing Wa shared as they sat in the private lounge.

"Would you like a liqueur, Madame?" The voice was clear, crisp. "Or we have Heineken beer, or J&B or Chivas Regal whiskies."

He was very young for a waiter.

"I already have a cognac, thank you," she said, then looked again. He wasn't wearing a waiter's uniform, but instead white evening formals, with a red rose.

The frog-faced bodyguard, engrossed in the band's performance, didn't seem to notice.

The youth smiled sweetly, with a feminine touch to his eyes. A playboy from the pool bar, perhaps?

"It's on me. And the next request, as well."

She looked at the request card, where the clean, pink finger pointed, and doubted what she saw: "As Time Goes By."

"You can't! . . . That song! . . ." she cried, but it had already started. "As Time Goes By," the flowing music of the Café Américain in *Casablanca*. "You mustn't! You can't play that song!"

"But why not?" he laughed. "Just like that old love story."

"It's forbidden!" Her voice roughened. "Only the Master can request that song!"

"Ah . . . If you prefer cognac, we also have Rémy Martin," he said nonchalantly, winking. "You must be tired of Napoleon by now?"

She felt ice slither down her spine.

She searched that sweet face again.

"Who are you?"

"A specter. A resident ghost of the hotel," he said. "Hah! It seems he cannot perceive me!"

She glanced at the bodyguard. The eyes in his strong, frog-like face were unquestionably open, eyeballs dry and pupils wide. Frozen, immobile. Except for the bubbles—Except for the bubbles of blood frothing out from between his teeth . . .

She froze.

"Why . . . Why did you come here?"

"You know full well," he said, chuckling.

The light in the playboy's eyes pierced like a cat stalking its prey.

"Time goes by, and the times change—as does your possessor."

The invader took her hand. "And once again, the modern age sweeps away the old! A man who drowns himself in the forgotten shades of beauty is not fit to be king."

Startled, she looked into his eyes. Deep, black pools stared back into hers.

"As Time Goes By" played on in elegance. The men in black ran closer, as if in time to the music. Some pulled guns from the bulges on their chests, others sported shotguns as if using a stick to dance with. The band played on as time went by.

"You can never escape," she said.

"I wonder," laughed the usurper, unafraid.

But already on four sides, encircling them, a dozen men with guns surrounded them.

"If you would be kind enough to return her?" asked the white-haired manager, carrying a gentle smile and a heavy shotgun of his own. His honey-like expression made him look like a homicidal maniac disguised as Santa Claus.

"We can promise you your life . . ." he started, and fell silent. Not only his voice, but his movements, and the motions of the surrounding men. They shook as if with the chills, fascinated and trapped by the outstretched pink finger of the young invader. An eerie magic bound them all in place, and from between clenched teeth bubbles began to foam. Just like crabs, she thought to herself. Crabs drowning in the supreme liquor of power.

"What, is the music over already?" he asked, turning to face the band, fallen silent in astonishment. "Play it again, Sam!"

The pink finger, thrust into space, drew back an invisible trigger, and the white-haired man's body stretched, squelching. A little *xiao long bao* dumpling, bitten open. In an instant his body flipped inside-out like a balloon, a waterfall of fresh blood. She could but stand and stare, receiving the crimson baptism with her face, her skin, the depths of her being. As if oblivious to the bloodshed, the band played on. Like beautiful music, the blood spraying onto her skin, toying with her. Still frothing, the men fired their guns, bones shaking violently enough to be heard, shooting each other but unable to fall under the impact. A furious dance. In his seat, the huge, ugly man brought to this Paris of the Orient from a distant and dark abandoned port spurted the thick blood of his ancestry like a geyser to the bullets pumped into his body.

"Well," said the man, taking her bloodstained hand. "The beginning of a new journey."

Ducking under the gunfire, he ran, drawing her along. Down the hall, the stairs, the art deco hallway.

The mother-of-pearl and tortoiseshell fragmented under the concentrated fire of the gunmen, shards of chandelier and glass artwork raining around them in a polychromatic shower.

And through it all, he ran, holding up his hand as a shield. Under that pink gust the men stopped, fascinated, and turned the sights of their machine guns on each other. She turned to see the black-suited men dancing in a frenzied rhythm, even as they chewed each other's bodies to rags with their bullets. The parallel cubes shattered, the pentagons slivered—the men gradually lost shape, their geometrically patterned organs bursting out as they danced on in a terrible cubism of the living dead . . .

"My master!" she cried, as they ran. "You've already killed him, haven't you?"

"Someone surely would have," he said, conversationally. "The most likely was the hotel manager."

"What!?"

"Hadn't you noticed?"

The bullets tore away the pentagram lampshade.

"It's just like an action movie!"

They flew like bullets themselves.

"And we are the movie stars!"

Long shadows leaped in the geometric ruin, landed. The safety zone waited near at hand.

"What are you doing?"

"The jazz already told you, didn't it?" he said, pointing at the limousine. "Take the A-Train!"

It was the first time she had ever ridden in the front. The seatbelt was wet with blood.

He put the car in gear and stood on the accelerator, surging the million-dollar tank forward.

And the circus began: pursuing cars full of machine guns. They raced into the city streets, colliding with taxicabs, overturning a trolley bus. And as they scraped off the pursuit and dodged machine-gun bullets, he still joked on.

"This scene really needs some music. I think we've had enough jazz, though. You must be pretty tired of the old man's taste by now. Hard rock! No, even better: heavy metal!"

They drove onto the elevated road, and the opposite lane was full of enemy cars, too. Being shot at from both sides now, she huddled down. He grinned and spun the wheel, soaring off the elevated roadway. Miniskirted girls stood rooted in place, staring at the antique limousine flying overhead as if at a UFO. Behind them, their pursuers crashed into each other, head on, followed by an explosion, bursting flame, then another, more massive blast.

"The Roman Empire in neon," he said, glancing into the rearview mirror at the road, now a raging inferno from the growing pile-up. "Once, a visionary perfectly described this city that way. An Englishman named J. G. Ballard. I dedicate this neon to all those of vision! In celebration of the crowning of a new Emperor!"

Looking at the century-old metropolis alight with explosions and flares, he put his arm across her where she lay, her head angled down.

"What's the matter? You don't seem to be in a very good mood, my bloodstained Empress."

" . . . "

"Perhaps you are unhappy to leave that old man? You don't want to become the property of the man who killed him?"

"I killed him," she said. "It is my fate to extinguish those who love me, horribly. My curse. A curse on me."

Looking out over the explosion-lit cityscape, she spoke.

"You, too—you, too, will come to understand. The tragic end awaiting all who love me."

She had tried to put a stop to the endless cycle, long, long ago. It had been impossible. She was not even allowed to die.

"The fate of those without the power to possess you," he said. "Dying like those without the qualifications to live in this city. But you . . . you are the very image of Shanghai."

She looked into his face automatically. Deeply. Into those eyes.

"You speak the Shanghai dialect very well."

"Would you prefer I spoke with a southern accent?" he asked, stealing a kiss. "In Chinese, kiss sounds much like *qi shi*, 'extraordinary man.'"

The sounds of fireworks and screams echoed faintly.

"The night is still long," he said. "There's a very interesting place just across the Hong Kou Bridge."

"An interesting place?"

"A movie theater," he explained. "Hmm, no, perhaps better to call it a cinema, in the old style."

They crossed the steel bridge, entering the old Japanese part of town.

The cinema lurked there, waiting.

Inside, the vast cinema walls were done in red.

The dome and arches were all art nouveau, quite unusual for this part of Shanghai. The curving, ivy-like decorations stretched out like blood vessels to the seats, in over a hundred shades of rouge-red.

She stared in amazement that there should be such a huge movie theater—no, a cinema—in the old settlement.

"I've never been here—to the Japanese settlement—before."

"Really?" countered the young playboy, surprised. "That old Napoleon was born around here, you know."

"He was?"

"You never knew anything about him, did you?"

The lights gradually faded out. The hundreds of seats, though, remained vacant . . .

"We're the only two watchers."

He stole another kiss, another extraordinary man.

"It's a love story, you see," he explained. He spoke as if he were the movie producer, as so many men do when explaining movies to women.

"The title is 'As Time Goes By.'" His white teeth flashed in the darkness. "Or, perhaps, 'Night Voices, Night Journeys.'"

The film began to whirl at his voice.

"And you are the star."

In the next instant—at the image writ so large on the screen—she gasped.

A man's face, gasping in terror.

His expression was driven by his nightmares, eyes bloodshot as if to burst.

She remembered him. No, she could never forget. A night journey from so long ago; he had been her possessor. And this scene—just before they parted.

Why? She turned to face him, but he merely squeezed her gently.

On the screen the man pleaded with someone in the darkness, trembling. She knew it was she herself. Behind him was a collection of oddities: antique mummies, skulls of all shapes in their niches. The voluminous black hangings, the headstones snatched from the oldest churchyards of the world. Yes. It was the museum they had owned, her masters. She had had two masters at once, then: collectors of decadence and beauty. She had belonged to them, with all together under a single room, the two of them savoring her flesh in turns. And the end . . . one of them died horribly on his way home from the railway station. Her flesh crept at the memory. The green jade amulet that no human should touch. Her body had sought it, that statue of a crouching winged hound stolen from the dead body. And then . . . *it* had come. One of them was horribly eaten, and the survivor disposed of the collection. He discarded even her, and fled. He fled, but he could not forget the touch of her. In the room on the screen he loved her yet again, a revolver gripped in one hand, ready to face the end, his end. He didn't die by the gun, though; instead, *it* came crashing through the window, with a flurry of monstrous wings and a hound's howl. The shriek had been cut off by snapping fangs, fresh blood spurting. On her skin, a crimson spray of the sacrifice. Just like what had happened to the other as he returned from the station, his body torn to gobbets. Her skin drank up the blood, like a desert painted by a bloody rain.

    . . . I hate it!

I never wanted this. I never wanted him to die, but . . . the sweet blood lured her, stirring her passion. The charnel odor brought her to climax, and over. She hated herself, hated the secret curse buried in her body. And yet . . .

The film played on. As time, going by . . .

A close-up of his face.

She could never forget that face, with beard and black-rimmed glasses. It was as he had looked toward the end, after they were together for a relatively long span. She, of course, vastly preferred the bold figure like that painted in a superb impressionist picture, but he had loved costumes, and had demanded them of her as well. She had donned an Islamic robe for him, plucking the Egyptian qanoon. There had been no doubting that the notes and the lure of her body had stimulated his research, but it could not be denied that gradually distortions began to appear. He had been a genius in chemistry. On the screen, surrounded by experimental gear from the era of King George, he entwined with the naked woman, her singed Islamic robe discarded. Bathed together in dark green vapor, he chanted the spells so crucial to his chemistry, blending them with the qanoon melody. Y'ai 'ng'ngah, Yog-Sothot'! The neatly-arranged lekythos urns suddenly shook as countless hideous creatures began to squirm. Monstrous arms gave form to the deformation that had twisted his destiny. Talons searching in the emptiness, overlapping with an image of his arm as he scrabbled against death in those final hours. Yog Sothoth! 'ng'ngah, y'ai zhro! His hand clutching air, his very body, melted away before her eyes. The waves of agony emanating from her lover as he transformed into the bluish-gray wall—more erotic than the blood of the thousand sacrifices he had throttled for her—melted the deepness inside her.

—*Stop the projector!*—

She was tormented by pity and remorse, and even more by the memories of passion that overwhelmed them.

But the film rolled on, and on.

There. That face. There was one who had died a horrible death before he even had the chance to meet her.

The young man, young enough to still seem like a child in ways, had come to find her.

He had heard a rumor of her beautiful portrait, and had come to the strong vault imprisoning her, with fervor to overcome the weakness of naivety. His wild, vital form—even though only seen through a slight crack into the thick steel door—so rich in animal magnetism, had promised a body so ripe it could not be disguised by the mean clothes he wore, and had stimulated her to new heights. Her possessor then, though—that old man had been the only one she never wanted to acknowledge as "master"—had refused to let them meet, or even to allow the youth to see the portrait.

She never did meet him, as it turned out. That night he had climbed over the walls of the university to steal her away, and had been savaged by the fierce guard dog; killed. Listening to his hopeless screams from the other side of the heavy steel door, she had shuddered in grief—even as she flamed with unbearable passion at his final, piercing shriek. She writhed with the onyx cause-and-effect of her existence, and from the depths of her soul she wanted to die.

Her master then—called The Professor—engaged in sterile research, on a table that reminded her of a dissection bench. She felt nothing at all even when he toyed with her body. He was the archetypical scientist, scribbling notes and musings on book margins, and even on their spines, earning the ridicule of his fellows. She knew, though—knew that he absolutely hated his "research material."

She had hoped he would kill her. She had probably asked him to, several times. A man such as he would have known how to kill something like her, no doubt. She had been burned in flames a number of times; by the hand of her master, regretting his ownership; by people tortured by her master; as a witch in a small village; once at the feet of the Pope. But—she could not escape to death. Since Constantinople in the tenth century she had had the chance to reproduce several times, but even though her offspring died in the flames she could not die. Her body, charred black, would flush with blood from deep inside instead of dispersing with the wind, and lush, sensuous skin would be reborn. Her body had never known death. And across the ages, she still had no choice but to continue her night journey. The night she had become the property of the twin sorcerers, who hated each other, and killed each other . . . the night she had been the catalyst that let a cursed artist realize his rare talent . . . the night she had revealed the hidden elixir to that young medical genius . . . The film kept on, and on. Even as she loved the men who mastered her, she was intoxicated by the screams and curses, the blood and flesh; those sobbing nights she reeled at the black abyss of her crimes.

"I never knew you like human beings that much, Nekkie," jibed one of her fellows in this underground room. He was another of her line; she'd met others like him before. That university research room. Later she'd escaped, to be acquired by yet another master, but until then she'd shared confinement with a host of others of her line, and with others from different lines altogether, all sharing a common fate.

"Don't call me that, Misty!"

"Human beings may say everything's black and white, like the Elder Gods, but that's only skin deep. On the inside they're harder to handle than the Great Old Ones themselves," chuckled de Vermis. "They're only here in this world for the blink of an eye, poor things. Compared to the truths of our existence, they're just dust on the wind."

"One thing you can say," broke in a voice as deep as crawling dust, startling them both. The oldster who so rarely spoke, with pieces of his body missing here and there, old Eibon, whom everyone respected. "We are always . . . together with the humans . . . that's the very purpose of our creation . . ."

And as he spoke those words, the film began to roll with a terrible sound.

On the screen suddenly appeared her creator.

The solitary man, standing in the nighttime desert. Listening to the demonic voices of the night as he molded the vermilion sand to form a woman's head. He lowered his head, as if to kiss her on the brow, and the voices of the daemonic insects howled and chittered. And in the next instant, the screen revealed sights beyond imagination: an infinite chaos, wider than the very galaxy . . . stygian terror from the abyss . . . eroticism sweeter than death . . . herself, writhing at her eternal curse.

—*Why?*—

She screamed. Words made blood gush from her lips.

—*Why did you create me?*—

As if in reply, another image formed. A dream, she thought. A scene from a dream. Though she could not die, she could dream. But this one, this dream she saw on the silver screen, was not the endless, frozen wasteland or the gate that surpassed Time.

It was an image as a youth.—*I am an Arab!*—he cried, sitting at his wretched desk, an illuminated copy of *The Thousand and One Arabian Nights* in his hand.—*I am Abdul Alhazred!*—His hand grasped a pen. In that instant, she was gripped by a deep and inexplicable emotion: she felt that she came into existence in this world the same instant the youth grasped that pen. Her countless night journeys, all the endless centuries, began with that pen stroke in the vermilion desert.

Shaking with an emotion she couldn't express, she suddenly noticed where she was. Not in the cinema seats any more, but propped in front of the screen. From the seats swelled the applause of an audience of hundreds. Surely there had been nobody there, in those wine-red seats?

No, wait: if she squinted, she could see them. The red audience, thronging the cinema, packing it with their blood-red presence. Faces as red as if they had been flayed, like silverfish wriggling in the ripples of a rich meat stew, looked at her. They waved at her, cheered, watching her eagerly. Yes. Those eyes. The same eyes as before. The eyes she had felt then, on the banks of the fog-cloaked canal. And for so many of them to be watching her at once . . .

"I said you were the star, remember?"

Climbing up from the first-row seats onto the stage was the playboy, garbed in his pristine white suit. Handing her a bouquet, he spoke: "They're your fans. They love you."

"But . . . those horrible faces . . ." she said, shivering. "They're all my sacrifices."

"No, your recipients. The recipients of your saga," he corrected. "Everyone looks that way, eventually. That's exactly why they are so enraptured by your story; they want to peer inside, and to help you weave the next chapter."

In the front row she could see the bespectacled young man, clutching his *Thousand and One Arabian Nights*. The darkness roiled like red fog, like the night voices.

"They all love you," he said, embracing her. As if to taste her tears he brought his lips closer. "But now, I am your master."

And then, his form slowly faded into darkness, the pink face and white clothes erased. As if melting into black, the packed seats, the cinema, all drained away. The applause and cheers dwindled, gone. All the shadows vanished from the theater.

She stood, numb.

Was this, then, all merely another dream?

Had she merely been fooled by shadows? Perhaps the playboy was indeed merely a phantasm.

Something was moving in the darkness. Dragging its feet like a toad that had been stepped on, the huge clot of blackness approached, halting in front of her to reveal its ruined visage. Qing Wa, his massive frame wrapped in the battered and torn chauffeur's uniform, was still leaking inky blood from gaping gunshot wounds. He caught her as she tipped over and fell.

Carrying her to where the night wind blew, to the waiting battle-scarred "A–Train." She turned toward the cinema once again, and under the light of the gravid moon was a looming ruin, cracked and shattered cement falling off, with only a solitary sign proclaiming this as the future site of a disco, casting a long shadow like a withered reed.

"Indeed, tonight was a very special night, Azia," came the hoarse voice of old Napoleon, lying in his canopied bed. It was the special room, the penthouse suite. At the doorway, Qing Wa stood with his melancholy steward's expression.

Merry flames were dancing in the fireplace, light more than sufficient to show the master's defenseless body, and the advanced state of his condition. The nightmare of his body was more hideous than even the grotesque carvings on the luxurious Chippendale bed. The face of the king of spades had been wrinkled like an old and faded poker card, but the imbalance between the waxwork precision of his features and the decaying body recalled the canvas of that accursed artist.

"It opened with dramatic, cinematic action, and ended as a horror film. Fleeing with your wraith must have been romantic indeed."

His fingers scrawled across her body.

He wasn't wearing gloves, and the transformation had progressed visibly in only hours. His colorless fingers, except for the gnarled knuckles, were the tentacles of some cephalopod of the ocean depths. There were more than a dozen of them—too many to easily count—intertwining with each other, but constantly moving dexterously. In the tiny suckers scattered across them like little pustules grew soft, barbed hooks.

Those skillful fingers caressed her to the sounds of old jazz: "Sentimental Journey," perhaps, or possibly "Stardust." Whichever; it didn't matter. The rhythm was his fingers, scribing poems on her skin.

"He must have been handsome, your young shade," said the King of Spades, seeking her lips, and suddenly—his face slipped, the celluloid mask peeling back onto the bed to reveal his naked, hideously changed face underneath. The visage, a travesty that would freeze a thousand guests at an evening ball in horror, whispered the droplets of its emotions: "He must have been beautiful, Azia."

—*You still are,*—she answered, and pressed herself to his lips, a continuation from the cinema. "Kiss" sounds like *qi shi,* "extraordinary man."

"You knew? All of it?" he croaked. "*You yin yang*: it is not intercourse with ghosts, but liberation of the corpse, living between the worlds of the living and the dead. To be trapped in this frail flesh, and become a specter still living."

The former playboy coughed, like a dog with no jaw.

"It was just possible, before I was destroyed entirely, but even so . . . there are limits."

He turned his eyes, scintillating as fireworks, toward the window, toward the phosphorescence of Venus, shining clearly.

"Tonight was special," he said. "The stars are right. The Gate of that star, too. And the final method that your body revealed . . ."

His skilled fingers attacked her. His incessant, gentle, ravenous fingers. No, those strange organs that could no longer be called fingers. Those unique fingertips, slick with saliva pungent with the scent of myrrh, would glide from the folds of her ears to her spine, and on through to that other place. Moving from page to page in her open body. The hot, brilliant garnet of her self would pulse red, and the chaos of the cosmos well up. Inside this ghostlike man, formless arousal quivered and writhed, huge mandibles and beaks. The radiant Sacrament of darkness was about to begin. He chanted the spells, and she panted in the mystery. Outside the window the voices of the nighthawks took up the melody of the old jazz.

"This time I will achieve *shi jie*: the liberation of the corpse."

A gasp of pleasure came simultaneously with his voice.

His form, staring into space, froze for an instant, looking almost like a demonic edifice transforming to yet a new form of modern architecture.

It seemed to all as if the demonic city itself had screamed.

His body collapsed in an instant, like shattered glass, and his indigo spirit howled like a formless sea creature, howled together with the mansions, the castles, the skyscrapers of the city. The rooftiles of the pavilion in Yu Yan Garden flipped, creeping like lizards, and the waters of the Bund bubbled furiously, revealing the unnatural facets and angles of an eerie fortress of dark, mucous green. The rocket-like Broadcasting Tower transformed into a huge sea lily, tentacles seeking. The neon-lit Stonehenge wriggled and writhed as one, and Chaos twisted into a vortex. And those eyes, the hot, red eyes of those countless watchers, sought her out.

Qing Wa's head, burned black, rolled past, clunking along the floor, and fell silent.

The curtains on the window, its lead cames melted, suddenly flurried.

Bathed in furious lights she lay on the Chippendale bed, facing upwards, stretching her body undefended. To the fingers of the wind. The fingers of the wind that could be he.

But this wind was not he; the night journey was not yet at an end.

She believed, never doubting that he would return.

She listened, still. She thought she could hear the cries of the nighthawks, calling together with the beat of heavy metal. Or was it just the howls of the insects on the wind? Straining to catch the footsteps of the wind, she listened, attentive, waiting. Listening. For an eternity . . . for the night voices of *Al Azif*.

FAREWELL PERFORMANCE
Nick Mamatas

What can I say about my own story, except that my dark masters at Dover Publications insisted I print one in these pages, and that "Farewell Performance" is dedicated to the memory of "Brother" Theodore Gottlieb—comedian, actor, genius, and my friend? He was plucked out of Dachau through the influence of his mother's illicit lover, one Albert Einstein, with whom young Teddy used to play chess ("Einshtein vas a very mediocre chess player," Theodore told me once), and from that near-fatal encounter with pure evil he made his living with that rarest of jobs: being himself, on stage and screen. He even edited a horror fiction anthology once. Get to know him. I hope my story helps. As Theodore liked to say, "As long as there is death, there is hope."

JASKEY WASN'T nervous. He had his flashlight. He had a few things to say. The sky felt low to the ground, dark and hazy. People were coming too, and not too many. Jaskey had spent a week putting up handwritten flyers. Skin flaked off the back of his hands like scales. He tried to make the flyers look professional; he kept it short, not like the ravings of so many other latter-day pamphleteers. Time as told by the setting of the sun, every evening until he could perform no more, no admission charge but trade goods greatly appreciated, in the oldest part of the old town. Come and see, come and see. It was twilight and when the last of the indigo was leached from the sky, there was enough of a crowd to begin.

Jaskey stepped onto the corpse of a vehicle—maybe it had been a very large SUV or a small Armored Personnel Carrier—and smiled out at the small crowd. His clothes were comfortably loose; dark against darker. The roll of his belly hung over a well-beaten pair of slacks. Jaskey turned on his flashlight; he stood up straight, his left foot ahead. He tilted the light under his own chin. There was a scattering of applause, and of other sounds—flesh against flesh anyway if not exactly palm against palm.

"I am a failure," he said. "But it is the failure you should all fear. You must know this by now." He could barely see the audience; they looked like underfed trees, all white branch and bone. "But with every failure, my friends," Jaskey said, "with every failure my plans come ever closer to fruition. My machinations are nearly complete." Jaskey's voice was a growl from the diaphragm. He knew how to project; he'd picked the old parking lot because the ruined buildings surrounding it would help the acoustics, because they towered over the audience.

"There are armed men surrounding you," he said. "Ready to rain down bullets, fire, bricks, dead cats ripe with buboes, letters by young women from all over this gray and ashen land that will *break your very hearts!*" He swung the flashlight; audience members flinched and flung up their arms to keep their eyes from the light.

"Do not be afraid," Jaskey continued, "all is proceeding according to plan. You and I, we are the lucky ones! We have a special mission. The human race, a group to which . . . *most of you* belong—" he stopped and waited through the titters, "exists on the edge of oblivion today. I am here today to speak of humanity.

"Its prevention.

"And cure."

Jaskey again swept the beam of the flashlight over the crowd. "Like most of you, I have two parents." He nodded, to himself, then added, "Both of my parents died many years before I was born." Some of the crowd chuckled. "My mother hated me. My father, he was far kinder. A warmhearted man, he only despised me. Let me tell you a story of my youth."

Jaskey lowered the flashlight. His feet were bare. He wiggled his toes, as if waving with them to the audience. "On one bright day in the midst of winter, when the snow glistened on the streets like great piles of diamonds, my parents brought me before this old man. He was old enough to be my grandmother." Jaskey chuckled because nobody else did. Finally, someone snorted in support. "And he told me the most horrid tale. When he was a boy my age, he lived in a camp. He was rarely fed. His parents were as thin as sticks. Men in uniforms ordered them about and threatened them with work and rifles. This boy had a job. There was a small stage made of scrap wood, and a frame painted like a proscenium. With some scraps of cloth and burlap, he and a few of the other children were allowed to put on a puppet theater. It was a Punch and Judy show, he believed. He remembered only one routine."

Jaskey again brought the light to the underside of his chin. His eyes were wide. "Punch threw his little baby, played by a dead and quickly rotting *mouse*, out the window, and the police were brought forth quickly to arrest him. The judge—another puppet of course, perhaps even an entire sock in order to present as regal a manner as possible—explained to Punch that he was to be hanged by the neck!"

Jaskey raised his arms, his fists tight, "Until dead! Dead, dead, dead!" Then he turned the light back onto himself, holding it arm's length, like a spotlight, like a firearm at his own head.

"'Am I supposed to die three times,' Punch asked in this play," Jaskey said, his voice a high squeak for Punch's sides. "'I don't know how to do that!' And then this old man laughed and laughed and laughed. He looked down at me, his young grandson, and asked me a question when he saw that I was not smiling and laughing." Jaskey shifted his weight to one foot and shrugged. An aside: "I didn't want to interrupt him, you see. He asked me, 'Do you get it?'"

Again Jaskey pointed his light toward the crowd. "Do you get it?"

Jaskey sighed and let his arms fall limply at his sides again. "I didn't get it." Jaskey shrugged, as his grandfather once did. "'Well,' the old man said to me, 'It was the Holocaust. I guess you had to be there.'"

The audience laughed, though an undercurrent of boos reverberated across the scene as well. A rock clunked against the hulk on which Jaskey stood. "Another failure!" he roared, the flashlight suddenly up again. "Who was it!" He pointed the flashlight at a member of the audience, a man with agitated flippers where arms once were. His face was narrow, too small for his flat head except for the nose, which was piggish. His eyes bulged from his head and glowed starry in the beam of Jaskey's torch. "It had to have been you! Who else wouldn't be able to throw a rock well enough to hit me?" For a moment he turned the light off. The click was loud. "You can try again if you like." Another rock did strike against something in the dark. Jaskey yelped a comical "Owie!" and the audience laughed again. He turned the light back on. In his free hand he held a rock and dropped it against his makeshift stage.

"I could not help but notice that the universe is getting stupider," he said. There were titters, chortles. Nervous laughter. "Have you noticed it too?" he asked. "Raise your hand if you have?" Then toward the fishy-looking fellow. "My apologies." More laughter. Even he giggled along, his whole body quivering.

"Yes, it isn't just us, though of course we humans are getting stupider too. There used to be so many of us—we split up our tasks. Some of us were doctors, others farmers. But could a lowly farmer amputate a limb?" He shook his head no, but then said, "Yes! Dozens if he wished to!" Downcast again. ". . . but grain threshers are not covered by most insurance policies."

"Ladies and gentlemen," Jaskey said, "today we are at our own wits' ends. We're taking a nap at the cosmic rest stop of nitwitdom. Half-wits on our way to total witlessness. Why even I," he continued, bowing deeply and stretching out one arm, "have forgotten to collect your ticket stubs. Some of you may sneak in tomorrow . . . if there is a tomorrow." Still bent over, Jaskey craned his neck toward the sky. "But I am afraid that there may not be, for the universe is getting stupider. The heavens mock us!"

Jaskey raised his flashlight high. It was growing dimmer, the beam was thick with orange, but in the particulate-heavy fog it still shone like a pillar reaching skyward. "We thought we were alone, though we did not want to be. We had our satellites, our nightlights, our spotlights, our telescopes and microscopes and Scope mouthwash so we'd be ready to kiss when we found someone else. Anyone else. And oh, they came, didn't they? But they weren't looking for us. Instead, they were only interested in making contact with an *intelligent* species. Such a family of beings is at a premium on Earth. Indeed, only one creature matched the description of wisdom sought out by the Outsiders who came to this world not so long ago. Of all the things that creepeth and flyeth, there was a single animal worthy of the attention of these old, old gods.

"I am, of course, referring to the octopus. Some of them can juggle, you know. You can't *learn* that from a book," Jaskey said. "They're not too bad for an invertebrate, really. If only we had had less backbone ourselves. Perhaps we would have surrendered, rather than launching our nuclear missiles at ethereal beings from beyond the stars. It was like trying to take out the infamous and illusory pink elephant of a drunkard's waking nightmare with a flyswatter. You simply end up—" Jaskey brought the light down on his head with a satisfying thump (and he stomped his foot in time as well), "braining yourself.

"Mother Earth herself is an organism. The brave and glorious octopus, the oceans are his. We were, perhaps, the brain cells of Mother Earth. And we're dying off now, a million a day. Intelligence, at least of the human sort, was an evolutionary wrong turn. We know that now, eh?" Jaskey said.

"After all, how did we hope to solve the problem of our visitors from beyond the stars?" He nodded solemnly. "That's right—the same way we tried to solve the problem of how to heat up a breakfast burrito: we nuked 'em." Then Jaskey put a hand to his stomach and winced. "And like that burrito of old, the tentacled Great Old Ones just came back an hour later, this time radioactive." He burped into the beam of the flashlight; the crowd laughed. "And we ended up more than a little radioactive too," Jaskey said, giving the flashlight a swing to illuminate the ruins and the deformed audience—a crumbled wall here, a twisted skull only half-covered with skin there.

"Hey!" someone called out in the dark as the flashlight's beam passed over the audience.

"Ah, a heckler," Jaskey said. "Finally." He turned the dimming light toward the crowd, looking for the person who had spoken. "Are you the chosen representative of the audience tonight?"

It was a woman, not quite so deformed as the other members of the audience. "Excuse me," she said, "but I have to say I found your flyer a little misleading—"

"Oh, madame," Jaskey said. "I must apologize for that. However, this is all that I have to offer. Failure."

She waved the paper, a leaf from an old broadsheet newspaper, its printed stories overrun with thick strokes of black ink, over her head. "You said you were going to talk about human achievement! About getting the world back on track. How we could succeed in reaching our potential?"

Jaskey put a palm to his chest, indignant. "But madame, I have. You want human achievement? You want a success story?" He lifted his arms high and wide, "You are positively soaking in it! This *is* the success story. There's no food in the cupboard, no mail in the mailbox. It is time for us to embrace failure! We have succeeded beyond our wildest dreams, now we must fail our way out of this nightmare.

"What you do not understand, madame, is that we—all of us—" Jaskey said, "have a certain power. The power to achieve whatever it is we most desire, so long as we want it and wish for it with all of our might." Jaskey stomped his foot, rattled the flashlight in his hand till it flickered as if shorting out. "What do you wish for, woman?"

Jaskey's knuckles were white against the cylinder of his torch. He turned his attention back to the audience as a whole. "I, ladies and gentlemen, have always wanted nothing, and now I nearly have it!" Scattered applause emerged from the crowd. The woman threw her copy of the flyer to the ground and from her waistband produced a pistol. Jaskey gestured toward her. "Ah, ladies and gentlemen, meet my future ex-wife!" The audience laughed and clapped again, but the woman looked nonplussed.

"And now, for my final trick, ladies and gentlemen," Jaskey said. "The light is growing dim." He shook the flashlight to get the light to spark up again, but it faded back to its dull orange glow. The woman marched up to him, her arm extended straight out, the gun pointed up at Jaskey's chest. "Please hold your applause, and assassination attempts, until the end of the performance. Thank you," Jaskey said with a curt nod.

The woman cocked the hammer on the gun. Jaskey hmmphed in response. "And now, the grand finale!" And with that, he pointed skyward and threw back his head and commanded, "Look!" All turned their heads up; even the fish-faced man, neckless, pushed himself onto his back to see the high black vault of the heavens and the scatter of strange new stars.

The flashlight went dark, like a match between two fingers. A shot rang out. Jaskey was gone, vanished from the rusted stage. Then small envelopes, pinkish in the new light of evening, fluttered to the ground from the windowsill of one of the buildings. One landed at the woman's feet. It wasn't addressed to her. Rather it was from her, written in a handwriting she no longer possessed, and had been meant to be delivered long ago to a man she no longer loved, but whom now, at the end of the world, she missed terribly.

For Theodore Gottlieb, 1906–2001

TRANSLATION
MICHAEL CISCO

The art of translation is a hard one. One might say that it is fundamentally impossible, except for the shortest utterances and only then if the translated language and the source language share a common ancestor. Every translation is a failure of some sort, even—especially!—if it improves on the source text. (Yes, I did spend over a decade editing science fiction in translation. How do you think I know it's always a failure?)

Michael Cisco has a knack for being simultaneously terrifying and humorous, academic and gritty. This is a story about the awesome power of writing, and the hard limits of understanding—"Translation" lives in the gap between composition and comprehension, and it's a gap you should know well, as you too live in it. Trapped in it, really. Forever.

IN THOSE anticipated days the Village was quiet, its streets were dim, the buildings that lined them were half-empty, where in an occasional window one might spot someone briefly parting black curtains, holding up a weak candle that would only feebly illuminate a face creased by anxiety, a thin lip of folded fabric where the curtain was held open, and no light streaming past from the invisible room. There was no sound of traffic, no sirens, horns, crowd noise, music, no man-made sound. Apart from your own footsteps, the coming and going of your breath, you would hear nothing but the wind folding around you like a parted curtain, and the sound of the air sliding through the trees. On the avenues, every now and then, a car did rush past, running the intersections, all the stoplights have been turned off, its headlights almost always turned off. In a so-far snowless December, the streets were completely derelict, except for the many feral cats that filled the city, most of them larger than usual, but harmless—they went everywhere, congregated silently, watched everything luminously. Also there were a great number of wild dogs in small packs; indigenous to the city, they had taken on their own traits of breed, more colorful than country dogs, more varied in appearance but generally favoring the lean, needle-headed variety. Most had no tongues, their mouths opened only slightly, at the front of their heads, and their teeth grew out the sides through their dewlaps, and through this modified mouth they would suck up steam from manholes, their only food. They would glide up and down each street in succession, in pairs or threesomes, completely silent, with wide saucerlike eyes, their heads veering regularly right and left.

On the sidewalk, only very rarely would you glimpse a half-imaginary walker, in the distance, or retracting into a doorway, where reflections of the dim streetlights would momentarily slide across the varnished surface of an otherwise invisible shutting door. In those days, one knocked at the doors of restaurants, and was admitted only after an up-and-down glance tossed from a high peephole. This glance was especially brief for X, here called Theodore, who was a regular at the E & C, which was like the inside of a wooden box, filled with small tables, each one lit with a tiny candle in a glass, the only light. He would sit by the window in an alcove and when the waitress would come and speak, her quiet voice would set the air ringing, because everyone else was quiet, and there were very few people. Theodore and the waitress would eye each other timidly, and, to spare their voices, or rather to spare the quiet, he would point out dishes on the menu, and she would nod, and then there would be no sound but the rasping of her pencil. The other diners, all sitting alone, kept their eyes down and ate furtively. When his food came, Theodore did the same.

Recently, Theodore had received word from Y, here called Eleanor, about a project. Eleanor had been working at the Jefferson Market Library, had suffered to see her job eliminated by the city, reducing the staff to one arthritic librarian. Eleanor nearly starved, there was no work. Now, in a letter lying whitely on the small table inserted between him and the sideboard, she wrote to Theodore of a translation project, she was required to select a partner, was he interested? Theodore, who had recently lost his job when the school collapsed, was on his way to see her, to accept the work eagerly. When he left the restaurant, the wind blew out his coat, the door locked behind him, the two gestures clockworkly linked.

Eleanor lived in a short alley, blocked at the far end by the sluggish overflow of the Hudson, half-clotted and eddying in mud and old rubbish across the concrete platform of West Avenue. The wind flued past her recessed door in transparent blue streaks, sucked hysterically cold by the water over which it had passed, over which it was passing. At present, Theodore stepped to the still cobbled lane, with its margin of dirt sprouting dingy trees to one side. Eleanor lived at #12, a two-story brick face covered over with dirty-white plaster. All along the lane, one illuminated window shed its light in dark space like a sonar ping, Eleanor's upstairs room. Theodore knocked and waited, the wind blasting him continuously, hardening his face and hands and making the flesh brittle and clear. The door was heavy, with a knocker but no handle and two keyholes, one on the side, one in the center. They both jostled and made a dull thud each, then the door opened and Eleanor waved him quickly inside.

They jammed together in the tiny aperture at the foot of the stairs, Theodore fumbling off his heavy coat with her faltering help, while the city loomed as empty as a desert for miles in every direction around them. The upstairs rooms were filled with smoke from a clogged flue and Eleanor tore holes in the cloud with her heavily bangled hands. She and Theodore were exactly the same age, and both Egyptologists, now more than ever before a subject with limitless horizons. Enormous federal budgets poured into frantic digs in the Sahara, new discoveries sluiced in every day, but competition was fierce and neither Theodore nor Eleanor had experience on-site, so they stayed at home and starved. They were free enough in each other's presence to be informally businesslike and candid; Theodore nakedly wanted to skip the formalities and get to work.

Eleanor brought Theodore immediately over to her desk, which filled half the room, which was not a small room, and introduced Theodore to a dozen neat piles of papers, explaining as she pulled up her stockings, "Steiniz uncovered this at Avaris—it's a Demotic translation of the Book of Nephren-Ka."

[This Ninth Dynasty text, written by the Pharaoh Nephren-Ka himself in either an unknown language or a private cypher, has remained untranslated.] Eleanor said, "No corresponding hieroglyphic translation of the Book was found, and this Demotic translation has only made things more confusing. The characters and vocabulary transpose for the most part, but the grammar is still incomprehensible. So my employer wants us to do two things—first, to determine if this Demotic translation is genuine, and if so, second, to reverse-engineer the grammar from comparison with the Demotic."

The pages she indicated, with a few rigorous and self-confident gestures, were high-resolution copies of the original scroll, shadowy edges crumbling in outline against the crisp borders of the printout pages, still totally legible. The body of the text was completely intact and filled eleven sheets, in small script, laid out in unusually perfect rows and columns.

"We should translate this into hieroglyphics first," Theodore said. Eleanor had already started—she showed him her sketchy results.

"There are no independent characters. Everything here is integral, so we can only go so far working word by word. Our translation will depend on whether or not we can get a sense of a pattern, then we'll have to combine all the elements in conformity with that pattern before any of it will take on sense."

They sat down together, and Theodore watched Eleanor's hair sweep gradually down from her shoulders strand by strand, hang vertically on either side of her face, waft finely in the warm drafts from the hearth, gleam a little with platinum gleams. Her bangs were fine and short and burlesquely arched to either side of the top of her forehead like a golden upper lip. He certainly noticed Eleanor closely. Her demeanor called up in him a coordinated clarity as he swept his gaze unchanged from her to the text.

They worked together, excitedly trying one tactic after another, even-tempered and unfrustrated but making little progress, until the sun came up. Theodore brought some things from his apartment and they ate sandwiches together. He slept at the foot of her bed, rolled on the floor in a blanket.

Without relenting they kept at the manuscript, showing no sign of strain and not getting bored, but the pattern that emerged came out in them, not in the translation. Having somehow divined from the first that the sense of the writing was spatial, he would establish regular grammatical clusters by means of small grids, and she would fill in the proper characters. Once he had isolated all the smaller clusters, he went to work grouping them into larger knots, and she filled out the contours as he drew them. At the end of the week they had organized the writing enough for Eleanor to decide that the Demotic was most likely a genuine translation, although an undeciphered one. She sent a letter to her employer, and some ration stamps and even a little paper money came back in the mail. Eleanor grinned and held out her palm, clicked her nails, coaxed out a handful of tokens from the rigid envelope, blue for sugar, red for meat.

Theodore took his afternoon walk that day, just before nightfall, along the river. He came back limping—bitten by a dog. The wound was small and deeply painful, but healed quickly. He and Eleanor stared at each other in silence, when he showed her. He could not afford rabies shots.

She commiserated with him a moment, and brewed him some milk steamed with tea—there was no coffee—before going back to review their results. Theodore washed his leg in the kitchen sink. When he rejoined her, Eleanor was bent nearly double over the desk and writing quickly. At a pause she waved the sleeves of her kimono at him, her eyes bright, saying, "I think the characters are grouped by number!"

Looking at her, the flush of her face became a brilliant cloud in which Theodore lost the next few days, overflowing them with intense work at the translation, as if it had sucked him in through her face. No fever developed, and Theodore forgot about the bite without noticing it. Incredibly alert, he and she both, filled with sharp and eager understanding, chafingly fitting and refitting characters, they worked numbered groupings at various orders, they turned avid attention increasingly to the arrangement of the glyphs in connected clustered strings, and days were spinning recklessly by unheeded outside the window when Theodore realized all at once, entirely, that the book was constructed in phases, such that one wave of grammatical morphology was superimposed upon another, making the text more dense than long. The entire book was a single passage which was to be read repeatedly in a predetermined sequence of grammatical modes and fully understood only at the last. The passage had to be read either over and over, using a different grammar each time (in the right evolutionary order), or simultaneously in all the grammars used, at once. When this unfolded in front of him, the page seemed to blossom out and enravel him, he could see that the grammar was not only symmetrical within each line, as a one-dimensional figure, but symmetrical for all characters on the page and in the book considered as an unfolded whole sheet like a multisymmetrical two-dimensional figure—and when he understood that, he understood that the grammar was also supersymmetrical, in that each element was balanced in each different grammatical reading, that when all readings were layered one atop another in the right order, it would harmonize like a supersymmetrical object in three dimensions—and when he understood that, he saw the entire text unfold in front of him in calculine symmetry as a single statement, a single word, a single name, and he felt his spirit being ravished half out of himself, to see such unanthropic order so impossible to grasp but close enough to intelligibility to flicker as intangibly as fire on his nerves, a firefaceted blossom in a shadowy spot just beyond possible reach, but nevertheless real and meaningful, a word written by a man blind and insane; to think of it all at once he felt pure abstract flavorless pleasure drain into him down his long nerves, feeling beautiful, anonymous, fainting back into a soft little aperture of pleasure in space, a sort of pain as if his soul were being gradually licked out of his heart in slow slow wonderful ebbs—deep satisfaction, just to have been given to understand that much, just to glimpse the problem clearly for once, a breakthrough in his mind that hummed real physical pleasure down in slow shivers into his cells, next to his nerves. And when he called to Eleanor, he felt his heart quicken, and when she looked up, he looked only at her face and especially her eyes, and when she finally came over and he showed her what he meant on the page, he watched her face, he watched her and watched her with his hands shaking and his heart rattling, also his breathing going faster and shallower, and then she saw it, it all unfolded for her just as it had for him; she all at once and entirely grasped the supersymmetry of the grammar, and confirmed it, and he could see with mental ecstasy that she was nearly swooned, she beamed and she looked up to the ceiling and patted her face, ran her fingers through her hair, thoroughly rapt in the inspiration of that total order. The sun was up by that time and was filling the room from the windows. With a voice that slid under the sunlight and at the same time chimed with pleasure she purred, "Yes…it's all total clarity to every horizon, on every level."

Together dream-drunk with the ready potentiality of that single name, brought within reach by a single organic insight, they began training their bodies to read it. Over the weekend, after a day lost to satisfied daydreaming in bland auburn sunlight, sitting together a little stunned and all at once out of practice with work, they resumed the project on Monday as if only just naturally discovering a mutual aptitude for it. They immediately began itemizing the name's grammatical elements on stacks of index cards, then sat, with their knees touching, swapping the cards back and forth, trying to assemble them in order, finding ways to reduce and homogenize them—even translated, the heterogeneous elements had to be fully homogenized—working with fewer and fewer cards as each steadily collapsed into each. They worked and collapsed into each other, so that, when he fell back in exhaustion, she fell back in exhaustion. The pace of collation slowed at regular intervals until they deadlocked at eight cards. These eight passed unceasingly back and forth for two days with no progress, until Eleanor broke free, drained. She undressed and rested.

Although he was weak, Theodore couldn't rest. He ended up on the street. The neighborhood was now entirely unfamiliar to him—at first, he hadn't walked too fast, looking anxiously around at the buildings, but as he continued to fail to recognize them he turned his eyes to the ground and quickened his pace; he realized he was afraid. His head felt soft, he put his hands to his head, when he could find his head—asking himself, what's wrong with who? Who is here? He looked back to find he had disappeared, he was watching himself not being there, where he had always been before—suddenly the panicky idea that he had never been there, that he had only ever been the fear in this one moment, happening to no one and wholly confined to itself. He looked at his body with surprise, and felt it, and then with relief he seized hold of it and calmed himself. His body had not changed, but he felt it differently, he was directly conscious of the ghostly life that was there in each smallest part. He tried to calm himself, standing absentmindedly on a deserted street corner, stilling himself with listening attention, trying at the same time to trace the new impressions back to the source, the new sense he was just now feeling. He felt himself directly connected with the weather, the ground, the light coming from the sun—he was all of a sudden aware of being only partially separate from them; this wasn't an idea, it was an exhilarating intuition. Now he knew he was crouching down beside a front stoop, staring at a planter directly in front of him. The tree that had been there was long uprooted for firewood, but there were a few tender shoots, even now, kept from freezing by a steam grate in the street, that were alive and growing there. Theodore could see, directly, the life that was in them, and he ate them, to feel them still alive in his mouth as he chewed, and to feel that life reorganize itself inside him as it merged with his own. The green breath of that life released him a while later at the foot of Eleanor's bed, and he collapsed there, senseless.

That night, like sleepwalkers, they rose together and feverishly began work again. The manuscript and the index cards were the first things and only things they saw. The name would not emerge gradually—they would have to have all the parts ready, and they would come together at once, in the one proper fashion, only then. Theodore worked until his head fell forward onto the table, out cold. Eleanor blinked up at weird-looking sunlight glancing in through the window, then impulsively stepped outside. She surprised a dog in the alley—it snarled, and then viciously snapped at her. Eleanor whipped a rock in its direction and unexpectedly struck its head; the dog staggered two steps sideways and dropped to the ground.

Without thinking, she went over to it, breathless, excited. The dog wasn't bleeding, but its head wobbled on its neck, dazed; something winked on in Eleanor as she looked at it. She saw its life directly, without needing any secondary motion of thought, but simply, like a color. Without seeing, feeling, or hearing it, without using any proper sense, she perceived it somehow and was fascinated. Even in this stray dog it was complicated, synchronized, elaborate, symmetrical. The dog recovered itself and stood up, barking explosively, cornered against the wall. The noise and sudden motion clanged against Eleanor's nerves and she stumbled back a little from where she had knelt. The dog barked and put its ears back. Eleanor somehow knew how active it was inside, but all the racket was too distracting. She had put her hand on another stone when she fell back, and now cracked the dog's head with it. The dog crumpled, mewling. Eleanor had only struck it a glancing blow and knelt over it, planting the rock solidly so that the impact jarred her arm, and a little blood came out onto the pavement. She could see it was still alive, then—her racing heart, her rapid, shallow breath—all at once opened out and down into herself that same sense, minute and precious chemistry in every part of her, orchestrated, living things arranged in symmetrical levels from cells to tissues to organs to organ systems and then to an organism, and now there was an appetite in her to extend further her own organism with another. Eleanor fetched a knife from the kitchen and cut the dog's throat, intuitively knowing where to cut, and caught the blood in a bowl she had brought, draining it every time it filled, delighted to feel the living blood in her mouth and inside her, merging its life with hers, its red breath simmering dry thermals in her brain like alcohol. And later, when she came inside, Theodore was awake, sitting with the index cards. She put away the knife and bowl and cleaned her face, then stood in the doorway, unnoticed, and watched his cool, white, dry hands flash, gleaming like knives, through the air at the ends of his black cuffs, where these cuffs were cinched at the wrist, so that none of the arm showed. Yes she watched him and certainly she felt it too, loved him—she saw something there that shocked her: she saw the name taking shape in him, partially, and realized by reflection that the name was taking shape in her, writing itself with their life. Nearly ecstatic, Eleanor understood the fathomless complexity of the life she was looking at, and now her other appetite was whetted, she wanted to join her life with his, and especially it struck her that she must experience pregnancy in this condition, what would it be like to feel so acutely the little shift that would start in her, then that internal extension of her own life growing and elaborating itself inexorably every day. Eleanor came into the room and, with her hand, she turned his head. With a start she clearly felt him inside touch her naked life in his mind. She brought him into her arms and to the bed without speaking and each of them fed back consciousness and pleasure.

Then announcements break through on the wireless—severe weather conditions imminent, a year-long blizzard on the way, the governor has signed an immediate evacuation order. Theodore and Eleanor stare at each other in panic and confusion, then start frantically packing up the manuscript, the notes, the cards.

"How much gas is there?"

"A gallon or two—enough to drop by your place and pick up a few things if you want. We should get to the phone first."

There are two working phones at the post office. After an hour in line, with more panicking citizens trailing in minute by minute, Theodore books a too-expensive flight to Los Angeles.

"I still have the keys to my cousin's house."

They make the bridge before the rush—the tunnels had begun leaking years ago and were by now knee-deep and impassible—dodging broken cables drooping over the lanes. Brooklyn flashes in their windows, overrun by trees.

Presently, the broken-jawed jumble of derelict buildings and hangars at JFK, bright orange signs with spray-stenciled directions to the one operating terminal. Eleanor beaches her car on the sidewalk at the loading zone, and they run together into the half-dark, drafty terminal. They check in at the gate.

Long delays on into the early morning. The floor is filling, knots of people in tiny patches of light, huddling together for warmth, shivered by icy gusts threading through them from the cracked, wall-sized windows. Outside, the runways and taxiways are littered with drooping and semicollapsed aircraft, a few prop planes are taking off from time to time. Then around sunrise a converted cargo plane rumbles up to the window and a steward appears at the gate with two armed security guards, calling for tickets over the earsplitting droning of the engines, ushering passengers onto the tarmac, turning away the standbys. Theodore and Eleanor hold their breath, pass the gate, and board, blowing steam and rubbing their hands as they file up the stairway. Moments later, the pilot slams the hatch behind them and rushes forward to the cockpit. The plane turns from the gate and threads its way through the hulks, the shadowy runway lit with freestanding lanterns, torches, and burning tires. Now a lurch forward at speed and with three brief jerks they're rising fast, then circling back over the airport—as they turn the sun appears behind them, its rays reflected back toward the horizon by a black hood of clouds closing in from the north.

The flight is full, but now the people are calm. Theodore and Eleanor have seats set off a bit from the rest, bolted down toward the back of the plane, where the windows are. They sit with their knees angled toward each other, swapping cards. They tick the six that are left back and forth from hand and eye to hand and eye, and below them the land changes from green to brown, now the earth is cryptically marked in sparse places, less obviously so many towns and roads, lights, sublimating into streaks and points at this middle altitude, and rarefying, the details of the landscape are less definite, each one has its own amorphous, isolating margin of empty country, these margins become clearer than the details over time and expand to form measureless gaps bordered by the horizon—the plane seems to be vibrating in space clear to every horizon above the ground. In the hours that follow, Theodore and Eleanor trade their index cards, reducing their number faster and faster, and with rising excitement to feel the Pacific rolling over the curvature of the earth, momentarily nearer to them, so that if they kept going, the brown field underneath would give way to chaotic blue-green frothed with white, seeming far vaster than dry land. Without announcement, the plane suddenly dips forward, peeling off momentum and altitude; they are circling down, sliding off slopes of air mounded up atop the mountains. The city appearing beneath them is clear and full of very bright sunlight—an untended fire sends an unwavering column of smoke straight up, and they descend through it at high altitude, sweeping down parallel to the coast. Eleanor has the window seat; she can see a vast herd of leopards running up the beach below them as so many dodging spots and almost invisible patches of blonde fur racing over blonde sand. The plane drops as if it was sliding off the edge of a titanic bubble and the engines shake the plane as if they and the tidal force were rattling it apart—Theodore and Eleanor shut their eyes and take each other by the hand, and by this they take each other completely, and hang in suspense until the runway flashes up beneath them and the plane batters down the air onto it. In their clenched hands, their index cards are straight and uncrumpled. Even frightened, the two of them have become so vivid, they're irradiating the passengers, vibrating cancer down into their cells. In the next few weeks, they will all begin growing again, sprouting fabulous new structures, tubefeet, heatsinks, and erogenous feelers and glands budding and fleshing out with euphoric industry in the tissues. The children they have spirited safely away from the storm will grow up more dramatically than expected.

On the ground, the terminal is calm and deserted. Theodore and Eleanor rent a car and leave at once, moving in straight lines down a calm and deserted freeway, toward the foothills, the manuscript lying between them as an adulterous secret. Something is watching over them like a jealous spouse, an angry parent, something that is also taking shape in them both—both taking shape in them and giving them shape, impatiently changing a shape given them long ago.

Theodore and Eleanor at the house: in a deserted neighborhood, in an empty canyon—coming to the house finally, their one and only place to go, it's where they've been heading together from the start, they'll go no farther, they both understand this intuitively as they sit in the car, watch the house appear at the end of the street. The wind is strongly blowing; the whole canyon is stirring.

Each the same can see clearly to the short time ahead, free if only to work and be changed some more, but the future has become decisive, with a definite direction and the word of their work at the end. Dried leaves, curled in on themselves like seashells, scrape up the drive before them on the wind as they come from the car together. The house is modest and plain, with a concrete porch. Inside, they will find some sticks of furniture, bare plaster walls perforated in places with painted-over nails, running water and electricity, a small store of canned food on the shelves in the pantry, a few boxes of books-paper-pens-paper clips and so on, one bed. With the wind rushing by outside, the low air turning pink as the sun sets across from them on the horizon, the hills embracing them are green and brown, the sky is perfect azure and clear—inside the house the light from the windows will intermittently dim down, amid shimmering shadows of leaves from the oaks growing all around to twice the height of Theodore's cousin's house, this shimmering light will suddenly die down, be dim for a few minutes, and then grow strong again; the light is synchronized with each new gust of wind, which hisses along the walls of the house. Together they move a table up against the wall, between and level with two windows, bring in a small lamp, set out the remaining cards, the manuscript in the middle on a writing desk. They sit beside each other, happy to be here, safely out of the way, where the work can be pursued to its end.

Here, the silence, the embrace of each other's presence, above that the embrace of the house, the scores of empty and embalmed houses hovering dreamlike on all sides, then the web of trees, then the hills all around, the wind, then the chrysalis of the sky and infinite distance, set them all the more calmly, and with a sense of inevitability, to the task. They slept and ate in modest turns. In a trance they now traded three index cards back and forth, in full view of their hieroglyphic translation and the Demotic copy laid side by side.

For a full day they mechanically stared at the three cards remaining, like dummies beside each other, like two translations from the same source laid side by side. Then at once they keyed the third card to the first, and were left with two. Coyotes were yipping under the streetlight outside. Their tightly-knotted pack burst apart as it happened, sending flashing streams of coyotes in all directions—a few insinuated themselves around the house, going swiftly by to the dark hillside on blinking feet, in columns of softly panting shadows.

The next morning, they woke to discover that a letter of congratulations had come, from Eleanor's employer, along with two tins of food. They ate hastily, with nothing to say to each other, and returned as quickly as possible to staring at the two cards that remained, that would combine in one name that they would both speak, with which they were both pregnant. Eleanor sat, flicking her eyes madly from one to the other, too excited to concentrate, unable to see anything more than two words lying on the table, too excited even to be frustrated; and Theodore could only see his shaking hands lying bunched up in front of him. When these two elements were harmonized, he and Eleanor would have made the movement of translating for the last time, and the change he had long been expecting would be finished. As long as he thought about that change, he was overwhelmed by the effort of considering it, and too exhausted to move forward. The two index cards outlined between them a gap that would be filled when the translation was done, and, transfixed by it, he lost track of time. He was certain Eleanor was fascinated by the same space between the cards. They both wanted to prolong their contact with it as it was just at the threshold, because they wouldn't be the same after it appeared.

Then Theodore looked up and saw a buck staring in through the window, with a long needle-shaped head and a mouth that opened only at the very front, black animal alien eyes under weirdly spreading antlers. Theodore was caught instantly in its unmoving gaze and saw something in this animal's face like a living desert with a yawning, indifferent stare, like the sunlight, or open space, nothing he hadn't seen before, nothing he had ever noticed, seeing him, with indifference. He saw the buck was alive and seeing him clearly, and he acutely felt Eleanor beside him as she looked up and joined in the triangle of looking eyes. All at once the buck moved weightlessly off—having looked, it passively looked elsewhere and disappeared in a continuous outpouring of wind out of nowhere.

Eleanor had seen the buck's eyes and was shocked, looked down at the cards with a cauterized mind, and seized Theodore's hand as his eyes automatically dropped down to the cards and, with one motion coordinated for the last time in two bodies, they combined the cards with a few pen scratches and the name silently appeared, clicked through them as they spoke it in gelatinous waves on fixed and timeless air. The wind dropped, the light from the windows steadily dimmed, the cards shone white and winked out on the completely darkened table. As they combined the cards, Theodore and Eleanor slid together and overlapped with a click, and what had been gestating in them appeared in their place—each of them perceived this separately as a contraction of the room, the door flying violently open and something like a jealous spouse storming in and almost completely darkening the room forever, and as it came in for them, Eleanor, with Theodore inside her and vice versa, said "My Employer!"

The Book

THE ORIGINAL text dated from the Ninth Dynasty, adding Nephren-Ka's name to the other three pharaonic names known from that period. It was written by Nephren-Ka himself, in an unknown language, possibly a cipher of his own making. The book remained an uncracked mystery until Steiniz uncovered a Demotic copy of the book, with an appended history from a Ninth Dynasty scribe, presumably an eyewitness, translated from a lost hieroglyphic account, and reproduced below. The Demotic translation of the Nephren-Ka text, from the scribe's original hieroglyphic translation, also lost, proved only slightly less impenetrable than the original—while the characters and some of the vocabulary could be made out, the crypto-grammar continues to frustrate all attempts at rendering the Book intelligible.

The Scribe's History

NEPHREN-KA WAS a beautiful child. Beloved of everyone and the best of hunters, he once killed a ten-foot crocodile.

When his older brother died, Nephren-Ka grieved. For days he stared into the desert and refused to see anyone.

When his father died, Nephren-Ka was made Pharaoh. He grieved for his father. The people rejoiced when Nephren-Ka became the Living Sun[1]. His beautiful face gave them pleasure.

In the second year of his reign, Nephren-Ka grieved the death of his sister, who would have been his wife. All his family had died. Nephren-Ka stared into the desert and refused to see anyone. He watched jackals in the desert and would look without blinking into their faces.

---

1. This designation was apparently unique to Nephren-Ka's reign.

At the end of the second year of his reign, Nephren-Ka saw the sun devoured [witnessed an eclipse]. Everywhere there was fear. Everyone was calling on Nephren-Ka. Nephren-Ka watched as the sun was devoured and he laughed, he gave his people no comfort. The sun returned and he was laughing, and the people saw that he had been blinded. At that time the people said that the Living Sun was blind and insane.

From that time Nephren-Ka [was] almost blind [could see only very dimly]. He watched the desert at night and during the day, and brought jackals and vultures into his house and watched them. In the third year of his reign, Nephren-Ka received Niarat-Hotep[2] of Uaghdas, the City of Wisdom[3]. This was a young Prince of Uaghdas who was white as ivory and whose hair was white as ivory, and who had lips and eyes the color of rubies, and who wore no clothes. Niarat-Hotep was young and beautiful. He danced for Nephren-Ka. Wide-eyed, Nephren-Ka saw Niarat-Hotep dancing and laughed.

Nephren-Ka and Niarat-Hotep were always together. Niarat-Hotep danced for Nephren-Ka. Nephren-Ka laughed.

At the beginning of the fourth year of his reign, Nephren-Ka began to make wars.

At that time, Nephren-Ka told the priests that the Living Sun was red and could see only red. The priests brought him a thousand slaves and he told the priests to kill the slaves and to allow their heart's blood to cover everything, so that he could see. The people said that the Living Sun was blind and insane.

The land was blighted. The Nile sank into the ground. Everyone starved and died in plagues.

Nephren-Ka stayed with Niarat-Hotep. At that time, he made many wars and captured thirty thousand slaves. The people ate the slaves. The people withered and became strange, and ate corpses. No one was

---

2. A proper name in a khartouche; one of the letters used is not identifiable, i.e., Niar*at-Hotep, possibly a foreign letter.

3. It is not known to what city this refers.

starving. With my own eyes I saw them do this. There was no one in the road who was not eating dead and living people. I saw dead people walking in the road.

Nephren-Ka stayed with Niarat-Hotep.

When I saw this, the morning was always red, the sky was red and stinking, the ground was red and steaming. There was no food or water but carrion and blood. Everywhere there were dead bodies and blood running on the ground. There were fires in the dried fields, and in the towns. The people burned and were eaten. The smoke covered the sun. The ground was black with flies.

The people ate with the flies. I saw them pursue dead people without heads running into the desert, and rotting and dead corpses ran from them and were caught and eaten. Nephren-Ka and Niarat-Hotep were eating their slaves. The people became strange/not people. I saw this with my own eyes. This is how the ghouls[4] were made.

Acagchemem was in the desert. He was one of the generals of Nephren-Ka. When he returned to the land, the ghouls attacked his army and killed a number of soldiers. He took his army back into the wilderness. He swore an oath to kill Nephren-Ka. I saw this with my own eyes. With the great Scribe[5], my teacher, I fled to be with Acagchemem in the wilderness.

In the wilderness, the Scribe made a phoor[6] against NephrenKa. He drew an eye in stone and made a phoor. I saw this.

This was the beginning of the fifth year of the reign of Nephren-Ka. Acagchemem went to war on Nephren-Ka. The Scribe made a phoor and the ghouls were all killed by the army of Acagchemem.

The ghouls all died or fled into the desert, or were also chased into the ocean, by Acagchemem and the armies of Acagchemem.

---

4. Word of uncertain origin. "Ghoul" is a substitution, from the Arabic word *ghul*, meaning ghost.

5. The Scribe's identity is not known.

6. A literal translation of an unknown word. There is no indication, other than the textual, of its meaning.

Acagchemem called Nephren-Ka out of his palace. NephrenKa was laughing. Acagchemem wrestled with Nephren-Ka for three days. After three days, Nephren-Ka was strangled.

Acagchemem went to find Niarat-Hotep. Niarat-Hotep had fled. Acagchemem died. His body was covered with incisions that stank of poison. When his body was washed he no longer stank. He was buried in a mastaba and an eye was carved by the Scribe in stone where he lay. The Scribe said all tombs must have this eye against the ghouls.

The lieutenant of Acagchemem, who was also his brother, told the priests to burn Nephren-Ka. One of the priests went mad when Nephren-Ka spoke as he was burned. The priests told the brother of Acagchemem that Nephren-Ka had spoken as he burned, and the brother of Acagchemem told the priests to cut Nephren-Ka apart and to grind his pieces to dust and destroy them, and to disperse the dust in the desert, and they did this.

The brother of Acagchemem was made Pharaoh. The good people came out from where they were hiding. He told them to take down the house of Nephren-Ka and bury the stones in the desert, and they did this. The land was restored.

WEIRD TALES
FRED CHAPPELL

There is a certain subgenre of Lovecraftian fiction that integrates the life of H. P. Lovecraft into the story—and most of these are predictable pulp fictions about how Lovecraft was really onto something with his goofy occult bullshit, and how he and his pals must stop the menace and save the world. In a way, Lovecraft encouraged this, as his bookish, fainting narrators—one would hesitate to call them protagonists, as they don't actually "protag" very much—are themselves clearly Lovecraft himself. Even in his wildest dreams, Lovecraft couldn't make himself look good. He left that work to his many epigones.

"Weird Tales" is the best possible version of a story about H. P. Lovecraft, whose life was indeed very interesting. But there's no pulp hero, and there's no world to save, or one worth saving. It is cult fiction about cult authors, and the dubious immortality of literary fame. Most of us will be instantly forgotten; Lovecraft will hang on a bit longer than most. But how long . . . ?

THE VISIONARY poet Hart Crane and the equally visionary horror-story writer H. P. Lovecraft met four times. The first time was in Cleveland on August 19, 1922, in the apartment of a mutual acquaintance, the mincing poetaster Samuel Loveman.

It was an awkward encounter. Loveman and four of his idle friends had departed around eleven o'clock to go in search of a late supper.

Lovecraft was sitting in an armchair under the lamp, a calico kitten asleep in his lap. He declined the invitation to accompany the others because he would not disturb the kitten; cats comprised another of his numerous manias. Shortly before midnight Crane blundered into the room. He was enjoying this night one of his regular fits of debauchery and was quite drunk. "'Lo," he said. "I'm Crane. Where's Sam?" He took no notice of Lovecraft's puzzled stare, but raked a half dozen volumes of French poetry from the sofa, lay down, and passed out.

Lovecraft was quite put off, though the poet's quick slide to oblivion had spared him a dilemma. He would have had to rise in order to present himself, and thus awaken the cat. Lovecraft insisted upon precise formality of address; it was part of his pose as an eighteenth-century esquire sadly comported into the Jazz Age. He was a fanatic teetotaler, and Crane's stuporous condition filled him with disgust.

When Loveman and two companions returned a half hour later, the cat had awakened and Lovecraft set it gently on the floor, rose, and walked to the door. He paused and pointed a finger at Crane, at the ungainly form overpowered with gin and rumpled by the attentions of sailors. "Samuel," he said to Loveman, "your friend is a *degenerate.*"

The effect of this melodramatic sentence was marred by the quality of Lovecraft's voice, a tremulous squeak. Loveman giggled. "Then I'm a degenerate, too, Howard," he said. "Maybe we all are. Maybe that's why no one takes us seriously."

Lovecraft's reply was a toss of his unhandsome head. He closed the door and walked out into the night, walked the seventeen blocks to the YMCA, to his cheerless room and narrow bed. He undressed and, after carefully laying his pants between the mattress and springs for pressing, fell asleep and began to dream his familiar dreams of vertiginous geometries and cyclopean half gods, vivid dreams that would have been anyone else's sweat-drenched nightmares.

After two days Lovecraft and Crane met again and attended a chamber-music concert. Crane was sober then and Lovecraft was quite charmed by his company.

It was an odd group of literary figures, these poets and fiction writers and amateur scholars stranded like survivors of a shipwreck on what they considered the hostile strand of American philistinism. They were not really congenial in temperament or purpose, but they all shared a common interest in newly discovered, newly reconstructed mythologies. They felt need to posit in history powerful but invisible alien forces that had made contemporary civilization such an inhumane shambles. This sort of notion may have been an index to acute loneliness.

Lovecraft's mythos is the most widely known. In a series of fictions soon to appear in the venerated pulp magazine *Weird Tales,* he told of several eras of prehistory when mankind vied with monstrous races of creatures with extraordinary powers for a foothold upon the earth. Man's present dominance was accidentally and precariously achieved; those alien beings were beginning to rearise from their dormancy. Lovecraft described a cosmos that threw dark Lucretian doubt on the proposition "that such things as organic life, good and evil, love and hate, and all such local attributes of a negligible and temporary race called mankind, have any existence at all."

Hart Crane's mythology was not systematic; in fact, it was hardly articulate. His sensibility was such that he was unnerved in his brushes with the ancient presences he detected, and he could not write or think clearly about them. But his old friends were interested to note in his later poems the occurrence of such lines as, "Couched on bloody basins, floating bones/ Of a dismounted people. . . ." Crane believed that Poe had gained best knowledge of the Elder Dominations and so paired him with Whitman in *The Bridge* as a primary avatar of American consciousness.

The most thorough and deliberate of these mythologers was Sterling Croydon, who might have stepped from the pages of one of Lovecraft's stories. He was such a recluse that not even Samuel Loveman saw him more than once or twice a month, though he occupied an apartment in the same building with Loveman, on the floor above. Croydon rarely ventured from his rooms; all those volumes of mathematics, physics, anthropology, and poetry were delivered to his door, and he prepared his scant meals with spirit lamp and a portable gas stove. He was gracious enough to allow occasional visitors, never more than two at a time, and Loveman would spend an evening now and then listening to Croydon elaborate his own system of frightening mythologies. He had been excited to learn that Lovecraft was coming to visit in Cleveland, abandoning for a week his beloved Providence, Rhode Island, and spoke of a strong desire to meet the writer. But when Lovecraft arrived, Croydon withdrew, fearing, no doubt, that to meet the inheritor of Poe's mantle would prove too great a strain for his nerves.

He didn't appear a nervous or high-strung person, but rather—like Lovecraft—a formal gentleman and the soul of composure. He was fastidious and kept himself neatly dressed in dark wool. He imagined that he was painfully photosensitive and ordinarily resorted to dark glasses. His complexion was pale and often flushed, his frame slender almost to the point of emaciation, his gestures quick but calculated. Yet there was a dreamy grandeur about him and when he held forth on various points of Boolean algebra or primitive religion, Loveman felt that he was in the presence of strong intellect and refined character, however neurasthenic.

It was Croydon's contention that his colleagues had but scratched the surface of the problem. He had read Tylor, Sir James Frazer, Leo Frobenius and had traced their sources; he knew thoroughly the more radical attempts of Lovecraft, Clark Ashton Smith, Henry Kuttner, Frank Belknap Long, and the others, but considered that they had done no more than dredge up scraps and splinters. He was convinced that one of Lovecraft's principal sources, the *Pnakotic Manuscripts*, was spurious, and that his descriptions of such cruel gods as Nyarlathotep and Yog-Sothoth were biased and vitiated by sensationalism and overwrought prose style.

He did not claim, of course, to know the whole truth. But he did know that Riemann's concept of elliptical geometry was indispensable to a correct theory and that the magnetic fluxions of the South Pole were important in a way no one had thought of. He had been eager to apprise Lovecraft of these ideas and of others, but at the last hour his shyness overcame him. Or maybe he had come to doubt the writer's seriousness.

We are forced to speculate about the outcome of this meeting that never took place; it might well have been of great aid to us, bringing to public notice Croydon's more comprehensive theories and engendering in Lovecraft a deeper sense of responsibility.

The one result we know, however, is that Croydon's life became even more reclusive than before. He almost never saw Loveman and his companions anymore, and no one was admitted now to his rooms. The single exception to this general exclusion was Hart Crane. Croydon thought that he saw qualities and capabilities in Crane lacking in his coarser-grained friends, and he would receive the poet anytime of the day or night. Drinking himself only a little wine, blackberry or elderberry, he kept a supply of gin for Crane, who never arrived sober and who would not stay unless there was something to drink.

So it was to Crane that Croydon poured out all his certainties, theories, and wild surmises. Almost all of it would have made no sense to Crane and would be distorted by his fever for poetry and disfigured by alcoholic forgetfulness. Yet he was impressed by this anomalous scholar, and bits and pieces of those midnight disquisitions lodged in his mind. Perhaps Croydon's talk impressed him in a way it might not have done if he had been sober. The poet was interested in pre-Columbian history, he had always had a yearning to travel in Mexico, and he was particularly taken with Croydon's notion that the Toltec, Mayan, and finally the Aztec religions were shadowy reflections of historical events that took place when mankind inhabited the Antarctic, when that region was steamy carboniferous forest. Those jaguar gods and feathered serpents that ornamented the temples had become highly stylized and symbolic, Croydon said, but long, long ago, when man and dinosaur and other less definable races coexisted at the bottom of the world, the first of these carvings and paintings had been attempts simply to represent literal appearance. Those creatures, and many others of unproducible aspect, had lived among us. Or rather, we had lived among them, as animal labor supply and as food source.

Crane discounted most of Croydon's notions. He did not believe, for example, that dinosaurs could have been intelligent warm-blooded creatures who had attempted to dislodge the alien gods who ruled among them. He did not believe the dinosaurs had died because their adversaries had infected them with an artificial bacterium that had spread like wildfire, wiping out every major saurian species in three generations. But he was fascinated by Croydon's accounts of tribal religions in South and Central America, caught up by the exotic imagery and the descriptions of ritual. Croydon was especially excited by an obscure tribe inhabiting the reaches of the upper Amazon who worshiped a panoply of gods they called collectively Dzhaimbú. Or perhaps they worshiped but one god who could take different shapes. Much was unclear. But it was clear that Croydon regarded Dzhaimbú as the most anciently rooted of religions, in a direct descent from mankind's prehistoric Antarctic experiences.

Crane was impressed, too, by another of Croydon's ideas. This scholar disagreed vehemently with Darwin's charming theory that man had learned speech by imitating the mating calls of birds. Not so, said Croydon; man was originally a vocally taciturn animal like the horse and the gorilla, and, like horse and gorilla, uttered few sounds except under duress of extreme pain or terror. But these sounds they learned to voice quite regularly when Dzhaimbú inflicted upon them unspeakable atrocities, practices that Croydon could not think of without shuddering. All human speech was merely the elaboration of an original shriek of terror.

"'S a shame, Sterling," Crane said, "that you can't board a ship and go down to the jungle and investigate. I bet you'd turn up some interesting stuff."

Croydon smiled. "Oh, I wouldn't bother with the jungle. I'd go to the Antarctic and look for direct archaeological evidence."

Crane took another swallow from his tumbler of neat gin. His eyes were slightly unfocused and his face was flushed and his neck red in the soft open collar. "Shame you can't go to the South Pole then, if that's where you want to go."

"No, I shouldn't make a very able sailor, I think," Croydon said. "But, after all, there are other ways to travel than by crawling over the globe like a termite."

And now he launched into a description of what he called spatial emplacement, by which means a man sitting in his room might visit any part of the earth. All that was required was delicate manipulation of complex and tenuous mathematical formulae, prediction of solar winds, polar magnetic fluxions, cosmic-ray vectors, and so forth. He began to pour out a rubble of numbers and Greek letters, all of which Crane disregarded, suspecting that they'd struck now upon the richest vein of his friend's lunacy. Croydon's idea seemed to be that every geographical location in the universe could be imagined as being located on the surface of its individual sphere, and that the problem was simply to turn these spheres until the desired points matched and touched. Touched, but did not conjoin; there would be disaster if they conjoined. The worst complication was that these mathematical spheres, once freed from Euclidean space, were also free in time. One might arrive to inspect Antarctica at the time he wished, which would be pleasant indeed; or he might arrive in the future, uncountable millennia from now. And that would be dangerous as well as inconvenient.

But all this murmur of number and mathematical theory had lulled Crane. He was asleep in the club chair. Croydon woke him gently and suggested that he might like to go home.

"Yeah, maybe I better," Crane said. He scratched his head, disheveling again his spiky hair. "But say, Sterling, I don't know about the travel by arithmetic. Better to get a berth on a ship and sail around and see the birds wheel overhead and the slow islands passing." The thought struck his enthusiasm. "That's what we'll do one of these days. We'll get on a ship and go explore these jungles."

"Good night, Hart," Croydon said.

This impulsive voyage was never to take place, of course. Crane's poetry had begun to attract important critical notice, and he soon moved to New York to further his melancholy but luminous literary career.

Croydon remained behind to pursue his researches ever more intensively. He was quite lost sight of to the world. Loveman would occasionally stop by but was not admitted.

It was on one of these infrequent visits that he felt a strangeness. The hall leading to Croydon's room was chilly and the air around the door very cold indeed. And the door was sweating cold water, had begun to collect ice around the edges. The brass nameplate was covered with hard frost, obliterating Croydon's name.

Loveman knocked and knocked again and heard no sound within but a low inhuman moan. He tried the icy knob, which finally turned, but could not force the door inward. He braced his feet, set his shoulder against the door, and strained, but was able to get it open only for the space of an inch or two. The noise increased—it was the howling of wind—and a blast of rumbling air swept over him and he saw in that small space only an area of white, a patch of snow. Then the wind thumped the door shut.

Loveman was at a loss. None of his usual friends was nearby to aid him, and he would not call upon others. He belonged to a circle in which there were many secrets they did not wish the larger world to know. He returned to his rooms on the lower floor, dressed himself in a winter woolen jacket and scarf and toboggan. After a brief search he found his gloves. He took a heavy ornamental brass poker from the hearth and returned to Croydon's door.

This time he set himself firmly and, when he had effected a slight opening, thrust the poker into the space and levered it back. The poker began to bend with the strain and he could feel the coldness of it through his gloves. Then the wind caught the edge of the door and flung it back suddenly and Loveman found himself staring into a snowy plain swept over by fierce Antarctic wind.

It was all very puzzling. Loveman could see into this windstorm and feel some force of the wind and cold, but he knew that what he felt was small indeed as compared to the fury of the weather into which he could see. Nor could he advance physically into this landscape. He could march forward, pushing against the wind, he could feel himself going forward, but he did not advance so much as an inch into that uproar of ice and snow.

It is in another space, he thought, but very, very close to my own.

He could see into it but he could not travel there. In fact, with the wild curtains of snow blowing he could see little, but what he could see was terrible enough.

There, seemingly not twenty feet from him, sat Croydon at his desk. The scholar was wearing only his burgundy velvet dressing gown and gray flannel trousers and bedroom slippers. The habitual dark glasses concealed his eyes, but the rest of his face was drawn into a tortured grimace.

Of course Loveman shouted out *"Croydon! Croydon!"* knowing it was useless.

He could not tell whether his friend was still alive. He did not think that he could be. Certainly if he was in the same space as this Antarctic temperature, he must have died a quick but painful death. Perhaps he was not in that space but in a space like Loveman's own, touching but not conjoining this polar location. Yet the Antarctic space intervened between them, an impassable barrier.

He wished now that he had paid more attention when Croydon had outlined his mathematical ideas. But Loveman, like Crane, had no talent for, no patience with, number. He could never have understood. And now those pages of painstaking calculation had blown away, stiff as steel blades, over the blue ice sheets.

He thought that if he could not walk forward then he might crawl, but when he went to his knees he found himself suspended a couple of feet above the plane of the floor. Something was wrong with the space he was in. He stood dizzily and stepped down to the floor again, and the descent was as hard a struggle as climbing an Alpine precipice.

There was no way to get to Croydon, and he wondered whether it would be possible to heave a rope to him—if he could find a rope.

It was impossible. The scholar had begun to recede in space, growing smaller and more distant, as if caught in the wrong end of a telescope. And the polar wind began to effect a bad transformation. The dressing gown was ripped from Croydon's body and he was blackening like a gardenia thrown into a fire. His skin and the layers of his flesh began to curl up and peel away, petal by petal. A savage gust tore off his scalp and the blood that welled there froze immediately, a skullcap of onyx. Soon he would be only a skeleton, tumbled knob and joint over the driving snow, but Loveman was spared the spectacle. The frozen figure receded more quickly and a swirl of ice grains blotted away the vision. Croydon was gone.

Loveman made his way into the hall, walking backward. His mouth was dully open and he found that he was sweating and that the sweat had begun to ice his clothing.

There came a crash as of thunder, the smell of ozone, and the Antarctic scene disappeared from the room and there was nothing there. Literally, nothing: no furniture, no walls, no floor. The door with Croydon's nameplate hung over a blue featureless abyss. There was nothing, no real space at all.

Loveman gathered his courage, reached in, and pulled the door closed. He went quietly down the hall, determined to get back into his own room before others showed up. He did not want to answer questions; he did not want anyone to know what he knew. He wanted to go to his room and sit down and think alone and reaffirm his sanity.

The disappearance of Croydon and of that part of the apartment building caused some little public stir. The recluse had no relatives, but scientists were interested, as well as the police. Loveman avoided as best he could any official notice, and in a few months the event, being unexplainable, was largely forgotten.

But the occurrence was not forgotten by the circle of Loveman's friends. For them it was a matter of great concern. They feared that Croydon's experiment had called attention to themselves. Would not those alien presences whose histories they had been studiously examining now turn their regard toward Cleveland? Had he not disturbed the web of space-time as a fly disturbs a spiderweb? It was true that they were indifferent to mankind, to species and individual alike. But there were some researchers who thought, as Lovecraft did, that the ancient race was planning a regeneration of its destiny and would act to keep its existence secret until the moment was ripe. The powers of these beings was immense; they could crush and destroy when and where they pleased, as casually as a man crushes out a cigarette in an ashtray.

It was actually at this early juncture that everything began to come apart. Though the pursuit among the seers and poets was leisurely by human standards, it was relentless. Lovecraft died in 1937, in painful loneliness. The official medical report listed the cause as intestinal cancer, but the little group of investigators was accustomed to greeting all such reports with deep skepticism. Hart Crane's more famous death had taken place five years earlier, the celebrated leap into the sea.

The men had since met twice again, during the period of what Lovecraft called his "New York exile." He was a little shocked at the changes in Crane's physical condition. "He looks more weatherbeaten & drink-puffed than he did in the past," Lovecraft wrote to his aunt, "tragically drink-riddled but now eminent." He predicted that Crane would find it difficult to write another major work. "After about three hours of acute & intelligent argument poor Crane left—to hunt up a new supply of whiskey & banish reality for the rest of the night!"

Lovecraft records this encounter as taking place May 24, 1930. They were not alone and had no opportunity to talk privately, so that Crane would not have told the other what he had learned of the circumstances of Croydon's death. He could not apprise Lovecraft that he alone was inheritor to Croydon's secret knowledge and that his identity must necessarily be known to that being, or series of beings, Dzhaimbú. He spoke of leaving New York and moving to Charleston, but Lovecraft did not pick up the hint, merely agreeing that such a move might be beneficial. Perhaps Crane's gallantry prevented his placing the other in danger.

Another interpretation is possible. We may guess that Crane did indeed communicate some of his information to the horror-story writer. It is just at this period that Lovecraft's mythos began to take its more coherent and credible shape in such works as "The Shadow Over Innsmouth" and "The Dreams in the Witch House." Certainly both Lovecraft and Loveman remarked that Crane now lived in a state of haunted terror, wild and frightful, dependent upon alcohol to keep his fear manageable. Crane must have known that he was being pursued—the signs were unmistakable—and decided to face the terror on its own grounds. For this reason he politicked to get the Guggenheim grant that would take him to Mexico.

But it was too late. Alcohol had disordered his nervous system; his strength was gone. On the voyage to Mexico he met the celebrated bacteriologist Dr. Hans Zinsser and imagined that he was an agent of Dzhaimbú sent to infect humanity by means of typhus-ridden rats. Zinsser's motives in dumping infected rats into the harbor at Havana remain unknown, but it is hardly probable that Crane's suspicions were correct.

In Mexico the poet's behavior was uncontrolled and incomprehensible, a series of shocking and violent incidents that landed him often in jail and caused his friends to distrust any sentence he uttered. His decision to meet the terror face-to-face was disastrous; he could not stand up under the strain. No man could. And his further decision to keep his knowledge and theories secret so as not to endanger others was a worse disaster.

In the end, he fled, unable to face the prospect of coming close to the source of the horror. The voyage home began with dreams and visions so terrifying that he could not bear to close his eyes and so stayed awake, drinking continuously. Embarrassing episodes followed of which he was numbly aware but past caring about. On April 27, 1932, Hart Crane jumped from the railing of the *Orizaba*. The sea received him and the immense serpentine manifestation of Dzhaimbú, which had been following in the unseen depths in the wake of the vessel, devoured him.

This fabulous shadow only the sea keeps.

It is inevitable that we read these sad histories as we do, as a catalogue of missed opportunities and broken communications. A present generation self-righteously decries the errors of its forefathers. But it is unlikely that any human effort would have changed the course of events. There still would have come about the reawakening of Dzhaimbú and the other worse gods, under whose charnel dominion we now suffer and despair.

Bright Crown of Joy
Livia Llewellyn

I think we can all agree that the world is going to end sooner rather than later. I'd say we'd had a good run, but really, we haven't. But even the inevitable and quickly rushing collapse won't lack for beauty. It may be beauty we find horrific (I say "may" because I am, like all Communists, an incurable optimist) or entirely beyond comprehension, but there will be beauty.

You're not going to appreciate it, though. Livia Llewellyn, on the other hand, will. Indeed, she already has.

[::AFTER::]

ONCE UPON a time, when I was a little girl, there were birds. Thin delicate arrows of bone and feather, crossing the dry horizons of the earth like the needles of the universe, stitching the planet together with their call. Billions of them, spiraling in coils like wind-swept dragons kissing the baby blue vault of the sky. Settling into the trees during cold nights like clusters of fluttering dark leaves, and bursting into high bright song every morning as the unstoppable sun breached the horizon like a volcanic god. Once upon a time, I was a girl and there were birds.

But those days have been gone for many long millennia. All warm-blooded life, all land once bone dry, all seasons once cold—all have been long banished from this warm water realm; and all the birds have died, along with most of the animals we few remaining half-humans remember, those magnificent amber-eyed creatures of feather and fur. Like childhood, they exist solely as memories, outdated maps to a country we can never return to. In the wake of His passage, all has been transformed.

When I sleep, I dream deep and hard, as we all do. Sleeping, I drink in and drown in memories, the last memories of the last survivor of a long-dead race. I awake still dreaming, the smell of pine pitch and rustlings of birds and trees lingering in the tendrils of those long-lost territories. Gradually, always, the sounds disappear into the soft song of stone chimes hanging from the arches of my roofless chamber, sounding out the passage of tiny cnidarians as they float and swim through the hot damp air. I rise up from my bed and watch their pulsing bodies push through the ceramic domes, tentacles trailing like strands of winking lights. Outside, larger beings, capillatas and medusas and creatures I have no names for, catch in the overgrown vegetation then burst free in silent explosions of gelatinous flight, disappearing into the pale sunless mists that have muted day and lightened night. These are the birds of the world now. And they are stupendous. They are beautiful.

The boy, hardly a boy anymore but something caught between boy and alien wonder, lingers in the crumbling remains of the other room, waiting for me to rise, his soft lips always in a slight smile that hides a mouth of teeth that ages ago fused together into a single ridged wall of bone. His reluctance at leaving me behind on the evolutionary ladder touches me. Sometimes I catch him slumbering, and I press my unclothed body against his, eyelids lowering as I join him in reverie. More and more, we remain like that for immeasurable passages of time, flickering images of past lives washing through our conjoining flesh and minds, breaking apart only when some mysterious creature brushes past us in its accidental perambulations through our home. No such lingering coupling for us this wan morning, though. Outside and far away, on the last and highest mountaintop in the world, our youngest children patiently await us, and as if in a dream I have realized that the time has come to meet them.

* * *

[::MEMORY #2724869.1::]
July 17, 24—, 11:38.52 PM
Roman Wall City, Mount Baker
PrionTech InterDiary #74543.01

[::WAKE::]
[::WAKE::]
[::WAKE::]
[::REMINDER: 12:15.00 AM CAR PICK-UP, 1:00.00 AM DESTINATION SUMMER CRATER ESTATES::]

HE IS COMING. *He is coming. He is coming.* The alarm is going off, but it's this nightmare that's really ripping the sleep from me, again. I'm waking up as I always do, trembling and panting, sheets all twisted around my body, the mattress and my t-shirt are so wet and slick that—no, I didn't wet the bed. Huh. Well, that was a horrifying moment. God, it's so hot. I bet the AC has gone out again. Let me check.

I was whispering when I woke up. *He is coming.* Repeating it, chanting, like a prayer. How long have I been saying those words? My mind keeps going over the dream. The horizon, the Pacific bulging up and out like a bowl until the waters break.

No, it's working, barely. Going through the motions. *[::REC OFF::]*

[::REC ON::] I went to the bathroom, and now I'm in front of the open food locker, letting this feeble chill wash over me as I drink the last of the filtered water—though I'd specifically saved it for my morning tea, and my grocery appointment isn't until the 19th. Oh well. I needed it. I probably shed five pounds of sweat onto my poor bed.

It's pitch black outside, so I'm rolling both the blinds and the UV shades up. I hope the video for all of this is uploading. No lights in the apartment, no reflection in the window except for a faint purple wink of the wireless implant at my left temple. I'm pressing my nose against the glass, I can see all the way across and down the southwest slopes to the edges. Autumn comes earlier every year, and already great swathes of gold and red run through the forests, needles and leaves falling faster than rain. People are saying this is the final die-off, that this is the start of the end. They say that every year, though. There are little pockets of light all the way down the mountain into the foothills and valleys, pockets of those like me who can afford 24-hour electricity and avoid the brownouts. The rest of the slope is dark as a tomb. Occasional flashes of light, though—probably fires. Sometimes police cars or ambulances.

Sometimes, though I don't know why I think this, the lights look like something else. Organic, almost bioluminescent, like the flashing of giant anglerfish, luring we few night owls outside, into our benthic doom. There they go, again.

[::M-FLASH::]
seven years ago, after the Pan-Pacific tsunami waters receded
valleys and rivers of green fire.
[::/M-FLASH::]

I DON'T KNOW if this is even uploading to my online diary or if I'm the only one who will ever read this, when I'm old and bored and out of memories to make. The aurora borealis—bands of bright orange and cold blue flickering high above the horizon. Unfolding and spiraling upwards in thin streams, like twisters of wildfire, like the ocean is unraveling. It's the wrong time of year for the lights. How odd.

Beyond the valley, beyond the peaks of the Olympic Mountain Archipelago and the Vancouver Island Ranges, is the Pacific. I can't see it from here, even as high up as I am and as much as the ocean has risen, but those even higher and far richer than me, those with homes at the summit with their high-powered telescopes, they can see the coast grow closer with every passing year, filling up valleys, sliding over low foot hills, filling in all the spaces of the world. In less than two hours I'll be in one of those summit homes, one of those guests of a guest affairs where I'll be granted access to the gated stronghold of one of the few remaining mega rich families via the arm of my handsome silver-haired date, a banking acquaintance further down the ridge at Colfax Peak, who's probably looking for a companion higher up the mountain he can move in with when the waves start knocking at his door. I'm not judging: tonight I'll be doing the same thing. We all spend our lives looking up now, much more than looking down. There's so much less to look up to anymore. I should get ready.

[::REMINDER!::] Pack my collapsible water bottle, in case there's no timer on their bathroom faucets.

OH, THE nightmare. I never got around to downloading that DreamCatcher app, way back before internet access got so slow and spotty, and so I was going to think it down when I woke up—that was the whole point of this entry. And of course, I've forgotten most of the details. All I remember now are bells, gigantic church bells or gongs, a constant thunderous ringing as all the oceans of the world pour up into the sky, and everything sinks below.

[::/MEMORY::]

* * *

[::AFTER::]

WE TAKE the long way, as always, across the great delta to the watery marshes that lap against the chain of ancient mountain peaks we and the other remaining elders have made our final home. I never need to remind or insist, the boy knows my every routine as if it is his own. Roads and trails have been reduced to shadows and suggestions of themselves, spectral threads of our previous passage that are only slightly less overgrown than the surrounding jungle. Our feet know the way only by instinct anymore. You could call it mere, but instinct seems more and more to be the wondrous order of our endless day. We sleep and dream and eat and breathe in the super-saturated air; and decades and centuries and perhaps even millennia go by before we stop and think, *I am doing this, I am picking up that, I remember that place and that time, I am here, right here, and it is now*. And we no longer remember the terrible, human limit of finite days and years, all that weight of decay and mortality. Time simply is, it stretches out like this wilderness, like the waters, like the river of stars that spirals across the sky, drawing ever closer with every phase of the moons. There is so much of it now. Sometimes the boy and I weep at the thought, the thought of us being within it and a part of it, of becoming vast and endless and, and. And.

So much endless becoming. We lap at the edges, daring to taste, to wonder: what will it be like, when we finally succumb, are subsumed? And then, like tiny fish, we dart away. For now.

Through jungles of gold and green ferns, high as trees, across warm rivers and wetlands, draped in brown hanging moss and blood red flowers. All the colors of a crisp northern fall, erupting out of an endlessly sub-tropic world. Masses of giant starfish-headed worms cling to boulders, their rows of bead-black eyes noting our progress as their suckered arms grind the smooth surfaces away. We find the skiff, an ancient hardwood beauty, tied to the tree that has grown higher and thicker with each greeting, and slip into the currents. Skeletal vestiges of the tips of skyscrapers glide past, covered in green, followed by slender tree trunks and vines mimicking the angular shapes of the towers they once latched onto and fed off of, towers that collapsed ages ago as the trees grew on. Our public spaces, our thoroughfares and byways are lush carpets of sea grass in shallow waters, waving us through the serene backwaters of what were once our last cities, our last homes.

Above the roof of the wilderness, three pale spires float into view. The fourth barely rises above the tree line, looking like the broken stub of a finger bone. And then: a column-lined stone road leading to an arched gateway that devours it like a mouth; and beyond the gate, the high stone and granite walls of the crumbling former holy palace that has become through all our ages and evolutions so many different kinds of schools, the crown that rests on the highest summit of the last remaining land mass in the world. Next to the water's edge, a figure sits at the broken base of a cyclopean Buddha, worn back down into the featureless aerolith from which it was born. The man. He spends all his time now with the children, watching them grow, teaching them and learning from them, embracing change almost as quickly as they do. I wonder which of the oldest I will no longer recognize. I wonder which of them will no longer recognize me. Someday, the boy and I will join them, as will the few remaining humans like us, the elders who still live alone in the lands; and then it will be all of us together, a colony of one, pulsing and expanding as one, drawing up all the waters of this world as our body becomes a sail with which to catch and ride the sonic songs of distant stars.

The skiff catches the shore, and the boy leaps out. The man moves forward, offering to me his graceful, fingerless hand. He sees and speaks and breaths solely through his limbs and soft skin now, his features long subsumed into the smooth brown of a hairless head that even now the ghost of a welcoming smile lingers within. He pulls me up with ease, and we stand together in the shadows of the leaves, arms encircling, foreheads touching. He still knows us, but he no longer knows who we are. A familiar fading purple light at the side of his head winks once, like a candle that sputtered into flame only to immediately die. He is trying to commit our faces to permanent memory again, his brain and the technology going through the motions without understanding that it is nothing more than a death rattle. Like the boy, and all the other Elders, whose ports died out at the start of the After, their past lives have vanished. There is only the present for them, a memory-free, streamlined evolution into the future. Only I still remember that even these moments will be wiped away clean. I have no choice. I cannot forget.

[::M-FLASH::]
his beautiful silver hair
[:://M-FLASH::]

* * *

[::MEMORY #2724869.3::]
July 18, 24—, 02:05.07 am
Ballad House, Summit Crater Estates, Mount Baker
PrionTech InterDiary #74543.04

[::FILE CORRUPTION::]
—by the standards of today, I'm rich and jaded and cruel, but even for me
it's a bit grotesque. I could never eat that. I politely decline and the waiter
gracefully moves away into the crowd with his silver tray. The first group
is back from their tour, moving through the double doors into the living
room, most of them excited and flushed, a few somber and quiet. People
forget their drinks and their important conversations, crowd around
them, touch their bright red cheeks and gasp and laugh. What they've
just seen, few people in the world have seen for hundreds of years—and
even the most powerful people on the planet, scientists and politicians
and queens, they have not seen, will never see this thing. Perhaps they
don't remember it exists anymore. We're all so busy running from the
ocean and cowering under the sun, there's no time for anything else
anymore. A shiver is running through me, despite the almost suffocating
heat in the room. I'm in group twelve. I don't mind waiting. I've found
out that when you're the last, it means you can find out little things the
ones who went before you didn't know, secrets and cheats. Sometimes
you learn how to stay as long as you want.

I'M WALKING over to the side of the room, now, to the bar. Except for my
date, I don't know any of these people here tonight. Not the usual crowd
that attends these events.

No more unlimited ice—they started rationing before the first half-hour was up. Our hosts have been gracious and apologetic, explaining the lack of usual amenities to the unusual temperature spikes, to the diverting of resources to other areas of the estate. Money can buy anything, but we've long been coming to the end of how much there is in the world to buy.

ANOTHER DRINK, with a single shard of ice, no larger than one of my nails. Gone. It's disappeared so quickly, I might have imagined it. I'm walking out into the square outdoor courtyard that sits in the middle of the house, and look up past the slashing lines of concrete and steel to the faint twinkle of stars pushing through the humidity and haze. God, what an ugly-looking building. Uglier than most. Certainly not a mansion, barely a house. More like some giant reached into the mountain, grabbed the top of a nuclear bunker and pulled it halfway out of the rock. It's been built to survive anything, I've heard—all of the buildings at Summit Crater have. Our hosts insist that they designed every last detail of their home, as well as all the other homes on the gated estate, but over the decades, rumors have flown.

[::M-FLASH::]
weapons testing facility
center for disease control
torture and detention center
?astro-archaeology?
[::/M-FLASH::] [::REC OFF::]

[::REC ON::] Boring conversation over with. It's almost my group's time to go. People are pointing up. The lights again, the aurora borealis, streamers of thick blue and white lights overhead like comet showers. What was the name of that famous one, that crossed the planet's path every century? *[::SEARCHING…SEARCHING…/SEARCH::]* No internet. Never mind. I'm standing in the middle of the courtyard with everyone else, staring

up at the moving sky. All the constellations, spiraling, circling. All of us, drifting like torn sea grass, falling up—

IN THE next room people are laughing, like waves over breaking glass. I'm stumbling over to a bench, my evening companion suddenly at my side, his hand around my bare arm. My head bent down. *It's okay, I'm not drunk*, I hear myself saying as I'm rubbing my eyes. *It's just the stars. It's just the bells.*

[::/MEMORY::]

✳ ✳ ✳

[::AFTER::]

ALL SCHOOLS look the same, smell the same, sound the same, I think as we walk through the echoing halls. Even after so many eons, even in air so thick with water that most days now the boy's and my too-slowly-evolving antediluvian lungs struggle to breath. The tiny purple and blue light that still sparks and winks at the side of my glabrous heads, it remembers for me. It lets me forget nothing. The colors of curled crayoned papers fluttering against cream and lime walls. The speckled linoleum, yellowed and cracked with blooms of algae and moss bursting between each square. The long hallways, silent and high and wide, lined with rusting lockers and dusty windows and open classroom doors. The miniature size of each round-edged wooden desk and rickety chair. All as familiar as if we were human children again. The only thing missing is the soft smell of chalk in the air.

I reach out with the tip of one long sticky digit, and touch the faded remains of a drawing of tall green plants. The paper is so delicate that it dissolves at my slightest touch, bursting into thousands of particles that hang in the air like insects. Had it been the work of one of my thousands of children, back in the early centuries of the post-transformation of the world, when we were still more human than not? The implant in the dissolving remnants of my brain comes up with no memories. As we move down the cracked stone floors, past pale branches with snapping flowers and clusters of tall sea grass erupting from lockers and doorways, a single bell peals gently from one of the towers. Wind, perhaps, or a school of floating polyps. The boy and I smile in unison.

Hallways and stairways converge, pouring into a roofless, multi-leveled atrium. Tiny lizards sleep on the balustrades and warm floors. The man heads off in another direction, down wide steps of graying marble that lead to underground rivers, bioluminescent rooms, and glittering nocturnal pools, where those children and elders reside as a single entity that is so far beyond and above us that the boy and I hear its song only as a faint impulse, a tug of the heart that catches only to release and melt away before we can join in.

Not yet. It's not my time just yet.

The boy and I continue down the steps toward the masses of supine bodies that cover the floor, drape across balustrades and up stairwells, hang over balcony railings like glistening tapestries. Toward the center of the room they begin to merge, bodies conjoining and melding together, forming a singular living mass that flows down through a wide, round fissure in the middle of the space. Beneath the collective breath and shifting of their bodies, the constant low roar of the ocean works its way up through the remains of the mountain, through the funnel of pulsing flesh that endlessly descends toward their brothers and sisters in the watery chambers below. Plumes of brine and sweet decay fill my lungs, the scents of my children and the elders as they begin their final journey into the ever-increasing being that shall someday span the ocean, that shall someday consume the entire planet, that shall someday take its place once again as a traveler of the dark river of stars, that shall someday find some other bright blue world in which to sink and shrink and settle and dream until the time is right once again for the cycle of life to repeat.

We make our way through ropes of softening bone, columns of vibrating limbs, our hands running over humming flesh as we pass through the room to the other side. I feel their thoughts vibrate into me like electrical currents, welcomes and salutations and declarations of familial love, equations and astral projections and all the cosmic revelations that come with pending godhood. The air becomes easier to breathe, and the myriad needle pains of my ageless body fade. These children of mine do not understand me, but they love me and they heal me, because I have shown each of them the wondrous and mind-altering glimpse of what is to come, of what we will all become. I alone contain the glimpse of our future-self.

✳ ✳ ✳

[::MEMORY #2724869.4::]
July 18, 24—, 04:12.08 am
[::SEARCHING::]
PrionTech InterDiary #74543.07

Dammit dammit I forgot to turn the diary back on until now. I'm standing at the end of a long underground hallway with one of my hosts, and the six other people in my group, my silver-haired date included. I'm looking back down the hallway, and I can't quite make out the door we entered through. That's how long it is. There's a steep slant to the floor. We went down.

My date is next to me, holding my hand, we're watching in silence as our host and their security team unlock the door. We're all looking away, respectfully, although they're not entering codes. The entire door is covered in locks and cogs and tumblers. It was built for a world without electricity—that's why there are small shell-shaped recesses in the walls. For candles or lamps, maybe. I bet this used to be a shelter. The higher the oceans drive us, the lower we sink. I can't help but feel we deserve this, that we brought this all on ourselves.

Enough of that. My date's hand is at the small of my back. He's smiling, and I'm returning it. This, right here and now, is an incredible, singular moment I'll remember for the rest of my life. This will shape and define me in ways I have yet to understand. It's only a few degrees cooler within the mountain, but I'm so unused to the difference, I'm almost high—and this is just the start. The vertigo and confusion of earlier in the night is gone—I was overheated, dehydrated, the alcohol didn't help. Guests always faint at these things, we don't know how to pace ourselves anymore. Now I'm practically levitating with excitement.

The door is clicking, our host—he's saying something . . . it was once one of only three in the Northern Hemisphere, but he has it on good authority that the other two are long gone, and there are no more in the south . . . something about quadruple-insulated glass walls, twenty-four-hour security, blast doors and walls . . . slow down, I missed a date. It's very old, the oldest thing you could imagine, created even before the Ice Age, whenever that was. One of the guards is ushering us through into a small antechamber, where we're being instructed to slip on long fur-lined coats with hoods, face masks, gloves, heavy booties that look like tree stumps. The room is growing cool, very cool, very quickly. We're crowding together, there's just enough room for all of us with all this fabric swaddling our fancy outfits. I'm pressed between my date and a young man, maybe fourteen or fifteen, with long blonde hair and a baby-soft face. Familiar—the host's son, or a donor clone? So hard to tell anymore. The door behind is clanking shut, and the door in front of us is now opening. *He is coming*, I whisper. Shaking my head, laughing like I told a stupid joke. I meant to say, *this is it*.

THE WOMAN in front of me is passing out as the door slowly opens—
—super-cold—
—murky heat of th—
—opens into the snow—

[::FILE CORRUPTION::]
—son-clone, is speaking to my date, I'm catching the end of their conversation, his amazing offer we're both now saying yes to in unison,

as we're directed back through the two-foot-thick doors. It seems our night of wonders has yet to end.

* * *

[::AFTER::]

PAST THE oculus of ocean-saturated flesh we wander, through the crumbling arch of a doorway and up wide stairs. More hallways, lined with worn stone doors. Rough bands of dead coral and the tiny bones of antediluvian sea creatures are embedded in the surface of the walls, creatures completely unfamiliar to me. After the After, there were waves of tsunamis that circled the surface of the world again and again, remaking it entirely new, there were epochs of monstrous and amazing creatures that thrived and died off in mass extinctions as the planet recalibrated again and again, as we who survived realized that we too had recalibrated, and were part of the chain of change. To our right, light pours in through rows of windows, the glass panes long cracked and worn away. Fog sifts over the sills in flowing bands of soft pure white, and our thin bodies turn it into coiling serpents that wilt and fade in our wake. That color is a rarity now, it reminds me of a moment so thoroughly buried in my past, that to access it takes lengths of time that spans the cycles of the moons. Only with the help of my children can I melt the eons away. But it is more than that. I want them all to know what it was to be awake, alive.

The boy stops before one partially open door. I follow him in. In this place, more than any other, sometimes the old thoughts and emotions reemerge, and curiosity comes to life again within us. This is the room with the globes, row after row of round, almost weightless planets and moons, perched on stands that allow them to spin and gyre in place. I don't know if the boy remembers what they represent anymore, but it is clear he remembers his pleasure in spinning them, in staring at the continents and islands and rivers and seas whirling with the touch of his hands. Most of the map features have vanished, some globes have rotted away into half-shells, others are simply dust. All are static snapshots of a planet whose surface has shifted countless times. Faint traces of maps cover the classroom walls, painted on the stone and plaster. Long ago, when they were legible, I could make out trails and calculations, the plans of routes and journeys, cuneiform scratches that spelled out destinations. There was a time we thought we could reverse the process, escape our fate. But from this place, the highest mountaintop in the world, there was nowhere else to run.

An elder appears before us in the doorway, its featureless head nodding as multiple arms beckon us forward. I don't recognize it. Are they someone I once knew, in our human life before the After? They have no mouth. Their port, if they ever had one, is dead, and their mind is already becoming attuned to the writhing confluence below, their body soon to follow. No urgency drives its movements, only instinct, and so we continue our circuit around the room, taking as much time as we need and desire, our fingers entwined, mesmerized by the thick layers of pasts crowding the space like ghosts. We let them wash over and through us until we are sated, until some restless primal human emotion or urge in each of us has subsided. I let the boy leave the room first, and I follow, both of us letting the elder lead us to the end of the hall and into a small classroom covered in soft rugs and lined with chains of bright prayer flags.

Multiple heads and eyes turn toward me. It always takes me by such surprise, it's a jolt to my heart I never can steel myself against. Multiple human heads, human faces. Is this what I looked like when I was a child? They came out of my body, but do they look like me? Small mouths and noses, rows of even teeth, pupils of blue and hazel and green that dilate beneath lids lined with delicate lashes of hair. Some of the children have no ears, a few have thinning hair, most have no genitals. That is the extent of their physical evolution. They have arrived at that moment in their lives when puberty once would have taken over and shaped them into adult human beings, but they are about to take a far different path to adulthood, if it can be called that anymore. They will grow and shift and morph and there will be ages of wandering and discovery of each other and what lies beyond the horizons of these waterlogged peaks. They shall dream, dream of an existence in which they never awaken. And eventually they shall return, and become part of the whole, become what I saw rising from the waves and its dreams so many, many countless ages ago.

The boy stands at the side of the room as I make my way to the middle. As I lay down, hands reach out and touch my naked skin. I settle in, relaxing as my children form a cocoon around me, bodies draped over me, each touching the other so that none of them are not in some way connected to the others. This is how they communicate, how they learn. I close my eyes. Eventually, I feel the delicate touch of fingers at my left temple. There is only a moment of unease, and th—

[::REC INTERRUPTED::]
[::REC OVERRIDE::]
[::ACCESS TRANSFER COMPLETE::]

✳ ✳ ✳

[::MEMORY #2724869.5::]
July 18, 24—, 05:32.08 am
Ballad House, Summit Crater Estates, Mount Baker
PrionTech InterDiary #74543.08

[::FILE CORRUPTION::]
—ver seen such lighting in the sky. Great bolts of it split the dark apart, each one so bright that we gasp in shock and clutch our eyes every time the sky lights up around us. And yet no thunder—this storm is completely silent. The aurora borealis has vanished, pushed away by whatever system is moving through the night. The boy is guiding the hands and face of my silver-haired date to the massive telescope that rests on the edge of the expansive covered terrace that crowns

the house. Their fingers move together and apart, the boy's hand rests against the back of the man's head as he adjusts the lens until the man nods slightly. They work well together. *[::DELETION::]* He's got the hang of it now, and the boy is moving away, letting the man aim the massive column of bright metal in a slow arc back and forth across the slopes of the mountain. He's exclaiming how he can see into people's apartments, halfway down Mount Baker, watching TV, arguing, having sex. He's looking for his apartment now—not his current home, the one he grew up in, that's long been subsumed by the Pacific. The boy is smiling. Everyone does this, apparently. They all want to see remnants of the places they once lived in, the towns their parents and grandparents came from, the waterlogged vestiges of Bellingham, Everett, Seattle, the cloudy peaks of the Olympic archipelago. Everyone wants to see their past.

DESPITE THE eerie weather, a few other people have joined us, close friends and family of the hosts only, the most private of parties within the most private of parties. Everyone has a drink in one hand, is ranting about the strange room half a mile below our feet, the odd lights in the southern sky, the restlessness and unease that none of us can seem to escape. I'm sitting down in a cushy chair, clutching the arms and staring up at the tiny votive candles that flicker on cocktail tables scattered across the space. I'm squeezing my eyes shut until all I see are orange flickerings of hot life that wink in and out of view.

SOMEONE IS talking softly about the bells.

THE BOY is tapping me on the shoulder, it's my turn now. The man is stepping aside, placing one hand on my back again as I take his place. I'm following his instructions, moving the levers around as I adjust the lens. *You won't see the old cities,* he's telling me, *except for the skyscrapers, most of them are gone. Further out,* I'm telling him. The boy is helping me turn the telescope—it moves easily but I'm surprised at the weight of it beneath my hands. Together we aim it south and east, just beyond the remaining mountain peaks. I'm looking for our enemy ocean. I want to see exactly what's coming for me.

LONG SLIVERS of silver. The light of the full moon, reflecting in the silky rippling dark. That's it. The ocean. A continent of water, nothing more. From here, it's so benign. I sense no malice in the horizon before me, no intent. Above it sits a night sky hazily studded with stars, stretching out forever. Everywhere, so much neutral, quiet water and space. I'm blinking, staring at the crest of the horizon again. The silver light quivers slightly—is it curving? Are the waters moving? *Whales*, I'm saying, *are there still whales out there because it looks like something's swimming across the surface*, and the man replies *no one's seen a whale in two hundred years* while the boy is reminding us of the floating cities, multitudes of ships sailing in unison from one land mass to the next and now it's hitting me oh god I know I know what's happening *He is coming I'm so cold I'm so cold I'm saying this out loud oh it's a wave it's a wave the light at the top of the wave tsunami it's a tsunami* and thunder, so loud it stops my hear—

[::FILE INTERRUPTION::]
—ailing of the tsunami sirens begins, echoing all up and down the mountainside. Behind me, screaming, crashing of chairs, the sounds of panicked people scattering like flies. *I'm going, are you coming because I'm not waiting*, the man is shouting at me, but I shrug his hand off my arm, *just go already*, I start to yell but he's already gone, I can hear his voice from far off telling people to get the fuck out of his way and the boy is placing his hands around my trembling tight fingers telling me *it's okay it's okay just let go I won't leave you I'll make sure you're safe* and silence now except for distant commotion from other parts of the house the squeal of car wheels and horns a single gun shot, and my breath sounds like some panting anim—

[::FILE INTERRUPTION::]
—oor beneath my feet, traveling up through my bones, as fast as those deep white lighting strikes ripping up through the night. A vast, heavy,

steady roll of the earth, so powerful my heart is matching it beat for beat, as if there is no other way to survive. My head is slamming against the telescope, I'm bouncing back against the boy. The building is moaning along with the earth, cracks ripping through the walls and sending dust and pebbles of concrete showering through the air, the glass terrace doors shattering. I *[::UNINTELLIGIBLE::]* and the boy and I start toward the doors, and freeze again. Blast plates are lowering. The building is a watertight box, impenetrable, it's how they've survived so many other waves. But we have to be on the ins—

[::FILE INTERRUPTION::]
—other massive strike rolls through the air, almost tugging us behind in its wake as it travels up through the mountain but lesser than the one before, and I grab the boy and he holds me tight. Lights and engines, shutting down all around us. I'm squinting in the dark, looking for any sign of life looking for any way out but I can't see it. We're standing at the top of a world that doesn't exist anymore. No wind. No quakes. No sirens. It's so quiet. So quiet.

WE'RE GOING *to die*, I'm saying, and the boy is replying *I know. He is coming*, I say. *Yes*, says the boy. We hold each other in the dark, listening for the coming wave, but it's still so far away. The aurora borealis is back, or whatever that light is, a deep and relentless green that I now see rises up out of the ocean. I have to, I can do this, I can move, I'm walking stiff choppy steps, the boy beside me always, I'm grasping the telescope handles again and he's helping me move it. *Is this what you want*, he's asking, I'm saying *yes I need to do this, I can't just stand here and wait. Tell me what you see*, he's saying, *don't stop talking, just keep telling me what you see*, and I'm telling him:

Great ribbons of fire dancing along the edges of the water, the edge of the water, a wall moving continually without breaking, green and blue, deep colors like a crown.

So beautiful.

Stars moving behind, or comets, little sparkles of white light like glass in the sun like glass on tar roads when the sun hits it you remember how that looks.

The water is lighting up now, can you see it? All the blues and greens are, it's like a wall of stained glass, liquid fire.

So fast. So fast. Sorry, I can hardly breathe, I didn't think it would be this fast.

Put your arms around, yes, tighter. Tighter.

This is it.

I can feel it now, yes, that, rumble, that roaring, louder, everything's trembling, OH MY GOD the wave is passing over the edges of the Olympics it's coming so fast now there's something in the water. Something in the—

OH GOD OH MY GOD IT'S NOT WATER THIS [::UNINTELLI-GIBLE::] NOT WATER THAT ISN'T LIGHT there are so many parts so much movement coming NONE OF THIS IS WATER it's so wide it so wide oh my god oh my god it's almost HE'S HE'S HE'S—
[::UNINTELLIGIBLE::]
EVERYWHERE EVERYWHERE EYES EYES EYES I SEE YOU I SEE YOU INSIDE INSIDE INSIDE I SEEEEEEEEEEEEEEE—

✳ ✳ ✳

[::AFTER::]

THE AIR is choked with green wisps of gossamer webbing, thread-thin streamers that catch against our bodies, collide and collect against the vines that have made their way up to the rooftop of the school. The boy and I pull them gently from our naked skin. There is no repulsion in our act, no curiosity. We only wish to set them free. Like us, they are a part of this world, they are some other version of our future, a component of our communal body whose purpose we cannot yet fathom, an integral part of the great After and in fact ourselves. The threads drift away in the slow breeze.

Downstairs, our children sleep in the classroom, dream in each others arms, their last afternoon surrounded by the ghost ruins of a human childhood they never experienced. Tomorrow they will be moved lower, closer to their conjoined siblings. Already their minds have processed the unimaginable, and it's sparked the beginnings of a physical transformation into the very thing they uncovered in my mind. Or so we believe. We will not know for certain until it is finished. Three floors above them, the boy and I spread out on the rooftop at the base of the broken spire, our bodies warming under the heat of a surprisingly strong sun that dares to occasionally break from behind the haze. The man sits somewhat apart from us, his head nodding back and forth slightly. More and more he does this, his earlier greeting already slipping from his mind as his thoughts become attuned to all our children below, those at the beginning of their journey and those nearing the end. By the time we leave the school, he'll remember little of our time together, if anything at all. The boy has these moments as well. There are long periods where he sits in our home, his thoughts adrift, his body trembling and shifting as he fights and accepts the biological call. What I feel inside, perhaps it was something I once called sorrow. I still remember everything that has happened in my life, before and After, except for one insignificant event that the loss of plagues my every waking thought, and I do not know why. Is it because I dared to look upon the face of an ancient, indefinable being? Was I the first living creature who dared to be seen by him? Is it his face my children need to discover within my mind, that one illusive memory that remains forever hidden to me?

Below, the jungle spreads out before us in a thick carpet, down to the river that winds in and out of the edges of the ocean, an ocean smoothed out and dampened with patches of bright and dark greens, bubbles and slicks of primordial flesh that crest the surface and slide back down silently to the nurturing depths. Where the river and ocean and vast marshes all come together in a torrent of untamed life, I can make out the remains of the low, flat fields where I and the other elders who had once been female lay on our backs in countless rows, where we watched the seasons pass and the moons circle the skies a million times over as eggs poured out of us, a torrent of latent life. The fields once spread to the horizon. Countless times I've sat on this roof with the man and the boy and others, watching elders tend our future children, moving our hatching brood into the school. Countless times I've walked into those school rooms, opened my mind to their probing thoughts, and inserted the image of what we once were and are once again becoming. There are so few eggs now, and the fields are being subsumed into the wide maw of the marshes and swamps. This part of the cycle is ending. Birthing has ended. There are no more females or males. Melancholy—is that the word? Perhaps, but also anticipation. Curiosity. Wonder and joy. All the things that oceans and mountains cannot hold, that nature cannot impart or receive, that universes cannot feel.

I stretch my arms high into the air. Who is to say what will happen when I am received into the oculus below, when my body and mind and that tiny bit of circuitry that will not die join everyone I have ever loved and birthed and known. Perhaps this time we will become a being that rejects nothing and accepts all. Perhaps this time no one will be forgotten, and everyone remembered. Perhaps there will be no more dreaming.

✳ ✳ ✳

[::MEMORY #2724869.4::]
July 18, 24—, 04:12.08 am
[::LOCATION UNKNOWN::]
PrionTech InterDiary #74543.07

[::/FILE CORRUPTION::]
[::FILE UNLOCKED::]
—passing out as the door slowly opens—she's the first to feel the super-cold air slashing through what now feels like the murky heat of the antechamber. She's falling against me, one of the guards is catching and moving her to the side as the door opens into the snow vault. Stupid, I'm

crying a little, I never ever thought I'd feel cold air again, the cruel cold air that squeezes your lungs and stings your eyes, not the sad semi-efforts of the food locker or the AC. Rows of dim track lighting illuminate the chamber, most of them pointed at the center of the room. I'm staring at the very last remaining pack of snow from Mount Baker. This is it. The heart of a glacier that once spanned the length of the mountain, that carved deep canyons that remain to this day. This is the last piece of glacier in the world. Even great Chomolungma at the top of the world lies naked and bare.

I'M STEPPING forward, slowly, one of the guards watching my every move. Someone is exclaiming as they walk to the other side, the host explaining how they moved it here thirty years ago from another facility—two more people are asking to leave the chamber, the sub-zero temperature is just too much for them. It's not what I imagined it would look like. Parts of it are dirty and gray and hard, pocked with thousands of tiny holes. I don't know what I was expecting—a mile-wide river of brilliant white and blue ribbons that glowed like a pearl, like in an old movie or book? It sort of looks like a chunk of cement the size of a delivery van. The man has pulled his face mask down, and he's sniffing the air. I do the same, even though our host advises against it. The air is so dry and crisp it hurts to breathe. I don't have any words for what it smells like. We smile and laugh and clouds of white jet out of our nostrils and mouths, hanging in the air like insects.

WE'RE WALKING around it in a circle now, the host rattling off a number of statistics and facts, I don't care about those. No, he laughs, they won't chip off bits for the drinks. The guards never take their eyes off us—they're all armed. There's a small round spot on one side of the rectangle, shiny as glass, no longer grey but pure brilliant white from years of supplicating hands wearing it away. So beautiful I almost gasp. One after another, we're removing a glove and placing our hand briefly in the hollow. It's my turn. Biting. Needle-pricks against my skin, wet-smooth ice, numbing, gelid. Life, ancient and incomprehensible, connected to all, to me. This *is* me.

WALKING AWAY, slipping the glove back on even though we'll be back in the antechamber and undressing in seconds. Feeling the warmth soak through the layers of freezing skin and stiffening muscle, burning through me in delicious pain as if I've dipped my hand in fire. My heart, racing. I'll never not be cold again. I've touched the heart of the world. I am this world. I'm not insignificant anymore.

[::LOCK::]

GHOST STORY
VICTOR LAVALLE

When Victor LaValle published The Ballad of Black Tom, *I was not surprised, because fifteen years earlier I had read "Ghost Story," which is not a Lovecraftian story, or a ghost story, or even any sort of fantastical genre story at all. And yet, it still belongs in this volume, because it feels like a Lovecraftian story, and one that traffics in the experience of awe and the sublime. It's simply a story where the person driven to madness is the victim of neurochemistry and circumstance instead of that oft-invoked invisible whistling octopus, or one or another field guide to him and his friends. Call it a realist proof-of-concept for the structure and motifs of a Lovecraft story, and you'll see what I mean.*

MOVE ANYWHERE, when you're from the Bronx, you're of the Bronx, it doesn't shed. The buildings are medium height: schools, factories, projects. It's not Manhattan, where everything's so tall you can't forget you're in a city; in the Bronx you can see the sky, it's not blotted out. The place isn't standing or on its back, the whole borough lies on its side. And when the wind goes through there, you can't kid yourself—there are voices. I was at war and I was in love. Of both, the second was harder to hide, there was evidence. Like beside my bed, a three-liter bottle, almost full. I rolled from under my covers, spun off the cap, pulled down my pants, held myself to the hole and let go.

Besides me and the bottle, my room had a bed, some clothes hanging in the closet, books spread out across the floor. Somewhere in that pile of texts and manifestos were two papers I had to turn in if I ever wanted to be a college graduate.

Cocoa was in the next room, snoring and farting. I listened to him, all his sounds were music.

I finished, pulled up my sweatpants and closed the bottle; inside, the stuff was so clear you could hold it to one eye and read a message magnified on the other side. I religiously removed the label from this one like I had all the others, so when I put it at the bottom of the closet with them, in formation (two rows of three), I could check how they went from dark to lighter to this one, sheer as a pane of glass; each was like a revision—with the new incarnation you're getting closer and closer to that uncluttered truth you might be hunting privately. I would show them all to a woman I loved, one I could trust; that had been tried three times already—the two stupid ones had asked me to empty them and change my life, the smart one had dressed right then and walked out. This was my proof, their intolerance, that people hate the body. But me, I was in love.

Cocoa and I had grown up poor and I was the stupid one; I believed that's how we were supposed to stay. That's why, when I saw him on the train two months before, with his girl, Helena, her stomach all fat with his seed, I didn't leave him alone. I walked right over. I was at war too, and needed the help.

She'd looked up before he did; the express cut corners and I fooled myself into thinking she was glad to see me. —Hey Sammy, she forced out. Cocoa was working, I was sure of that; she was rocking three new gold fronts on her bottom teeth.

I asked, —You going to be a mommy?

Started telling me how many months along she was but I'd stopped listening; soon she wasn't talking. Her jewelry disappeared behind her closed mouth. Cocoa hugged me tight like when we were fourteen: me and him coming out of the crap church on the corner of 163rd, the one with neon-bright red bricks, the painted sign on the door, misspelling the most important word ("cherch"). It was when his mother died, quick, and we were leaving the ceremony, behind us the thirty more people who'd cared to come. It had been a nice day so fellas were hanging out in crews everywhere and despite them Cocoa hadn't been able to hide his crying like his father and uncles had. I put my hand on his shoulder, patted it hard like men do, but it wasn't enough. So I wrapped my arms around his neck and hugged, on the corner, like even his pops would never care: publicly. When Dorice walked by I didn't stop and she probably thought we looked gay; still, I didn't force him back and try to catch up to her. And Cocoa? He didn't push me away, he leaned closer. He hugged me like that when I saw him on the train, like there was a death nearby. He looked right at me.

—We need to chill again, I said.

The way Cocoa grinned, it was like I'd given him cash. He was small, but he had the kind of smile it takes two or three generations of good breeding to grow; the one descendants of the *Mayflower* had after four centuries of feeding themselves fruit I'd never get my lips around (the kind where fresh means just picked, not just brought out for display). It was a good smile that made people trust him, think he was going places. Helena touched his leg, but he brushed her back, saying, —I'm just getting his number.

I watched Helena's back curl like it would when the stomach got grander, the baby inside pushing out its little legs like it might kick a hole; as she sank I told Cocoa my number and he gave me his; he was living with Helena and her family, back in the Bronx.

—Wake up! I yelled out to the living room.

There was a class today. Physics, I think, but me passing that now was like a dude trying to be monogamous—impossible. Cocoa hadn't missed a lecture or seminar all year, he'd bragged about it, so the last three days he'd been with me were only getting him in trouble with the mother-to-be. When she beeped him, every few hours, and he called back, she'd say she needed errands run, but her cousin Zulma was around, and her aunt; she was just on that ultrahorny pregnant-woman program and Cocoa knew. He would say, over the phone, —You know I can't sleep with you when you're pregnant, that would be wrong. I might give the baby a dent in its head. He laughed with me when he hung up, but while they were talking I said nothing; I listened from the kitchen to every syllable; if I'd had a pen and paper nearby I would have written it all down.

He stood in my doorway. He was slim as well as short but still seemed to take up all the space. Cocoa said, —You're messing me up. That stuff from last night is still bothering me. What did we drink?

—I had a bugged dream, I muttered.

—I'd hate to hear it, Cocoa said. I'm going to make some breakfast.

My hand, I placed it against the window to see how cold it was out. It wasn't a snowy winter. When I'd enrolled at City College it had been a big deal. I'd be getting my own place. My mother and sister were against it, but when you hit eighteen they call that adulthood and a lot more decisions are yours to make. Plus, you know how it is with boys in a family of women, they won't let go. When I'd first moved in, Mom and Karen were coming by once a week to check on me, but after two years of staying on top of things, schedules, they had no choice, they let me be.

Three nights ago, when Cocoa had come to hang out, I'd made him wait outside while I got things in place: threw my pillows and sheets back on my bed, plugged everything in. I kept up with news, they were doing renovations all over the Bronx: new buildings, the parks reseeded with grass and imported trees, you could almost pretend there wasn't a past.

AFTER BREAKFAST, for an hour, Cocoa and I took trains up and down the spines of Manhattan. Then we stood outside Washington Square Park, on the side farthest from NYU (Cocoa's school), staring at three women he thought he knew. I was shaking my head. —No, no. You don't know them. They're way too pretty to be talking to you.

He spat, —You criticize when you get them herpes sores off your lips.

I touched my chin. —They're only pimples.

—Then wash your face.

He'd been giving me advice since we were kids. He had thought that if he just told me how to be better I could be. Age ten was the first time for either of us that I acted up: when people whispering into telephones were talking about only me, a radio announcer was making personal threats (—Someone out there, right now, is suffering and won't get relief until they're our ninety-eighth caller and gets these tickets to Bermuda!). And Cocoa grabbed me tight as I dialed and redialed the pay phone in front of our building, screaming for someone to lend me twenty cents.

Cocoa walked and I moved beside him; we entered the park. The day was a cold one so the place wasn't way too full like summers when you couldn't move ten feet without having to dodge some moron with a snake on his shoulders or a cipher of kids pretending they're freestyling lyrics they'd written down and memorized months before. —I saw Evette the other day, I told him.

He smiled. —What are you telling me that for? Anyway, she married someone didn't she?

—Well, you staring at them three girls, I thought I'd tell you about one you actually got.

We had come to an NYU building and he told me to wait outside; he was angry that I'd brought up this woman with him trying so hard to be good; really, I don't know why I did. When I'd called him a few days earlier, it had been because I knew I needed help, but once he was with me I avoided the issue.

My hands in my coat pockets, they were full of those used tissues from the flu in March. I had planned to keep them in a pillowcase under my bed when I got better, but those were all filled with the hairs I clipped off and saved, so it was September and I had never truly healed and my hands were full of dried snot.

Maybe if he hadn't been doing so well, if his girl hadn't been so pretty, if his grades weren't soaring, if he'd been unhealthy, anything, but I couldn't confide in someone doing so much better than me. I wouldn't feel like I was asking for help, more like charity. The man he was now, I couldn't sit down with him and go through all the events in my day to figure out which thing was damning me: that I woke up every day, alarmless, at seven-forty? that I couldn't stand the taste of milk anymore? that I kept putting off a trip to the supermarket and so the cupboards and fridge were empty? that I had two pillowcases under my bed, one full of cut hair, the other full of old tissues? They all made sense to me.

They all had reasons: 1) for two years I'd had nine A.M. classes so now my body, even though I'd stopped attending, had found a pattern; 2) on campus two women had pulled me aside and shown me pamphlets about the haphazard pasteurization process, pictures of what a cow's milk does to human lungs so that even just a commercial for cereal made my chest tighten; 3) I'd dated a woman who worked at the market two blocks away, had been too open in explaining my collections to her one night, sat dejected and embarrassed as she dressed and walked out forever, so I couldn't go back in there even if it was silly pride; there wasn't another grocery for blocks, when I needed food I just bought something already made and I was mostly drinking water now (to watch a cleansing process in myself) and you could get that from a tap. And 4) it wasn't just my body, but The Body that I loved. So where others saw clippings as waste and mucus as excess, all to be collected and thrown away, spend no time on them, to me they were records of the past, they were treasures. Just tossing them out was like burying a corpse too quickly—rub your face against the cold skin, kiss the stony elbows, there is still majesty in that clay. People hate the body, especially those who praise the life of the mind. But even fingernails are miracles. Even odors. Everything of or in the body is a celebration of itself, even the worst is a holy prayer.

I found, as soon as he spoke, as I considered opening myself, I hated him again; I wanted to mention anything that would ruin his happiness. Like that, I brought up Evette and the night before it had been Wilma. Cocoa came out the building, pushing the glass door with power. Smiling.

—Your divorce come through? I asked.

He stopped, composed himself back to pleasure. —Today, a little boy was born.

—Yours? I thought it wasn't for three or four more months. I was suddenly hopeful for the pain of something premature; I could talk to a man who was living through that kind of hurt.

—Not mine. Once a week I find out the name of a baby, a boy if I can, that was born. Newspaper, radio, Internet. This kid was born today, his father already posted pictures. Nine pounds seven ounces, man. Benjamin August something. He looked healthy. It's good luck.

I laughed. —I bet that kid wasn't born in the Bronx. If he was he'd have come out coughing. One fear of every South Bronx parent: asthma. It was enough to make Cocoa tap me one, hard, in the chest and I fell back onto a parked car. His child would be born in the Bronx, he didn't want to be reminded of the dangers. I put my fists out, up. I'd been planning for this, not with him, but with someone. Had been eating calcium tablets every day, fifteen of them (student loan refund checks are a blessing), and now my bones were hard like dictionaries.

He didn't hit anymore. It's what I wanted.

Do you remember the hospital? Not torturous (well, maybe one time), no beatings though; it wasn't even the drugs; try one word: boredom. You could move around but there was nothing to chase the mind, hardly even television if you weren't always good. Just the hours that were eons sitting on a couch, a row of you, ten or twenty, no books, magazines too simple for the mildly retarded and your active mind leaps further and further over an empty cosmos, as lonely as the satellites sent to find life in the universe. But in there, at least, was when I'd realized how they waged their war, my enemies: through sockets and plugs, through a current.

We balanced on a corner as cabs passed by in yellow brilliance. It was late morning. I noticed how much energy was on: some streetlights never went off, people passing spoke on phones and the charged batteries glowed, radios came on and stayed on, computers were being run, every floor of every building. The taxi horns, engine-powered, began to sound like my name being called; I kept turning my head; the sounds bounced around inside my body, leafing through my bastard anatomy like I was a book of poems.

He spoke but the words were coming out of his mouth now all orange. I could see them, like the cones put out on the road at night to veer traffic away from a troubled spot. He said, —Look, let's not get craz, uh, let's not get agitated. I know someplace we could hang out. It'll be real good.

The NYU banners flapped with the wind, loud enough to sound like teeth cracking in your head. And how many times had I heard that noise! Like in the last month maybe five; whenever the remote control wasn't working or the phone bloopblopbleeped in my ear about no more Basic Service and I took each instrument between my teeth and bit down, trying to chew my anger out, that rage of mine which could take on such proportions.

THOUGHT WE'D catch the 4 to 149th and Grand Concourse—everybody out, everybody home. We could pass the murals of young men painted outside candy stores and supermarkets, where a thoughtful friend might have set out a new candle, where mourning seemed like a lifestyle. Instead we took the 6 and got out at 116th, walked blocks, then left, to Pleasant Avenue. My sister's home.

Cocoa saw me turn, flinch like someone had set off a car alarm in my ear, but then he put his arm on my shoulder and pushed hard, said, —Come on. Keep going. Cocoa kept pushing until we got upstairs, to the door, green, on it the numbers had been nailed in and the air had oxidized their faux-gold paint into that blackened color so familiar to buildings across our income level. He rang the bell. (Are they artificially powered?) The sound was so shrill I guessed they were part of the enemy army. Our first battle, twelve years before in the drab brown medical ward, had been so quick I'm sure they'd thought I'd forget. But I'd squirmed after they set those wires against my little forehead, so when they flipped the charge that one time, the lines slipped and burned both cheeks black; years later the spots were still there.

She opened the door. The whole place was going: television, microwave, coffeemaker, VCR. Karen was surprised to see me, but still, expecting it in some way. She was used to this.

I went to the bathroom but didn't shut the door. I filled my mouth with water and let it trickle out through my pursed lips, down into the toilet bowl so they'd think I was busy, held open the door some and my ears more:

Karen: How did you end up with him?

Cocoa: I ran into Sammy a few weeks ago, gave him my number, then he wouldn't leave me alone.

Karen: You think he's starting up?

Cocoa: I don't know what else. It's got to be. He hasn't done this nonsense in years. He calls me one morning and in an hour he's at my door, ringing the bell. I'm living with my girl's family, you know? He started kicking the door if I didn't answer. So I been with him three days.

Karen: You should have called me or something.

Cocoa: Called who? I wasn't even sure if you still lived here. I got lucky you and your man didn't get promoted or relocated. I called your mom but the number was disconnected.

Karen: She needed to get away.

Cocoa: Well, I know how she feels. You know I love that kid, but I can't keep this up. My son is about to drop in a few months. I'm trying to take care of this school thing. He's bugging, that's all I can say.

Karen: You think you could help me out here, until Masai comes?

Cocoa: I can't take five more minutes. I'm sorry Karen, I am, but I can't be around him no more. I'm through.

I listened to him walk to the door, open and shut it quietly. That thing was a big metal one, if he'd just let it swing closed behind him it would have rattled and thundered, so my last thought of Cocoa was of him being delicate.

Washed my hands and crept out, pulled the door closed and left the light on so she'd think I was still in there and snuck into her bedroom. On the door was the family portrait everyone has from Sears. A big poster of my sister, her husband and that baby of theirs. My niece. There was enough daylight coming in from outside that I didn't need the bulbs; besides, the light would have been like my rat-fink friend Cocoa, squealing to my sister about my goings-on.

There was a big bed in this big room, a crib in the corner, clothes in piles, just washed, on top of a long dresser. I walked to the crib and looked down at Kezia. She was wrapped up tightly, put to bed in a tiny green nightdress. Her diaper bulged and made noise when she moved. Dreaming little girl, she had dimples for laughing. I should have been able to make her smile even in her sleep.

From the hallway a slamming door, then, —Sammy? Samuel? Karen kicked into the room like a S.W.A.T. team. I looked, but she didn't have a rifle. She flicked on the light and ran to me, but not concerned with me, looked down at Kezia and rolled her over, touched her face, pulled her up and onto Mommy's shoulder. The big light shook Kezia into crying and it was loud, torturous. I laughed because my sister had done some harm even though there was love in it.

—What are you . . . is everything all right?

I looked at her and said, —Of course. I was just looking at my niece.

—You might have woken her up.

—Seems like you did that just fine, I told her.

Kezia turned toward me and then looked to her crib, twisted and latched on to it, pulled at that because she wanted back in. Karen finally acquiesced and returned her. The tiny one watched me, remembering, remembering and broke out in a smile. You know why kids love me so much? Because all kids are very, very stupid.

—She'll never get to sleep now.

I thought Karen was wrong. I pointed. —Look at her eyes. She's still drowsy. Kezia was looking at me, intently. I started rocking from left to right on the balls of my feet and Kezia mimicked me. She held the crib's rail to keep her balance but when I leaned too far right she followed, tipped over on her side, huffed, grabbed the bars and pulled herself back up to try again. She made a gurgle noise and I returned it, she went louder and I went louder, she screamed and I screamed; Karen flopped back against her married bed, holding her face, laughing.

My hands went around Kezia's middle, then I lifted her up as high as my arms would allow, brought her belly to my mouth and bit her there. She kicked her feet happily, caught me, two good shots right in the nose; that thing would be flaring up later. But she laughed and I did it again. I dropped her down two feet, quickly, like I'd lost my grip, and across her face came the look that precedes vomit, then a pause and like I knew it would, laughter.

Put her back in the crib and we returned to yelling, added movements with our hands and feet. Whenever I threw my palms in the air she did the same, lost her balance and fell backward; she lay there, rocking side to side so she could get some momentum for rising. I tickled her under the chin. We did it like this while Karen left the room and returned (repeat three times). Finally Kezia sat, watching me. I twirled in arms-open circles and she still had enough energy to smile, but not much else, and then she didn't have energy enough even for that and she watched me, silent, as she lay on her back, then Karen had to tap my shoulder and shush me because the kid was sleeping.

The lights were still on: around the crib there were pictures taped up. Of our family and Masai's, all watching over; the picture of me rested closer to Kezia than all the rest, but in it I was only a boy. Looking at my crooked smile I felt detached from that child—like we could cannibalize his whole life and you still wouldn't have tasted me. Every memory would someday make the catalogue I kept in my room, eleven small green notebooks.

Me and Karen sat in the kitchen. She had been preparing dinner. I started making a plate. —Leave a lot for Masai. He'll be home from work soon.

I covered all the pots and poured myself some berry Kool-Aid. Karen's Kool-Aid was the only thing I would drink besides water. After I gulped I told her, —You need more sugar.

She sucked her teeth. —Masai and me decided we should still have teeth when Kezia gets to be seven. Karen finished her rice. You look awful, she said.

—Yeah, but I've always looked bad. You got the beauty and I got everything else.

She smacked me, gentle, across the chin. —I had my bachelor's before you had been left back for the first time. Have you thought about coming to stay with us?

—I like where I'm at.

—You need to be around your family. You're acting stupid out there.

—Whatever. I shrugged. You don't know what I'm doing.

—I can see what you're not doing: washing, changing your clothes. Probably not going to class.

—Man, I said. You don't understand subtlety. You've got to bring these things up cool, easy, otherwise you'll close all avenues of communication.

THAT'S HOW long she paused, watching me. Then she went to the fridge, found a green plastic cup. She put it on the table, sat, sounded stern, — How about you take the medication mixed with something? You still like it with orange juice? I'll make it.

I looked at the cup, the white film on top, that clump and beneath it the actual Tropicana Original. There had been plenty at my apartment, taken regular for two years, on my own. But someday you want to rest. —How about you put some vodka in there?

On top of the fridge Karen had left a Tupperware bowl of the boiled egg whites she'd been cutting up for her next day's meal. Even in the light blue bowl they seemed too bright. She wasn't kidding around. —Drink it. You told us you would. You were doing so well.

—It makes my head feel like rocks.

—But at least it keeps you thinking right. Just drink this cup. It'll be a new start. Come on.

See, but I was supposed to take that medicine twice a day, every day. She wanted me to drink this one glass and everything would go right but you can't dam a river with just one brick.

I said, —Karen, you can't stop the electric soldiers.

I was twenty-two years old and Karen was thirty. How long before it's just frustration in her, screaming to get out, wishing whatever was the pain would go away.

—Can you? she asked.

Blissfully the goddamn fridge worked, I could hear its engine going, regular like a heartbeat, mumming along and I was so jealous. When I got up she draped herself across the table, spilling the juice and the orchids she had in a vase, the ones her husband had bought two days ago, purple like lips too long exposed to the cold.

It was lucky Masai was at work. I was much bigger than Karen and I could simply pluck her off my arm and leave, but if Masai had been there it would have gotten louder, the trouble in this kitchen would have been contagious, contaminating the living room, the bathroom, their bedroom. We would have been all over the place. But at some point, as I was tugging, she let go. She could fight harder, she had before. Her hands fell to her sides; she opened the door for me.

I HAD other people I could have seen, but I kept forgetting their addresses. I might have passed four or five out on Malcolm X Boulevard. Later, I walked by the mosque, the brothers in their suits and bow ties selling the *Final Call*; I wanted to buy one, help them out; walked over to a short one in a gold suit; he pushed me a paper like it would save my life. —Only a dollar.

—And what do I get? I asked.

—You get the truth. All the news the white media won't show you.

I leaned close to him, he pulled back some. —You don't know that all this stuff is past tense? I asked.

Now he looked away, to his boy at the other corner, in green, white shirt, black shoes, talking with two older women; each nodded and smiled, one brought out her glasses to read the headlines. —So you want to buy this or what? My friend held it out again, the other twenty copies he pulled close to his chest. I could see on his face that his legs were tired.

But for what would I be buying that paper? Or if a Christian was selling Bibles? Name another religion, I had no use for any. I wanted to pull my man close, by the collar (for effect) and tell him I knew of a new god, who was collecting everything he saw around him and stashing it in his apartment on Amsterdam Avenue; who walked home from the 1 train stealing bouts of Spanish being spoken in front of stores and when he came home prodigiously copied them down; who stole the remnants of empty beer bottles that had been shattered into thirty-seven pieces, took the glass and placed it in his living room, in a jar, with the greens and browns of others—in the morning he sat there and watched the fragments, imagined what life had come along and done such destruction.

Instead I walked backward until I got to a corner, hugged myself tight against a phone booth with no phone in it as the people swam around me and ignored everything but the single-minded purposes of their lives. After an hour was up my brain sent signals to my feet: move.

I stood in front of my apartment again, had a paper to hand in. Go upstairs and slide it in an envelope, address it to the woman who led my seminar on black liberation movements. The one who lectured me only when I missed class and never remembered to mark it in her book. The one who had assured me that if I wrote it all down this mind would be soothed, salvaged. One Tuesday (Tues. & Thur. 9:00–10:45 A.M.) she had pulled me aside when lessons were over, confided, —These days, the most revolutionary thing you can be is articulate.

I had told her honestly, —I'm trying. I'm trying.

I touched the front door before opening it. I'd been struck by the fear that the building was on fire; a church and a mosque had been burned recently. In the secret hours of night they'd been turned to ash and in the daylight their destruction was like a screaming message to us all. Had the door been hot I would have run farther than I needed to, but it was cold so I walked in.

The elevator was still broken. I had ten stories to climb; my legs felt stiff and proud. I moved effortlessly until I reached the sixth floor and Helena stopped me. She was with her girls, they were coming down the stairs. As pregnant as she was I knew the climb couldn't have been easy, but the look on her face had nothing to do with exertion. It was all for me. —I was coming to talk to you Sammy, she said. Helena's cousin Zulma stood beside me; she was so big I felt boxed in.

—You should be out looking for your man, I told Helena.

Zulma looked like she wanted to leave, bored, but was there to get her cousin's back in case it was needed. If Helena had been alone I wouldn't

have had any problem kicking her in the gut and running. When she'd
rumbled to the bottom of the stairs I would have crawled down beside
her and in her ear asked, —Now tell me, what does this feel like? Tell me
every detail.

—Why you causing so much problems? another of Helena's girls
asked, but I didn't answer. Instead I told them one of my philosophies
to live by. —I never tell a pretty woman I think she's pretty unless we're
already holding hands.

Helena rubbed her face with frustration. —You need to leave Ramon
alone. He's good when he's not around you. Her watch beeped, not loudly,
but it echoed through the stairwell. Its face was glowing. Batteries gave
it power.

—Have you been drafted too? I asked Helena.

—Fuck this, Zulma muttered, then her elbow was in my chest.

As the five girls got all over different parts of me I swung wild.
Caught Zulma in the mouth and the first drops of blood on my face were
hers. They were yelling as I kicked out with both legs. Then I was burning
everywhere and I knew without looking that the off-silver colors in my
eyes were the box cutters finding whole parts of me to separate. Fabric
was tearing as they removed swatches of my clothing so they could get
nearer to my skin. Zulma and Helena were at my face; neither of them
smiled as they did the cutting. They didn't seem angry. Their faces were
so still.

I grabbed and reached for something, dipping my fingers in
everything spilling out of me. The colors were hard to make out in the
bad light, but the stuff was beautiful and thick, it pooled. The girls rose
and ran; I listened to five sets of sneakers move quickly down those stairs
to the emergency exit; the door swung out and stuck, there was the flood
of an empty wind up the staircase.

GO, GO, GO, SAID THE BYAKHEE
MOLLY TANZER

There are songs of innocence, and songs of experience, but rarely is a story both songs at once, arranged as a perfect mash-up. This story is about the end of our world, and the beginning of the next; it's fabulism in the voice of the young, and speaks of the dark and ancient. This is the rare Lovecraftian tale that rewards rereading—in lesser hands even the sublime can be a mere "twist ending," but in Molly Tanzer's it's an enticement to wind back time and start at the beginning-slash-end.

> *. . . human kind*
> *cannot bear very much reality.*
> *Time past and time future.*
> *What might have been and what has been.*
> *Point to one end, which is always present.*
>
> —T. S. Eliot

WRIGGLER LIVED in the lake, and when you didn't throw stones at him too much he would bring up purple-scaled balık and tiny scuttling yengeç for roasty crunchings. Feathers lived in a hut in the treetops and she would help pick the highest-up kayısı when they were ripe and juicy— sometimes. Feathers was mean. Half the time if you so much as looked at her funny she would open her mouth wide like an O and birdy squawks would come out, *eee eee eee*, which, true, were the only words she ever said since she changed, but she could make them sound so *angry*! No one cared if she was angry, though, because even with the wings, she couldn't fly. Wriggler could breathe underwater, and Whee! could swing from branch to branch with his long fuzzy tail, and Mister Pinch could bruise you with the handy claw on his extra arm if he ever got mad at you. Ouch! Feathers, she looked like a birdy, but wasn't quite. Everybody said it was because she didn't pray hard enough when she went on pilgrimage to Tuz Gölü to see the Mother in the Salt.

Dicle was still a two-legs two-hands two-eyes upright skin-wearer, so she still had her cradle-name that said nothing at all about who she really was. Bo-*ring!* But that would change soon, she knew it. When she went to fetch water she could see in the shiny surface of the well two of the protuberances mammals and mostly-mammals got when they were ready to give live birth and suckle their young, and she'd had a dream about Wriggler coming to the surface and touching her between the legs with one of his long bendy arms. Those were the signs, Whee! had said, but then again, Whee! couldn't be trusted, not completely. Whee! wanted to be the one Dicle took as a snuggler once she was given her true shape by the Mother in the Salt. But Dicle knew she'd rather snuggle with Wriggler, even if they had to do it mostly underwater so he could huff and puff through his gills.

But Stag-Face said Dicle wasn't ready for pilgrimage, or for huff-and-puff. Stag-Face said she was still a baby-girl, and since Stag-Face was the boss of everybody—those who'd visited the Mother in the Salt, those who hadn't yet, and *especially* those who failed—she had to heed him. She hated it, though! Ugh! Kids like her, they couldn't dance in the nightly revels, and they had to do all the worst chores, like climbing up the burning rocks to every single one of the hill-caves to dump out the piss-pots, or sweeping away the rubble to find the empty meat-shells when the earth shook and there were cave-ins, or weave reeds into wind-shields so people could sleep out of the dusty gusting breezes. But Dicle didn't like climbing, and she didn't like to clear away rocks to find meat-shells, and she didn't like weaving, either. She liked to run as fast as she could, and she could run sooooo fast! Stag-Face said maybe she could be a messenger once she was old enough. But she *was* old enough, and that's why she'd come up with the secret plan.

Well, it wasn't a *total* secret. Wriggler knew, but he'd promised not to gurgle it to anyone else. In fact, he'd helped her by catching balık a-plenty, just for her. Dicle had built little fires and smoked them so she'd have food for the overnight journey to Tuz Gölü. She knew it was wrong to disobey Stag-Face, but ever since her mama had been crushed to death in the cave-in during the shivery months, Dicle had been restless. She was going to go on pilgrimage, whether mean old Stag-Face liked it or not, and when she went, she'd take her mama's bones to the Mother in the Salt, so Mama could really rest. The Mother in the Salt would be so very pleased she'd change Dicle just how she'd always wanted, and then Dicle would come home and snuggle with Wriggler and everything would be wonderful.

THE MORNING she left, early-early she awoke, after the revelers were all in bed and before even the dawn-time scurriers were out and about. She snuck away at a run, the rucksack she'd stuffed full of Mama's bones and smoked balık bouncing on her back, the skin full of water slapping her hip. She'd also strapped a gleaming knife to her arm so the beasties of the wood and the ghouls of the salt flats would see she was one dangerous girl. She bared her teeth as she ran, *grr!*

The path was made of cracked black stuff, and was smooth from ages and ages of people going to Tuz Gölü and elsewheres. Dicle wasn't scared, though—at least, not at first. Back during the shivery months, right after Mama had died, she'd gone down the path a fair way before Whee! had caught her and told Stag-Face. Stag-Face had beat her, bad, and Whee! had laughed at her. That, more than anything, was why he'd never-*ever* be her snuggler.

Everybody, even little unchanged girlies like Dicle knew that time and space were the same thing, except when they weren't. There were a few places around K'pah-doh-K'yah everyone knew to avoid, where, if your eyes worked right—which was no promise!—you could see how the trees grew backwards in time, and would gobble you up if you got too close to them. Stag-Face said those places were holy, because if you looked at them too long, or thought about them too hard while you were there, you'd get a nosebleed, and that was the sign of the Mother in the Salt. Also, if an animal or person went there and he or she had a baby inside them, the baby would grow so fast it would tear its way out and make its mama or papa a meat-shell instead of a mama or a papa, and the baby would be a ghoul and never know anything except hunger. That was a bad thing, and it happened a few times a year even if everybody was careful, since time isn't always the same and therefore neither is space.

Dicle ran through a few of those Mother-places the first day of her pilgrimage (she ran as fast as she could, so time didn't slow down too much for her and make her journey take too long), but she saw more and more of them on the second day, as she drew closer to Tuz Gölü. She knew she was getting closer because all the trees had gone away, and she could taste salt on her lips when she licked them, and she was thirsty. She wasn't scared, though, because she didn't have a baby inside her, and if any of the ghouls said *boo!* to her she showed them her knife and they slithered away back to their hidey-holes.

Then Dicle crested a hill as the sun climbed as high as it could in the white-hot sky, and when she looked down into the valley her eyes started to hurt from too much brightness. Ouch! But that was what Wriggler said would happen, so she knew she was in the right place. Below her stretched endless white: the Tuz Gölü at last. When she shaded her eyes with her hand she could see the altar at the edge of the pale lake, sitting a bit back from the shore. It was a rectangular box the size of the meeting-cave, with all these poles jutting from the top, holding up a big empty circle. The rectangular part had lots of holes in the side that Wriggler said weren't caves but little peep-holes covered in clear stuff that kept the wind out better than woven reeds. That was strange, but Dicle fought her urge to explore. Her business was with the sacred stair and what was at the top of it. She'd show the Mother how dedicated she was by keeping focused.

So Dicle ran toward the altar, her bare feet pounding the earth, every cut or scrape on her body smarting from the salty wind, but as she drew closer she saw something and stopped so quickly she almost stumble-tumbled—something was crawling out of the Tuz Gölü, and nothing was supposed to come out of the Tuz Gölü except the Mother!

For the first time Dicle felt really scared, but she also felt curious. The thing—no, she realized, as she peered slit-eyed and scuttled closer sideways, just like a yengeç—*things*, were not happy, not at all. One was screaming and flailing and seemed to be missing a leg at the knee, and the other one was dragging the first as fast as it could away from the shore of the Tuz Gölü. As the dragger dragged the screamer further from the edge of the lake, Dicle saw they were leaving a big brown blood-smear behind them. But Dicle had seen wounds that bad before, and knew just what to do. She ran closer to help them, only to feel more scared and curious than she ever had in her whole life when she realized that the things looked *just like her*, even though they were obviously long past the time when they should have made their pilgrimage and been changed by the Mother in the Salt.

Still, Dicle remembered her manners.

"Merhaba!" she called, approaching them cautiously.

"Get away from the lake!" said the dragger, and Dicle understood what she was saying, even though she spoke the words in a funny way. "There's something in there!"

"Of course, there is, silly," said Dicle. "That's the Mother! Don't you know?"

The screamer looked up at her and spit up a big bubble of blood, then went limp in the dragger's arms. The dragger, who wasn't dragging any more, fell to her knees and vomited everywhere. Then she looked up at Dicle. Her mouth hung open, making shapes but no sound, and her eyes were glassy, empty, and bulging. She looked just like a balık! Dicle laughed, and unsheathed her glinty knife.

The dragger wiped her mouth. "But we just left *yesterday*," she said.

When Dicle's mama died, Stag-Face had comforted Dicle in her distress and helped her perform the rituals after they'd dug out her meat-shell from underneath the rocks. Dicle was happy to do the same for the dragger.

"Don't worry!" said Dicle, and she patted the dragger on the shoulder, to comfort her in her distress. Then, as was proper, Dicle plunged the knife into the right thigh of the (now quiet) screamer, slicing through skin and flesh. Working quickly, she cut a long strip of meat from his shell.

"What are you doing," whispered the dragger. "Oh god, oh *god*, what are you *doing?*"

This person *must* be a stranger if she didn't know the sorts of things even the littlest babies knew! Dicle decided to be Teacher and help her to understand. Leading by example, Dicle dipped her thumb in the (now quiet) screamer's cooling blood and drew the insignia of the Mother in the Salt on the dragger's forehead, then adorned herself the same way.

"The Mother knows our hearts, and loves us all, her children," said Dicle, and then began to gobble up the meat.

ONCE DICLE had given the stranger some water to rinse out her mouth—she'd vomited again as Dicle gobbled—she'd told Dicle her name was Yıldız, and forbidden Dicle from cutting the rest of the (now quiet) screamer's flesh from his bones, even though that's what was supposed to happen.

"I don't understand," she kept saying, over and over and over again. Bo-*ring!* Dicle didn't know what there was to understand, so she gave Yıldız a roasted balık to munch on, and it looked so good, Dicle ate one herself.

After Yıldız ate, she said, again, "we just left yesterday."

"How can that be?" Dicle was getting impatient. The sun was hot, and she wanted to clamber up the sacred stair to summon the Mother in the Salt so she could pray and change and then start home again. "You could not have left yesterday. You are all grown up, but you don't know about the Mother and you haven't changed. Did you fail on your pilgrimage?"

Yıldız laughed, but it wasn't a happy-sounding laugh. "Maybe so," she said. Then she pulled her knees into her chest and put her forehead on them. "This looks like the Tuz Gölü Research Station, but maybe. . ." Yıldız looked up at Dicle. "Where are you from?"

"I am on pilgrimage from K'pah-doh-K'yah," said Dicle. "Where are *you* from? There's not another village for a million billion klickers."

"*Cappadocia?*" Yıldız looked upset. "Where in Cappadocia?"

Dicle frowned. She *must* be from far away.

"K'*pah*-doh-K'*yah* is how you say it," she said, Miss Matter-of-Fact. "I live in the caves, of course, and Stag-Face is our boss. Everybody lives in the caves unless they're like Wriggler, who has to live in the lake so he can breathe."

"No one's lived in those caves for centuries," said Yıldız, as if she knew anything! "There were too many earthquakes, they were unsafe to live in. The government forced everyone to evacuate."

"Government?"

"Yes, the government. Do you not know what that means? Do you even know where we are?"

"Tuz Gölü."

"And where is Tuz Gölü?"

"Here?" Duh!

"It's in *Turkey*. That's the name of this country. What … but time dilation wasn't supposed to…" Yıldız got all glassy-eyed again and went quiet. Dicle wondered if she'd have to slap Yıldız to get her to wake up, until Yıldız started talking again, but it was like she was a tiny baby reciting lessons. "Tuz Gölü is an endoheric basin, so if there was any runoff from the Hypersaline Resonator, it shouldn't have gotten into the rivers—"

"But the music brought the Mother, who came here but was always here, and she gave us our true shapes. The Mother knows our hearts, and loves us all, her children," recited Dicle.

"The music what? The Mother?" Yıldız bit her lip. "I saw something down there… too big, it was too big, though. The lake is less than a meter deep in the summer, and yet…"

"Come with me!" Dicle grabbed Yıldız's arm and yanked her to her feet. "Space and time are the same thing. The Mother has always been there, forever and ever through time, so it's deep and big enough for her! Don't you know *anything*?"

Dicle took off running toward the altar, dragging Yıldız behind her. She was jitter-jumpy and restless, and anyways, the Mother would explain better, once she was summoned.

"Where are we—"

"Just come *on*!"

"What the hell is that?!"

Even though Dicle had reached the bottom of the sacred stair, which was made of hard rusty-crusty iron and ran zig-zag up the side of the altar, she turned around to see where Yıldız was pointing. There, at the top of the hill, terrible and looming against the bright afternoon sun was Stag-Face. Dicle could see his antlers. He'd spotted her, and was running pell-mell down the salty sand to get to her. She began to tremble.

"Stag-Face," she whispered. "Oh no!"

"He has a deer's head!"

"Come on!" Dicle would not be thwarted. She yanked Yıldız up up up the sacred stair, until they reached the flat top of the altar. She heard clomping on the stairs behind them as Stag-Face's hooves rung on the iron. Mean old Stag-Foot! He wouldn't stop her, not now!

Dicle rummaged in her bag and under the roasted balık found the sack of her mama's bones. She placed those at the base of the big circle, and found the thing that Wriggler said was called a *lever*—it was just where he said it would be, on the left-hand side.

"No!" cried Stag-Face. He had reached the top, and was pointing. "Dicle, Whee! told me you'd be here! Such a bad girlie! You don't know enough yet! You haven't purified your heart, you haven't learned the right songs! The Mother will *not* accept you for changing! She will punish us all!"

"The Mother knows our hearts, and loves us *all*, her children," shouted Dicle, as she wrapped her hands round the lever.

"Stop!" cried Stag-Face, and Dicle heard his hooves pounding on the roof.

"He's got a knife!" shrieked Yıldız. She was fumbling with something hanging on her belt. "Wait! *Wait!*"

But Dicle wouldn't wait, even if Stag-Face had a knife. She yanked on the lever, and big crackling shafts of lightning began to curl around the circle, writhing and touching each other just like Wriggler's arms, and they were even the same purple-blue color. Dicle felt a burst of heat behind her, she heard the angry sound of Stag-Face in pain, and then the salt began to sing. It was so beautiful it made Dicle's heart shudder and her skin crawl all over, and she felt a sudden gush of sticky hot wet over her face as she pressed her hands to the sides of her head in agony. It was blood, flowing from her eyes and ears and nose—*ugh!* But that was the sign of the Mother, and as the Mother emerged, Dicle began to pray, harder than anyone had ever prayed before.

Yıldız, who was now Spots, came back to K'pah-doh-K'yah with Dicle, who was now Jackrabbit. Spots took over bossing everyone because she had teeth and claws like a leopard, and she'd also killed Stag-Face with what she told Jackrabbit was called a "laser pistol." And anyways, now that the Mother had made her understand, it turned out Spots was the smartest of them all.

"Ahmet and I went through the Hypersaline Resonator, thinking we could visit this other place, a place up there in the sky that the star-watchers had said was okay for us to breathe and see," Spots had explained. "The Resonator was supposed to help with the problem of too much time passing here while we were gone. But when we got there, we saw a Mother—a different Mother, or maybe the same one, I dunno—and we were afraid it would come back here through the Resonator, because we didn't understand that the Mother loves us all, her children, and that would be a *good* thing! Silly us! But now everything is better."

Jackrabbit, who had been Dicle, was sure that Mother loved everyone, but she wasn't sure everything was better, even though she was finally changed. It was true that the Mother had granted her prayers to be the fastest of everybody, but she was now also the scaredest, and rarely wanted to come out of her hidey-hole in the caves. All the sounds were so *loud* in her big ears! She'd almost gotten gobbled by the ghouls on the journey back home because every time she heard something or saw something it terrified her and she couldn't always control her urge to run away and get deep under ground.

But, she reminded herself every day, at least she could dance in the revels, and she could jump higher than anyone. Not that she felt like jumping or reveling much, even for the sake of the Mother. She was very sad. Wriggler hadn't lived more than a few months after snuggling with her. When he'd seen her true self he'd said she was so pretty, and they'd done the huff-and-puff a lot, but only for a few weeks. All of a sudden he'd gotten sick and pale and told her to go away, so she'd gone away. When she next worked up the courage to bolt down to the lake, she'd found his corpse washed up and rotten on the bank. No one had eaten his meat, and that was sad. All Jackrabbit could do for him was clean his bones and put them with the rest, for the time when the next little babies grew up and made their pilgrimage to the Mother in the Salt. And nobody else wanted to be her snuggler, not even Whee!, because Wriggler had put a baby inside her, but when it had come out, she'd gotten so scared when everyone had crowded around to see it that she'd gobbled it right up!

Being changed was sure not like she'd thought it would be. Jackrabbit was always frightened, and always alone. Nothing was wonderful. Not at all.

THE CITY OF THE SINGING FLAME
CLARK ASHTON SMITH

As we begin, so we end, with a classic—this from Lovecraft's
close associate, Clark Ashton Smith. Perhaps Smith is read today
thanks only to his connection with Lovecraft, and that is a sad
mistake. He was not a mere acolyte, but a poet, artist, and
writer with a unique aesthetic. "The City of the Singing Flame"
is broadly Lovecraftian, of course, but so much more. It was one
of the first, and favorite, fantasy stories Harlan Ellison ever read,
and got him "into this miserable game" of writing as once declared
on the radio program Hour 25, *so let us see what reprinting the*
story here does to raise up and mutate the next, and likely final,
generation of the cult of weird-fiction authors.

I'm waiting.

Foreword

When Giles Angarth disappeared, nearly two years ago, we had been friends for a decade or more, and I knew him as well as anyone could purport to know him. Yet the thing was no less a mystery to me than to others at the time, and until now, it has remained a mystery.

Like the rest, I sometimes thought that he and Ebbonly had designed it all between them as a huge, insoluble hoax; that they were still alive, somewhere, and laughing at the world that was so sorely baffled by their disappearance. And, until I at last decided to visit Crater Ridge and find, if I could, the two boulders mentioned in Angarth's narrative, no one had uncovered any trace of the missing men or heard even the faintest rumor concerning them. The whole affair, it seemed then, was likely to remain a most singular and exasperating riddle.

Angarth, whose fame as a writer of fantastic fiction was already very considerable, had been spending that summer among the Sierras, and had been living alone until the artist, Felix Ebbonly, went to visit him. Ebbonly, whom I had never met, was well known for his imaginative paintings and drawings, and had illustrated more than one of Angarth's novels.

When neighboring campers became alarmed over the prolonged absence of the two men, and the cabin was searched for some possible clue, a package addressed to me was found lying on the table; and I received it in due course of time, after reading many newspaper speculations concerning the double vanishment. The package contained a small, leather-bound note-book, and Angarth had written on the fly-leaf:

"Dear Hastane, You can publish this journal sometime, if you like. People will think it the last and wildest of all my fictions—unless they take it for one of your own. In either case, it will be just as well. Good-bye."

Faithfully, GILES ANGARTH.

FEELING THAT it would certainly meet with the reception he anticipated, and being unsure, myself, whether the tale was truth or fabrication, I delayed publishing his journal. Now, from my own experience, I have become satisfied of its reality; and am finally printing it, together with an account of my personal adventures. Perhaps, the double publication, preceded as it is by Angarth's return to mundane surroundings, will help to ensure the acceptance of the whole story for more than mere fantasy.

Still, when I recall my own doubts, I wonder. . . . But let the reader decide for himself. And first, as to Giles Angarth's journal:

I. The Dimension Beyond

July 31st, 1938.—I have never acquired the diary-keeping habit—mainly, because of my uneventful, mode of existence, in which there has seldom been anything to chronicle. But the thing which happened this morning is so extravagantly strange, so remote from mundane laws and parallels, that I feel impelled to write it down to the best of my understanding and ability. Also, I shall keep account of the possible repetition and continuation of my experience. It will be perfectly safe to do this, for no one who ever reads the record will be likely to believe it. . . .

I had gone for a walk on Crater Ridge, which lies a mile or less to the north of my cabin near Summit. Though differing markedly in its character from the usual landscapes round about, it is one of my favorite places. It is exceptionally bare and desolate, with little more in the way of vegetation than mountain sunflowers, wild currant bushes, and a few sturdy, wind-warped pines and supple tamaracks.

Geologists deny it a volcanic origin; yet its outcroppings of rough, nodular stone and enormous rubble-heaps have all the air of scoriac remains—at least, to my non-scientific eye. They look like the slag and refuse of Cyclopean furnaces, poured out in pre-human years, to cool and harden into shapes of limitless grotesquerie.

Among them are stones that suggest the fragments of primordial bas-reliefs, or small prehistoric idols and figurines; and others that seem to have been graven with lost letters of an indecipherable script. Unexpectedly, there is a little tarn lying on one end of the long, dry Ridge—a tarn that has never been fathomed. The hill is an odd interlude among the granite sheets and crags, and the fir-clothed ravines and valleys of this region.

It was a clear, windless morning, and I paused often to view the magnificent perspectives of varied scenery that were visible on every hand —the titan battlements of Castle Peak; the rude masses of Donner Peak, with its dividing pass of hemlocks; the remote, luminous blue of the

Nevada Mountains, and the soft green of willows in the valley at my feet. It was an aloof, silent world, and I heard no sound other than the dry, crackling noise of cicadas among the currant-bushes.

I strolled on in a zigzag manner for some distance, and coming to one of the rubble-fields with which the Ridge is interstrewn, I began to search the ground closely, hoping to find a stone that was sufficiently quaint and grotesque in its form to be worth keeping as a curiosity: I had found several such in my previous wanderings. Suddenly, I came to a clear space amid the rubble, in which nothing grew—a space that was round as an artificial ring. In the center were two isolated boulders, queerly alike in shape, and lying about five feet apart.

I paused to examine them. Their substance, a dull, greenish-grey stone, seemed to be different from anything else in the neighborhood; and I conceived at once the weird, unwarrantable fancy that they might be the pedestals of vanished columns, worn away by incalculable years till there remained only these sunken ends. Certainly, the perfect roundness and uniformity of the boulders was peculiar, and though I possess a smattering of geology, I could not identify their smooth, soapy material.

My imagination was excited, and I began to indulge in some rather overheated fantasies. But the wildest of these was a homely commonplace in comparison with the thing that happened when I took a single step forward in the vacant space immediately between the two boulders. I shall try to describe it to the utmost of my ability; though human language is naturally wanting in words that are adequate for the delineation of events and sensations beyond the normal scope of human experience.

Nothing is more disconcerting than to miscalculate the degree of descent in taking a step. Imagine, then, what it was like to step forward on level, open ground, and find utter nothingness underfoot! I seemed to be going down into an empty gulf; and, at the same time, the landscape before me vanished in a swirl of broken images and everything went blind. There was a feeling of intense, hyperborean cold, and an indescribable sickness and vertigo possessed me, due, no doubt, to the profound disturbance of equilibrium. Either from the speed of my descent or for some other reason, I was, too, totally unable to draw breath.

My thoughts and feelings were unutterably confused, and half the time it seemed to me that I was falling upward rather than downward, or was sliding horizontally or at some oblique angle. At last, I had the sensation of turning a complete somersault; and then I found myself standing erect on solid ground once more, without the least shock or jar of impact. The darkness cleared away from my vision, but I was still dizzy, and the optical images I received were altogether meaningless for some moments.

When, finally, I recovered the power of cognisance and was able to view my surroundings with a measure of perception, I experienced a mental confusion equivalent to that of a man who might find himself cast without warning on the shore of some foreign planet. There was the same sense of utter loss and alienation which would assuredly be felt in such a case; the same vertiginous, overwhelming bewilderment, the same ghastly sense of separation from all the familiar environmental details that give color, form and definition to our lives and even determine our very personalities.

I was standing in the midst of a landscape which bore no degree or manner of resemblance to Crater Ridge. A long, gradual slope, covered with violet grass and studded at intervals with stones of monolithic size and shape, ran undulantly away beneath me to a broad plain with sinuous, open meadows and high, stately forests of an unknown vegetation whose predominant hues were purple and yellow. The plain seemed to end in a wall of impenetrable, golden-brownish mist, that rose with phantom pinnacles to dissolve on a sky of luminescent amber in which there was no sun.

In the foreground of this amazing scene, not more than two or three miles away, there loomed a city whose massive towers and mountainous ramparts of red stone were such as the Anakim of undiscovered worlds might build. Wall on beetling wall, spire on giant spire, it soared to confront the heavens, maintaining everywhere the severe and solemn lines of a rectilinear architecture. It seemed to overwhelm and crush down the beholder with its stern and crag-like imminence.

As I viewed this city, I forgot my initial sense of bewildering loss and alienage, in an awe with which something of actual terror was mingled; and, at the same time, I felt an obscure but profound allurement, the cryptic emanation of some enslaving spell. But after I had gazed awhile, the cosmic strangeness and bafflement of my unthinkable position returned upon me, and I felt only a wild desire to escape from the maddeningly oppressive bizarrerie of this region and regain my own world. In an effort to fight down my agitation I tried to figure out, if possible, what had really happened.

I had read a number of transdimensional stories—in fact, I had written one or two myself; and I had often pondered the possibility of other worlds or material planes which may exist in the same space with ours, invisible and impalpable to human senses. Of course, I realized at once that I had fallen into some such dimension. Doubtless, when I took that step forward between the boulders, I had been precipitated into some sort of flaw or fissure in space, to emerge at the bottom in this alien sphere—in a totally different kind of space.

It sounded simple enough, in a way, but not simple enough to make the modus operandi anything but a brainracking mystery, and in a further effort to collect myself, I studied my immediate surroundings with a close attention. This time, I was impressed by the arrangement of the monolithic stones I have spoken of, many of which were disposed at fairly regular intervals in two parallel lines running down the hill, as if to mark the course of some ancient road obliterated by the purple grass.

Turning to follow its ascent, I saw right behind me two columns, standing at precisely the same distance apart as the two odd boulders on Crater Ridge, and formed of the same soapy, greenish-gray stone. The pillars were perhaps nine feet high, and had been taller at one time, since the tops were splintered and broken away. Not far above them, the mounting slope vanished from view in a great bank of the same golden-brown mist that enveloped the remoter plain. But there were no more monoliths, and it seemed as if the road had ended with those pillars.

Inevitably, I began to speculate as to the relationship between the columns in this new dimension and the boulders in my own world. Surely, the resemblance could not be a matter of mere chance. If I stepped between the columns, could I return to the human sphere by a reversal of my precipitation therefrom? And if so, by what inconceivable beings from foreign time and space had the columns and boulders been established as the portals of a gateway between the two worlds? Who could have used the gateway, and for what purpose?

My brain reeled before the infinite vistas of surmise that were opened by such questions. However, what concerned me most was the problem of getting back to Crater Ridge. The weirdness of it all, the monstrous walls of the near-by town, the unnatural hues and forms of the outlandish scenery, were too much for human nerves, and I felt that I should go mad if forced to remain long in such a milieu. Also, there was no telling what hostile powers or entities I might encounter if I stayed.

The slope and plain were devoid of animate life, as far as I could see; but the great city was presumptive proof of its existence. Unlike the heroes in my own tales, who were wont to visit the Fifth Dimension or the worlds of Algol with perfect sangfroid, I did not feel in the least adventurous, and I shrank back with man's instinctive recoil before the unknown. With one fearful glance at the looming city and the wide plain with its lofty gorgeous vegetation, I turned and stepped back between the columns.

There was the same instantaneous plunge into blind and freezing gulfs, the same indeterminate falling and twisting, which had marked my descent into this new dimension. At the end I found myself standing, very dizzy and shaken, on the same spot from which I had taken my forward step between the greenish-gray boulders. Crater Ridge was swirling and reeling about me as if in the throes of an earthquake, and I had to sit down for a minute or two before I could recover my equilibrium.

I came back to the cabin like a man in a dream. The experience seemed, and still seems, incredible and unreal; and yet it has overshadowed everything else, and has colored and dominated all my thoughts. Perhaps, by writing it down, I can shake it off a little. It has unsettled me more than any previous experience in my whole life, and the world about me seems hardly less improbable and nightmarish than the one which I have penetrated in a fashion so fortuitous.

August 2nd.—I have done a lot of thinking in the past few days, and the more I ponder and puzzle, the more mysterious it all becomes. Granting the flaw in space, which must be an absolute vacuum, impervious to air, ether, light and matter, how was it possible for me to fall into it? And having fallen in, how could I fall out—particularly into a sphere that has no certifiable relationship with ours?

But, after all, one process would be as easy as the other, in theory. The main objection is: how could one move in a vacuum, either up or down, or backward or forward? The whole thing would baffle the comprehension of an Einstein, and I cannot feel that I have even approached the true solution.

Also, I have been fighting the temptation to go back, if only to convince myself that the thing really occurred. But, after all, why shouldn't I go back? An opportunity has been vouchsafed to me such as no man may even have been given before, and the wonders I shall see, the secrets I shall learn, are beyond imagining. My nervous trepidation is inexcusably childish under the circumstances. . . .

II. The Titan City

AUGUST 3RD.—I went back this morning, armed with a revolver. Somehow, without thinking that it might make a difference, I did not step in the very middle of the space between the boulders. Undoubtedly, as a result of this, my descent was more prolonged and impetuous than before, and seemed to consist mainly of a series of spiral somersaults. It must have taken me several minutes to recover from the ensuing vertigo, and when I came to, I was lying on the violet grass.

This time, I went boldly down the slope, and keeping as much as I could in the shelter of the bizarre purple and yellow vegetation, I stole toward the looming city. All was very still; there was no breath of wind in those exotic trees, which appeared to imitate, in their lofty, upright boles and horizontal foliage, the severe architectural lines of the Cyclopean buildings.

I had not gone far when I came to a road in the forest—a road paved with stupendous blocks of stone at least twenty feet square. It ran toward the city. I thought for a while that it was wholly deserted, perhaps disused; and I even dared to walk upon it, till I heard a noise behind me and, turning, saw the approach of several singular entities. Terrified, I sprang back and hid myself in a thicket, from which I watched the passing of those creatures, wondering fearfully if they had seen me. Apparently, my fears were groundless, for they did not even glance at my hiding place.

It is hard for me to describe or even visualize them now, for they were totally unlike anything that we are accustomed to think of as human or animal. They must have been ten feet tall, and they were moving along with colossal strides that took them from sight in a few instants, beyond a turn of the road. Their bodies were bright and shining, as if encased in some sort of armor, and their heads were equipped with high, curving appendages of opalescent hues which nodded above them like fantastic plumes, but may have been antennae or other sense-organs of a novel type. Trembling with excitement and wonder, I continued my progress through the richly-colored undergrowth. As I went on, I perceived for the first time that there were no shadows anywhere. The light came from all portions of the sunless, amber heaven, pervading everything with a soft, uniform luminosity. All was motionless and silent, as before; and there was no evidence of bird, insect or animal life in all this preternatural landscape.

But, when I had advanced to within a mile of the city—as well as I could judge the distance in a realm where the very proportions of objects were unfamiliar—I became aware of something which at first was recognizable as a vibration rather than a sound. There was a queer thrilling in my nerves; the disquieting sense of some unknown force or emanation flowing through my body. This was perceptible for some time before I heard the music, but having heard it, my auditory nerves identified it at once with the vibration.

It was faint and far-off, and seemed to emanate from the very heart of the Titan city. The melody was piercingly sweet, and resembled at times the singing of some voluptuous feminine voice. However, no human voice could have possessed that unearthly pitch, the shrill, perpetually sustained notes that somehow suggested the light of remote worlds and stars translated into sound.

Ordinarily, I am not very sensitive to music; I have even been reproached for not reacting more strongly to it. But I had not gone much farther when I realized the peculiar mental and emotional spell which the far-off sound was beginning to exert upon me. There was a siren-like allurement which drew me on, forgetful of the strangeness and potential perils of my situation; and I felt a slow, drug-like intoxication of brain and senses.

In some insidious manner, I know not how nor why, the music conveyed the ideas of vast but attainable space and altitude, of superhuman freedom and exultation; and it seemed to promise all the impossible splendors of which my imagination has vaguely dreamt. . . .

The forest continued almost to the city walls. Peering from behind the final boscage, I saw their overwhelming battlements in the sky above me, and noted the flawless jointure of their prodigious blocks. I was near the great road, which entered an open gate large enough to admit the passage of behemoths. There were no guards in sight, and several more of the tall, gleaming entities came striding along and went in as I watched.

From where I stood, I was unable to see inside the gate, for the wall was stupendously thick. The music poured from that mysterious entrance in an ever-strengthening flood, and sought to draw me on with its weird seduction, eager for unimaginable things. It was hard to resist; hard to rally my will-power and turn back. I tried to concentrate on the thought of danger—but the thought was tenuously unreal.

At last, I tore myself away and retraced my footsteps, very slowly and lingeringly, till I was beyond reach of the music. Even then, the spell persisted, like the effects of a drug; and all the way home I was tempted to return and follow those shining giants into the city.

August 5th.—I have visited the new dimension once more. I thought I could resist that summoning music, and I even took some cotton-wadding with which to stuff my ears if it should affect me too strongly. I began to hear the supernal melody at the same distance as before, and was drawn onward in the same manner. But, this time, I entered the open gate!

I wonder if I can describe that city? I felt like a crawling ant upon its mammoth pavements, amid the measureless Babel of its buildings, of its streets and arcades. Everywhere there were columns, obelisks and the perpendicular pylons of fane-like structures that would have dwarfed those of Thebes and Heliopolis. And the people of the city! How is one to depict them, or give them a name!

I think that the gleaming entities I first saw are not the true inhabitants, but are only visitors, perhaps from some other world or dimension, like myself. The real people are giants, too; but they move slowly, with solemn, hieratic paces. Their bodies are nude and swart, and their limbs are those of caryatides—massive enough, it would seem, to uphold the roofs and lintels of their own buildings. I fear to describe them minutely, for human words would give the idea of something monstrous and uncouth, and these beings are not monstrous, but they have merely developed in obedience to the laws of another evolution than ours; the environmental forces and conditions of a different world.

Somehow, I was not afraid when I saw then—perhaps the music had dragged me till I was beyond fear. There was a group of them just inside the gate, and they seemed to pay me no attention whatever as I passed them. The opaque, jet-like orbs of their huge eyes were impassive as the carven eyes of androsphinxes, and they uttered no sound from their heavy, straight, expressionless lips. Perhaps they lack the sense of hearing, for their strange, semi-rectangular heads were devoid of anything in the nature of external ears.

I followed the music, which was still remote and seemed to increase little in loudness. I was soon overtaken by several of those beings whom I had previously seen on the road outside the walls; and they passed me quickly and disappeared in the labyrinth of buildings. After them there came other beings of a less gigantic kind, and without the bright shards or armor worn by the first-comers. Then, overhead, two creatures with long, translucent, blood-colored wings, intricately veined and ribbed, came flying side by side and vanished behind the others. Their faces, featured with organs of unsurmisable use, were not those of animals, and I felt sure that they were beings of a high order of development.

I saw hundreds of those slow-moving, somber entities whom I have identified as the true inhabitants, but none of them appeared to notice me. Doubtless they were accustomed to seeing far weirder and more unusual kinds of life than humanity. As I went on, I was overtaken by dozens of improbable-looking creatures, all going in the same direction as myself, as if drawn by the same siren melody.

Deeper and deeper I went into the wilderness of colossal architecture, led by that remote, ethereal, opiate music. I soon noticed a sort of gradual ebb and flow in the sound, occupying an interval of ten minutes or more; but, by imperceptible degrees, it grew sweeter and nearer. I wondered how it could penetrate that manifold maze of builded stone and be heard outside the walls. . . .

I must have walked for miles, in the ceaseless gloom of those rectangular structures that hung above me, tier on tier, at an awful height in the amber zenith. Then, at length, I came to the core and secret of it all. Preceded and followed by a number of those chimerical entities, I emerged on a great square, in whose center was a temple-like building more immense than the others. The music poured, imperiously shrill and loud, from its many-columned entrance.

I felt the thrill of one who approaches the sanctum of some hierarchal mystery, when I entered the halls of that building. People who must have come from many different worlds or dimensions went with me, and before me, along the titanic colonnades, whose pillars were graven with indecipherable runes and enigmatic bas-reliefs. The dark, colossal inhabitants of the town were standing or roaming about, intent, like all the others, on their own affairs. None of these beings spoke, either to me or to one another, and though several eyed me casually, my presence was evidently taken for granted.

There are no words to convey the incomprehensible wonder of it all. And the music? I have utterly failed to describe that, also. It was as if some marvelous elixir had been turned into sound-waves—an elixir conferring the gift of superhuman life, and the high, magnificent dreams which are dreamt by the Immortals. It mounted in my brain like a supernal drunkenness, as I approached the hidden source. I do not know what obscure warning prompted me, now, to stuff my ears with cotton before I went any farther. Though I could still hear it, still feel its peculiar, penetrant vibration, the sound became muted when I had done this, and its influence was less powerful henceforth. There is little doubt that I owe my life to this simple and homely precaution.

The endless rows of columns grew dim for a while as the interior of a long, basaltic cavern; and then, some distance ahead, I perceived the glimmering of a soft light on the floor and pillars. The light soon became an over-flooding radiance, as if gigantic lamps were being lit in the temple's heart; and the vibrations of the hidden music pulsed more strongly in my nerves.

The hall ended in a chamber of immense, indefinite scope, whose walls and roof were doubtful with unremoving shadows. In the center, amid the pavement of mammoth blocks, there was a circular pit, above which seemed to float a fountain of flame that soared in one perpetual, slowly lengthening jet. This flame was the sole illumination, and also, was the source of the wild, unearthly music. Even with my purposely deafened ears, I was wooed by the shrill and starry sweetness of its singing; and I felt the voluptuous lure and the high, vertiginous exaltation.

I knew immediately that the place was a shrine, and that the transdimensional beings who accompanied me were visiting pilgrims. There were scores of them—perhaps hundreds; but all were dwarfed in the cosmic immensity of that chamber. They were gathered before the flame in various attitudes of worship; they bowed their exotic heads, or made mysterious gestures or adoration with unhuman hands and members. And the voices of several, deep as booming drums, or sharp as the stridulation of giant insects, were audible amid the singing of the fountain.

Spellbound, I went forward and joined them. Enthralled by the music and by the vision of the soaring flame, I paid as little heed to my outlandish companions as they to me. The fountain rose and rose, until its light flickered on the limbs and features of throned, colossal, statues behind it—of heroes, gods or demons from the earlier cycles of alien time, staring in stone from a dusk of illimitable mystery.

The fire was green and dazzling, pure as the central flame of a star; it blinded me, and when I turned my eyes away, the air was filled with webs of intricate colour, with swiftly changing arabesques whose numberless, unwonted hues and patterns were such as no mundane eye had ever beheld. And I felt a stimulating warmth that filled my very marrow with intenser life. . . .

III. The Lure of the Flame

THE MUSIC mounted with the flame; and I understood, now, its recurrent ebb and flow. As I looked and listened, a mad thought was born in my mind—the thought of how marvelous and ecstatical it would be to run forward and leap headlong into the singing fire. The music seemed to tell me that I should find in that moment of flaring dissolution all the delight and triumph, all the splendor and exaltation it had promised from afar. It besought me; it pleaded with tones of supernal melody, and despite the wadding in my ears, the seduction was well-nigh irresistible.

However, it had not robbed me of all sanity. With a sudden start of terror, like one who has been tempted to fling himself from a high precipice, I drew back. Then I saw that the same dreadful impulse was shared by some of my companions. The two entities with scarlet wings, whom I have previously mentioned, were standing a little apart from the rest of us. Now, with a great fluttering, they rose and flew toward the flame like moths toward a candle. For a brief moment the light shone redly through their half-transparent wings, ere they disappeared in the leaping incandescence, which flared briefly and then burned as before.

Then, in rapid succession, a number of other beings, who represented the most divergent trends of biology, sprang forward and immolated themselves in the flame. There were creatures with translucent bodies, and some that shone with all the hues of the opal; there were winged colossi, and Titans who strode as with seven-league boots; and there was one being with useless, abortive wings, who crawled rather than ran, to seek the same glorious doom as the rest. But among them there were none of the city's people: these merely stood and looked on, impassive and statue-like as ever.

I saw that the fountain had now reached its greatest height, and was beginning to decline. It sank steadily, but slowly, to half its former elevation. During this interval, there were no more acts of self-sacrifice, and several of the beings beside me turned abruptly and went away, as if they had overcome the lethal spell.

One of the tall, armored entities, as he left, addressed me in words that were like clarion-notes, with unmistakable accents of warning. By a mighty effort of will, in a turmoil of conflicting emotions, I followed him. At every step, the madness and delirium of the music warred with my instincts of self-preservation. More than once, I started to go back. My homeward journey was blurred and doubtful as the wanderings of a man in opium-trance; and the music sang behind me, and told me of the rapture I had missed, of, the flaming dissolution whose brief instant was better than aeons of mortal life. . . .

August 9th.—I have tried to go on with a new story, but have made no progress. Anything that I can imagine, or frame in language, seems flat and puerile beside the world of unsearchable mystery to which I have found admission. The temptation to return is more cogent than ever; the call of that remembered music is sweeter than the voice of a loved woman. And always I am tormented by the problem of it all, and tantalized by the little which I have perceived and understood.

What forces are these whose existence and working I have merely apprehended? Who are the inhabitants of the city? And who are the beings that visit the enshrined flame? What rumor or legend has drawn them from outland realms and ulterior planets to that place of inenarrable danger and destruction? And what is the fountain itself, what the secret of its lure and its deadly singing? These problems admit of infinite surmise, but no conceivable solution.

I am planning to go back once more . . . but not alone. Someone must go with me, this time, as a witness to the wonder and the peril. It is all too strange for credence: I must have human corroboration of what I have seen and felt and conjectured. Also, another might understand where I have failed to do more than apprehend.

Who shall I take? It will be necessary to invite someone here from the outer world—someone of high intellectual and aesthetic capacity. Shall I ask Philip Hastane, my fellow fiction-writer? He would be too busy, I fear. But there is the Californian artist, Felix Ebbonly, who has illustrated some of my fantastic novels. . . .

Ebbonly would be the man to see and appreciate the new dimension, if he can come. With his bent for the bizarre and unearthly, the spectacle of that plain and city, the Babelian buildings and arcades, and the Temple of the Flame, will simply enthrall him. I shall write immediately to his San Francisco address.

August 12th.—Ebbonly is here: the mysterious hints in my letter, regarding some novel pictorial subjects along his own line, were too provocative for him to resist. Now, I have explained fully and given him a detailed account of my adventures. I can see that he is a little incredulous, for which I hardly blame him. But he will not remain incredulous for long, for tomorrow we shall visit together the City of the Singing Flame.

August 13th.—I must concentrate my disordered faculties, must choose my words and write with exceeding care. This will be the last entry in my journal, and the last writing I shall ever do. When I have finished, I shall wrap the journal up and address it to Philip Hastane, who can make such disposition of it as he sees fit.

I took Ebbonly into the other dimension today. He was impressed, even as I had been, by the two isolated boulders on Crater Ridge.

"They look like the guttered ends of columns established by pre-human gods," he remarked. "I begin to believe you now."

I told him to go first, and indicated the place where he should step. He obeyed without hesitation, and I had the singular experience of seeing a man melt into utter, instantaneous nothingness. One moment he was there—the next, there was only bare ground, and the far-off tamaracks whose view his body had obstructed. I followed, and found him standing, in speechless awe, on the violet grass.

"This," he said at last, "is the sort of thing whose existence I have hitherto merely suspected, and have never been able to hint at in my most imaginative drawings."

We spoke little as we followed the range of monolithic boulders toward the plain. Far in the distance, beyond those high and stately trees, with their sumptuous foliage, the golden-brown vapors had parted, showing vistas of an immense horizon; and past the horizon were range on range of gleaming orbs and fiery, flying motes in the depth of that amber heaven. It was as if the veil of another universe than ours had been drawn back.

We crossed the plain, and came at length within earshot of the siren music. I warned Ebbonly to stuff his ears with cotton-wadding, but he refused. "I don't want to deaden any new sensation I may experience," he observed.

We entered the city. My companion was in a veritable rhapsody of artistic delight when he beheld the enormous buildings and the people. I could see, too, that the music had taken hold upon him: his look soon became fixed and dreamy as that of an opium-eater.

At first, he made many comments on the architecture and the various beings who passed us, and called my attention to details which I had not perceived before. However, as we drew nearer the Temple of the Flame, his observational interest seemed to flag, and was replaced by more and more of an ecstatic inward absorption. His remarks became fewer and briefer, and he did not even seem to hear my questions. It was evident that the sound had wholly bemused and bewitched him.

Even as on my former visit, there were many pilgrims going toward the shrine—and few that were coming away from it. Most of them belonged to evolutionary types that I had seen before. Among those that were new to me, I recall one gorgeous creature with golden and cerulean wings like those of a giant lepidoptera, and scintillating, jewel-like eyes that must have been designed to mirror the glories of some Edenic world.

I felt, too, as before, the captious thraldom and bewitchment, the insidious, gradual perversion of thought and instinct, as if the music were working in my brain like a subtle alkaloid. Since I had taken my usual precaution, my subjection to the influence was less complete than that of Ebbonly; but, nevertheless, it was enough to make me forget a number of things—among them, the initial concern which I had felt when my companion refused to employ the same mode of protection as myself. I no longer thought of his danger, or my own, except as something very distant and immaterial.

The streets were like the prolonged and bewildering labyrinth of a nightmare. But the music led us forthrightly, and always there were other pilgrims. Like men in the grip of some powerful current, we were drawn to our destination. As we passed along the hall of gigantic columns and neared the abode of the fiery fountain, a sense of our peril quickened momentarily in my brain, and I sought to warn Ebbonly once more. But all my protests and remonstrances were futile: he was deaf as a machine, and wholly impervious to anything but the lethal music. His expression and movements were those of a somnambulist. Even when I seized and shook him with such violence as I could muster, he remained oblivious of my presence.

The throng of worshippers was larger than upon my first visit. The jet of pure, incandescent flame was mounting steadily as we entered, and it sang with the pure ardor and ecstasy of a star alone in space. Again, with ineffable tones, it told me the rapture of a moth-like death in its lofty soaring, the exultation and triumph of a momentary union with its elemental essence.

The flame rose to its apex; and even for me, the mesmeric lure was well-nigh irresistible. Many of our companions succumbed, and the first to immolate himself was the giant lepidopterous being. Four others, of diverse evolutionary types, followed in appallingly swift succession.

In my own partial subjection to the music, my own effort to resist that deadly enslavement, I had almost forgotten the very presence of Ebbonly. It was too late for me to even think of stopping him, when he ran forward in a series of leaps that were both solemn and frenzied, like the beginnings of some sacerdotal dance, and hurled himself headlong into the flame. The fire enveloped him; it flared up for an instant with a more dazzling greenness, and that was all.

Slowly, as if from benumbed brain centers, a horror crept upon my conscious mind, and helped to annul the perilous mesmerism. I turned, while many others were following Ebbonly's example, and fled from the shrine and from the city. But somehow the horror diminished as I went; more and more, I found myself envying my companion's fate, and wondering as to the sensations he had felt in that moment of fiery dissolution. . . .

Now, as I write this, I am wondering why I came back again to the human world. Words are futile to express what I have beheld and experienced, and the change that has come upon me, beneath the play of incalculable forces in a world of which no other mortal is even cognisant. Literature is nothing more than a shadow. Life, with its drawn-out length of monotonous, reiterative days, is unreal and without meaning, now, in comparison with the splendid death which I might have had—the glorious doom which is still in store.

I have no longer any will to fight the ever-insistent music which I hear in memory. And there seems to be no reason at all why I should fight it. . . . Tomorrow, I shall return to the city.

IV. The Third Venturer

EVEN WHEN I, Philip Hastane, had read through the journal of my friend, Giles Angarth, so many times that I had almost learned it by heart, I was still doubtful as to whether the incidents related therein were fiction or verity. The transdimensional adventures of Angarth and Ebbonly; the City of the Flame, with its strange residents and pilgrims; the immolation of Ebbonly, and the hinted return of the narrator himself for a like purpose, in the last entry of the diary, were very much the sort of thing that Angarth might have imagined in one of the fantastic novels for which he had become so justly famous. Add to this the seemingly impossible and incredible nature of the whole tale, and my hesitancy in accepting it as veridical will easily be understood.

However, on the other hand, there was the unsolved and recalcitrant enigma offered by the disappearance of the two men. Both were well known, one as a writer, the other as an artist; both were in flourishing circumstances, with no serious cares or troubles; and their vanishment, all things considered, was difficult to explain on the ground of any motive less unusual or extraordinary than the one assigned in the journal. At first, as I have mentioned in my foreword to the diary, I thought the whole affair might well have been devised as a somewhat elaborate practical joke; but this theory became less and less tenable as weeks and months went by, and linked themselves slowly into a year, without the reappearance of the presumptive jokers.

Now, at last, I can testify to the truth of all that Angarth wrote—and more. For I, too, have been in Ydmos, the City of Singing Flame, and have known also the supernal glories and raptures of the Inner Dimension. And of these I must tell, however falteringly and inadequately, with mere human words, before the vision fades. For these are things which neither I, nor any other, shall behold or experience again.

Ydmos itself is now a riven ruin; the Temple of the Flame has been blasted to its foundations in the basic rock, and the fountain of singing fire has been stricken at its source. The Inner Dimension has perished like a broken bubble, in the great war that was made upon Ydmos by the rulers of the Outer Lands. . . .

After having finally laid down Angarth's journal, I was unable to forget the peculiar and tantalizing problems it raised. The vague, but infinitely suggestive vistas opened by the tale were such as to haunt my imagination recurrently with a hint of half-revealed mysteries. I was troubled by the possibility of some great and mystic meaning behind it all; some cosmic actuality of which the narrator had perceived merely the external veils and fringes. As time went on, I found myself pondering it perpetually, and becoming more and more possessed by an overwhelming wonder, and a sense of something which no mere action-weaver would have been likely to invent.

In the early summer of 1939, after finishing a new novel, I felt able for the first time to take the necessary leisure for the execution of a project that had often occurred to me. Putting all my affairs in order, and knitting all the loose ends of my literary labours and correspondence, in case I should not return, I left my home in Auburn, ostensibly for a week's vacation. Actually, I went to Summit, with the idea of investigating closely the milieu in which Angarth and Ebbonly had disappeared from human ken.

With strange emotions, I visited the forsaken cabin south of Crater Ridge, that had been occupied by Angarth, and saw the rough table of pine boards upon which my friend had written his journal, and then left the sealed package containing it to be forwarded to me after his departure.

There was a weird and brooding loneliness about the place, as if the non-human infinitudes had already claimed it for their own. The unlocked door had sagged inward from the pressure of high-piled winter snows, and fir needles had sifted across the sill to strew the unswept floor. Somehow, I know not why, the bizarre narrative became more real and more credible to me, while I stood there, as if an occult intimation of all that had happened to its author still lingered around the cabin.

This mysterious intimation grew stronger when I came to visit
Crater Ridge itself, and to search amid its miles of pseudo-volcanic
rubble for the two boulders so explicitly described by Angarth as having
a likeness to the pedestals of ruined columns. Following the northward
path which he must have taken from his cabin, and trying to retrace his
wanderings of the long, barren hill, I combed it thoroughly from end to
end and from side to side, since he had not specified the location of the
boulders. And after two mornings spent in this manner, without result,
I was almost ready to abandon the quest and dismiss the queer, soapy,
greenish-gray column-ends as one of Angarth's most provocative and
deceptive fictions.

It must have been the formless, haunting intuition to which I have
referred, that made me renew the search on the third morning. This
time, after crossing and re-crossing the hill-top for an hour or more, and
weaving tortuously among the cicada-haunted wild-currant bushes and
sunflowers on the dusty slopes, I came at last to an open, circular, rock-
surrounded space that was totally unfamiliar. I had somehow missed it
in all my previous roamings. It was the place of which Angarth had told;
and I saw, with an inexpressible thrill, the two rounded, worn-looking
boulders that were situated in the center of the ring.

I believe that I trembled a little with excitement, as I went forward
to inspect the curious stones. Bending over, but not daring to enter the
bare, pebbly space between them, I touched one of them with my hand,
and received a sensation of preternatural smoothness, together with a
coolness that was inexplicable, considering that the boulders and the
soil about them must have lain unshaded from the sultry August sun for
many hours.

From that moment, I became fully persuaded that Angarth's account
was no mere fable. Just why I should have felt so certain of this, I am
powerless to say. But it seemed to me that I stood on the threshold of
an ultramundane mystery, on the brink of uncharted gulfs. I looked
about at the familiar Sierran valleys and mountains, wondering that they
still preserved their wonted outlines, and were still unchanged by the

contiguity of alien worlds, still untouched by the luminous glories of arcanic dimensions.

Convinced that I had indeed found the gateway between the worlds, I was prompted to strange reflections. What, and where, was this other sphere to which my friend had attained entrance? Was it near at hand, like a secret room in the structure of space? Or was it, in reality, millions or trillions of light-years away, by the reckoning of astronomic distance, in a planet of some ulterior galaxy?

After all, we know little or nothing of the actual nature of space; and, perhaps, in some way that we cannot imagine, the infinite is doubled upon itself in places, with dimensional folds and tucks, and short-cuts whereby the distance to Algenib or Aldebaran is but a step. Perhaps, also, there is more than one infinity. The spatial 'flaw' into which Angarth had fallen might well be a sort of super-dimension, abridging the cosmic intervals and connecting universe with universe.

However, because of this very certitude that I had found the inter-spheric portals, and could follow Angarth and Ebbonly if I so desired, I hesitated before trying the experiment. I was mindful of the mystic danger and irrefragable lure that had overcome the others. I was consumed by imaginative curiosity, by an avid, well-nigh feverish longing to behold the wonders of this exotic realm; but I did not purpose to become a victim to the opiate power and fascination of the Singing Flame.

I stood for a long time, eyeing the odd boulders and the barren, pebble-littered spot that gave admission to the unknown. At length, I went away, deciding to defer my venture till the following morning. Visualizing the weird doom to which the others had gone so voluntarily, and even gladly, I must confess that I was afraid. On the other hand, I was drawn by the fateful allurement that leads an explorer into far places . . . and, perhaps, by something more than this.

I slept badly that night, with nerves and brain excited by formless, glowing premonitions, by intimations of half-conceived perils, and splendors and vastnesses. Early the next morning, while the sun was still hanging above the Nevada Mountains, I returned to Crater Ridge.

I carried a strong hunting-knife and a Colt revolver, and wore a filled cartridge-belt, with a knapsack containing sandwiches and a thermos bottle of coffee.

Before starting, I had stuffed my ears tightly with cotton soaked in a new anaesthetic fluid, mild but efficacious, which would serve to deafen me completely for many hours. In this way, I felt that I should be immune to the demoralizing music of the fiery fountain. I peered about at the rugged landscape with its far-flung vistas, wondering if I should ever see it again. Then, resolutely, but with the eerie thrilling and sinking of one who throws himself from a high cliff into some bottomless chasm, I stepped forward into the space between the grayish-green boulders.

My sensations, generally speaking, were similar to those described by Angarth in his diary. Blackness and illimitable emptiness seemed to wrap me round in a dizzy swirl as of rushing wind or milling water, and I went down and down in a spiral descent whose duration I have never been able to estimate. Intolerably stifled, and without even the power to gasp for breath, in the chill, airless vacuum that froze my very muscles and marrow, I felt that I should lose consciousness in another moment and descend into the greater gulf of death or oblivion.

Something seemed to arrest my fall, and I became aware that I was standing still, though I was troubled for some time by a queer doubt as to whether my position was vertical, horizontal or upside-down in relation to the solid substance that my feet had encountered. Then, the blackness lifted slowly like a dissolving cloud, and I saw the slope of violet grass, the rows of irregular monoliths running downward from where I stood, and the gray-green columns near at hand. Beyond was the titan, perpendicular city of red stone that was dominant above the high and multi-coloured vegetation of the plain.

It was all very much as Angarth had depicted it; but somehow, even then, I became aware of differences that were not immediately or clearly definable, of scenic details and atmospheric elements for which his account had not prepared me. And, at the moment I was too thoroughly disequilibrated and overpowered by the vision of it all to even speculate concerning the character of these differences.

As I gazed at the city, with its crowding tiers of battlements and its multitude of overlooming spires I felt the invisible threads of a secret attraction, was seized by an imperative longing to know the mysteries hidden behind the massive walls and the myriad buildings. Then, a moment later, my gaze was drawn to the remote, opposite horizon of the plain, as if by some conflicting impulse whose nature and origin were undiscoverable.

It must have been because I had formed so clear and definite a picture of the scene from my friend's narrative, that I was surprised, and even a little disturbed as if by something wrong or irrelevant, when I saw in the far distance the shining towers of what seemed to be another city—a city of which Angarth had not written. The towers rose in serried lines, reaching for many miles in a curious arclike formation, and were sharply defined against a blackish mass of cloud that had reared behind them and was spreading out on the luminous, amber sky in sullen webs and sinister, crawling filaments.

Subtle disquietude and repulsion seemed to emanate from the far-off, glittering spires, even as attraction emanated from those of the nearer city. I saw them quiver and pulse with an evil light, like living and moving things, through what I assumed to be some refractive trick of the atmosphere. Then, for an instant, the black cloud behind them glowed with dull, angry crimson throughout its whole mass, and even its questing webs and tendrils were turned into lurid threads of fire.

The crimson faded, leaving the cloud inert and lumpish as before; but from many of the vanward towers, lines of red and violet flame had leaped, like out-thrust lances, at the bosom of the plain beneath them. They were held thus for at least a minute, moving slowly across a wide area, before they vanished. In the spaces between the towers, I now perceived a multitude of gleaming, restless particles, like armies of militant atoms, and wondered if perchance they were living things. If the idea had not appeared so fantastical, I could have sworn, even then, that the far city had already changed its position and was advancing toward the other on the plain.

V. The Striding Doom

APART FROM the fulguration of the cloud, the flames that had sprung from the towers, and the quiverings which I deemed a refractive phenomenon, the whole landscape before and about me was unnaturally still. On the strange amber air, the Tyrian-tinted grasses, and the proud, opulent foliage of the unknown trees, where lay the dead calm that precedes the stupendous turmoil of typhonic storm or seismic cataclysm. The brooding sky was permeated with intuitions of cosmic menace, and weighed down by a dim, elemental despair.

Alarmed by this ominous atmosphere, I looked behind me at the two pillars which, according to Angarth, were the gateway of return to the human world. For an instant, I was tempted to go back. Then, I turned once more to the near-by city, and the feelings I have mentioned were lost in an oversurging awesomeness and wonder. I felt the thrill of a deep, supernal exaltation before the magnitude of the mighty buildings; a compelling sorcery was laid upon me by the very lines of their construction, by the harmonies of a solemn architectural music. I forgot my impulse to return to Crater Ridge, and started down the slope toward the city.

Soon the boughs of the purple and yellow forest arched above me like the altitudes of Titan-builded aisles, with leaves that fretted the rich heaven in gorgeous arabesques. Beyond them, ever and anon, I caught glimpses of the piled ramparts of my destination; but looking back in the direction of that other city on the horizon, I found that its fulgurating towers were now lost to view.

I saw, however, that the masses of the great somber cloud were rising steadily on the sky, and once again they flared to a swart, malignant red, as if with some unearthly form of sheet-lightning; and though I could hear nothing with my deadened ears, the ground beneath me trembled with long vibrations as of thunder. There was a queer quality in the vibrations, that seemed to tear my nerves and set my teeth on edge with its throbbing, lancinating discord, painful as broken glass or the torment of a tightened rack.

Like Angarth before me, I came to the paved Cyclopean highway. Following it, in the stillness after the unheard peals of thunder, I felt another and subtler vibration, which I knew to be that of the Singing Flame in the temple at the city's core. It seemed to soothe and exalt and bear me on, to erase with soft caresses the ache that still lingered in my nerves from the torturing pulsations of the thunder.

I met no one on the road, and was not passed by any of the trans-dimensional pilgrims such as had overtaken Angarth; and when the accumulated ramparts loomed above the highest trees I came forth from the wood in their very shadow, I saw that the great gate of the city was closed, leaving no crevice through which a pygmy like myself might obtain entrance.

Feeling a profound and peculiar discomfiture, such as one would experience in a dream that had gone wrong, I stared at the grim, unrelenting blackness of the gate, which seemed to be wrought from one enormous sheet of somber and lustreless metal. Then, I peered upward at the sheerness of the wall, which rose above me like an alpine cliff, and saw that the battlements were seemingly deserted. Was the city forsaken by its people, by the guardians of the Flame? Was it no longer open to the pilgrims who came from outlying lands to worship the Flame and immolate themselves?

With a curious reluctance, after lingering there for many minutes in a sort of stupor, I turned away to retrace my steps. In the interim of my journey, the black cloud had drawn immeasurably nearer, and was now blotting out half the heaven with two portentous, wing-like formations. It was a sinister and terrible sight; and it lightened again with that ominous, wrathful flaming, with a detonation that beat upon my deaf ears like waves of disintegrative force, and seemed to lacerate the inmost fibers of my body.

I hesitated, fearing that the storm would burst upon me before I could reach the inter-dimensional portals, for I saw that I should be exposed to an elemental disturbance of unfamiliar character and supreme violence. Then, in mid-air before the imminent, ever-rising cloud, I perceived two flying creatures whom I can compare only to gigantic moths. With bright, luminous wings, upon the ebon forefront of the storm, they approached me in level but precipitate flight, and would have crashed headlong against the shut gate if they had not checked themselves with sudden, easy poise.

With hardly a flutter, they descended and paused on the ground beside me, supporting themselves on queer, delicate legs that branched at the knee-joints in floating antennae and waving tentacles. Their wings were sumptuously mottled webs of pearl and madder, opal and orange; their heads were circled by a series of convex and concave eyes, and fringed with coiling, horn-like organs from whose hollow ends there hung aerial filaments. I was startled and amazed by their aspect; but somehow, by an obscure telepathy I felt assured that their intentions toward me were friendly.

I knew that they wished to enter the city, and also that they understood my predicament. Nevertheless, I was not prepared for what happened. With movements of utmost celerity and grace, one of the giant, moth-like beings stationed himself at my right hand, and the other at my left. Then, before I could even suspect their intention, they enfolded my limbs and body with their long tentacles, wrapping me round and round as if with powerful ropes; and carrying me between them as if my weight were a mere trifle, they rose in the air and soared at the mighty ramparts!

In that swift and effortless ascent, the wall seemed to flow downward beside and beneath us, like a wave of molten stone. Dizzily, I watched the falling away of the mammoth blocks in endless recession. Then, we were level with the broad ramparts, were flying across the unguarded parapets and over a canyon-like space, toward the immense rectangular buildings and numberless square towers.

We had hardly crossed the walls when a weird, flickering glow was cast on the edifices before us by another lightening of the great cloud. The moth-like beings paid no apparent heed, and flew steadily on into the city with their strange faces toward an unseen goal. But, turning my head to peer backward at the storm, I beheld an astounding and appalling spectacle. Beyond the city ramparts, as if wrought by black magic or the toil of genii, another city had reared, and its high towers were moving swiftly forward beneath the rubescent dome of the burning cloud!

A second glance, and I perceived that the towers were identical with those I had beheld afar on the plain. In the interim of my passage through the woods, they had traveled over an expanse of many miles, by means of some unknown motive-power, and had closed in on the City of the Flame. Looking more closely, to determine the manner of their locomotion, I saw that they were not mounted on wheels, but on short, massy legs like jointed columns of metal, that gave them the stride of ungainly colossi. There were six or more of these legs to each tower, and near the tops of the towers were rows of huge eye-like openings, from which issued the bolts of red and violet flame I have mentioned before.

The many-colored forest had been burned away by these flames in a league-wide swath of devastation, even to the walls, and there was nothing but a stretch of black, vaporing desert between the mobile towers and the city. Then, even as I gazed, the long, leaping beams began to assail the craggy ramparts, and the topmost parapets were melting like lava beneath them. It was a scene of utmost terror and grandeur; but, a moment later, it was blotted from my vision by the buildings among which we had now plunged. The great lepidopterous creatures who bore me went on with the speed of eyrie-questing eagles. In the course of that flight, I was hardly capable of conscious thought or volition; I lived only in the breathless and giddy freedom of aerial movement, or dream-like levitation above the labyrinthine maze of stone immensitudes and marvels. I was without actual cognisance of much that I beheld in that stupendous Babel of architectural imageries, and only afterward, in the more tranquil light of recollection, could I give coherent form and meaning to many of my impressions.

My senses were stunned by the vastness and strangeness of it all; I realized but dimly the cataclysmic ruin that was being loosed upon the city behind us, and the doom from which we were fleeing. I knew that war was being made with unearthly weapons and engineries, by inimical powers that I could not imagine, for a purpose beyond my conception; but, to me, it all had the elemental confusion and vague, impersonal horror of some cosmic catastrophe.

We flew deeper and deeper into the city. Broad, platform roofs and terrace-like tiers of balconies flowed away beneath us, and the pavements raced like darkling streams at some enormous depth. Severe cubicular spires and square monoliths were all about and above us; and we saw on some of the roofs the dark, Atlantean people of the city, moving slowly and statuesquely, or standing in attitudes of cryptic resignation and despair, with their faces toward the flaming cloud. All were weaponless, and I saw no engineries anywhere such as might be used for purposes of military defense.

Swiftly as we flew, the climbing cloud was swifter, and the darkness of its intermittently glowing dome had overarched the town while its spidery filaments had meshed the further heavens and would soon attach themselves to the opposite horizon. The buildings darkened and lightened with the recurrent fulguration, and I felt in all my tissues the painful pulsing of the thunderous vibrations.

Dully and vaguely, I realized that the winged beings who carried me between then were pilgrims to the Temple of the Flame. More and more, I became aware of an influence that must have been that of the starry music emanating from the temple's heart, There were soft, soothing vibrations in the air, that seemed to absorb and nullify the tearing discords of the unheard thunder. I felt that we were entering a zone of mystic refuge, or sidereal and celestial security, and my troubled senses were both lulled and exalted.

The gorgeous wings of the giant lepidopters began to slant downward. Before and beneath us, at some distance, I perceived a mammoth pile which I knew at once for the Temple of the Flame. Down, still down we went, in the awesome space of the surrounding square; and then I was borne in through the lofty, ever-open entrance, and along the high hall with its thousand columns. Pregnant with strange balsams, the dim, mysterious dusk enfolded us, and we seemed to be entering realms of pre-mundane antiquity and trans-stellar immensity; to be following a pillared cavern that led to the core of some ultimate star.

It seemed that we were the last and only pilgrims, and also that the temple was deserted by its guardians, for we met no one in the whole extent of that column-crowded gloom. After a while, the dusk began to lighten, and we plunged into a widening beam of radiance, and then into the vast central chamber in which soared the fountain of green fire.

I remember only the impression of shadowy, flickering space, of a vault that was lost in the azure of infinity, of colossal and Memnonian statues that looked down from Himalaya-like altitudes; and, above all, the dazzling jet of flame that aspired from a pit in the pavement and rose into the air like the visible rapture of gods. But all this I saw for an instant only. Then, I realized that the beings who bore me were flying straight toward the Flame on level wings, without the slightest pause or flutter of hesitation.

VI. The Inner Sphere

THERE WAS no room for fear, no time for alarm, in the dazed and chaotic turmoil of my sensations. I was stupefied by all that I had experienced, and moreover, the drug-like spell of the Flame was upon me, even though I could not hear its fatal singing. I believe that I struggled a little, by some sort of mechanical muscular revulsion, against the tentacular arms that were wound about me. But the lepidopters gave no heed; it was plain that they were conscious of nothing but the mounting fire and its seductive music.

I remember, however, that there was no sensation of actual heat, such as might have been expected, when we neared the soaring column. Instead, I felt the most ineffable thrilling in all my fibers, as if I were being permeated by waves of celestial energy and demiurgic ecstasy. Then we entered the Flame . . . .

Like Angarth before me, I had taken it for granted that the fate of all those who flung themselves into the Flame was an instant though blissful destruction. I expected to undergo a briefly flaring dissolution, followed by the nothingness of utter annihilation. The thing which really happened was beyond the boldest reach of speculative thought, and to give even a meager idea of my sensations would beggar the resources of language.

The Flame enfolded us like a green curtain, blotting from view the great chamber. Then it seemed to me that I was caught and carried to supercelestial heights, in an upward-rushing cataract of quintessential force and deific rapture, and an all-illuminating light. It seemed that I, and my companions, had achieved a god-like union with the Flame; that every atom of our bodies had undergone a transcendental expansion, and was winged with ethereal lightness.

It was as if we no longer existed, except as one divine, indivisible entity, soaring beyond the trammels of matter, beyond the limits of time and space, to attain undreamable shores. Unspeakable was the joy, and infinite the freedom of that ascent, in which we seemed to overpass the zenith of the highest star. Then, as if we had risen with the Flame to its culmination, had reached its very apex, we emerged and came to a pause.

My senses were faint with exaltation, my eyes blind with the glory of the fire; and the world on which I now gazed was a vast arabesque of unfamiliar forms and bewildering hues from another spectrum than the one to which our eyes are habituated. It swirled before my dizzy eyes like a labyrinth of gigantic jewels, with interweaving rays and tangled lustres, and only by slow degrees was I able to establish order and distinguish detail in the surging riot of my perceptions.

All about me were endless avenues of super-prismatic opal and jacinth; arches and pillars of ultra-violet gems, of transcendent sapphire, of unearthly ruby and amethyst, all suffused with a multi-tinted splendor. I appeared to be treading on jewels, and above me was a jeweled sky.

Presently, with recovered equilibrium, with eyes adjusted to a new range of cognition, I began to perceive the actual features of the landscape. With the two moth-like beings still beside me, I was standing on a million-flowered grass, among trees of a paradisal vegetation, with fruit, foliage, blossoms and trunks whose very forms were beyond the conception of tridimensional life. The grace of their drooping boughs, of their fretted fronds, was inexpressible in terms of earthly line and contour, and they seemed to be wrought of pure, ethereal substance, half-translucent to the empyrean light, which accounted for the gem-like impression I had first received.

I breathed a nectar-laden air, and the ground beneath me was ineffably soft and resilient, as if it were composed of some higher form of matter than ours. My physical sensations were those of the utmost buoyancy and well-being, with no trace of fatigue or nervousness, such as might have been looked for after the unparalleled and marvellous events in which I had played a part. I felt no sense of mental dislocation or confusion; and, apart from my ability to recognize unknown colors and non-Euclidean forms, I began to experience a queer alteration and extension of tactility, through which it seemed that I was able to touch remote objects.

The radiant sky was filled with many-colored suns, like those that might shine on a world of some multiple solar system; but as I gazed, their glory became softer and dimmer, and the brilliant lustre of the trees and grass was gradually subdued, as if by encroaching twilight. I was beyond surprise, in the boundless marvel and mystery of it all, and nothing, perhaps, would have seemed incredible. But if anything could have amazed me or defied belief, it was the human face—the face of my vanished friend, Giles Angarth, which now emerged from among the waning jewels of the forest, followed by that of another man whom I recognized from photographs as Felix Ebbonly.

They came out from beneath the gorgeous boughs, and paused before me. Both were clad in lustrous fabrics, finer than Oriental silk, and of no earthly cut or pattern. Their look was both joyous and meditative, and their faces had taken on a hint of the same translucency that characterized the ethereal fruits and blossoms.

"We have been looking for you," said Angarth. "It occurred to me that, after reading my journal, you might be tempted to try the same experiment, if only to make sure whether the account was truth or fiction. This is Felix Ebbonly, whom I believe you have never met."

It surprised me when I found that I could hear his voice with perfect ease and clearness, and I wondered why the effect of the drug-soaked cotton should have died out so soon in my auditory nerves. Yet such details were trivial in the face of the astounding fact that I had found Angarth and Ebbonly; that they, as well as I, had survived the unearthly rapture of the Flame.

"Where are we?" I asked, after acknowledging his introduction. "I confess that I am totally at a loss to comprehend what has happened."

"We are now in what is called the Inner Dimension," explained Angarth. "It is a higher sphere of space and energy and matter than the one into which we were precipitated from Crater Ridge, and the only entrance is through the Singing Flame in the city of Ydmos. The Inner Dimension is born of the fiery fountain, and sustained by it; and those who fling themselves into the Flame are lifted thereby to this superior plane of vibration. For them, the Outer Worlds no longer exist. The nature of the Flame itself is not known, except that it is a fountain of pure energy springing from the central rock beneath Ydmos, and passing beyond mortal ken by virtue of its own ardency."

He paused, and seemed to be peering attentively at the winged entities, who still lingered at my side. Then, he continued:

"I haven't been here long enough to learn very much, myself; but I have found out a few things, and Ebbonly and I have established a sort of telepathic communication with the other beings who have passed through the Flame. Many of them have no spoken language, nor organs of speech, and their very methods of thought are basically different from ours, because of their divergent lines of sense-development and the varying conditions of the worlds from which they come. But we are able to communicate a few images.

"The persons who came with you are trying to tell me something," he went on. "You and they, it seems, are the last pilgrims who will enter Ydmos and attain the Inner Dimension. War is being made on the Flame and its guardians by the rulers of the Outer Lands, because so many of their people have obeyed the lure of the singing fountain and vanished into the higher sphere. Even now, their armies have closed in upon Ydmos and are blasting the city's ramparts with the force-bolts of their moving towers."

I told him what I had seen, comprehending, now, much that had been obscure heretofore. He listened gravely, and then said:

"It has long been feared that such war would be made sooner or later. There are many legends in the Outer Lands concerning the Flame and the fate of those who succumb to its attraction, but the truth is not known, or is guessed only by a few. Many believe, as I did, that the end is destruction; and by some who suspect its existence, the Inner Dimension is hated as a thing that lures idle dreamers away from worldly reality. It is regarded as a lethal and pernicious chimera, as a mere poetic dream, or a sort of opium paradise.

"There are a thousand things to tell you regarding the Inner Sphere, and the laws and conditions of being to which we are now subject after the revibration of all our component atoms in the Flame. But at present there is no time to speak further, since it is highly probable that we are all in grave danger—that the very existence of the Inner Dimension, as well as our own, is threatened by the inimical forces that are destroying Ydmos.

"There are some who say that the Flame is impregnable, that its pure essence will defy the blasting of all inferior beams, and its source remain impenetrable to the lightnings of the Outer Lords. But most are fearful of disaster, and expect the failure of the fountain itself when Ydmos is riven to the central rock.

"Because of this imminent peril, we must not tarry longer. There is a way which affords egress from the Inner Sphere to another and remoter Cosmos in a second infinity—a Cosmos unconceived by mundane astronomers, or by the astronomers of the worlds about Ydmos. The majority of the pilgrims, after a term of sojourn here, have gone on to the worlds of this other universe; and Ebbonly and I have waited only for your coming before following them. We must make haste, and delay no more, or doom will overtake us."

Even as he spoke, the two moth-like entities, seeming to resign me to the care of my human friends, arose on the jewel-tinted air and sailed in long, level flight above the paradisal perspectives whose remoter avenues were lost in glory. Angarth and Ebbonly had now stationed themselves beside me, and one took me by the left arm, and the other by the right.

"Try to imagine that you are flying," said Angarth. "In this sphere, levitation and flight are possible through willpower, and you will soon acquire the ability. We shall support and guide you, however, till you have grown accustomed to the new conditions and are independent of such help."

I obeyed his injunction, and formed a mental image of myself in the act of flying. I was amazed by the clearness and verisimilitude of the thought-picture, and still more by the fact that the picture was becoming an actuality! With little sense of effort, but with exactly the same feeling that characterizes a levitational dream, the three of us were soaring from the jeweled ground, slanting easily and swiftly upward through the glowing air.

Any attempt to describe the experience would be foredoomed to futility, since it seemed that a whole range of new senses had been opened up in me, together with corresponding thought-symbols for which there are no words in human speech. I was no longer Philip Hastane, but a larger, stronger and freer entity, differing as much from my former self as the personality developed beneath the influence of hashish or kava would differ. The dominant feeling was one of immense joy and liberation, coupled with a sense of imperative haste, of the need to escape into other realms where the joy would endure eternal and unthreatened.

My visual perceptions, as we flew above the burning, lucent woods, were marked by intense, aesthetic pleasure. It was as far above the normal delight afforded by agreeable imagery as the forms and colours of this world were beyond the cognition of normal eyes. Every changing image was a source of veritable ecstasy; and the ecstasy mounted as the whole landscape began to brighten again and returned to the flashing, scintillating glory it had worn when I first beheld it.

VII. The Destruction of Ydmos

WE SOARED at a lofty elevation, looking down on numberless miles of labyrinthine forest, on long, luxurious meadows, on voluptuously folded hills, on palatial buildings, and waters that were clear as the pristine lakes and rivers of Eden. It all seemed to quiver and pulsate like one living effulgent, ethereal entity, and waves of radiant rapture passed from sun to sun in the splendor-crowded heaven.

As we went on, I noticed again, after an interval, that partial dimming of the light; that somnolent, dreamy saddening of the colors, to be followed by another period of ecstatic brightening. The slow tidal rhythm of this process appeared to correspond to the rising and falling of the Flame, as Angarth had described it in his journal, and I suspected immediately that there was some connection. No sooner had I formulated this thought, than I became aware that Angarth was speaking. And yet, I am not sure whether he spoke, or whether his worded thought was perceptible to me through another sense than that of physical audition. At any rate, I was cognisant of his comment:

"You are right. The waning and waxing of the fountain and its music is perceived in the Inner Dimension as a clouding and lightening of all visual images."

Our flight began to swiften, and I realized that my companions were employing all their psychic energies in an effort to redouble our speed. The lands below us blurred to a cataract of streaming color, a sea of flowing luminosity; and we seemed to be hurtling onward like stars through the fiery air. The ecstasy of that endless soaring, the anxiety of that precipitate flight from an unknown doom, are incommunicable. But I shall never forget them, nor the state of ineffable communion and understanding that existed between the three of us. The memory of it all is housed in the deepest, most abiding cells of my brain.

Others were flying beside and above and beneath us, now, in the fluctuant glory: pilgrims of hidden worlds and occult dimensions, proceeding as we ourselves toward that other Cosmos of which the Inner Sphere was the antechamber. These beings were strange and outré beyond belief, in their corporeal forms and attributes; and yet I took no thought of their strangeness, but felt toward them the same conviction of fraternity that I felt toward Angarth and Ebbonly.

As we still went on, it appeared to me that my two companions were telling me many things; communicating, by what means I am not sure, much that they had learned in their new existence. With a grave urgency as if, perhaps, the time for imparting this information might well be brief, ideas were expressed and conveyed which I could never have understood amid terrestrial circumstances. Things that were inconceivable in terms of the five senses, or in abstract symbols of philosophic or mathematic thought, were made plain to me as the letters of the alphabet.

Certain of these data, however, are roughly conveyable or suggestible in language. I was told of the gradual process of initiation into the life of the new dimension, of the powers gained by the neophyte during his term of adaptation, of the various recondite, aesthetic joys experienced through a mingling and multiplying of all the perceptions, of the control acquired over natural forces and over matter itself, so that raiment could be woven and buildings reared solely through an act of volition.

I learned, also, of the laws that would control our passage to the further Cosmos, and the fact that such passage was difficult and dangerous for anyone who had not lived a certain length of time in the Inner Dimension. Likewise, I was told that no one could return to our present plane from the higher Cosmos, even as no one could go backward through the Flame into Ydmos.

Angarth and Ebbonly had dwelt long enough in the Inner Dimension, they said, to be eligible for entrance to the worlds beyond; and they thought that I, too, could escape through their assistance, even though I had not yet developed the faculty of spatial equilibrium necessary to sustain those who dared the interspheric path and its dreadful subjacent gulfs alone. There were boundless, unforeseeable realms, planet on planet, universe on universe, to which we might attain, and among whose prodigies and marvels we could dwell or wander indefinitely. In these worlds, our brains would be attuned to the comprehension of vaster and higher scientific laws, and states of entity beyond those of our present dimensional milieu.

I have no idea of the duration of our flight; since, like everything else, my sense of time was completely altered and transfigured. Relatively speaking, we may have gone on for hours; but it seemed to me that we had crossed an area of that supernal terrain for whose transit many years, or even centuries, might well have been required.

Even before we came within sight of it, a clear pictorial image of our destination had arisen in my mind, doubtless through some sort of thought-transference. I seemed to envision a stupendous mountain range, with alp on celestial alp, higher than the summer cumuli on Earth; and above them all the horn of an ultra-violet peak whose head was enfolded in a hueless and spiral cloud, touched with the sense of invisible chromatic overtones, that seemed to come down upon it from skies beyond the zenith. I knew that the way to the Outer Cosmos was hidden in the high cloud. . . .

On and on we soared; and at length the mountain range appeared on the far horizon, and I saw the paramount peak of ultra-violet with its dazzling crown of cumulus. Nearer still we came, till the strange volutes of cloud were almost above us, towering to the heavens and vanishing among the vari-colored suns; and we saw the gleaming forms of pilgrims who preceded us, as they entered the swirling folds. At this moment, the sky and the landscape had flamed again to their culminating brilliance; they burned with a thousand hues and lusters, so that the sudden, unlooked-for eclipse which now occurred was all the more complete and terrible. Before I was conscious of anything amiss, I seemed to hear a despairing cry from my friends, who must have felt the oncoming calamity through a subtler sense than any of which I was yet capable. Then, beyond the high and luminescent alp of our destination, I saw the mounting of a wall of darkness, dreadful and instant, positive and palpable, that rose everywhere and toppled like some Atlantean wave upon the irised suns and the fiery-colored vistas of the Inner Dimension.

We hung irresolute in the shadowed air, powerless and hopeless before the impending catastrophe, and saw that the darkness had surrounded the entire world and was rushing upon us from all sides. It ate the heavens, blotted the outer suns, and the vast perspectives over which we had flown appeared to shrink and shrivel like a fire-blackened paper. We seemed to wait alone, for one terrible instant, in a center of dwindling light on which the cyclonic forces of night and destruction were impinging with torrential rapidity.

The center shrank to a mere point—and then the darkness was upon us like an overwhelming maelstrom, like the falling and crashing of Cyclopean walls. I seemed to go down with the wreck of shattered worlds in a roaring sea of vortical space and force, to descend into some infra-stellar pit, some ultimate limbo to which the shards of forgotten suns and systems are flung. Then, after a measureless interval, there came the sensation of violent impact, as if I had fallen among these shards, at the bottom of the universal night.

I struggled back to consciousness with slow, prodigious effort, as if I were crushed beneath some irremovable weight, beneath the lightless and inert débris of galaxies. It seemed to require the labors of a Titan to lift my lids, and my body and limbs were heavy, as if they had been turned to some denser element than human flesh, or had been subjected to the gravitation of a grosser planet than the Earth.

My mental processes were benumbed and painful, and confused to the last degree; but at length I realized that I was lying on a riven and tilted pavement, among gigantic blocks of fallen stone. Above me, the light of a livid heaven came down among over-turned and jagged walls that no longer supported their colossal dome. Close beside me, I saw a fuming pit from which a ragged rift extended through the floor, like the chasm wrought by an earthquake.

I could not recognize my surroundings for a time; but at last, with a toilsome groping of thought, I understood that I was lying in the ruined temple of Ydmos, and that the pit whose gray and acrid vapours rose beside me was that from which the fountain of singing flame had issued. It was a scene of stupendous havoc and devastation: the wrath that had been visited upon Ydmos had left no wall nor pylon of the temple standing. I stared at the blighted heavens from an architectural ruin in which the remains of On and Angkor would have been mere rubble-heaps.

With Herculean effort, I turned my head away from the smoking pit, whose thin, sluggish fumes curled upward in phantasmal coils where the green ardour of the Flame had soared and sung. Not until then did I perceive my companions. Angarth, still insensible, was lying near at hand, and just beyond him I saw the pale, contorted face of Ebbonly, whose lower limbs and body were pinned down by the rough and broken pediment of a fallen pillar.

Striving, as in some eternal nightmare, to throw off the leaden-clinging weight of my inertia, and able to bestir myself only with the most painful slowness and laboriousness, I got to my feet and went over to Ebbonly. Angarth, I saw at a glance, was uninjured and would presently regain consciousness, but Ebbonly, crushed by the monolithic mass of stone, was dying swiftly, and even with the help of a dozen men I could not have released him from his imprisonment; nor could I have done anything to palliate his agony.

He tried to smile, with gallant and piteous courage, as I stooped above him.

"It's no use—I'm going in a moment," he whispered. "Good-bye, Hastane—and tell Angarth good-bye for me, too."

His tortured lips relaxed, his eyelids dropped and his head fell back on the temple pavement. With an unreal dreamlike horror, almost without emotion, I saw that he was dead. The exhaustion that still beset me was too profound to permit of thought or feeling; it was like the first reaction that follows the awakening from a drug-debauch. My nerves were like burnt-out wires, my muscles dead and unresponsive as clay;

my brain was ashen and gutted, as if a great fire had burned within it and gone out.

Somehow, after an interval of whose length my memory is uncertain, I managed to revive Angarth, and he sat up dully and dazedly. When I told him that Ebbonly was dead, my words appeared to make no impression upon him, and I wondered for a while if he understood. Finally, rousing himself a little with evident difficulty, he peered at the body of our friend, and seemed to realize in some measure the horror of the situation. But I think he would have remained there for hours, or perhaps for all time, in his utter despair and lassitude, if I had not taken the initiative.

"Come," I said, with an attempt at firmness. "We must get out of this."

"Where to?" he queried, dully. "The Flame has failed at its source, and the Inner Dimension is no more. I wish I were dead, like Ebbonly—I might as well be, judging from the way I feel."

"We must find our way back to Crater Ridge," I said. "Surely we can do it, if the inter-dimensional portals have not been destroyed."

Angarth did not seem to hear me, but he followed obediently when I took him by the arm and began to seek an exit from the temple's heart, among the roofless halls and overturned columns. . . .

My recollections of our return are dim and confused, and full of the tediousness of some interminable delirium. I remember looking back at Ebbonly, lying white and still beneath the massive pillar that would serve as his eternal monument; and I recall the mountainous ruins of the city, in which it seemed that we were the only living beings. It was a wilderness of chaotic stone, of fused, obsidian-like blocks, where streams of molten lava still ran in the mighty chasms, or poured like torrents adown unfathomable pits that had opened in the ground. And I remember seeing, amid the wreckage, the charred bodies of those dark colossi who were the people of Ydmos and the warders of the Flame.

Like pygmies lost in some shattered fortalice of the giants, we stumbled onward, strangling in mephitic and metallic vapors, reeling with weariness, dizzy with the heat that emanated everywhere to surge upon us in buffeting waves. The way was blocked by overthrown buildings, by toppled towers and battlements, over which we climbed precariously and toilsomely; and often we were compelled to divagate from our direct course by enormous rifts that seemed to cleave the foundations of the world.

The moving towers of the wrathful Outer Lords had withdrawn; their armies had disappeared on the plain beyond Ydmos, when we staggered over the riven, shapeless and scoriac crags that had formed the city's ramparts. Before us was nothing but desolation—a fire-blackened and vapor-vaulted expanse in which no tree or blade of grass remained.

Across this waste we found our way to the slope of violet grass above the plain, which had lain beyond the path of the invader's bolts. There the guiding monoliths, reared by a people of whom we were never to learn even the name, still looked down upon the fuming desert and the mounded wrack of Ydmos. And there, at length, we came once more to the grayish-green columns that were the gateway between the worlds.

CONTRIBUTOR BIOGRAPHIES

Laird Barron is the author of several books, including *The Beautiful Thing That Awaits Us All*, *Swift to Chase*, and *Worse Angels*. His work has also appeared in many magazines and anthologies. Barron currently resides in the Rondout Valley in New York, writing stories about the evil that men do.

Nadia Bulkin writes stories, thirteen of which appear in her debut collection, *She Said Destroy* (Word Horde, 2017). Her short stories have been included in editions of *The Year's Best Weird Fiction*, *The Year's Best Horror*, and *The Year's Best Dark Fantasy & Horror*. She has been nominated for the Shirley Jackson Award five times. She grew up in Jakarta, Indonesia, with her Javanese father and American mother, before relocating to Lincoln, Nebraska. She has a BA in political science and an MA in international affairs, and she lives in Washington, D.C.

Fred Chappell is the award-winning author of more than twenty books of poetry and fiction, including *I Am One of You Forever*, *Brighten the Corner Where You Are*, and *Look Back All the Green Valley*. He has received many major prizes, including the Bollingen Prize in Poetry from Yale University and the Award in Literature from the National Institute of Arts and Letters. He lives with his wife, Susan, in Greensboro, North Carolina.

Michael Cisco has published ten novels, including *The Divinity Student*, *The Great Lover*, *The Narrator*, *ANIMAL MONEY*, and *UNLANGUAGE*, and a short story collection called *Secret Hours*. His short fiction has appeared in *The Thackery T. Lambshead Pocket*

263

Guide to Eccentric & Discredited Diseases, Lovecraft Unbound, Black Wings, Blood and Other Cravings, THE WEIRD, The Grimscribe's Puppets, and *Aickman's Heirs,* among others. He teaches at CUNY Hostos, New York.

Masahiko Inoue (井上 雅彦) was born in Tokyo in 1960. In 1983, his submission to the Hoshi Shinichi Short-Short Contest won an award for excellence and was included in the contest's best-of anthology. Drawn to the subgenre of historical dark fantasy Ryō Hanmura helped create, Inoue's first novel featured a young Abraham Van Helsing hunting *yōkai* in Edo-period Nagasaki. In addition to his own prolific output as a novelist, he supervised the paperback horror anthology series *Freak-Out Collection,* running for almost fifty volumes from 1998, providing a place for countless emerging and established authors to unveil weird and macabre creations of their own.

Victor LaValle is the author of the short story collection *Slapboxing with Jesus;* four novels, *The Ecstatic, Big Machine, The Devil in Silver,* and *The Changeling;* and two novellas, *Lucretia and the Kroons* and *The Ballad of Black Tom.* He is also the creator and writer of a comic book *Victor LaValle's DESTROYER.* He has been the recipient of numerous awards, including the World Fantasy Award, British World Fantasy Award, Bram Stoker Award, Whiting Writers' Award, a Guggenheim Fellowship, Shirley Jackson Award, American Book Award, and the key to Southeast Queens. He was raised in Queens, New York. He now lives in Washington Heights, New York, with his wife and kids and teaches at Columbia University.

Livia Llewellyn's fiction has appeared in over forty anthologies and magazines and been reprinted in *The Best Horror of the Year, Year's Best Weird Fiction,* and *The Mammoth Book of Best New Erotica.* Her short fiction collections *Engines of Desire: Tales of Love & Other Horrors* and *Furnace* were both nominated for the Shirley Jackson Award, and her story "One of These Nights" won the 2020 Edgar Award for Best

Short Story. You can find her online at liviallewellyn.com and on Twitter and Instagram.

H. P. Lovecraft was born in 1890 in Providence, Rhode Island. He started his career writing poetry and essays, but turned to fiction in 1917 and found his niche as a writer of horror and the supernatural. Although he wasn't widely read during his lifetime, his reputation—and readership—grew quickly after his death in 1937. Often compared to Edgar Allan Poe, Lovecraft is considered to be one of the most important horror writers of the twentieth century.

Nick Mamatas is an author, editor, and anthologist. His novels include the Beat Lovecraft mash-up *Move Under Ground*, the Lovecraftian murder mystery *I Am Providence*, and the speculative thriller *The Second Shooter*. *Haunted Legends*, his anthology coedited with Ellen Datlow, won the Bram Stoker Award, and *The Future Is Japanese* and *Hanzai Japan*, coedited with Masumi Washington, were both nominated for the Locus Award. His own short fiction has been published in *Best American Mystery Stories*, *Year's Best Science Fiction and Fantasy*, and dozens of other venues. Nick's fiction and editorial work has been variously nominated for the Hugo, World Fantasy, Shirley Jackson, and International Horror Guild awards.

Erica L. Satifka's short fiction has appeared in *Clarkesworld*, *Shimmer*, and *Interzone*. Her debut novel *Stay Crazy* won the 2017 British Fantasy Award for Best Newcomer, and her rural cyberpunk novella *Busted Synapses* is forthcoming from Broken Eye Books. She lives in Portland, Oregon, with her husband, Rob, and several adorable talking cats.

Clark Ashton Smith was a self-educated artist, poet, and author best remembered for his short stories of fantasy, horror, and the supernatural published in genre pulp magazines such as *Wonder Stories* and *Weird Tales* in the late 1920s and 1930s. Smith died in 1961 in California.

Molly Tanzer is the author of the Diabolist's Library trilogy: *Creatures of Will and Temper*, the Locus Award–nominated *Creatures of Want and Ruin*, and *Creatures of Charm and Hunger*. She is also the author of the weird Western *Vermilion*, an io9 and NPR "Best Book" of 2015, and the British Fantasy Award–nominated collection *A Pretty Mouth*, as well as many critically acclaimed short stories. Follow her adventures at @molly_tanzer on Instagram or @molly_the_tanz on Twitter. She lives outside of Boulder, Colorado, with her cat, Toad.

PUBLICATION INFORMATION

The Shadow Over Innsmouth, by H. P. Lovecraft, was originally published by Visionary Publishing Co., Everett, Pennsylvania, in 1936.

"Seven Minutes in Heaven," by Nadia Bulkin, was originally published in *Aickman's Heirs,* Undertow Publications, Pickering, Ontario, Canada, in 2015.

"Vastation," by Laird Barron, was originally published in *Cthulhu's Reign,* DAW Books, Inc., New York, in 2010.

"You Will Never Be the Same," by Erica L. Satifka, was originally published in *Whispers from the Abyss,* 01 Publishing, San Diego, in 2013.

"Night Voices, Night Journeys," by Masahiko Inoue, was originally published in *Hishinkai—Rekishihen,* Sogen Suiri Bunko, Tokyo, Japan, in 2002. The Edward Lipsett English translation was originally published in *Night Voices, Night Journeys,* by Kurodahan Press, Kumamoto, Japan, in 2005.

"Farewell Performance," by Nick Mamatas, was originally published on Tor.com, December 31, 2009.

"Translation," by Michael Cisco, was originally published in *Tales of Lovecraftian Horror* #8, Eastertide, in 1998.

"Weird Tales," by Fred Chappell, was originally published in *The Texas Review*, Summer 1984.

"Bright Crown of Joy," by Livia Llewellyn, was originally published in *Children of Lovecraft*, Dark Horse Books, Milwaukie, Oregon, in 2016.

"Ghost Story," by Victor LaValle, was originally published in *Slapboxing with Jesus*, Vintage Contemporaries, New York, in 1999.

"Go, Go, Go, Said the Byakhee," by Molly Tanzer, was originally published in *Future Lovecraft*, Innsmouth Free Press, Vancouver, British Columbia, Canada, in 2011.

"The City of the Singing Flame," by Clark Ashton Smith, was originally published as "The City of the Singing Flame" in *Wonder Stories*, July 1931, and "Beyond the Singing Flame" in *Wonder Stories*, November 1931. As a single piece, "The City of the Singing Flame" was originally published in *Out of Space and Time*, Arkham House, Sauk City, Wisconsin, in 1942.